A WITCH TO CHANGE THE WORLD

Winner, 2025 Golden Leaf Award
Best Paranormal Romance & Best First Book
New Jersey Romance Writers

SUZANNE SNOWDEN

A Witch to Change the World
(The Witch Wars, Book 1)
Suzanne Snowden

Published by Industry Books

Cover art by Danielle Fine

ISBN: 979-8991440226

The story, all names, characters, and incidents portrayed in this production are fictitious. No identification with actual persons (living or deceased), places, buildings, and products is intended or should be inferred.

No artificial intelligence programs ("A.I.") were used in the writing of this book. Without in any way limiting the author's exclusive rights under copyright, any use of this publication to "train" generative artificial intelligence (AI) technologies to generate text is expressly prohibited.

DEDICATION

For Desiree, who made me read a romance to perk me up during the pandemic. Five hundred romances later, I decided to write my own. This book would never have been written if not for you, my good friend and best recommender of books.

Content Notes

I wrote this book mainly because I was mad about the lack of representation for mature characters in romance novels. Seriously, I was like, if I have to read one more sex scene where the twenty-something protagonist wets her pants at the sight of the hero... I may die. Specifically, I was not seeing *any* depictions of older characters having sex. And by 'older characters' I mean fifty and up. I'm here to spread the good news that people over fifty can still have sex, and it can be hot.

This book features open-door, consensual sex between mature characters. So, if you are uncomfortable with steamy sex scenes, maybe don't read this book. It's okay.

There is a reference to a rape that occurred off page, years ago. There is a storyline that deals with cancer, and there are scenes in a children's hospital depicting patients suffering from cancer. Also, if you get offended by reading or hearing 'bad words', then I want you to know, they are *all* in here. The F word, the P word, the other P word, the C word, the other C word, the D word, the V word, the W, X, Y and Z words... all here. Not all over the place and not gratuitously, but they're here.

And now for quite possibly the strangest trigger warning of all time:

This book takes place in the United States in the year 2024. Anyone alive right now in the U.S. knows what a long, strange trip the past decade has been. It's crazy out there. The main character in this book has a liberal bent, and I want you good readers to know about that before jumping in. It's not a main plot point; it's just a facet of his personality that I couldn't ignore. He lives in Washington, D.C.! His house is right behind the Supreme Court. He has opinions. If you are a conservative-leaning friend, I get it if you just can't even bring yourself to read about a liberal-leaning doctor. But if you can, I hope you enjoy it!

And if you'd like some music for the adventure you're about to embark upon...check out *"Adam's Playlist for Vivienne."* Get the Spotify link at: https://www.suzannesnowden.com.

CHAPTER ONE

Adam

June 5th, 2024

There is exactly one good chair in the main reading room of the Library of Congress. I twirled around in it slowly, staring up at the dome above and relishing the solitude.

Every Wednesday night, I liked to meet my son Grant there while he finished a regular online meeting in his office. It wasn't a real meeting, more like Dungeons & Dragons with a few of his librarian friends scattered across the country. I think some of his former army buddies were in there, too.

Flashing my name tag from Children's National Hospital in D.C., which reads *Adam Parrish, Oncology,* I mentioned meeting Grant Parrish upstairs. Whoever was on duty usually reminded me that closing was in ten minutes and to please leave on time. After making sure the staff was gone, I'd head to the main reading room and pull out the good chair from behind the reference desk. Placing it dead center under the dome, I leaned back and tried to relax.

Every Wednesday, I just tried to relax.

If I heard that anyone was still around, I'd cloak myself with a shield. A magic shield. Like invisibility, but more of a suggestion to the other person that nothing is really there where I'm sitting. It works better on some people than on others. The power of suggestion and the ability to create illusions are the gifts I was born with. Grant has them too. They're rare talents that were passed down to me from my mother, Isabelle, who is also a witch. I have dozens more specialties, but no one else knows that. Too much power is something to conceal, not brag about.

That's one reason I haunt the library like I do. It's something I can do alone, for fun. I like being surrounded by all the stories in that room. In 1815, Thomas Jefferson sold his personal library to Congress after the British burned the building and destroyed their collection. Those books are displayed just outside the reading room. The main collection of their books is housed on a double ring of shelves that circle the chamber. Sometimes I go there on the weekends and sit in one of the private alcoves within the ring and just read some history.

That night, I twirled in the chair and stopped short when I saw my son standing in the aisle about ten feet away.

"I can see you perfectly clearly. That cloaking is pitiful." He walked toward me and pulled out a chair to sit at the reference desk.

"Whatever. You and your grandmother are the only people on earth who could see through it, so I'm fine with that. I'm just hiding from security guards. Are they gone?"

"I think so. But Mark is upstairs. We're both in the same meeting online. Him in his office, and me in mine. We're on a ten-minute break and then we'll do another twenty minutes. Are you good to hang out?"

"Of course. This is the very serious meeting of dragon enthusiasts, right?"

"Don't forget the dungeons."

"Obviously." I leaned back in the chair and said, "I'm fine. Take your time."

But he wasn't ready to go back. In fact, I felt a lecture coming on.

"Dad, I know a lady here in reference who you would love..."

"Grant." I winced. "Stop this. Please."

"I'm just saying it would be nice if you had somebody you could share your interests with."

"Are you talking about Mary? Because she actually hates my guts. And she does not deserve this chair."

That slowed his roll a little, but I could tell when he decided not to pick up what I was laying down, and he plowed right on.

"I know you're traveling a lot. Internationally. That's got to be hard. Hard to relax, hard to have a social life..."

He waited for me to chime in. I did not. He rolled his eyes. "Fine. I'll be back in a little bit."

When he was gone, I closed my eyes and took a few deep breaths in through the nose and out through the mouth, trying to leave behind my day full of very sick children. Meditation wasn't really working for me, but I was out of other options. Valium for anxiety, Prozac for depression, melatonin to sleep. Turned out none of those fix a deeply repressed crisis of conscience. So, meditation it was. But as usual, no matter how still I sat or for how long, my brain refused to shut down.

Grant was right. The problem was that I had two jobs, and they were both becoming too much to handle. Helping sick children survive during the day and enforcing witchcraft council death sentences at night was a pair of vocations not in alignment, to say the least. But I couldn't give either of them up.

Being a physician is my calling. Dealing with cancer in babies and children takes a toll, as any oncologist will agree. Sometimes patients die. But sending kids home to their families after they beat cancer... that's the good stuff. A man could put up with anything to do that.

People also die while I'm on the night job, but that's because of me, not in spite of me. I tell myself that what those witches have done in this world justifies me taking them out of it. And I mean it. But I guess somewhere deep in my brain, there's a pious little imp tallying the good versus the bad and pointing emphatically at the Hippocratic Oath.

I'd like to kill him too, but I can't get to him.

Bottom line, I wasn't handling the stress well, and something needed to change. I wasn't suicidal, but I did find myself wondering pretty frequently what the fuck was the point of it all? My assistant Maria also tried to help, always joking with me about my love life and giving me advice on how to improve it. I told her it was fine, and that I dated more than she or any Millennials even thought about dating. Which was true, but the quality of my dating life was lackluster. I thought about the few women I had dated recently. They were beautiful. The sex was good.

But none of them had made me think twice. I tried to remember the last time I was truly interested in a woman and found myself back at the beginning of the relationship I'd had with Connie, Grant's mother. She was brilliant, beautiful, and ambitious. When she got pregnant with Grant, we were thrilled. I thought we'd make a lifetime of it, but she was on a tenure track at her teaching hospital and didn't want to marry. We grew apart after Grant was born. I remembered her caustic wit and how she turned it on me, and I was once again grateful that we ended it when we did. But... thirty years. Jesus. That's a biblical drought. That's the relationship equivalent of the Cubs not winning the World Series for a hundred and eight years.

My peace ended abruptly when a muffled crash and the sound of glass breaking came from the floor below. I sat up straight. The guards had gone home, so what was that? Grant was on duty to set the alarms on Wednesday, so no one else should be downstairs. I hurried to one of the metal spiral staircases and peered over the railing. It was dark, but there was definitely something down there making noise. I tried to keep my footsteps silent on the way down.

The Library of Congress basement holds the old wooden card catalogs and sometimes special exhibits that are being moved from different locations. I'd seen the Gutenberg Bible up close one time down there. Stepping off the last stair, I took note of a couple of nineteen-fifties metal desks and chairs pushed up against the wall to my left. I pulled the chain to turn on a reading lamp with a green glass shade on one of the desks.

To my right was a vast space with a low ceiling. I flipped a switch on the wall and a single row of fluorescent lighting that ran between two endless aisles of cards began to light up in sequence. The sounds stopped. Floor to ceiling metal racks held the wooden cabinets in stacks of four. A paper taped to the end of the first row of cabinets proclaimed there were twenty-two million cards in the main card catalog and none had been added since 1980. Debris spilled out into the aisle about halfway down the way.

Once there, I stepped around the side of a case and saw a woman huddled over an enormous book, glass scattered around it on the floor. I noticed her clothing first. She wore a floor length blue dress and had long silver hair. It fell to her waist and was gathered in a loose braid at the end.

"Are you okay?" I asked.

The woman twirled around, her gray eyes piercing mine. Instantly, a wall of force pulsed from her body and froze me in place. And then there I was, encased in what felt like jelly. I couldn't move a finger. A foot of energy with an amber glow surrounded me. It smelled a bit like a chemical fire, and I hoped whatever was burning wasn't me.

She's a witch. Son of a bitch.

Not able to move or speak, I watched her as she made her way toward me, feet crunching on the broken glass. She kept eye contact, and I saw that she was battle-ready. She circled me and checked out the corridor behind me.

My mind flipped through every trick I knew to break a binding spell, but nothing came close to weakening what she had on me. I briefly entertained the possibility that the Council of Witches had found somebody better than me to do their dirty work, and this was their way of letting me know. But her magic was earthy and rich and stronger than anything I had ever encountered. Witches with that much power all know of each other. There was no way in hell the Council could keep this woman a secret.

The spell continued to press in on me and I felt myself relaxing and sinking into it. I stopped struggling and actually closed my eyes to feel it fully. Another scent had joined the mix. *God, what was that?* It smelled amazing. If I wasn't ninety-five percent sure I was about to die, I might have let myself enjoy that shit.

After a moment she said, "I shall release thee."

I must have appeared harmless to her, but her accent was so strange that it took me a moment to understand. As she loosened her spell, she told me not to touch her or shout for help. I leaned against the card catalog to regroup and pulled every ounce of my power together to shield myself against any other type of strange magic she might hit me with. Her eyes narrowed at that, and she began to pepper me with questions.

"Who art thou?"

"Adam Parrish. Who the fuck are you?"

She didn't answer. "What is this place?" she asked. Her body was taut, fierce as she faced me down.

"The Library of Congress."

"Where is it?"

"Washington, D.C."

She paused at that and then asked for what appeared to be the most important piece of information to her.

"What is the date?"

"June 5th, 2024."

The woman exhaled sharply and bent over. I took advantage of her distraction and waved my hand in a circle in her direction.

She didn't even have to make a motion to do this.

Her eyes widened as she realized she was unable to move.

CHAPTER TWO

Vivienne

He is a witch? How can he be?

I recognized the force surrounding me. It was my own spell. He had copied it precisely and added something of his own. A warmth. It calmed me. The man was attempting to put me at ease, and it was working. I felt my body relaxing like a traitor as my mind raced on.

He was not harmless. I had assessed him wrong. But in all my earthly years, I had never seen a man wield magic. Did not know it was possible for men to hold magic within them. This shock was almost greater than my fear of the power that held me in place. Did he know this could kill if administered too long? He was talking. His accent was strange, and I made myself focus on his words.

"Who are you? How did you get here?" He loosened the spell the slightest bit so I could move my head and speak.

"Free me now! I will be free or I will not speak!"

I was being loud and he did not like it. He frowned and surveyed the corridor.

"I'll let go of the spell. But be quiet. You aren't supposed to be here." He scanned my eyes to see if I would agree. I gave a brief nod and felt his magic drop softly to the ground. I moved away from him, back down the aisle.

He reached into his pocket and brought out a glowing box. I squinted at him.

"Wait!" He held his other hand out toward me. "This is not harmful. I need to fix things."

I glanced behind me. The book was still there, opened to the page I needed. He pushed at the box in his hand, and sound came from each touch. He held it to his ear.

"Grant? I have a situation downstairs in the card catalog section." His eyes did not leave my face as he spoke. "No... I'll take care of it. Nobody else is here, right?" He studied the debris around my book. "Yep. Go find them and be sure to say goodbye. Now how do I get out without being on camera?" I heard a faint voice coming from the box. "Okay. Don't go down to the catalogs. Make sure the cameras see you setting the alarm and leaving. And come over later." He pushed the box again. It made another sound, and he put it back in his pocket.

We stared at each other.

He broke the silence. "Your name?"

We stood for another moment, each surveying the other. He was handsome. A man of my own age. Taller than most men I knew, he had dark hair cut close to his head with some gray at the temples. He was close-shaven but wore a day's growth of beard.

The way he waited for my response interested me. This was a man who would hear me. He did not like it, but he would listen. Despite the circumstances and the fact that a male witch from the future stood in front of me, something in me decided to trust him. I answered, "Vivienne."

"How did you get here?" he asked.

I gazed back at the large manuscript my father had illustrated. I stepped back over the broken glass and squatted down to stroke the mini paintings around the large letter *V*. There was a riot of color at the top left of the page. Deep blues and greens, magenta and gold leaf. A small girl held a bouquet of flowers on one side of the *V* and kneeled in prayer on the other. Nobles hired my father to paint their manuscripts because of his skill with vibrant colors and delicate designs. He chose this page in the manuscript to paint me because the letter *V* began my name. I had been at the monastery, lightly running my hand over this *V* when I was thrown through time to this new and foreign place.

But now it was not taking me back to my place.

I ignored the witch and placed my entire hand over the *V*.

"Heavenly Father," I prayed silently, *"please let me return to where I am needed."*

Heavy footsteps sounded on a staircase down the hall.

"The library is closed. No one is supposed to be here," a man's voice began.

The witch in front of me held out a hand and worked another spell. It was strong and laden with a command to obey. The spell was not aimed at me, but I felt myself agreeing with what he said and wanting to comply.

"Everything is fine," he said. "We are leaving now, but you never saw us. You did not even come down here. Good to see you, though." He waved him away. "Have a great night!"

"Right, you too!" The other man's voice faded as he climbed the stairs again.

Dear God. That was a skill.

I would not give him a chance to use that magic on me. I would come back later for the book. And figure out how to make it take me home.

"We have to go." The witch stared at me pointedly. "Now, before anyone else sees us."

He took the small box out of his pocket, held it over the manuscript directly over the *V*, and pushed on it again. He stored the box again on his person and pointed for me to back away from the mess.

I watched as he raised both his hands toward the manuscript. The pieces of glass rose slowly and rearranged themselves into a solid case around the manuscript, which was lifted and laid on the wooden podium. I heard a muffled sound, and I felt pressure in my ears. He seemed to struggle too, frowning as the podium settled. The magic was taxing him. Minutes later, it was done, and the glass case was reassembled around the manuscript. But he shook his head slightly, dissatisfied with the result.

"Let's go," he said. He waited for me to walk beside him, not turning his back on me, as I would not turn my back on him. I glanced back at the display case and wondered if his repair had made the glass more solid. Hurrying along next to him, I considered ways to break that case again when I returned.

CHAPTER THREE

Adam

The walk home was interesting. From the Library of Congress on First Street to my home on Second Street should have been just a five-minute walk. It took longer with Vivienne because she was cataloging everything she encountered. She stood in front of a lamppost and gave it a good thirty seconds of intense scrutiny, then moved on to the streetlight and watched as I pushed the button to cross. When the recording prompted us to walk, her eyes darted to mine. She stopped still in the middle of the street when a black Escalade blasting hip hop jerked to a stop in front of us. I tugged on her sleeve to move her along.

My house on Capitol Hill is one of the oldest in the city. Prized for its location across the street from the back side of the Supreme Court Building, it sits in the center of a block with five other houses. All of them stand at least three stories tall, made of carefully placed stone, large wooden doors, and a liberal sprinkling of stained and beveled glass windows. My house has a wide porch in the front that wraps around the right side of the building. On the left front corner stands a gray stone tower with a turret room on top. The turret was mine as a child and Grant's after that.

I'm the third generation to live in the house, and it's the same story with three other families on the street. We grew up together, went to school together and have seen each other through marriages, divorces and deaths. Recently, one of the Justices bought the house at the south end of the street. We don't talk about him. Or *to* him.

The lights were on as we approached, as was the protective shield of magic I always kept in place. I pointed to the house and watched the woman with me. When her eyes took in the whole of the shield, I wasn't surprised. No one else had ever seen it, not even Grant. But I knew somehow she'd see it, and she did.

Once inside, I motioned for her to sit on the couch in my study. Plush, the color of wine, it was one of my favorite things in the house. That and my books. They filled the inlaid mahogany shelves lining two of the walls. The front of the room held a window seat looking out over the porch and the street. At the back of the room, there were a few family pictures on a roll-top desk. The bookshelves bordered a small gas fireplace. Persian rugs covered the dark cherry floors that ran throughout the place. I watched her as she absorbed it all.

I said, "I'll be right back," then headed toward the kitchen at the rear of the house. She was still standing in the center of the room when I returned a few minutes later with two mugs of tea and a tray of crackers and cheese. I handed her one of the mugs, and she nodded her head in thanks when she took it from me. I motioned again for her to sit on the couch, and this time she did. Placing the plate down on the small table next to her, I went to sit at the other end of the couch. We regarded each other, and both took a sip of tea.

I decided to start. "As I said, my name is Adam Parrish." I placed a hand on my chest. "Adam. This is my house." I made a small circle in the air, indicating the whole building.

She acknowledged that and said, "Vivienne." She placed a hand on her chest.

We looked at each other some more. She had delicate features. Full lips. Intense eyes.

"Vivienne," I said to myself. I wondered if she was French. Her accent was foreign, but from where I couldn't tell. Mostly, I just wondered how she ended up in the lower level of the Library of Congress, but she spoke before I could ask.

"And when?" It was a demand. "When is this?"

I had already told her the date, but the walk home had obviously been slightly overwhelming for her, and I imagined she was trying to come to terms with it all. She was clearly disoriented. Maybe she suffered a head injury and was experiencing amnesia. There were documented cases of concussed people waking to find they had developed a foreign accent. I wondered if she might think she was here from another time.

"The year is 2024."

Her face paled as that sank in. I went to the desk and wrote it down on a notepad. Bringing it back to her, I showed her the paper. She took the pad from me and set the mug down. She placed two fingers on her temple as if to ward off a headache.

I asked her, "What year are you from?"

Reaching for the pencil I held, she examined it carefully before placing the tip on the paper. Moving the pencil lightly over the pad, she wrote her year. Holding it up for me, she said, "My year is 1502."

Jesus. The Middle Ages?

She dropped the pencil, and I bent to pick it up before she did. I took the pad from her and went back to my side of the couch. We both lifted our tea and had another long sip, looking at each other over the tip of our cups. Her eyes were slightly wider than before. They were lovely, I noticed. Gray, with a dark ring around the iris and heavy eyelashes. Oh no, she was crying.

I stood and held my finger up, as if asking her to wait. Going down the hallway, I cursed myself for not being prepared for that. *Of course she was crying! For Christ's sake, she thinks she's just been yanked through time—*I did the math quickly—*522 years!*

I imagined myself stepping into medieval times, and it was not pretty. I'd cry too. Poor woman.

In the bathroom, I closed my eyes and wondered, not for the first time, *What the fuck just happened?* And where the hell was Grant, anyway? He minored in history and loved the Middle Ages enough to act them out on the weekends with his larping friends.

I began to make a mental list of psychiatrists I knew who were witches and who might make a house call this late at night. The list was short. The only person I could come up with was Sharon Waltman, and I was not her favorite. We dated for a while many years ago and it ended with a lengthy session, right here in this very house, where she employed her professional understanding of psychology to detail all my faults. But she had been married for ten years or so and maybe that memory had faded.

Reaching for a box of tissues for Vivienne, I wondered if she might like a bath. I started the hot water running and tossed in some lavender soap to make bubbles. I thought again about the odds that this was a setup, but then shook my head. If so, it was very fucking creative. Hurrying back down the hall, I saw that she had composed herself. I set the tissue box next to her on the couch and pulled one out. Dabbing it at my eyes to show her the proper usage of such an item, I was rewarded with a small smile and... did she actually laugh at me a bit?

I sat on the couch again, spread my hands wide and said, "How did this happen?"

Vivienne took a tissue from the box, gave a small shrug and said, "I touched a book."

We sat in silence for a few moments. She clearly believed what she was saying. My magic could usually tell when an obvious lie was spoken, and I was getting no alarms from this woman. I tried to apply some logic to the situation. 1.) Time travel has been theorized but not proven. 2.) Witchcraft is real but is believed to exist only in fables. 3.) Vivienne's magic was otherworldly. Also, what was up with her clothes? The dress she wore was ankle-length and stained at the bottom, and it looked like her shoes were covered in dried mud. I frowned when I realized she had me almost believing her story.

To appease her, I said, "Well, time travel has not been disproved. And I do believe that you believe you are here from 1502."

Her eyes teared up again.

"Hast thou ever...?" She held up her hand, palm up.

"Heard of someone actually traveling through time? No," I said. "I have not."

She closed her eyes then and wiped a hand over them.

"You're tired," I said, standing again and walking back to the bathroom. "We'll fix this in the morning," I said over my shoulder. When the bath was full and I had set out a towel and washcloth for her on the sink, I stepped out of the bathroom and motioned for her to come to me.

Too late, I realized I was going to have to explain the toilet to this woman who thought she was here from 1502 and I had no idea how to do so. I quickly pulled out my cell phone and texted Grant.

Emergency request—what did people call shit in the middle ages? 1502—what did they call the toilet?

I had no doubt Grant would know this or find the correct answer using his librarian skills faster than I could by doing a Google search.

Also, where the hell are you? Get over here.

Vivienne stopped at the bathroom door, and her eyes swept the room. When her gaze landed on the mirror, I heard her breath catch. In the mirror our eyes met, and she gave a small nod, reaching over slowly to touch it. I started my pitch for her with the bath.

"I made you a bath." I pointed to the water with bubbles. Picking up the towel, I said, "And here is a towel and a washcloth." Damn, what about when she was done? Her clothes were filthy. She couldn't sleep in those. I looked behind the door.

"And here is a robe to wear when you are done." I pulled it out to show her. It wasn't mine, but it was a woman's, and it would do.

My phone dinged. "About time," I muttered. Grant's message was short.

They called it a garderobe room, if in a castle—the place they shit. Gong farmers were guys who took waste away.

And then:

Stop texting me. I have a date.

I put the phone in my pocket. "All right," I started, pointing at the toilet. "This is the place you make your waste go away. Like a garderobe?" I ripped off some toilet paper and tossed it in the bowl. Then I pushed the handle down and she leaned in to watch the water swirl. Her eyebrows rose at that. She smelled good.

"Where..." she seemed to struggle to find the words. Pointing to the toilet, she said, "To where?"

"Where does it go?" I repeated. *Good question. Where the hell does it go?*

"To a water treatment plant," I said, having no earthly idea if this was, in fact, where it went. She looked at me as if she recognized my complete bullshit and wondered what kind of special idiot she had found in the future. "Far away," I motioned with my hands as if dispersing something over the wind to a land somewhere in the distance. She nodded, clearly unconvinced.

I pulled the door back against the wall and stepped around her, trying not to touch her as I exited the room. Standing at the threshold, I showed her the lock on the inside handle and turned it so it was locked and demonstrated that the handle would not turn. Then turned it back to unlock it and showed the handle was loose. Then back to locked. She stared at me. As if daring me to do it again and pretend that a lock on a door mattered to the likes of us. I realized it would not, and that I was expecting her to bare herself in my home with no real protection.

"You can shield the door," I said. "I'll stay in the study."

Again, she stared at me in silence. Tonight, I had stolen the secret of her shield. Did she know that, I wondered? She must have felt it when I used it on her. I stepped away from the bathroom, into the hall, and faced her.

"We both know your power is stronger. Significantly stronger, from what I've felt so far." She raised her eyebrows but did not agree or disagree.

"You can trust me," I said. And again, "I will stay in the study."

She nodded once. When the door closed, she raised a shield around it from the inside that was so powerful it leaked through the cracks and glowed orange in the hallway.

Damn. That was a much stronger wall of energy than she had used before. She had upped her game considerably. I imagined waking up to find her standing over me, ready to strike a death blow. This woman was a threat.

That fucking shield smelled great, though. It was more likely to bring bad guys to it than away from it. Until I found out who she was and where she was from, I'd have to ask her to tone down that magic. It occurred to me that a death blow from that magic might be interesting.

And once again I asked myself, *"What the fuck is happening tonight?"*

CHAPTER FOUR

June 6th, 2024

My first sleep in the twenty-first century was surprisingly untroubled. I woke in a four-poster bed under a puffy white blanket. Sunlight streamed in from three large windows that ended in a cushioned seat. Fighting my way out from under a sea of fluffy white pillows, I used the wooden steps to get down from the bed.

In the daylight, I admired the rounded room Adam had called "the turret." Directly across from the bed was a fireplace with two chairs facing it. Opposite the windows was the door leading downstairs. A small desk and armoire stood against the wall between the bed and windows. Adam had managed to let me know that I was in his son's room, but it seemed like his son was away. I was dressed in his son's clothes, too. They were soft but ill-fitting. I wore the robe over top of them, not knowing what was correct in this age, and not wanting to be dressed inappropriately.

Floorboards creaked under me as I made my way down a narrow staircase and then followed a delicious scent in the hallway. Adam's house was sparsely decorated. No pictures lined the walls. A scarlet carpet adorned the gleaming floorboards. Through the kitchen doorway, I saw him pouring something hot into a mug. My gaze was drawn again to the floor to ceiling wall of books straight ahead in his main room. I approached and could not resist running my hand lightly over one set of leather covered books. The green spines were ridged, the letters in gold leaf.

"Those were my father's," Adam said from the doorway. He held a small tray with three mugs on it and placed it down on a cushioned footstool. "Would you like some coffee? Or tea? I made you both." He picked up his mug and gestured at the green set of books. "He was a lawyer. My father." I just stared at him.

"Would you like to sit?" He waved at the couch and sat down in the soft leather chair across from it. I admired the beautiful silver tray in front of me and picked up a white cup with delicate flowers lining the outside and inside. I breathed deep the comforting aroma and sat down at the end of the couch nearest him. "Grant's clothes from high school are a bit big on you. I'll get you some clothes today."

Something about clothes. He is going to get me clothes for a woman.

"I thank thee," I said. *He is kind. And very learned to have all these books.*

"Thy son?" I asked and raised up a piece of my shirt sleeve to show I understood.

"Yes," Adam said. "He lives in his own house. About ten minutes away." I had trouble following him. "And my mother, she lives about twenty minutes away. By car." *What is a car? I am only understanding the end of his words.*

"Wait, I have a picture of him." He got up and went over to the desk in the back corner of the room. Two framed portraits sat on the desk, along with a cup of sticks and a stack of bound parchment.

He brought me the portraits. He handed me one that could have been a younger version of himself.

"This is Grant, my son. At his graduation from the University of Maryland, where he got his master's degree in library science. He's a librarian," Adam said. I heard the pride in his voice, though I did not gather much of the meaning of his words. I touched the glass tentatively and studied the portrait. It was so realistic, I wondered if it was made with magic. It had to be. His son was smiling, accepting a book from an older man and shaking his hand. He wore a black robe and a black cap with fabric hanging from it. A handsome young man. Like his father.

"He is a monk?" I asked.

Adam gave a short laugh and shook his head emphatically. "No, not that one." He took the portrait and fixed his own gaze on it. "He is a librarian." I took a biscuit from the tray and waited for him to explain. He sat down and started over.

"His work is with books. To organize and protect books. To find information from books. A whole building of books."

That was interesting. A building of books. That's where my father's book was. Where we were last night.

When I took a bite of the biscuit, I was pleasantly surprised. It was moist and had berries mixed in. I pointed at the other portrait. It was a lovely woman who had reached a great age. She was smiling at the artist, holding a cat and sitting in what appeared to be a garden. "Her name is Isabelle, my mother," he said.

"Thou art blessed," I said.

He asked, "Do you have family?"

"I have a granddaughter. She is thirteen years of age. Alice." I handed him back the portrait of his mother. Then I picked up the parchment from the night before and the writing instrument and I began to draw. The lines of her features came into view and then her face became clear. To reach my creativity, I had to release a bit of the hold I kept on my magic, but I was monitoring it and kept watch for Adam's reaction. And then there she was, my Alice, a girl of thirteen years with shoulder-length red, wavy hair.

"She hath blue eyes," I said. "And beautiful red hair and a dimple that shows in her cheek when she smiles." Adam appeared to be mesmerized by the image. Alice raised her eyebrows a bit, as if interacting with someone.

He said, "She's moving. Is this her right now, or are you projecting a memory?"

He spoke so fast I still was not understanding everything.

"Memory," I said. I did get that part. "It is a memory."

"She's lovely," he said.

My heart ached as I continued to look at her face. "I thank thee," I said. "She will be wondering where I am. I know the sisters will take care of her, but..." I set the paper down on the table and strengthened again the shield on my magic. The drawing ceased to move.

Adam was looking at me with a new intensity, and I felt a twinge of concern that I had shared more about my magic with this male witch than I should have. But I needed him to know how imperative it was that I return to my time.

He was clearly struggling in the presence of my magic. His pupils were dilated, he was staring a little too long, and his heart was beating at an elevated rate. I had used the smallest amount possible that would allow me to create an image, but my magic has always been enticing to those who are exposed to it. Men and women. I often have to work with patients while they sleep.

"Is there no one else?" Adam asked.

"Nay. My husband died long ago. My daughter and her husband were taken by the sweating sickness. I have only Alice." I said it without emotion. "I must return to her."

Adam focused on me as if I were a puzzle and the fate of the world depended upon him solving it.

After a moment of silence, I broke in with, "And what of thy wife?"

Adam dispelled that notion immediately. "Oh, no. God. No. I was never married to Grant's mother. We are not together." He went on to explain that. "For a long time, we have been separated."

It was all I could do not to roll my eyes. *Men.*

"Vivienne," he said with purpose, trying to move on, "I have an idea. Would you be willing to teach me some of your spells and, in return, I will do everything I can to help you get home?"

I got most of that. I spoke slowly and countered with, "I am a healer. I can show thee but do not know if thou can learn. I am a nun and a midwife in my time. I would like to know about childbirth and medicine in thy time."

He frowned slightly. Then he surprised me with, "I am a doctor and can tell you all you want to know about medicine and childbirth."

He had my interest. Adam followed with, "I work at a hospital and make treatment plans for the sickest of children there. Those who have cancer." *What is cancer?* I leaned the tiniest bit closer and waited for more. He stared into my eyes, and I made sure he saw that I really wanted this. Brown eyes, very intent on mine. "It may be difficult to take you there," he said, "but I'll figure it out."

He stood up and went to the bookshelves on the wall directly behind his desk. "These are my medical texts. And I think I have one here with some writing in Middle English." His eyes scanned the rows as if trying to remember what it was called. "It was a gift from my mother..." he bent down to the bottom shelf, "Ah! This is it. Maybe." He pulled out a book with a soft cover, and read the title aloud, "*A Leechbook or Collection of Medical Recipes of the Fifteenth Century*. It has medieval recipes for all illnesses." He opened it to the middle and pointed to the text there. "What to do for a headache lasting days?" Adam read the answer to himself and laughed. "This cure seems way worse than the illness."

My mouth fell open. "I know this book," I said. "There is one at the monastery. I am allowed to read it when I help the monks with illnesses." I paused to let that sink in. "I am the only woman who is allowed to see it. I know all the cures in this book."

Adam raised his eyebrows and sat down next to me on the couch. "Do you mind if I ask you some questions?"

He wants to test me? "Fine," I shrugged.

"What do you give a woman who has had many miscarriages?"

"Baneswort to the stomach," I replied immediately. I recited the entire recipe for the cure as Adam attempted to follow the Middle English translation.

"That's very impressive," he said when I had finished, "But we need to discuss some better methods for helping a woman after miscarriage." I frowned at him, but he did not see.

While he focused on the page, I stole a glance at his profile. He had a strong jaw and was closely shaved. He was very fit for a man of his age. His shoulders were broad and muscled, as were his arms. But he was lean, like a laborer. I wondered what activities he pursued to achieve this state.

His brows drew together, and he was concentrating so hard on the passage that I decided to draw the book onto my lap and read it out loud for him while following along with my finger. Adam pointed and said, "What is this letter?" I made the sound "ssss" and he said, "It looks like an f."

On one side of the page, the medicinal recipe was in English from my time, on the other side it was written in English from his time. They were very different. No wonder we had to speak so slowly to each other. And I was still not getting most of what he said.

He took the book back, flipping to other areas and asking what to do for other maladies. I recited the cures word for word. He raised his eyebrows each time I was correct and then asked me, "Have you read this a million times or does your brain remember everything you see the first time you see it?"

This was a compliment, and I shook my head to dismiss it.

I was aware of his scent as we sat so near to each other. He smelled like a forest of pine trees and I wondered where there was such a place near his house. I resisted drawing a deep breath of him. He glanced up then, his face close to mine. "Well, this book is yours now, so you can read it all you want, whenever you want."

I could not help myself. I brought the book to my chest in gratitude. "I thank thee, Adam. I will learn thy English from this." *But I cannot take too long, Alice will grow into her powers soon. I will need to be there to guide her.*

"There is one more thing." He seemed to choose his words carefully. "Your magic is very different from any magic I have ever experienced. It's stronger. And unique. I think it is best if you do not practice your magic in public or around other witches while you're here. I think they would want it and I don't want to give anyone a reason to seek you out or try to use you for your magic."

As if they could.

But it was good of him to worry about it, so I said, "I understand."

"Come on," he stood. "Let's eat breakfast. I made a quiche."

CHAPTER FIVE

Adam

After breakfast, I called Grant to find out the condition of the case and the manuscript itself. The night before, I had only covered the basics with him of what was happening with Vivienne. It was very abbreviated (broken glass case, there was a witch from the sixteenth century there, fixed the case, took her home) and, to his credit, he rolled with it. He did say, though, that he'd check with me today to see if my fever had broken yet.

He said he had not heard one word about the illuminated manuscript down in the card catalog area, and today when he went to look for it, they had already moved it to be on display in the great hall of the Library of Congress.

"Did it look all right?" I asked him.

"I mean, all right enough to put on display. So, yeah."

"I put that shit back together," I said. "That glass was completely shattered."

"Oh my god," he laughed at me. "Great work, most exalted witch on high."

"Hey, I didn't even know what it looked like before! That's some magic right there!"

"Yes," he said in a monotone. "You are a god of magic. Again, great work."

I asked him to come to dinner later, and he said he'd be over after work. Vivienne watched me from the kitchen table as I spoke to him on the phone.

"That was thy son?" she asked.

"Yes."

Then I sent a text to Maria, asking if she would get me some clothes for a friend from Europe whose luggage got lost. I sent some guesses at sizes, and she texted back:

Where am I shopping? Target or Nordstrom's?

Nordstrom's

So we like this lady. Got it.

Am I also getting undies?

I paused.
What the hell?
Very carefully keeping my eyes on the phone, I estimated a bra size and raised my eyebrows at my conclusion. But I was pretty sure I got that right. For a second I contemplated what it said about me that I had noticed a bra size for my guest who was a nun, but then I pushed that uncomfortable thought far away.

I didn't know she was a nun at first. And Vivienne is beautiful. I'm only human. And it's not like it was the first thing I noticed about her!

After I was done justifying my observations, I texted Maria the measurement. And then:

Victoria's Secret

Oh my god, who is this lady?

Then:

A girlfriend?

Then:

Please let me meet your girlfriend!

Then:

It is HIGH TIME.

I shook my head.

Stop it

I paused, again.

Also, make it lace

I thought Vivienne would appreciate lace work.
Also, I appreciate lace work.
*Also, seriously, what the hell is wrong with me? This is for
a nun.*

YES SIR. When do you need it?

Tonight, if possible

Thanks, Maria

Have fun with mystery lady (Who you will
introduce me to tonight or else.)

I looked up to see Vivienne watching me as I was texting.
"I'm communicating with my assistant," I said.
She gave me a blank look that somehow also conveyed
irritation.
"Maria is her name. She works for me."
Another blank stare. Then she said, "Like a clerk?"
"Yes," I said.
"What sayest thou?" she asked.
"I'm asking her to get you some clothes."

She pursed her lips as if she was unsure of this situation. Then she seemed to conclude that it was for the best and said, "I thank thee." She stood and brought her plate to the sink. Turning to me, Vivienne said, "I have many questions."

I bet you do.

I got her set up in the study on the daybed with my laptop and enough medical books for a first-year med student. I thought she might want to take some notes, so I gave her a pen and a few notebooks.

"These are here in case you want to write notes."

She looked like she wanted to say something. I waited.

Then she said, "Our letters are different."

That was a good point. Some had appeared very different as we compared the two sides of the Leechbook. I nodded. I turned the laptop my way and looked for alphabet sheets I could print for her. When I heard them printing, I turned it back toward her and went to pick them up off the printer. I handed her the sheet.

"This is what all our letters look like. Now you can compare."

She gave it a once over and pointed at the bottom half.

"What is this?"

"Cursive," I said. "Cursive is for adults and printing is for children. But you may want to start with printing to write. That's what you'll be using to read."

Her look told me I could shove the print letters up my ass, she would be learning cursive.

I was wondering how a head injury or amnesia could actually result in a person not being able to recognize letters and whether this could possibly be a thing when the doorbell rang. Vivienne nearly jumped out of her chair. I felt her magic rise and the look in her eyes was that of a soldier ready to storm a beach. It was immense, her power. And right there under the surface of her skin. She clearly did not have to command it, it just instantly reacted to her emotion.

"It's fine," I said. "It's just the doorbell. Someone is at the door, that's all."

"Sorry," she said.

I thought it delightful how murderous the nun had become in .5 seconds.

"Okay. Well, shut that magic down," I said. "I'm answering the door."

I checked back on her before I opened it, and her small smile seemed like an indicator that she was fine.

It was Marshall Smith, the Executive Director of the North American Council of Witches and my contact there. He gave me the jobs that no one else could take care of, and I agreed to do some of them. He was an ambitious little snot and not at all like his mother. Margaret Smith was a friend of my mother's and Marshall and I had spent some time together as kids.

I guess some people considered him handsome. He had black, never out of place hair and dark-framed glasses. I hated the fact that Marshall Smith was on my doorstep when I had the most powerful witch I'd ever met right in the study. It was terrible timing. His main power as a witch was to identify the powers of other witches. Which was why he was the absolute worst person to know about Vivienne being here. He'd sniff her out in a minute and know she was something rare.

"Hello, Adam. Got a job for you." He stepped into the hallway, uninvited. I boosted the shield on my powers as I always did in the presence of Smith. He dropped a folder on the hallway table.

"Hello." He took stock of Vivienne for a moment and then was in motion toward her with his hand outstretched. "I'm Marshall Smith."

She did not smile. God, I really did like this woman.

"Vivienne," she said, giving him her hand. When she didn't shake his hand Marshall pivoted and brought her hand to his lips for a kiss.

"Vivienne," he said, smiling. "That's a beautiful name. Nice to meet you."

Don't touch her and shut up you cocksucker.

Vivienne arched a brow at me, and I was suddenly worried she could read minds.

"Are you from Europe? I thought I heard a slight accent there," he said with all kinds of interest.

"I am from England," she said.

"What else do you want, Smith?" I needed him to go.

Marshall was still looking at Vivienne. He widened his eyes and laughed as if I was overreacting. "That's all, don't worry. Just needed to drop something off. Wonderful to meet you, Vivienne."

On the front step, he turned and said, "I like your friend. She's interesting." He searched my expression. "You don't know how interesting, do you?"

I kept my face neutral, and he laughed softly. "Priceless," he said. When I didn't respond, he started down the stairs. "Need to hear from you soon on this."

"Yep. Bye." I shut the door loudly behind him.

Vivienne was at the window watching him walk away.

"There are probably thousands of delightful people in this city," I said. "Marshall Smith is not one of them."

"Hmm," she murmured.

"He's a Diviner," I said. She turned to me and I explained, "A witch who can read other witches."

She frowned. "Read them?"

"He knows what abilities witches have."

Vivienne raised her eyebrows. "More than the amount of power?"

"Yes. Witches can discern the level of power other witches possess, but not the type. Marshall can tell both the level and the type." I observed her look of surprise and thought to myself again that if this was an act of hers, it was a good one.

"Yeah, it's unpleasant as hell every time I have to see him. I spend the whole time blocking his feelers. I couldn't block you because I don't know..." I gestured at her from her toes to her head. "Your magic is so different it's hard to tell what you can do. I mean, beyond healing. Did you feel anything?"

"I did," she said. "But I strengthened my shield when I noticed. It was..." she seemed to be looking for the right word. Then she said, "Invasive."

I scowled. *God damn it. That motherfucker would never see her again.*

"So I sent him away with something from me," she said.

"What?"

"Nausea." She smiled.

God, yes. Marshall deserved nausea.

I approved. "So you can heal and harm? Excellent. How about today we talk about all your gifts?"

To keep Vivienne busy, I showed her how to use the dictionary on the laptop and how to have the word and definition read aloud. I picked an American woman's voice to read the definitions for her. She picked it up quickly and was going through the Leechbook vocabulary, ignoring me completely, when the doorbell rang again. When it did, she raised her head to me, as if asking if I needed backup.

I said, "I got this."

I opened the door and shook Sharon Waltman's hand. She was dressed for work, a black suit under her white medical coat. She wore her brown hair different from when I last saw her. It was longer and in a ponytail.

"Thanks for coming," I said.

"Of course!" Stepping inside, she took a look around and said, "This is a flashback."

"About that," I started, "If I was an ass, which I probably was, back when we were together …"

"Jesus. Parrish." She stopped me with an incredulous look. "That was a lifetime ago. No need to grovel."

"All right." *That was a relief.* "Well, I just want you to know how much I appreciate you coming over."

"I'm glad I could make it. Where's my patient?"

I walked her into the study and Vivienne stood up. Sharon took in the weird outfit of a woman's bathrobe over a teen boy's sweatpants and t-shirt. She smiled at Vivienne and introduced herself.

"Hello, I'm Dr. Sharon Waltman." Vivienne shook Sharon's hand when she offered it.

"Sorry," I said. "Vivienne, this is Sharon. I called her last night to see if she could have a look at you and see how you're doing today. Sharon, this is Vivienne Lanier."

"Nice to meet you," Sharon said to Vivienne. Vivienne was clearly assessing Sharon and deciding if she would participate in this exercise. She looked to me.

"I am a little fatigued this morning. Otherwise, I feel fine."

Sharon said, "That's good. Glad to hear it. I hope you don't mind, but Adam shared some of your story with me and I would like to help you make some sense of it, if I may."

Vivienne's face reflected irritation that I had told someone her story but also a curiosity about Sharon's offer to make sense of things. After a moment, she said, "I will allow that."

Sharon turned to me with a big smile and said, "Great! Adam will leave us now so we can speak in confidence."

I don't know why I didn't see that coming. But knowing Sharon, there was not going to be any movement on that demand. "I'll be out on the porch if you need anything."

I sat down on the porch swing on the right side of the house and gently pushed off with my toe, over and over, swinging slow and thinking fast. Reviewing the facts. Running through scenarios that Sharon might give me. What if she said Vivienne needed to be committed? Would she advise psychotropic meds? I rebelled at the thought. What Vivienne was saying was crazy, but Vivienne herself did not seem at all crazy.

Forty-five minutes later, I heard Sharon saying goodbye to Vivienne. Sitting down next to me on the swing, she said, "Well, that was one for the books." She sat her purse between us. "Vivienne has given me permission to speak to you about her situation."

"Good," I said. "What are you thinking?"

She shook her head. "First, I'm sure you get this. She is a witch of enormous power. That's something to consider. What that sort of power might do to an ego, to relationships." She contemplated me. "Actually, you might know something about that."

"Ouch," I said.

"Oh, you know what I mean." She patted my leg. "You still out there trying to save the world while simultaneously pushing it away?" She laughed at my unamused face.

"Fine. This isn't about you." She went on. "It does not appear to me that Vivienne is running from anything. She's focused on a goal to return to her family. It's all very sensible and admirable. Until you add in the time travel aspect and then it feels like crazy town."

She swung her legs out with me and we picked up a little steam in our swing. She stared off down the street. My neighbor Linda's husband Phil jogged down their front steps and gave me a wave as he took off down the sidewalk.

"I don't know. Her delusional thinking is thorough. That Middle English accent and delivery is consistent. Like, if you had a linguist analyze it, I'm betting it would be spot on."

"She has the whole Leechbook memorized," I said. "All the medieval ailments and their cures. She can recite them all in Middle English." I nodded my head at her as Sharon's eyes got wide. "She knows that book front to back."

Sharon shook her head at that. "She's incredibly smart. She could have engineered this entire situation."

"Do you think she did?" I asked. "Is she making it all up?"

Sharon turned to me. "Nope. She is not making it up. She really believes everything she's saying. The question is why?"

Holding up her hand, she ticked off items with her fingers as she listed them. "I don't see any evidence of physical trauma. Without a brain scan, we can't be sure, but I don't think that's what we're dealing with. She does not seem concussed. I do think she could have gotten here from emotional trauma, like losing her husband and daughter and son-in-law. Which is what she says has happened to her. That seems very possible."

I waited while she ran things through her psych filter. Sharon was skilled in her field. I'd believe what she had to say.

"She is deeply committed to this story. Her involvement with the manuscript, her clothing, her insistence that she's not from this era. It all means something." She stared off down the street, then looked back at me. "She asked me how far Washington, D.C. was from London. I showed her on your globe. Explained the ocean between our continents. She tried to hide it but that freaked her out pretty bad."

We were silent for a moment. Then she asked, "Have you checked with the police?"

"Yes. Nobody appears to be missing a woman from the middle ages."

"Okay. Well." She paused. "If it were anybody else, I'd say they need to be in the hospital. This woman needs therapy. But she's a witch, who is obviously out of her mind at the moment, and I don't want to report her to the Council." She glared at me. "She's too powerful, and they would take advantage of her."

I held my hands up. "Agreed! That's why I called you!"

"All right then." She approved of that response. "Here's what you need to do. Keep a watch on her to make sure the reading doesn't give her headaches. I checked her head and didn't notice anything but just in case… keep a lookout for symptoms of concussion."

"Okay. What else?"

"I believe she is probably British. I think you should take her to England. Take her somewhere she would recognize and see what happens."

"See what *happens?*" I asked.

"Yes. See what happens." Sharon stopped the swing abruptly with her foot and stood up. "Like it or not, Parrish, this woman is in your care and you are responsible for her wellbeing and recovery." She pointed two fingers at her eyes and then at mine. "I'm watching you."

As she walked down the porch steps, she called back to me, "I'll check in again next week."

I wondered how many days leave from the hospital I would need and what excuse I could give to take a quick trip to England.

CHAPTER SIX

Vivienne

When Adam came back into the house, he sat down in one of his chairs and began looking at the box he used last night.

"Doctor Waltman said the modern word for thou is 'you.' Why did you not tell me this?"

He looked up from the box he was holding.

"You think I am mad," I said to him.

He sat back in his chair and addressed me. "No. But I do think you need help. Sharon was the best person to begin the process of getting you help."

"She is a doctor who treats ailments of the mind. You think I have an ailment of the mind."

He shook his head. "I don't know what you have. Sharon says you completely believe what you're saying, so that means we need to investigate further. I'm looking for flights to England now. She thinks we should go see something from 1502 that you might have some connection to and maybe that will jog your memory. Or help you figure out how you got here."

"But the manuscript is here." I stood up. "I just need to touch it again."

Adam stood as well. "Hang on. For one thing, you can't go out looking like that."

"What is wrong with how I look? Are these not clothes from this time and place?"

"It's just…" he appeared to be at a loss for words. "The clothes you have on now are a mixture of nighttime and daytime and woman and man. Can we just wait until tomorrow when I will have some more appropriate clothes for you?"

I felt my frustration rising. "Why do I have this on then?"

He closed his eyes at that and I realized I needed to get a handle on things before I angered him.

"Adam, all I need is to see the manuscript. Today. Will you help me?"

Although his own frustration was evident, he agreed to my request, as I knew he would.

"Yes. After lunch, though. I'll take you. Let me get you a jacket to wear instead of that robe." He opened a door in the hallway and pulled out a cloak that appeared to be small enough for me.

As he handed it to me, I said, "Thank you."

"No problem. I'm just going to go make some lunch, then we can go."

When Adam was out of the room, I slipped off the robe, put on the cloak and closed the front door quietly as I left. I believed him that he would take me there later. But I did not know what would be necessary for me to do when I saw it. And I did not want Adam there to stop me.

CHAPTER SEVEN

Adam

When I called Vivienne to the kitchen for lunch, she didn't come. I looked for her in the study and the bathroom. I started to worry when she wasn't in the other bedrooms or the turret room. When I stepped out on the porch and she wasn't there either, I knew she had flown the coop. I took off on a jog over to the Library of Congress.

A few minutes later, I was at the back entrance and was showing my ID to the guard. He let me in and I headed straight for the great hall where I knew the manuscript was being displayed. There, to my relief and horror, I saw her.

Vivienne stood in front of the manuscript, radiating power like I had never seen. The five or six other people there stayed to the displays on the outskirts of the room, avoiding the waves of sheer energy she was putting out. She was making them uncomfortable, but they would not understand why. It was lucky there were no witches present to observe this impressive display, but even so, it was only a matter of time before someone noticed the woman standing still and staring directly at the manuscript without blinking.

"Vivienne." I said it low, hoping to catch her before she did anything to it. "You can't do this in public."

She ignored me. I walked to within a foot of her.

"There are rules. You are breaking them by practicing in public. This is unacceptable in our time and in your time. Stop now. I won't ask again, but I will make you stop."

She didn't move, but her eyes slid to mine. "I do not answer to you." And then, "I do not know why I cannot reach it. I can barely feel it." She closed her eyes and sent out another wave of power that almost took me down, but it was Vivienne who fell. I caught her just before she hit the floor. When my hands touched her arms, I felt a jolt that made me almost drop her. My hands tingled, and I felt it spread throughout my body.

I had no time to figure that out because now we really had caused a scene, and I had to persuade the guards that everything was fine. I said that Vivienne was my wife, we lived just around the corner, and I just wanted to get her home to eat some lunch. Some of that was true, so it was accepted fairly quickly.

My body buzzed the whole way home, and I knew it was the proximity to her, but I didn't know why. Was she still putting out that power I felt at the library? My skin on hers had stimulated every cell in my body somehow and I felt the great store of my magic rising to the surface, completely unbidden by me.

Well, this is new and different.

My concentration was shot by the time we got home. I laid her on the daybed and went to get a washcloth from the kitchen. Running it under some water I brought it back and placed it over her forehead. The pulse at her wrist was rapid and her eyelids jumped as if she was in the deepest REM.

I murmured to her, "What's happening in there, Vivienne? It's Adam. Wake up now."

I patted her hand. Then her cheek. She jerked away, and I thought it best that I not be touching her when she came to, so I stood and went back to the kitchen to get her some water. Her eyes were open when I came back and handed over the bottle of water. She took a sip and then leaned back on the daybed pillows. I turned my leather chair toward her and sat.

She gave a small shake of her head. "My power...it seems shallow. I could barely sense the manuscript."

I arched an eyebrow. "That was shallow?" *Fuck.*

"Yes. But it is replenishing." Then she fixed her gaze on the street outside the window and said, "I am sorry."

"You need to understand that if word got out, there was a witch using that kind of magic in front of mortals, she would be hunted down by the Council of Witches and she would be killed. No questions asked." I paused. "You are living with me, so I would be the one to do it."

"You think you could?" Her eyes met mine. She wasn't asking if I had the stomach for it. She was wondering how confident I was that I could take her.

"That's tough talk for somebody who just knocked her own self out. Yes. I could, and I would, end your life. My life would also be forfeited for harboring you."

She closed her eyes.

"Practicing magic in public is one of the most common ways for a witch to die today. There is no tolerance for risking the entire witch population of the world. With video, it's even harder to contain an incident and harder to explain."

She rubbed a hand over her eyes. "What is video?" she asked.

"Moving pictures. A record of what happened that looks like you were there."

She shook her head slightly as if wondering what next fresh hell 2024 might offer.

"You also need to know that I do not think you have an ailment of the mind. I just want to help you. Ask yourself, if I showed up in 1502 dressed like I am today and said I was from 2024... what would you think?"

Vivienne smiled at that; her eyes still closed. After a moment, she opened her eyes and said, "I may think you had an ailment of the mind."

"Yeah you would," I said. "But you'd help me, just like I'm going to help you."

She focused on the street again. "I understand not to practice magic in public." She paused and then looked at me. "But I will need to see the manuscript again." Another pause. Then she seemed to come to a conclusion.

"Thank you, Adam. I will accept your help."

I suggested she take a nap until dinner time. Grant was coming over and I wanted some time with him before she came back down from the turret. I opened the door to Grant and was surprised to see Maria standing next to him. She held up two giant shopping bags and said, "Got your clothes delivery!" So much had happened during the day that I had completely forgotten about asking her to shop for Vivienne.

Maria was a beautiful girl and a fashion fanatic, so I knew she'd love that assignment. She had long, honey blond hair and big blue eyes that were currently busy looking over my shoulder at Vivienne, who had heard the doorbell, no doubt, and probably wanted to offer her assistance.

I shot a look at Grant to say, *Maria hasn't heard about this time travel stuff.* He read my look correctly and gave a small shrug as if to say, *She can handle it and may even be of some help.* I agreed that Maria could handle it. She was an extremely intelligent witch who I was lucky to get on my payroll. I just didn't know if I should be discussing the idea of time travel with very many people.

A slow smile spread across Maria's face and she said, "Oh my *god,* she is so *pretty!*" She tried to stage whisper at me but was too excited and it was heard perfectly clearly by all.

"I'm aware," I said in a low voice. "Regain some chill, please."

Vivienne gave Maria a hint of a smile.

"Maria, Grant, this is my friend Vivienne. She's from London."

Maria hurried inside to take her hand. "It is so nice to meet you."

I watched their hands as they shook. Maria did not appear to have any reaction to Vivienne's touch. I realized that Marshall and Sharon had not seemed to feel anything different, either.

Grant was staring, and I had to nudge him inside. It was funny to see my son at a loss for words. He stood an inch taller than me and had my same brown hair and eyes. Grant looked so much like me that sometimes I felt caught in my own time warp remembering times when I had probably worn the same expressions. But I had never seen this one. It said, "What do I say to the lady from 1502? Has she seen a jousting tournament? Has she met the king? What kind of alcohol do they really drink?"

I addressed Vivienne. "Maria is my assistant, and Grant is my son. He works at the Library of Congress where you and I were today." Vivienne also shook Grant's outstretched hand.

Maria was soaking in this information like a sponge and with Vivienne's permission I was about to blow her mind.

"Vivienne, there are about five or six people I trust in the world and standing before you are two of them. Do you approve of me telling your story to them both?" Imagining hearing this tale for the first time, we shared an amused glance.

"Yes, that will be fine," she said. "But I do think you had better let them sit first."

Ten minutes later, Grant and Maria sat next to each other on the couch, their eyes wide. Vivienne and I sat in my leather chairs facing them.

"So here's the situation," I started. "There's some question about whether or not Vivienne is really from the past." She shot me a dirty look. I continued. "But no matter what, she needs our help to get back to her family. Also, her magic is completely different from ours, and I do not want anyone to know about it." I could see they both gathered immediately what I meant.

Vivienne said to Maria, "My granddaughter Alice is thirteen. I am her only relative."

Maria's brow furrowed. She understood what it meant to be a teen and suddenly gain your power. Whether it was 1502 or 2024, without guidance, it could be dangerous. It also seemed like Maria was one hundred percent 'Team Vivienne' on the time travel story.

"If anyone can figure out how to get you home, it's this guy," she pointed at me with confidence. "Let me show you the clothes I brought for you," she stood and picked up her giant bags. "Are you in Grant's old room?"

Vivienne went with her, thanking her for buying the clothes, and Maria gave me credit for the purchase.

"Maria," I got her attention as she headed to the stairs. "Maybe tell her about bras?"

"No problem," she said. "And I'll be sure to tell her about your special lace request."

Well, shit. That was probably a mistake.

Over dinner we realized that Vivienne was not understanding most of what we said, even when we slowed it down to snail speed. We had communicated so much better during the day, but now she seemed to get only the beginnings and endings of sentences. Or maybe it was just that she got a few important words and answered as best as she could. She was difficult to understand too, and I called it after about an hour when I saw how tired she was.

"Let's give Vivienne a break." I turned to her. "How about we let you study some of our modern English for a while and then we give it a good effort to figure out how to get you back home?"

She paused for a moment, processing what she could from that statement.

"I will learn your English." She looked at me to confirm that was right.

"Yes," I said. "Study some books. And then we will try again to make a plan. You will recognize more words then."

She said firmly. "Yes, I will."

I had no doubt that she would. And that was a good thing. Because now that Marshall knew she was here, soon the Council of Witches would know. And, although I wasn't worried about anyone there, the more witches who learned about Vivienne's magic, the more likely someone would come looking to recruit or capture her to harness that power for their needs. Vivienne would need to be at her best in the coming days.

CHAPTER EIGHT

Vivienne

June 20th, 2024

In two weeks, I had made it through most of the books I wanted to read about childbirth. I started with the Leechbook, comparing the words on both sides of the book. It was astounding to me how many words were similar in spelling but sounded so very different. The way I determined this was to type the letters into Adam's laptop, which he opened to an online dictionary where a woman's voice spoke them to me aloud. I worked eighteen hours a day, only stopping for the meals Adam brought to me.

I now understood what a laptop was, what the Internet was, and what 'online' meant. Somewhat. Adam was still not sure I was from the past, I could tell, but he very kindly described the scientific achievements of the current era to me. I could not help but shake my head in awe at some of the things he said.

Long before the Internet, a scientist figured out there were invisible waves all around us, and that man could use these to turn electrical sparks into messages that could be sent all over the world instantly. This led to the cell phones everyone used today to communicate.

Then, men made vehicles with things called engines in the front of them that used fuel and bursts of fire to move down the roadways. These were the cars I saw on the street in front of his house. Then they invented airplanes that flew dozens of people in a cabin in the sky. Then they sent man, in what was called a spacecraft, to the moon, where he did not stay but he did plant the American flag. It did not wave because there is no air on the moon or in space.

Most remarkable of all was that none of these things came about because of magic. Mortals were the inventors and creators of all the miracles of 2024. Adam had a great regard for mortals and said they were his best friends. He said that not all witches today respected mortals like he did, and these witches were to be avoided.

Adam spent time telling me about the world today so that he could prepare me for our trip. He had gotten us passage on an airplane to England so I could see where I was from and hopefully find a way back there. He said the nunnery where I lived was no longer in existence, but there was a monastery like I described south of the city of London and we could go there for a tour. We would need to fly over the ocean for a long while and then land in London. I was both excited and terrified. I wished there was some magic involved in the holding up of the airplane in the sky.

When the day came to leave, I brought my case down the stairs from the turret, and Adam gave me a stern look when I opened the door.

"I told you I'd come get that for you."

"And I told you I could carry a case down some stairs."

We engaged in a staring contest, which he won when I realized I had just been rude.

"I'm sorry. That was kind of you to offer."

He shook his head. "Oh, no. You don't ever have to back down from an honest opinion with me. I prefer it. Just tell me when I'm an ass, I can take it."

I nodded. "When you were trying to be chivalrous, you were also an ass."

He broke into a wide smile at that and then threw his head back and laughed. "Oh, I see. It's going to be like that?"

"You asked for it to be like that."

We were smiling at each other, comfortable in our sparring, when his eyes roamed over me, taking in my hair and my features.

"You look different," he said.

"Maria gave me a spray for my hair that makes it smooth. And I'm wearing eye makeup and lipstick." I wanted to look correct in 2024. Even though she had demonstrated what to do, suddenly I worried that I had done it wrong. He was still staring. I touched my hair. "Is it acceptable?"

He huffed out a laugh but still did not reply.

"Am I to take your silence as a compliment?" I didn't want to belabor the point, but I wanted to be sure how I looked was right for the situation and time.

"Yes. How you look is very acceptable." He reached for my bag to place a tag on it.

Handing me a thin blue book, Adam said, "Here's your passport. I had a witch make it. These are papers that allow you to travel between different countries."

I opened it to the first page and saw my portrait there.

"It's important that you memorize this address and some other information that you may be asked if we're stopped at the airport." I frowned at that, wondering why we would be stopped.

He noticed my concern and said, "Police, or guards, monitor the airports to make sure no one..." he seemed to rethink how to say something. "Police are at the airports to ensure security for all the passengers. So they routinely interview people to check on their travel plans."

I felt that he was going to say more, but he left it at that. I memorized his address and the information on my passport.

"My date of birth appears to be wrong," I said.

He studied me. Then laughed at me. "Oh is it? Maybe by five hundred years or so? Sorry. Maybe your next passport will be more accurate. When is your birthday?"

"October fifteenth. You made me younger than I am."

"Really? I just thought you looked a lot younger than me."

He picked up our bags and said, "Come on, we need to be there two hours before liftoff."

As we walked down the stairs of his front porch, Adam set the bags down and shook hands with a man who was walking in front of us.

"Herb," he said. "This is my friend Vivienne. She's British and we're headed off to visit her family for a day or two. Vivienne, this is Herb Tolley. He lives next door."

The man had brown skin and hair and a large smile. He held out his hand to me. "Wow, Vivienne. Getting this guy to vacation is a feat I don't think I've ever witnessed. And I've known him my whole life. You may deserve a medal."

I shook his hand and said, "I think we will be gone for only a few days."

He laughed and said, "Well, that's better than nothing. Have fun."

Adam ushered me into the back of the car and went to place our bags in the back part. I heard Herb mention he was worried when he saw Adam carrying me into the house a couple of weeks ago and Adam replying something about low blood sugar.

When he got in beside me, he said, "Herb is a good friend. He's not a witch. But if you ever need anything, you can trust him to help."

As the driver pulled the car away from Adam's house, I paid close attention to all the scenery that we passed. Huge buildings lined the streets. The walkways in front of the buildings were full of people moving so quickly. Cars surrounded ours on the roadway and they traveled at speeds I had never thought possible. I was almost grateful when night fell and the only thing left visible were the lights from the cars all around us.

The airport was also a shock. It was a giant building made up of glaring white spaces that assaulted my eyes. We stood in line so that our luggage could be scanned by machines that saw right through them without even opening them, then we sat in a waiting area until our airplane began letting passengers in it.

When we got there, a woman directed us to seats in the front. Adam helped me to secure a belt over my lap and opened the window shade so I could look out.

"You won't see much in the dark. We should sleep while we can because when we land, it will be the middle of the night still."

I said yes to the woman attending to us when she asked if I would like something to drink. Adam ordered champagne for me, which is a kind of wine, and water and the chicken dish they were serving for dinner.

A voice came out from above us, discussing where exits were and what to do in the event of an emergency landing. I looked at Adam sharply and he saw that I needed him to address this concept with me.

"This is the standard message they give on every flight that goes anywhere. This plane is safe, I promise." I searched his eyes and saw that he meant what he said.

That did not make it any easier when the plane started to move and then pick up speed. I felt uprooted as the plane lifted from the earth. My body yearned to be grounded again. My mind ran through the scientific principles of flight that Adam had shared with me the night before. But those scientific principles did not change the fact that birds flapped their wings when they flew and airplanes did not.

And how was any of this possible?

I didn't want Adam to know I was afraid, so I kept my eyes on the window. Adam reached over and squeezed my arm to reassure me that everything was fine. Lights below fell away and then I could see only darkness.

We ate our dinner and then I slept long and hard in that aircraft flying six miles above the ocean. I woke with my head on Adam's shoulder and my hand in his lap. This had always been my way, gravitating toward my spouse in the night and sleeping as close to him as I could. Adam had placed a blanket over me while I slept. Still groggy, I patted his leg and said, "Sorry," as I withdrew to my own space.

"Not a problem." He paused and then said, "You were smiling. Did you dream?"

I tried to recreate my thoughts upon waking, but they were elusive. I shook my head. "I don't remember."

"That's a shame," he said. "I'd like to know what made you smile like that."

That coaxed a small smile from me and, as I looked him in the eyes, I thought that I would like to explore that with him. People had mistaken us for husband and wife at every turn on our trip. We did not correct them.

No, a voice in my head reminded me. *You are not here to stay.*

I turned back to the window and watched the activity outside the airplane.

Chapter Nine

Adam

June 21st, 2024

Thankfully, our London inn had a bar. I sat on a stool and drank my second cup of coffee while waiting for Vivienne. I checked my email and sent some texts back to the nursing staff at my hospital. One of my patients had not gotten what I ordered and here I was halfway around the world trying to fix that. It wasn't the first time my travel had interfered with work but I had things covered at the hospital. And the travel couldn't be helped. There was no way I was leaving Vivienne to solve her problem alone. I admired that woman and the way she was tackling her situation. She was tough. She was just full steam ahead, all day, every day. It was fucking impressive.

We had agreed to meet in the lobby once we were both settled into our rooms and had slept for a few hours. I picked the inn for its proximity to the Tower of London, her first choice of a place to visit. I stood when I saw her at the top of the staircase. She was wearing flowing beige pants and a sleeveless white silk blouse. She had on some sort of walking shoes with a wedge heel and her beautiful silver hair was up in a messy bun.

I had to give it to Maria. Vivienne looked sexy as hell. Which did not seem right for a nun, but I was not about to say anything. I was doing my best to be professional and non-observant of her qualities as a woman. Not having spent much time around beautiful nuns, this was proving to be somewhat confusing for me.

She glanced down at herself and said, "This is normal?" I assured her it was.

We had a quick breakfast in the bar at our inn, then took a car I had rented to the Tower of London. Our chauffeur gave us some background as we drove. In a quiet moment, she murmured that there was something at the Tower she wanted to show me. I said, "Good. If it's not on our tour and we need help getting to it, just tell me."

The Tower was impressive. I had a pretty good handle on British history, having been raised by David Parrish, Washington, D.C.'s premier European history nerd. My father made sure I knew the basics of all European kingdoms and dynasties. But I didn't know a lot about London itself and, even though I brushed up on it during the plane ride over, I was not expecting the sheer size of the Tower complex.

Vivienne listened with deep concentration to the words of our tour guide. He told us he was a Yeoman Warder, or Beefeater, a guard of the Tower. He said their order had been founded in 1485 and had been continuously operating since then. She gave a small nod of affirmation to some of his facts. I realized that time period would have been when she said she lived here.

Stories about the Tower were mostly grim. "I regret to tell you now, what is for many the most distressing story of those who were imprisoned here." The Beefeater paused at that and lowered his voice for the rest of the tale. "We stand before the White Tower, the place where many royal foes were imprisoned and met their fate. The saddest of these stories involves a young king to be and his brother. Edward the Fifth was just twelve when his father, King Edward the Fourth, died. To 'protect' him, his uncle Richard housed him in this very tower. If you've read your Shakespeare, you know that Richard the Third was up to no good. It is believed that he ordered the killing of both Edward and his younger brother Richard, Duke of York, who was also imprisoned here. The two princes were never seen again after Richard the Third's coronation in 1483. Then in 1676, not far from here, archeologists found buried ten feet deep in a wooden chest, the bones of what appeared to be two boys believed to be the ages of ten and twelve."

Vivienne closed her eyes.

The Beefeater moved our group along until we stood back at the site where the tour began. Vivienne waited for others to thank him and disperse and then she approached. "Thank you, sir, for your time. I wonder if I might ask to see another place here in the Tower? A door in the highest level? There is a carved message."

The guard's eyes darted down to hers. When he did not reply, she said, "It's a secret recently discovered in some family correspondence. A carving for an anniversary." She waited for him to acknowledge what she said. My magic heard that she was telling the truth as she believed it. I wondered if I would need to persuade him to take us there. But he moved then, bowing deeply to her.

"Pardon me, Miss, while I go and get my superior." He gave a sharp turn on his heels and walked toward an administrative building. Vivienne avoided my eyes, looking around the grounds instead. I counted the six Ravens in the courtyard trees as they watched the people below them. The Beefeater had told us it was believed that if the ravens ever left the tower, the kingdom would fall. To protect them, a raven master was in charge of their care and feeding every day. I wrinkled my nose at the thought of their blood biscuit breakfasts.

Our tour guide was returning at a rapid pace with another man beside him. His superior was dressed in a suit instead of the full red regalia. He regarded us with suspicion and introduced himself.

"My name is Reginald Cord. I am the Chief Warder. Collins tells me you'd like to see a door in the Tower?" This guy was clearly not interested in helping out a tourist.

"My family tells a story of a message carved at the base of a door, at the very top of the White Tower." Vivienne paused.

Cord frowned. "Is there more?"

"Yes. The message was for an anniversary."

He knew what she was talking about. "I'm afraid I'll need some more information. If you have any?"

This asshole was stonewalling her. I started to speak, but Vivienne held up her hand.

"The message says, 'For V, my love of 20 years, yours J' and it ends with a heart." She kept her eyes trained on him as he absorbed this information. I watched his face turn from suspicion to disbelief, then eager curiosity.

"Good lord," he said. "I thought it was just a story."

He set off for the Tower entrance, taking Vivienne with him. "Collins, get the Governor and meet us up there." The other man took off at a jog. "We have kept the secret of this message since our origins. It's one piece of knowledge about the Tower that only we have. Beefeaters do not tell of the message on the door. Unless someone who knows of the message asks." He stopped and looked down at her in shock. "You are the first person to ever do so!" He took a step back. "Do you know anyone who is or has been a Beefeater?"

Vivienne shook her head. "No, I only know of this tale from my family."

The Chief Warder spoke to a guide once we reached the top and asked her to cancel any more tours for the next hour. When the group had all left, he locked the door behind them and walked to another door across the Tower. It seemed like it would be a door to nowhere, but he reached into his pocket and pulled out an ancient looking key to open the lock.

Someone pounded at the door behind me and both Vivienne and I reacted by drawing our power close to the surface. The Chief Warder raised his chin to me. "Open it," he said.

Collins was back with another man in a suit who said, "Are you crazy? Don't do this!"

Chief Warder Cord scoffed at the new man and opened the door. "This woman knows the message. Our duty is clear. We are to share it with anyone who knows about it."

The space it opened up to was barely larger than a closet. Vivienne crouched down and placed her hand over the etchings in the wood on the lowest panel of the door. She touched the J and the heart. Then she ran her hand over the whole message. I felt a stab of jealousy and wondered why it hurt my chest to see her remember something from her past. And this was definitely from the past.

So was Vivienne. She was telling the truth.

I stepped closer to her and pulled out my phone. As I snapped a picture of her next to the message, all three of the men behind us began to clamor that I could not take a picture here and that the message must remain a secret. I turned to them and said with persuasion, "You will give her ten minutes of privacy to view the message. I did not and will not take a picture. You will wait for us outside."

They filed out of the room and left us alone at the top of the White Tower while Vivienne took in the message from her long-dead husband. She sat on the floor in front of it and kept a hand trained on the grooves. She closed her eyes. I sat in a too small chair and wondered how old it was.

Finally, she spoke. "I healed the princes once in this tower." My eyebrows shot up. She opened her eyes and smiled a little sadly. "They were not cared for well. The guards didn't like it and asked my husband if I could come. John was the chief mason for the Tower and these buildings for most of the time we were married."

I tried to picture her here in 1485. Mothering sick boys and going home to a husband and family. This was real. Vivienne had been ripped through time and somehow survived.

Her eyes surveyed the rest of the room. "A lack of food was the main problem when I was brought here. I comforted them and got a message out to a friend to send back some stew. They sat here and ate and were happy boys."

She shook her head. "Now it is clear they were not long for this world."

After a few more minutes of her sitting with closed eyes and communing with the past, she kissed her fingertips and placed them on the J.

Standing up, she said, "Those were different times."

CHAPTER TEN

Vivienne

When we returned to our inn from the Tower, I told Adam I would like to rest awhile. I woke a couple of hours later to find that he had left me a snack and a note in the living space between our two bedrooms.

Vivienne, I want to do some research on the monastery we are going to visit tomorrow. I'll be back later. I left you a snack. Also, here's a book on the musculoskeletal system. Be prepared for a test on the plane ride home.

I lifted the cloth to find a blueberry muffin.

Folding the note, I put it in the pocket of my sweater. As I ate the muffin, I admired the beauty of the sitting room between us with its gold accents everywhere and the rich wooden trim. I smiled to think about Adam packing the giant Oxford Textbook of Musculoskeletal Medicine in his case. I brought the heavy book down to my lap to use. I would miss Adam's library when I returned to my time.

The few books I had ever seen in my life had all been at the monastery. When I was a child, and after my mother died, my father would take me with him to his art studio there. The monks did not approve, and I spent the majority of those days playing at a table in the back that I could hide under at a moment's notice. Some of them would look the other way, mindful of the prestige they were awarded by hosting a man of my father's talent. Patrons of my father were often also inclined to patronize the monastery. But, as my father said, some monks loved the rules too much, and they were the ones who hounded me to leave whenever they saw me without him.

So I stayed close. I didn't mind. I listened to the monks sing their prayers three times a day and felt transported to another place I had not seen or learned of yet but desired to know with all my fervent ten-year-old being. I felt closest to our Heavenly Father during their chants and even began to sing them myself when at home with Father. He was delighted in my singing and somehow got a schoolbook for me that taught Latin words. Then he got me an actual songbook the monks used when in the chapel. Over time, I learned all their chants and had fair control of my own voice when singing them.

But my singing was all done under my breath when at the monastery. Even though my father did not love the rules as other men did, he made sure I knew a woman's place was not to sing with men. And as I grew older, he was detailed in explaining to me the ways of the world and the expectations of a girl, and then a woman, in our village.

On her deathbed, my mother had confided to me that she was a witch and that was how she was able to help so many people as a healer. She said my father would explain the rest. What he explained was that I should never say the word witch and I should never admit to knowing one. His plan was to have another witch tell me the ways of magic when it came close to my time to learn about it.

One rainy night just before my fourteenth birthday, a woman named Rebecca appeared on our doorstep. To me, she seemed very old, and I was more than a little afraid of her. She was the tallest woman I had ever seen, taller even than my father. She had long, curly black hair with streaks of white running through it.

My father had not prepared me for her visit. Her dark eyes seemed to know that.

"I am a witch," Rebecca said. She placed her wet bag on the floor and removed the hood from her head. "You are also a witch. As was your mother." She watched as my eyes filled with tears. "It is not a bad thing to be a witch. All beings are created by God and are just as he intends them to be. That is the first thing for you to know."

My father reached over to prod the logs from his chair by the fire. Our cottage was small but filled with the color of my father's paintings and my mother's woven rugs. Father gave me one reassuring nod before Rebecca commanded my attention again.

"Your mother was a healer. The most powerful witch I have ever known. If you have half of your mother's abilities, you will be formidable. Once you have your first cycle, you will come into those same powers. If you have a daughter, she will also be a witch and will gain your powers."

My head was spinning. Rebecca recognized my state and poured me a cup of ale from the pitcher on the table. "Drink it," she said. "All of it."

When I finished drinking, she sat back and told me the rest.

"To be a witch is to be lonely in this life. We are feared and reviled." She paused and seemed to look straight through me, as if she could see what I was made of. "Witches do not speak of their craft to anyone but other witches." She turned to my father, and he grew pale at her inspection. "Your mother chose to betray this oath by informing your father about our sisterhood."

Then she looked down for a few moments, and tapped one finger on the table, as if trying to decide something. "Our laws dictate that those who are not witches, but learn of our existence, should be put to death."

I slowly stood and placed my hands on the table. I didn't know what I was going to do, but I would not sit still and let her kill my father in front of me.

Rebecca nodded her approval at my reaction. "That was good. A good decision. You may sit. I will not act on this law. Your mother was kind to me and I will return the favor to her."

That night, Rebecca opened my eyes to the world of witchcraft I was about to enter. She said to be a witch is to hold power, and that power is hard to resist. I learned from her that not all witches had the same skills and that not all witches are good. Knowing this, and not having any witches in my family to discuss witchcraft with, she advised me to keep my secret to myself. Witches would recognize my power and I would recognize theirs, but I could ignore them.

When she was leaving, my father thanked her and tried to pay her for her time. She refused his coins. The last thing she said was, if my power should ever be shown to mortals, I would be dooming us both to certain death. My father blanched as she described some of the ways witches were being crucified in our own land and kingdoms across the water. If I was accused of witchcraft in our village, Rebecca told us we should leave in the middle of the night and never be seen there again.

Decades later, I realized that Rebecca's experience of what it meant to be a witch had informed her characterization of it to me. Her description of a bleak, lonely life that was very likely to end in a blaze of fire and death on a stake was not encouraging, to say the least. But my life, and my mother's life, had been full of love, sacrifice and gratitude for the witchcraft that allowed us to help others. I never knew what sort of powers Rebecca had, but it was clear that for her, being a witch had been a very different experience.

When she left, my father and I sat in stunned silence. Our introduction to witchcraft had been terrifying. My father said, "We will never discuss this again." And we never did.

I thought of him in his studio, the morning light streaming in through the large windows. He would gently mix his paint and then say a silent prayer before he hunched over and touched his paintbrush to the manuscript.

He was a good father. He prepared me as well as he could for the world we lived in.

I have never faulted him for what happened later.

CHAPTER ELEVEN

Adam

June 22nd, 2024

What remained of the monastery where Vivienne grew up was south of London and would be a two-hour drive. She was shocked to hear that, recalling that the journey had taken days for her and her new husband to complete. He had been at Bayham Old Abbey to consult on some of the artistic features being added and had sprained an ankle which Vivienne had been asked to treat. He had fallen hard for her and pressed her father to give his consent for them to marry, even though she was just seventeen.

"And your father allowed that?"

She kept her eyes trained out the window of our limo on the London streets as if waiting to recognize something. Anything.

"We were in love. My father saw that John was sincere. And he knew John could provide for me."

She turned her head my way. "Am I correct in thinking that you believe me now that I'm here from the year 1502?"

I was glad there was a partition between us and the driver. Because what I was about to say defied all logic.

"Yes. I thought it was insane. I didn't believe there was any way this could be happening. But it's clear you've been telling the truth. And after yesterday..."

"You were wrong." Her eyes met mine, and she waited.

I gave her a flat look. When her gaze did not leave my face, I conceded, "Yes. I was wrong."

She nodded. "I understand. As you pointed out, it would be a hard thing for me to accept if our positions were reversed." Her expression became serious. "Thank you, Adam, for all you have done for me. And thank you for yesterday." She turned back to the window. "But I don't know what seeing Bayham Abbey will do for us. I still think the key to my going home is the manuscript."

"You may be right. But let's give it a go and then get back to Washington and figure out the rest."

When the car reached the country and there were no more landmarks to look for, Vivienne opened a book and started reading. I felt some satisfaction when I saw it was the book I had brought for her on the musculoskeletal system. I pulled out my phone to type up some questions I could ask her about it on the ride home.

When we reached the abbey, our driver parked the limo, and I told him he could take a break for about an hour while we walked the grounds. Vivienne was silent as she took in the ruins of the abbey. The night before, I had shown her the website with a clear aerial view of what remained, and she had narrowed her eyes at it, trying to reconcile what she saw with what she remembered.

As we walked toward the ruins, I felt something wash over me, a wave of it at first and then a constant presence around me. I focused on Vivienne and was struck by the faint glow to her skin, the shine on her hair, her eyes alert and searching for something.

I was overcome with desire for her. *Holy shit.* I had been attracted to her over the past couple of weeks but, of course, did not pursue that because I'm not an ass who hits on women of the cloth. Also, she was a guest in my house and her circumstances made her vulnerable.

What the fuck was this?

I reminded myself of these things as I tried to get a grip. She commented on the size of the arches, something about the stained glass that would have been there. The effort not to touch her was so great I found myself struggling to respond. Finally, trying to formulate a question, I reached out and took her hand between mine. The buzz was there again. We both looked down at our hands. I felt my magic responding to her touch again.

"Vivienne. What are you doing to me?"

She frowned down at our clasped hands.

"No. It's good. It's unbelievable, really." I gave a small laugh. "I can barely speak." I studied her face. "Did you use your magic on me?" I hoped I was saying what I meant. It was hard to think. I wanted more than anything to pull her to me.

Her face remained neutral as she answered. "I'm casting my magic outward to see if anything calls to me. I'm sorry, I know it can be strong. But no one else is near and I need to use this time to find out what I can."

"What is that scent? It feels like a drug. And this? What is this?" I turned her palm over and rubbed my thumb along the lines there. Every stroke made my magic hum. She was watching our hands clasped together with fascination.

Then she ran her eyes over my face. "You seem to be handling it."

I frowned at her. "Barely. And you know it. What are you doing?"

She stared past my shoulder, over toward the abbey and a couple walking to it from the parking lot, as if debating whether to waste more time continuing the conversation. After a moment, she met my eyes.

"It's my magic. I relaxed my guard and am casting it to discover what I can. That's why we're here, is it not?" She studied my face and saw that I was not happy. She clarified, "You're experiencing the effects of my magic as it calms and heals."

I said sharply, "It does more than calm or heal. You know that, too."

Vivienne's reply was just as sharp. "For patients, I don't release it for anything but calming and healing. I shared it with my husband, with lovers. But never to bind them or render them weak."

Husband. Lovers.

"Well, it sure as hell made me weak! And I don't recall asking for your healing."

She said patiently, "I'm sorry. I thought it might be acceptable here. Out in the open where people wouldn't know where the feeling was coming from. I know my magic is potent. The magic I used at the library was to communicate, and you withstood that, so I hoped my healing magic might be the same. It's the best I have."

I scowled at her. If she was telling the truth, I was in some deep shit. The full force of her magic unleashed was more than any man on earth would be able to resist. Probably any woman, too. I'd never been so distracted in my entire life as the few minutes since we began our walk. And here stood the culprit, in front of me and sleeping in my house. To top it off, she was a nun.

She watched me as I processed her words.

"Adam, this is the best magic I have to locate something. Isn't that why we're here?"

"Don't try to tell me you didn't know what that would do." She hardened her stare. "And don't do it again. People will come looking for this when they sense it."

And I don't want them to, I realized. *I want it for myself.*

Two men who were somehow now just a dozen feet in front of us had stopped and were frowning in my direction.

Vivienne and I stared at each other for a tense moment. I wondered what she was thinking. My own thoughts raced ahead to her, in my bed, wearing that teal lace bra and panty set I had washed with her laundry at home.

"I'll guard my magic," she said and ripped her hand from mine. I felt the loss as soon as she shielded herself again.

She turned away from me. I took a deep breath and released it slowly.

Nothing to see here, folks.

Just a total shift in world view and a complete re-ordering of life priorities.

After a minute, I said to her back, "When everyone leaves, you can try again. I'll stand farther away."

She gave a derisive laugh and shook her head. She walked on and I followed her in silence. One of the men ahead of us asked her if she was okay.

As Vivienne assured the stranger that she was fine, I wondered how I was going to handle this new threat to my sanity. And my power. Because as of now, without any question, this sixteenth century witch had the upper hand.

She sat on a bench near the parking lot, waiting for other tourists to clear the area. I leaned against the limo and watched her. Once the other three cars in the parking lot were gone,

Vivienne stood and slowly took the gravel walkway on her own toward the ruins. I followed at what I hoped was a respectful distance. She was putting out that magic again, and I caught myself straining to feel it, hoping to have it wash over me like it did before, to smell that intoxicating perfume just once more.

Jesus Fucking Christ. I'm a fucking junkie.

Just then, a man rounded the corner of the ruins and walked directly toward Vivienne. She saw him and reined in her magic immediately. I caught up to them just as he was introducing himself. His hand outstretched, he said, "Father Andrew Barry. How are you? I felt the magic you were using and wanted to meet you." He was in his forties or fifties, tall, handsome, with brown curly hair and blue eyes.

He's a goddamn witch. Could this get any worse?

"Vivienne," she said as she shook his hand reluctantly. He held his hand out to me then.

"Samuel Marsh," I said and shook it. Vivienne did not acknowledge my lie, but I hoped she had picked up that we were now on the defensive and nothing more was to be said about who we were or our purpose there.

"You don't meet many witches who are priests," I said as an opener.

He laughed at that and said with his Irish accent, "No, you don't. I am a unicorn, that's for certain. That's why I was thrilled to sense your presence here."

When neither of us responded to that, he asked, "Would you like me to give you a tour? I'm in this area doing research about the history of witchcraft. I've learned an incredible amount since I've been here." He smiled at Vivienne. "Where are you from?"

"The United States," she answered, most unhelpfully. She began to stroll again along the path toward the back of the abbey, away from the parking lot. I followed them, not liking the closeness of this priest.

"Is that your job in the church?" Vivienne asked. "Research?"

"I'm a professor," he replied. "And this is my area of expertise. Early witchcraft. How it developed and how it differed from our magical abilities today."

Vivienne stopped to look at the arches still standing on one side of the abbey. Her gaze swept from the front to the back and I knew she was filling in the windows with stained glass and replacing doors. He watched her, too.

"If you don't mind my saying so, your magic is very different from anything I've experienced before. The intensity of it nearly knocked me down."

She ignored him and began to walk again. He kept pace with her. "It's theorized that early magic was just that strong. That the witches of the medieval era were mostly elemental, gifted in the use of earth magic and water and weather." He studied her profile and added, "Blood."

She stopped and turned to him with confusion on her face. "What does that mean?"

"Well, there aren't many documents still around, as you can imagine. But those we do have seem to imply that witches in the distant past were tied more to the healing arts. To magic that was more beneficial to mankind than abusive or selfish."

He turned to me and said, "You have to admit... present day magic can be used to further incredibly selfish goals."

He was right about that. But my instinct was telling me that everything else was wrong about that man. Despite wanting to keep a low profile, I sent my magic out to read him. He glanced back at me when I did. His shielding was strong. Some of the best I had ever felt. The priest wasn't giving anything away, and now all my inner alarms were going off.

"Today's witchcraft is thought to be a diluted version of what was possible for witches at their beginning." He motioned us toward a small, one-story building that said, 'Old Bayham Abbey Welcome Center.' Pulling the door open for Vivienne, he said, "The most common modern areas of witchcraft are physical. Even the least powerful witch can raise a shield to block their opponents from harming them or reading them. It's led to us remaining a secret society. We hide from mortals and ourselves."

He walked around the room, pulling out brochures from stands lining the walls. The Welcome Center was empty, and Father Barry appeared to know where everything was.

"Do you disagree with our secrecy?" I asked. If so, that in itself would make him a danger to us. There was no room for that kind of talk in witch society.

"Not necessarily," he said. "I just think that if we shared our gifts, we, as a people, could do more with them." He handed Vivienne a pile of brochures. "I hope you enjoy these. There's some fascinating history in this old abbey."

She took the brochures with a wry smile and placed them in her bag.

I held the door for them as we left.

Father Barry continued his lecture. "Modern witchcraft is composed of mostly mild physical talents with some rare mental abilities. But witchcraft in the middle ages appears to have been enormously powerful and, as I said, rooted in the elements. Witches then pulled power from Earth." His eyes shifted over Vivienne. "I've been searching for the origin of that ability. For the instance where the first magic was used. What was the source of that magic?"

That stopped Vivienne in her tracks.

Uh oh, Father Barry was about to get it. I smiled.

She reprimanded him. "As a man of God, it should be apparent to you that Our Heavenly Father is the source of all magic and any other talents mankind has been gifted."

His ass having been handed to him, he said, "Of course," and motioned for her to walk ahead of him on the path.

Vivienne walked under an archway and stood in what would have been the center of Bayham Old Abbey. It was now a green field. Staring at the opposite end of the field, she asked him, "What have you discovered about the origins of our craft?"

We followed her as she strolled along. I knew she was trying to place herself there over five hundred years ago.

Father Barry said, "What origins? Oral histories indicate it was almost certainly in existence as long as man has lived. But it flourished here in Britain. Around the time of the Tudors. The persecution of witches in the middle ages was so prevalent because there were so many of us. Witchcraft was growing, evolving. I assume you've read the Malleus Maleficarum?"

Vivienne shivered. He noticed. "Yes, that was not a time to be accused of witchcraft. I would hope witches today would fare better."

I said, "There you go again with the references to witchcraft being revealed to mortals. Is that something kids are doing today? Talking about a revolution?"

The priest leveled a look at me that said he wanted me dead. *There he was. The real Father Barry.*

I smiled and turned away to look back at the entrance of the abbey. It looked like the groundskeeper for Old Bayham Abbey had gone missing. Weeds pushed up through cracks between stones on the pathway. The sun disappeared behind some fast-moving clouds and a swift breeze rattled the trees nearby. I tried to imagine the abbey filled with pews and parishioners. Some with hands clasped in prayer and heads bowed. Some sitting upright listening to the service.

Vivienne and the priest had made their way to the exit, some fifteen feet from where I stood. As she stepped around the corner to the back of the abbey and he followed, I lost sight of them for a moment. I heard her cry out, and I ran to the exit to find Vivienne on the ground, a cord of her magic glowing with silver and golden light stretching from her chest to his. He held an arm outstretched in my direction, but I moved in time and his strike missed.

My own strike was true, and he collapsed as soon as it hit him. I pulled Vivienne a few feet away from him and into my arms. She was unconscious. Her face had no color. He had only been connected to her for a moment, but she was seriously hurt.

The priest was out. A blow like that could definitely have killed him, but it looked like he was still breathing. Having been connected to Vivienne's magic might have saved him. I wished I'd thrown everything at him, but I'd been worried about Vivienne.

He needs to die.

But my desire to get Vivienne to safety overcame my instinct to kill the priest. I gathered her up and walked to the limo as fast as I could without calling any attention to us. I didn't see anyone in the lot, and I wondered again where the priest had come from. Our driver dropped his food when he saw us and ran around to open the back door.

"She's fine," I said. "Just needs some juice. Get us back on the road, will you?"

"Yes, sir."

I got Vivienne secured in the back, her head on my leg and my hand running over her hair and over her forehead. "Vivienne, talk to me."

She was breathing fine, but her pulse was still too high. I got out my phone and dialed. "Reeger. I need something fast. A priest, maybe working at Bayham Old Abbey in England. He's Irish, name is Andrew Barry. Said he was a professor and was an expert in old magic." I paused as he wrote it down. I added, "Powerful."

He said he'd get right on it and when I hung up, my anxiety eased a bit. Tom would find anything there was about this guy.

But I knew I should have gone back to kill him.

The limo sped through the countryside, and I thought about our new reality. Vivienne was no closer to getting home and now her power was a known commodity.

And until I saw her magic flowing into that priest, I didn't know there was another witch on the planet who could do what I could.

CHAPTER TWELVE

I was aware of Adam carrying me into the inn and persuading everyone around us that everything was fine as he did. He laid me on my bed and began to take off my coat. "Adam," my eyes still closed, I reached for his arm.

"Thank God," he said, and I felt him kneel next to the bed. "Your vital signs are better now, but you've been out for two hours. What do you need?"

I opened my eyes. I was relieved to see the woodland wallpaper of my room at the inn and the luxurious linens and pillows surrounding me.

"Time," I said. "My body needs time to heal itself. It was a grave injury." His face darkened, and I knew he wanted to find the priest.

"I'll be fine," I assured him. He was gentle as he helped me with the coat. I cried out a little at the pain in my side. Adam moved on to my feet then and gently removed my shoes. He sat back on his heels.

"What else?"

"Tell me what it looked like. What did he do to me?"

He hesitated. "It seemed like your power was flowing into him. It could only have been a few seconds."

That's what it had felt like. A severe blow to my core to stun me, then him pulling my power. It was depleted, but not by much.

"What happened then?"

"I hit him with a strike. It should have killed him, but he was connected to you. Could he have been healed by it?"

I gave a slight nod. "I need some water."

Adam brought me a bottle of water and helped me sit up to take a sip. The pain was formidable, and I knew this was going to take some time. Then he laid me back down and felt my forehead. He frowned and headed for the bathroom. I heard him running water at the sink. He brought a cool cloth back and laid it gently on my forehead.

"What can I do?" he asked.

This would be the hard part. Getting this man to sit back and do nothing was not going to be easy.

"I need you to seal the room with your strongest spell. I'll be sleeping while my body works to heal me. My magic will be strong without me holding onto it." I saw that he understood what that would be like. "I need to lower my shield so I can use its magic, too. It may be all day. You can stay in your room, or the room between us, if you like."

"I can help you," he said. "Or we can get another doctor who is a witch to come, an internist."

He did not want me to be unconscious again, and I understood that.

"The only thing I need you to do is to seal the room and then go."

He shook his head. "No. I won't leave."

I gave a short laugh. "I didn't think so."

He began to seal the room, using a touch of my own magic and I marveled at how he wove our shield spells together to create something completely impenetrable. A golden thread darted in and out, binding our spells. There was an artistry to it. We would not be interrupted.

"Now you should sit by the door and not move."

His brow knit, he asked, "Why?"

"Adam, I know you would never act in an inappropriate manner. But I would like to take the struggle from you."

I saw him processing that and was relieved when he said, "Fine." He pulled an armchair over to the door and placed it directly in front of it.

Sitting down, he said, "I'll be here if you need anything."

I closed my eyes and began to repair my damaged body.

I awoke some hours later to a darkened room. Streetlight filtered in through the windows. Adam was still sitting across the room from me, his gaze intense.

"How do you feel?"

I tested my body, reached for the depths of my magic, and realized my stores were replenished. I felt as good as new. "Back to normal," I said.

He wiped a hand over his face. "Good."

I sat up and turned, putting my legs over the side of the bed and stretching my back.

"How long was I out?"

He checked his watch. "Almost eight hours."

I reached under the lamp shade and turned the switch. Light flooded the room and I could not help my smile at that modern-day miracle.

From across the room, he said in a tight voice, "Could you turn it off now?"

I frowned and wondered why. But looking at him, I saw that he meant my magic, not the light. I replaced my shield, and he sat back in relief.

"Jesus Christ," he said and covered his face with both his hands. After a moment, pulling them down, he said, "Does your shield stay up when you're just sleeping? It would have to. Otherwise, your safety would be compromised every fucking night."

I regarded him with sympathy. "You did very well. Eight hours is a long time to withstand my magic."

Adam closed his eyes and shook his head. "I cannot do that again."

He got up and placed the chair by the window.

"I need a walk. Lock the bolt behind me."

CHAPTER THIRTEEN

Adam

June 23rd, 2024

I chartered a private jet for the trip home. I used a fake passport but did not have anything different for Vivienne. Which was unfortunate because now her power had been sampled by a bad guy and she had a giant target on her back. Having spent eight hours being completely ruled by that power, I knew the priest was not going to give it up.

I sipped my whiskey and wondered if it affected him the same. *Does a priest get hard for a woman?*

He's a man. Of course he would.

But did it bother him? Or would he spend every waking minute of the day reveling in her nearness and wanting to touch her? Like me. Then there was the fact of her being a nun. Would that change things for a priest? Sadly, it did not change a thing for me.

She sat in the front of the plane and read her medical text while I sat in the back and made a mental list of things to do. I'd have to put security in place now. Guards for her whenever she left the house. Guards for Maria and Grant. More guards at mother's home.

Remembering that I gave my best friend Samuel's name to the priest instead of my own, I realized poor Marsh was a target now, too. Not my best moment. I held the glass against my forehead, thinking about the conversation I'd have to have with him to alert him to the fact that he could be in danger but not give him any details about why. Marsh and I had been best friends since day one of medical school and, although he was not a witch, he was used to my 'shady dealings,' as he called them. He'd roll with it.

I called Reeger again and asked him to arrange coverage for everyone, including Marsh, and told him to use the best. I knew he'd find me witches with impeccable background checks and devastating skill sets to put on guard. It would cost a fortune, but he knew I was good for it.

He still had not been able to find anything about Andrew Barry. Which made me wonder if one of Barry's skills was persuasion. It was the perfect magic for criminals. Persuasion could get a man out of any situation and leave no trail of his presence. The only thing tripping up persuaders was video evidence and even that could be avoided or explained away by a thorough persuader.

After Reeger, I called Grant and told him about the attack on Vivienne. I wanted him to be on alert and to keep an eye out for Maria and mother.

Vivienne made her way to the back of the plane and sat in the seat across from me.

"You have not had much sleep in the past day and night."

"Is that a nice way of saying I look like hell?"

"I've seen you looking better." I laughed at that, and she smiled. "Do you regret now that you told me to be honest?"

"Not at all. I always want to hear the truth from you." I motioned for the flight attendant who stood at the front. "I'll have water. Vivienne, would you like anything?"

She asked, "Do you have champagne?"

"Of course," the flight attendant made her way back to the front.

While we waited, Vivienne said, "May I ask you a question, Adam?"

"Anything," I said.

"Your power. To persuade people to your cause." She paused and met my gaze while she composed her next words. "Is it the reason you are able to have your own plane?"

I clasped my hands in front of me. "That's a loaded question. Are you asking, do I abuse the power to persuade people? Do I use it to my advantage and to the disadvantage of others? If so, then I'd say no. I do not choose to do that."

"I would not expect that you would. No, I mean, is it the reason you have wealth?"

"Ah." Without a doubt, persuasion was part of the reason for my family's generational wealth. "That's very observant of you. I would say yes to that. But I can't be responsible now for choices previous generations made to get ahead. I'm sure stock tips were acquired. Contracts awarded. All I can do with the power I hold today is to use it responsibly. Ethically. And teach my son to do the same."

We sat in a comfortable silence for a moment.

I said, "You must know something about this, though. I'm thinking your magic must be extremely persuasive when you want it to be."

She tipped her head slightly in acknowledgement. "I only use my magic to convince another to do something when safety is a concern. For myself, or others."

She changed the topic then.

"Why are you not married?"

I was not expecting that. My eyebrows raised. I thought for a second, then shrugged and said, "Just haven't met the right woman, I guess."

She looked skeptical. "You are handsome, smart, accomplished. Kind." She shook her head as if trying to put the pieces together, but they were not fitting. "I don't understand. Is marriage not something that is desirable to do, in this time?"

My sleep deprived self was having a tough time tackling this one. "I mean, I date. I date women."

She was amused by my inability to explain this. I tried to get my brain in gear. "Yes, people do still get married. It's still something people want to do. I think."

Luckily, the flight attendant came back with our drinks then and we thanked her and each took a sip. I asked, "Are you a fan of champagne now?"

Vivienne took another drink. Her newly smooth hair framed her face and hung in a silky curtain over her shoulders. "I love it." She smiled.

We sat in silence for a minute or two and I gazed out the window in an effort to stop cataloging the properties of those eyes. Light gray with a dark gray ring around the iris. Maybe some flecks of blue. She flipped through a magazine left on the seat beside her.

"How do you find the women you date?"

I turned back to her and saw that she was not done with this line of questioning. I sighed. "Today, people mostly meet in bars or in their professional environment or online."

Her brows drew together. "Online? How do you meet online?"

I picked up my phone and looked for a dating app. "Mostly it's younger people who meet online but, because I don't go to bars and seeing anyone from work is out of the question, I also look at apps." I opened one and held it out to show her. She leaned in and I got a whiff of her scent that stopped me cold. *Dear God, please more of that.*

She looked up at me when I didn't say any more.

Get your shit together, Parrish.

"People post their profiles online and then if someone likes your profile and you like theirs, you can meet in person." I demonstrated swiping. She took the phone and began swiping.

After a few swipes, she said, "This woman is lovely. She is also a doctor." She turned the phone around to me to show a beautiful dark-haired woman, forty-five or over, because those were my parameters.

"Yes," I agreed. She turned the phone back around, narrowed her eyes and continued to scrutinize the profile.

Adorable. I enjoyed the free time to examine every feature of her face. I thought that she was perfection, and I realized I was in trouble.

"Are you interested?" I teased her.

"Not in a woman," she said, still looking down at the phone. Then she handed it back to me quickly, as if she had said too much.

"Can I ask you a question, Vivienne?"

"Anything," she said back to me.

"How did you become a nun?"

She sat back and crossed one leg over the other. "I was widowed and despondent. I needed the structure and comfort that the sisters in the convent gave me. I needed so much. And they gave it to me. They helped me." My magic heard the truth in that statement. She was full of gratitude for her fellow sisters.

I took a drink of my water.

She gave me a thoughtful look. "You haven't slept, have you?" She leaned in a bit and said, "I can help you."

I took another drink. She reached out and placed her hand on my hand, holding the glass. There was that beautiful hum of recognition again as our skin met and the surprise in her eyes showed that she felt it, too. The last thing I saw was her face near to mine as an invisible blanket of warmth and comfort gently covered me. Vivienne helped me lean back in my chair and I fell into a glorious, deep sleep.

CHAPTER FOURTEEN

Vivienne

June 26th, 2024

Adam had a servant. Her name was Sonya. She was a young lady from Cuba, and she usually came once a week, but Adam had told her not to come the past few weeks. Sonya was short and curvy, with long curly hair that she tried to tame into a ponytail high on her head. She moved through the house with such purpose I felt I was being swept along with the wind.

Her husband Fausto (his mother was Italian) had come over from Cuba on a boat when he was a child, but she came by plane and had lived here for seven years. Fausto was older than her. They had a six-year-old son, Eduardo, with curly hair and big dark eyes. Eduardo was with her for the afternoon while she cleaned.

She was a witch, with a not very significant level of magic, who recognized my large store of power right away. I learned of her life while she was cleaning Adam's house. When she was almost done, we sat to enjoy iced tea together. She had been shocked to see that Adam had a guest.

"He's very private, Mr. Adam. He does not have guests who live here."

I observed the supplies she used and where she stored them so that I could be of some use in maintaining his household myself. She noticed my attention.

"Don't you go getting any ideas to start cleaning here, Miss Vivienne. I see you taking notes! I need this job! Mr. Adam pays better than anyone I've ever worked for. And he's a good man. I love my job here."

"I understand. I will not clean."

For a while we sat at the kitchen table with a globe from Adam's study between us. Sonya had been showing me where her family was from in Cuba. Then Eduardo sat in my lap and drew in a coloring book while she cleaned the counters and the floor. He had a slight cough that I took from him easily and dispersed toward the screen door that was open to the backyard. Sonya's head turned sharply toward us as she sensed a change in her child.

"He is better," I assured her. She scanned him herself and then smiled as she observed me handing him individual crayons that he then used on his artwork. When he set one down, I gave him another. I swayed my legs slightly and hummed a song for him as he colored.

Adam came in just then and set his briefcase down in the hallway. He watched as I handed Eduardo another crayon and ran my hand over his soft curls. Sitting down in the chair across from us, he flipped one of the coloring books around and grabbed the group of crayons discarded by Eduardo.

"Hello, ladies." Then he narrowed his eyes and looked at the boy in my lap. With suspicion, he said, "Eduardo."

The boy giggled.

Sonya turned the water off at the sink and ran a cloth over the counter to dry it. "Don't pay attention to them, Miss Vivienne. They have a strange rivalry no one understands."

Eduardo narrowed his eyes right back at Adam and then dissolved in laughter again.

Sonya said, "Mr. Adam, he is in heaven right now. Eduardo doesn't have an abuela or abuelo. You both have a way with little boys."

Adam caught Eduardo's eye. "My father used to say little girls were made of sugar and spice and everything nice. But little boys were made of frogs and snails and puppy dog tails." He leaned in. "Do you have frogs in your tummy, Eduardo?"

I poked the boy's stomach, and he squealed with laughter.

"No! I don't eat frogs!"

Adam laughed and began to color in a picture of an extinct creature I had learned was called a dinosaur.

I said, "What about snails?" Poke. "Or puppy dog tails?" Poke.

"No! Just spaghetti!"

We all laughed at that.

Sonya said, "Would you like to go outside now, buddy? You can play in the backyard for twenty minutes while I finish."

When Eduardo scrambled to get out the back door, Adam concentrated on his drawing for a bit longer, then gathered up the crayons, ripped out his finished artwork, and pushed it to me. I smiled as I examined his meticulous pink and green coloring, all inside the lines. It was a creature with a huge body and impossibly long neck that he labeled "Vivienne" at the top.

"Very nice," I said.

"Thank you. I drew it just for you. That's an apatosaurus. He eats leaves, like you."

"I have never been likened to an apatosaurus. Thank you?"

He nodded. "You're welcome. I think it might be the nice long neck you have in common. And the leaves."

We smiled at each other over the kitchen table.

Sonya called Fausto then to see when and if he would be available to pick her up or if she would need to take the metro home. Fausto was a policeman at the Capitol building. I listened to her rapid-fire Spanish with interest. I understood some French, having spent some time with a noblewoman who hosted French friends. But Spanish seemed faster and more intense. From the amount of times I heard "metro" it sounded as though she was going to need to take the metro.

Adam placed the crayons back in the box and left for his room. Since our time in England, he had been avoiding being in my presence for very long.

God help me, I loved seeing his desire for me on that field at the abbey. It had been a while since I had taken a lover, and that beautiful man was tempting me like no one ever had. And when his hand touched mine... it felt as though my magic was rushing to meet his. It coursed through my veins, and I thought I would catch fire from the force of it. It was exquisite. My entire body awakened at that single touch. It was a feeling like no other, and I wanted more.

I was not lying when I said I hoped it would be different there, that maybe my magic would not overpower every person around me. But I didn't really expect that to be the case. And as far as I could tell, Adam was affected by my magic the same as others always had been. But the added sensation when our skin met... that was something new. And dangerous. When we touched it was explosive and I didn't know why.

I am devout. But I have learned to trust my instinct more than the written word of man. And the truth is, I have a better understanding of God's grace and his will, having been made more in his likeness than other humans are. He gave me this magic of mine; of that I have no doubt. He trusts me with it. And if something does not ring true to me, I do not give it credence. I trust in my decision making, whether that be to protect a life by taking a life, or by taking a lover when I want to. I know God will judge me in the end.

In my world, I would have had no problem acting on my attraction to Adam. His intelligence was an intoxicating distraction for me every day. When he first was touched by my magic, I relished the knowledge of my power over him. I even played out in my mind how it would go if we were in a different setting. How his kiss would taste. What he would like from a lover.

But this world was still unknown to me, and I knew Adam was probably the most dangerous thing in it. I felt his anger when I raised my guard again at the abbey. He did not like having a vulnerability to my magic any more than I did with his.

My instinct said I could trust him. But I was better off keeping my distance while here and keeping my cover as a nun. The attack from the priest was even more proof of the risks I faced in this world.

God willing, I would be home soon enough with all this new knowledge to put to use in my healing. It would have to do.

I lifted a magnet and placed his drawing on the refrigerator.

Chapter Fifteen

Adam

July 1st, 2024

The trip to England hadn't helped Vivienne connect to her past, but it did help me to believe her story that she was here from the past. And I could no longer avoid checking in with the International Council of Witches to see what, if anything, Marshall had said to them about Vivienne. After her stunt at the Library of Congress and after the attack on us at the abbey, I had to make sure she wasn't on some wanted list.

I called for a car. Usually I took the metro over, but I needed to get that meeting done and get back home. It was a luxury to be driven around and I took endless grief about it from my neighbor Herb. But I didn't care. Time was precious, I had the money for it and I put that back seat time to good use. "Bigshot!" he would shout if he saw me getting in or out of the back of a limo. "Dumbass!" I would shout back and we would both laugh.

The ICW was hidden in plain sight on the top floor of a mirror covered building in Crystal City, Virginia. Louise Carmichael was at the front desk. I always liked her. What's not to love about a gorgeous blond with impeccable taste in her dress and makeup who could be counted on to flirt with me? But it was subtle. We both understood we were just playing. I tried to keep a low profile when visiting that office and it would be stupid to date someone so crucial to the operation.

"Hello, my favorite person in Crystal City," I greeted her.

"Hello, my favorite doctor of little people," she responded.

"How's everything?"

She rolled her eyes. "Connor told his teacher he was better than the principal at making decisions. This was after the principal told him he had to stop throwing shade at some asshole kids in an upper grade."

I laughed. "Connor should tell those kids to fuck right off."

"I believe he did." Her son, Connor, was fourteen or fifteen, on the spectrum and wicked smart. "He recognizes shitheads right away, that kid. And he calls them on it."

"The House could use a shithead detector. Let's groom him for public office."

She laughed at that. "Dear God, can you imagine?"

"Yes. It's a great plan." I tapped on her desk. "I'm on it. It's happening." She shook her head. I pointed to the back. "Is he in?"

"He is," she said, reaching under her desk to hit the switch to open the door to the hall of offices. Richard Cole was the CEO of the Council. His office was behind a pair of massive oak doors at the end of the hall. To the right were four offices for witches with exceptional skills. To the left were four offices for witches with useful everyday administrative skills. I ignored the open doors on each side and headed for Richard's office. His door was slightly ajar, and I heard Marshall Smith's voice.

God damn it. I strengthened the shield I held around my power when I was in public.

Marshall finished what he was telling Cole as I walked in. I pushed open the door and locked eyes with him.

"What's up, Marshall?" I asked.

His mouth flattened when he saw me. I turned to Richard. "Cole," I acknowledged him and looked back at Smith.

"How's your friend?" he asked. "Her power is off the charts. But you wouldn't know that unless she told you. Has she told you?"

She didn't need to because I can also divine powers like you, jackass. I can do everything any other witch in this building can do.

"Why don't you fill me in?" I said.

"She's a healer. Maybe strong enough to bring people back from the dead." He waited for my reaction.

"And?" I asked.

"And that's all I got..." he didn't finish the sentence.

I raised my eyebrows. "That's all you got?"

After a moment, he said, "I was sick that day." And then, "But I'd get what to look for now. Wouldn't be bombarded by that first shock. Could you feel anything?"

In other words, did you fuck her and did anything weird happen when she came?

"She's an old family friend. I didn't interrogate her about her powers. That's considered uncool in most of the world. How the fuck do you not know that?"

He shook his head. "Why are you such an ass? You are our whole department. I have no other options sometimes with the worst cases." When I didn't respond, he said, "You could give us some names of other people who can do what you can do."

Smith saw from my face that naming names was not about to happen. He said to Cole, "I'll be back later." He walked past and bumped me slightly as he left the room. I broke into a big smile and couldn't help laughing out loud when he was gone. I raised my hands to Richard as if to say, *what?*

Richard Cole was over seventy, with deep frown lines between his brows and wrinkles at the eyes and mouth. He was working the frown lines just then, not amused by my antics. He shook his head. "Can you please not rile him up like that? I'm going to have to hear about you more than I want to now. He's been bugging me about your friend for weeks." He walked around his giant oak desk and motioned toward the door. It closed softly, and he moved back to sit in his massive leather chair. Richard Cole was not a big man, but he was of the opinion that he was an important man and he decorated his office accordingly. I sat in the less comfortable chair across from him and admired the view of the river below.

Cole ran a hand over his bald head and said, "Give the guy a break, maybe. Marshall's not wrong. We have more and more serious cases these days and really just you to handle them."

"Tell me about it," I said. "I have two local ones I'm investigating right now." Richard knew I wouldn't just take a case without having my own investigator make sure it was necessary. I always did the research before accepting a job. "Tell Smith to stay the fuck away. He grossed my friend out with his creepy feelers."

Richard raised his eyebrows. "As a rule, I don't go ordering Marshall around. He's sensitive. And you know I need him."

I made a face. *Oh please.* "Whatever. I'll tell him myself if he comes back around. I came today to say I need some time off. While Vivienne's here. I'll still do the two local cases if needed."

He kept his eyes down, reviewing the contents of a blue folder. The type of folder that Smith delivered to me almost once a month now. Closing it, he pushed the folder toward me and asked, "You think this can wait for you to have time off?"

I reached for it and flipped it open. It didn't take long for me to realize that no, it couldn't wait. But I asked anyway, "Is there nobody else that could handle this?" I looked up at him.

Shaking his head no, he said, "I wish there was somebody. This one is too dangerous for anybody but you." At my skeptical look, he said, "I'm not stroking you here. You know it's true. I'd be sending anybody else on a mission to die if I gave them this." He gestured at the folder I held. "Shit, I don't even want to give it to you! But this asshole needs to be gone."

I agreed. This was a witch in Chicago who was known to have relationships with underage girls. Caught by another witch, whose investigation showed a pattern of more than a dozen such relationships by the man. He clearly believed he was bullet proof. The report showed he had the same power I was born with, an ability to persuade someone to do your bidding. I'd be immune to his commands, but anyone else would be susceptible.

"What else can he do?" I asked.

Richard shrugged. "That's all we got."

"Sloppy," I said. Most witches were born with a combination of two talents at the very least. You could expect a child to develop some powers from each parent. Meaning this son of a bitch in Chicago could most definitely do more than persuade people. I'd need to have some idea of what his other skills were before approaching him. I'd also want much more detail than that report contained about his daily activities and relationships. Once Tom could get that information for me, I could plan a trip.

Cole raised his hands up in a question. "So you'll do it?"

"Does it look like he has anything planned? Any prospects he's grooming?"

"No. Do you want to hold off until it looks like there's a situation?"

"Yes. I'll get a better report on him and be ready. Keep somebody on him. Also, you need to get somebody else on your payroll with persuasion."

"That's true. But you guys aren't that easy to find. How about Grant?"

I closed my eyes and tried to clamp down my fury that a representative from the Council of Witches had just mentioned the name of my son as a possible enforcer for one of their sentences. It was one thing for me to do it. I had a rare set of skills that helped me survive confrontations with bad guys. Grant was not suited for this work and Richard Cole would understand that before I left.

"Richard." I opened my eyes. "Grant has never declared his talents to anyone outside of the family. And he is not an option for you, or anyone from this council, to ever approach for any reason whatsoever." I paused. "Is that clear?"

He gave a wry smile. "Crystal clear. Thanks for taking this. Now tell me about this friend of yours who has Marshall so excited."

I put the folder in my bag and sat back. "Her name is Vivienne. She's from England. I knew her when we were kids. Her parents were friends with mine. They're private, though." He would get what private meant. Any witch with a lot of power didn't want the world to know and come asking for it. "She does have remarkable healing powers. He's right to be excited about that."

This was the delicate part. I needed intel on the priest but did not want to reveal why I was asking.

"In fact, we were in England for a couple of days and had someone express real interest in her powers. A priest named Andrew Barry." It was subtle, but his eyes shifted when I said the name. Cole knew something about a powerful priest or someone with that name.

We sat in silence for a few moments while he fiddled with a legal pad and I stared him down. Finally, he said, "You know I can't share any information from the database. The privacy is for everyone's good. Nobody can see your records either."

The International Database of Witches was not all-knowing, but it would have what I needed on Barry. At its core, it was just a list of known witches throughout the world, their names, occupations, and addresses. The most important piece of information it provided was the level of magic each infant had been born with. That score would grow over time as witches came into their power at puberty and, as they became aware of and developed their skills. But that first dose of power, the level detected at birth, was the single most important indicator in the realization of significant power later in life. I had a pretty good idea of his specialty, but I wanted that birth score and I needed a location to start looking for him.

Cole came to a decision. "I can't do a search. There's not enough reason."

"How about he tried to kill Vivienne?" I was enraged that Cole was not going to help with this.

Shocked, Cole asked, "What?" And then, "Why?"

"He felt her power. Went insane trying to get it."

Cole stared at me. "He would have to have been insane to try that with you there. Did he immobilize her or persuade her to go with him?"

I realized my problem right then and there. I couldn't tell Cole that the priest was pulling her power and wanting to make it all his own because then Cole would know that was a possibility. It was the way I had built my power to such a level that I was almost invincible. I worked very hard to keep that secret. I wasn't going to out myself now.

"He tried to take me out, too. I don't think he had a plan. I just know that he hurt her, and that is unacceptable."

"There are ways to dispute that..." he tried to tell me.

"Dispute it?" My voice raised. I stood up. "I was there. There's nothing to dispute." I could see he wasn't going to budge. That settled it.

"Vivienne has asked for my protection. I'll take care of it from here."

Cole stood too, alarmed now that I was invoking an arcane method of resolution for witch feuds. Offering someone protection meant giving a formal declaration that you were going to get rid of a problem for them and no one could get in your way. It was sanctioned blood feuding for witches. It had not been used to my knowledge in a very long time and never in North America. We were supposedly more civilized than Eastern Europe.

"Are you fucking crazy?" His voice raised. "Why would you make this public? You're going to cause an international incident. I do not want those mother fuckers coming over here again looking into our affairs."

"Then you should have offered to help when I asked." I was not sorry Richard Cole's life would get messy. But I was relieved by my decision. I didn't know where I'd be when I took care of the priest and in the event it was in public, I'd need the official declaration of protection in place to do what was necessary and not end up in trouble with the council. I'd find the priest and kill him so Vivienne would be safe. She wasn't safe with the witches of today knowing about her power.

Richard saw that I was not going to take it back. "God damn it," he sat back down in his chair. After a minute, he reached over and slammed a stack of papers and pens off his desk. Without looking at me, he said, "She's your problem while in the states. You're on your own with this."

I walked out of Cole's office with a new mission. I'd get the priest out of the way and no one could interfere. The only other people outside of the family who knew about Vivienne's magic were Sharon, Marshall and Richard, and they wouldn't share that knowledge. Once the priest was dead, I'd help her get back to 1502 where, ironically, she would be much more safe.

CHAPTER SIXTEEN

Vivienne

July 4th, 2024

We were going to celebrate a holiday called Independence Day. It was an event held every year since 1776, when the United States of America won their independence from England.

Adam wanted me to understand just how significant an accomplishment that was. "We beat the pants off England, Vivienne. I need you to know this. England had the money, the armies, the weapons. But we had a thing called heart."

I recognized a lecture when I heard one but did not really care that America had beaten England in a war after my lifetime. We were crossing a large green lawn in front of the Supreme Court Building. It was hot and crowded, and it took us a while to find a section large enough for our group. When Adam saw that our security detail intended to surround us and remain standing through the evening festivities, he argued with the head man.

Adam set up a chair for me, said, "I'll be right back," and walked back toward the house. He came back ten minutes later with four chairs in bags slung over his shoulders. Handing the extra chairs off to our guards, Adam spread a maroon and white blanket down and then set our chairs on top. The security detail sat stiffly beside us, standing every once in a while, to stretch and turn and scan the entire field.

Adam poured me a glass of champagne then one for himself and set the bottle back in the box full of ice he rolled over with us. He extended his glass toward my glass and said, "To Benjamin Franklin, who knew that keeping a Republic would be hard."

He clicked his glass with mine and took a long drink.

In front of us was a young couple, clearly just getting to know one another and struggling to hold a conversation. Behind us was a young couple so enamored with each other they could not stop kissing and only broke for air and to drink from their bottles of ale.

Adam stared ahead, deep in thought.

"What does that mean?" I asked. "Keeping a republic is hard?"

He glanced back at the Supreme Court.

"The Justices made a bad decision yesterday that could jeopardize our Democracy and allow a despot to be President again. He'd be crowned King if he could."

That was interesting. It seemed like the President was equal to a King in England. And it was not popular for him to want to be King. Adam saw me sorting through the possibilities.

"America was founded as a sovereign country that's governed by the people. It was a rejection of a monarchy. We have three branches of government. Congress, they work in the Capitol," he pointed at the domed building straight ahead, "the President, he lives in the White House," he gave a wave off to the right, "and the Supreme Court," without looking back, he pointed his thumb toward the building behind us. "They're supposed to provide checks and balances on each other. But the country has become divided into two camps that despise each other, so no governing gets done. And the Supreme Court just gave the Office of the President immunity for his actions while in office. Which is like naming him king." He shook his head. "The Supreme Court hasn't been very supreme since RBG died."

"Who is that?"

"She was a wise justice. She fought many a good battle."

"A woman?" I asked.

He nodded. "There are four of them on the Court now."

"Can a woman also be President?"

His mouth drew to the side. "Theoretically. Not yet. But we do have a woman Vice President. The office just under President."

"Interesting."

He laughed. "Yes. You're visiting America at a very interesting time."

We each drank some more of our champagne.

After a moment I asked, "Is everyone in America as fraught as you?"

When that sank in he gave a genuine laugh and said, "Fraught! That's a great word for it. Yes. Everyone in America has become very fraught."

Adam had described for me the fireworks that were traditional for the United States to set off on the occasion of their victory over England. He said when it became dark, the explosions high in the sky would begin and we would see colored lights there for at least thirty minutes.

The couple in front of us abandoned their attempts to talk to each other, and both had their heads down, tapping at their phones. Adam and I shared a look at their unsuccessful evening and he leaned over to me.

"Poor guy should have learned some poetry."

I saw Tony, the head security man next to me, nod his head. He said in a low voice, "Or brought flowers, or candy, or a stuffed animal. Something." Adam laughed.

"Did twenty-year-old Adam have some poetry ready for a girl?" I wished there were pictures of a twenty-year-old Adam in his house.

"Obviously. But only because my dad made me memorize a few."

"And what were they?"

"Well, it's been a while." He tilted his head back, thinking. "A long while." He closed his eyes. "Getting the first line is always the hardest part."

I took a sip of champagne and then laughed as his struggle to remember stretched on.

"Be quiet, nun. I'm getting there."

That only made me laugh more.

"Why do you call me 'nun'?"

"It seems like nuns shouldn't be as sassy as you are." He tapped his forehead, and then, "Got it!" Holding up his hand, he gave me a triumphant look. "This is a good one."

Adam leaned closer, closed his eyes again, and recited the poem.

"O my Luve is like a red, red rose

That's newly sprung in June;
O my Luve is like the melody
That's sweetly played in tune.
So fair art thou, my bonnie lass,
So deep in luve am I;
And I will luve thee still, my dear,
Till a' the seas gang dry.
Till a' the seas gang dry, my dear,
And the rocks melt wi' the sun;
I will love thee still, my dear,
While the sands o' life shall run.
And fare thee weel, my only luve!
And fare thee weel awhile!
And I will come again, my luve,
Though it were ten thousand mile."

When he opened his eyes again, I was looking into them. Those warm, brown eyes with the dark lashes. He smiled, then sat back, satisfied that he had remembered it all.

"Though it were ten thousand mile," I quoted the last line again. "Yes, that's a good one."

"Who's that by?" Tony had his phone out, ready to type in the poet's name.

Adam said, "That's Robert Burns, Tony. A great old Scotsman, he was. But you should check out Shakespeare's sonnets, numbers eighteen or twenty-nine. *That's* some romance."

Tony nodded, typing away at his phone. I wondered who that big burly man would be reciting poetry to. Adam was finding something on his phone in order for us to listen to music when the fireworks began. I sipped more champagne and found myself excited to see the display.

After he found the place to hear the music, Adam handed me a bowl of berries and a spoon and opened a tray of crackers with cheese. He had observed these were my favorite foods to snack on and had been supplying me daily with sustenance as I read through his books.

I dug into the tray of treats with relish and was finishing a large bite of cheese and crackers when I saw him watching me and trying to hide a smile.

"What?" I asked, my mouth still full.

He said, "Where do you put it all? You're about five feet tall and weigh as much as a teenager. But you put away as much food as a linebacker."

I continued to chew. He saw that I was waiting for a definition for linebacker.

"A very large man playing on a football team."

I didn't know football either.

"Like Tony," Adam said helpfully.

I took a sip of champagne and then said, "Thank you for that compliment. It's shocking that you haven't found a wife yet."

"I'm just saying… the way you eat is impressive."

"It's my magic use. It takes a lot of energy." I put a palm up and shrugged.

He laughed at that and shook his head. "It won't be long before the show starts." Reaching over, he stole a strawberry from my bowl and ate it. "It's crowded here but on the other side of the Capitol, all along the Mall, it's completely full of people. That grass will not even be visible right now."

It was such a huge space, I was surprised.

"Yeah," he said. "It's one of the best perks of living where I do. Not having to drive to Fourth of July." He smiled. "Greg and Herb and I used to hit the Mall celebration every year. You met Herb." He looked at me and I nodded. "Greg lives on the other side of his house. When we got old enough to go on our own, we'd try to meet some girls on Fourth of July every year. We were not that successful." He laughed. "One year it was about a hundred and five degrees and were out there all day with a bottle of rum and no ice. I have never forgotten to appreciate ice since that day."

I pictured three teen boys with their warm bottle of spirits on a hot day. "I can imagine. I also appreciate your ice very much."

He smiled again and turned his attention to me full blast. I had experienced this a few times with him now and when he did it, I could hardly breathe. I wondered how any teen girls had ever withstood that smile.

"What holidays do you celebrate, Vivienne?"

What made him lock in like this and concentrate on me so intensely, I didn't know. I just tried to hold on and make it through the interaction with some sense of normalcy.

I took another sip of my champagne. "May Day. We dance then. Shrovetide, before Lent. We eat and make merry then." He reached over and poured me more champagne.

"Before Lent? So 'making merry' is a euphemism for debauchery?"

I searched my brain for the meaning of euphemism and debauchery.

Adam helped. "Immoral activities?"

I thought about it and had to agree with that description. He laughed when he saw my acknowledgement.

"What else?"

"Winter Solstice."

He nodded. "A very witch holiday to celebrate."

Just then, the music paused and the first firework was shot into the night. I held my breath as the music began again and the sky in front of us exploded into sparks of white and red and blue that then fell to the ground. I worried those below would be hit by the fire and turned to Adam to ask about them. He was watching me, not the show above us.

"Will the people underneath be hurt by the falling debris?"

"No, it burns away in the sky."

I turned back to the display and exclaimed when a brilliant gold burst lit up the sky and fell in soft sparkles for what seemed like forever.

"It's so beautiful," I murmured.

Still looking at my profile, Adam nodded.

"So beautiful," he said.

CHAPTER SEVENTEEN

Adam

July 7th, 2024

I needed to get back to seeing some patients at the hospital. Vivienne had spent the last couple of days reading medical texts and I was running out of ways to avoid her, so this was good timing. I'd make it a point to be home each day by early afternoon.

I had dispatched the local jobs from the Council in the middle of the night a couple of times, and even though there was a round-the-clock stakeout of the house being conducted, I hated leaving her there alone. There also had not been any filing of protection for Vivienne with the Council of Witches but I'd need to go there again and do that soon. I was waiting to see my mother and hoping she had some books I could reference about it. While I had my father's law books, as far as I knew, she had his collection of books pertaining to Witch Law.

I bought a simple flip phone from Amazon so Vivienne could call me or Grant if she needed anything while I was out. The knock on the door from the Amazon delivery person made her start in her seat at the breakfast table.

"It's fine. It's just a delivery. I ordered a package." After I signed for it, I brought the box back to the kitchen and set it on the counter.

I sat back down and took a drink of my coffee. Then I asked, "Why are you scared of someone knocking at the door?"

She took a moment and thought about her answer.

"It was loud. I've reacted poorly to loud sounds before. To the people who make loud sounds at a door."

I waited.

She emphasized, "I have reacted very poorly."

"Have you?" Now I was interested. "What have you done that was so bad?"

"In my time… I don't think you can understand. It's dangerous for a woman alone. And when I'm threatened, I react."

When she saw that I was waiting for her to elucidate, she said, "People have died."

There it was. She spoke what I knew to be true, even in this era. Great power requires you to use it sometimes.

"Vivienne, even knowing you for the very short time I have, I am positive that anyone who met his end from your magic deserved it."

After a moment, she surprised me with, "I know." She raised one shoulder slightly. "I've done what was necessary. But it's still a sin."

"No," I said. "Someone trying to harm you is a sin." She looked at me with skepticism. I doubled down. "You're a healer. People need you. Alice needs you. It's okay for you to want to stay alive."

She shook her head. "It's not a small thing."

"What do you do, make it look like a heart attack?"

She gave me an incredulous look. I smiled.

"I suppose you could only do that so many times, though." Her face turned disapproving.

I asked her, with some heat behind it, "Are you telling me they didn't deserve it? Because some people do. Did Father Andrew Barry not deserve it? There is real evil. I'm sure you've seen it." She tightened her mouth but did not agree.

"There is a cost to this much magic. This much power," I said. "I'm sorry you've had to pay it. But you have to know it's better that you have it than someone else. You'll do more good than bad."

She considered that and said, "Is that how you justify it? You save more lives than you take?"

Well, that was a leap. How did she know I had taken any lives?

Our eyes met. "It's complicated," I said.

It was interesting to talk about this. With someone who might actually understand. But I'd said as much as I would.

"Well." She laughed without any humor. "This is frowned upon, and we are going to be judged."

"Me? Definitely. You? Never."

I changed the subject.

"I bought this for you. Do you want to open it?" I got the package from the counter and pushed it her way.

She had no trouble opening the box, but then got stopped by the hard shell around the package and I had to laugh.

"Sorry Vivienne, you've just encountered the hardest task of modern times. How to open plastic wrapping with just your hands." I pulled open a kitchen drawer and found scissors. I cut off the top of the plastic shell. Vivienne watched it all with great attention.

"What's this?" she asked, touching the clear coating of the package.

"Plastic," I said. "Many things are made of plastics. Including the outer shell of items for sale."

I handed her the package. "Be careful. It's sharp on the top."

"Plastic," she said, filing the new word away in that steel trap brain of hers. She slowly drew the plastic apart and a black shiny object fell out onto the kitchen table.

She picked it up and turned it over in her hands. "What is it?" she asked.

I thought that I would never get tired of seeing Vivienne experience things for the first time. I loved trying to see things through her eyes.

"Open it," I said.

Her brow furrowed, she found the seam and pulled on the phone. It opened with a click, and she gasped. Red and white lights lit up inside it. When she ran her finger along the keys, they made a beep.

She said, "It's a cell phone."

"You can call me on it if you need anything when I'm not here."

Vivienne glanced up at me. "You won't be here?"

"I need to go to the hospital to see my patients."

"I understand," she said. "I'm sorry to have taken so much of your time."

"Vivienne, I have enjoyed every minute of it."

It was true. I had enjoyed the time with her. Especially evenings in my study reading together. I sometimes found myself watching her. She was so engrossed, she only looked up occasionally to ask me a question. And even then, she began with, "Adam, I am sorry to interrupt your reading, but…"

I loved seeing her face when I described a successful treatment for common baby ailments. She listened with such intensity that I had to make sure to give her the most detailed description possible because I knew she was filing that information away to use someday on a patient.

The phone was a hit. We practiced placing cell phone calls for thirty minutes or so. First, I had to try to explain how Amazon was able to bring me a phone the day after I placed the order. I agreed with her that it seemed like a miracle. Then, despite her protests that she was perfectly able to remember some numbers in a row, I had her write down my phone number, Grant's phone number, and 911. Vivienne pushed the end of the pen about twenty-five times to make it click. It seemed like pens might be her favorite twenty-first century invention. She put the list on the refrigerator under a magnet of the Washington Monument.

She turned to me with sparkling eyes, holding her phone with both hands. "You have been so generous. Thank you, Adam. I will treasure my phone."

I was struck then with the overwhelming desire to buy Vivienne everything under the sun. Phones, jewelry, books, dinners, trips. They all passed before my eyes, and I lost a few seconds to staring at her face while they did. I tried to recover with, "You are very welcome."

She walked to the study then with her new phone. I leaned against the kitchen sink, wondering at how my life had changed in the past month and realizing with some shock that life could still offer up surprises.

Chapter Eighteen

Vivienne

July 13th, 2024

We settled into a routine after Adam returned to work full time. I knew he was still looking for the priest and that he had people guarding me and his family. I hoped he included himself in that circle of protection. Adam seemed to be a caretaker for the world to the detriment of his own well-being. This was apparent when he watched the evening news with me and helped to clarify the current events of the day. We sat in his two leather chairs that faced the fireplace and watched a television screen that stood on the mantle.

One of the candidates running for President had been injured in an attack that took place outdoors. Adam's eyes did not leave the television screen, and I felt his blood pressure rise as the hour progressed. His expression grim, he finally spoke. "Everything is so much worse now."

I placed my hand on his and sent a wave of healing throughout his entire body. I flooded him with waves of cool and peaceful energy. He took a deep breath in and then released it slowly.

"That was nice," he looked down at my hand on his. I lifted it and sat back in my chair. "Did you just lower my blood pressure?"

"Yes. You needed it."

He nodded and turned the television off. "I did," he said. He sat back.

I tapped the arm of his chair. "Why do you watch things that make you feel sick?"

Clasping his hands in front of him, he shook his head. "I don't know." He laughed at himself. "You must think it's crazy."

We sat in silence for a minute. I listened to the click of a second hand as it worked its way around a clock in the hallway.

Then he said, "I can't seem to look away." He leaned his head back and scrubbed his hands over his face a couple of times. "But I need to. You're right."

I said, "The idea of having some agency in your laws...in decisions of state. I can understand it could be intoxicating."

"Back in 1776 it was intoxicating. We've gotten used to it. We expect it now. To see it all going to hell..." he shook his head.

I gave him a sympathetic smile. "It's not my country that's changing. Change is difficult." I added, "But nothing lasts forever."

He tilted his head in acknowledgment.

I said, "And if the worst happens? What will you do the next day?"

His mouth quirked up a bit. "Go to work. Help sick kids." He sat up straight then and placed his hands on the arms of his chair.

"Right," he said. "I'll look away. Is it ok with you if we don't watch the news from now on?"

"Of course. I won't always be here to lower your blood pressure. You need to take care of that."

He gave me a wry smile. "Well, I think not watching the spectacle might help me with that. Good advice, Doctor Lanier."

I smiled back at him. "My pleasure, Doctor Parrish."

The one thing Adam did do to care for himself was to exercise. Every morning, he went running just before sunrise. I determined this schedule during the first week of my stay. Once I understood what it was he was doing, I decided it would be fine for me to sleep in. He was always dressed in shorts and a light short-sleeved shirt, and he wore shoes that were made of rubber. He returned an hour later in clothes soaked with sweat and his hair curly and damp on his neck. He explained it to me when he found me reading on the porch once as he ran up his steps.

He collapsed in the chair next to me, opened a bottle of water he had left on the porch table, and took a long drink of it. "Running keeps me healthy. It has all kinds of benefits."

I raised an eyebrow. "You look near to death at the moment."

He laughed and pulled his shirt up to wipe the sweat from his brow. I observed his flat stomach and the hair on his chest and then remembered a nun does not do that.

"I'm sure I do look like death warmed over," he said. "But I feel great. Do you not exercise in your time?"

I shook my head and tried to express why we did not. "It seems something of a luxury to spend time this way."

"I can understand that it would. We do have too much time on our hands in this era. But exercise is the one thing I have to do every day, or I start to feel terrible."

He gave a small grimace and rubbed his right knee.

"Is your knee troubling you?" I asked.

He waved a hand as if it was nothing. "It does sometimes if I push it too hard. I'll have to take the day off from running tomorrow. Maybe a couple of days."

Without asking, I reached over and held my hand over his knee. I felt the inflammation and the disorder of the joint. I let my hand hover there for a moment, then moved it lightly over the area, flipping it this way and that to get a better idea of the problem. Then my magic knew what to do, and I placed my hand directly on his knee. I sensed the repair happen fairly quickly and knew it was back to proper in a matter of seconds. I waited for a moment, though, and glanced up to see how Adam was handling it. He was reacting a bit to the release of my magic, but his curiosity about the process was counteracting that.

He was looking at his knee. I withdrew my hand and his eyes searched mine.

"It feels better," he said. "How did you do that?"

"My magic felt the problem within your joint and repaired it to the intended state."

"But..." he said, "how did you know what that state was?"

"I didn't know," I replied. "My magic knew."

He was stretching his knee out straight. He stood on it and looked at me closely.

"How long will this last?" he asked.

"Probably until you injure it again," I said with a laugh.

Adam stared at me and I could almost see his mind racing with all the possibilities. He lifted his head then and stared out across the street at the building he called the Supreme Court. After pacing back and forth a bit, he made his way around to the other side of the porch and back to end up in front of me again.

"Oh my God. Vivienne. This is such a gift. Thank you."

He sat back down and drank some of his water. We sat for a bit and then he said, "Even though you lowered my blood pressure and I saw you heal yourself in London, I can't get over what you just did. It's incredible."

"Thank you," I said. We spent a few more moments in a comfortable silence.

Then, "Are there limits? Is there anything you can't do?"

I contemplated that. "There are limits. When an illness has progressed too far, I won't interfere. At the end and a person can no longer speak...then I know God has spoken for that soul and I simply ease their pain as they go."

Adam was a doctor. I could see that he understood that moment when a soul leaves the body.

"It's a miracle, though. What you can do. How do you keep it a secret? I want to call everybody I know right now and tell them I have a new knee. How do you not reveal yourself as a witch?"

"I'm careful. I use a lot of herbs and sometimes I take longer to administer healing than I have to. It's why I need to understand how my healing works. When I know this... I'll be able to encourage preventative measures for health. Maybe there will be less need for my healing." I looked to him to see if he agreed.

He nodded. "Less chance to reveal your magic." He studied me. "That's a pretty tall order. Educating all of medieval Europe as to modern medical theory."

"I thought I'd start with just my village."

He laughed. A warm breeze graced the porch then, and I leaned back and closed my eyes to enjoy it. When I opened them again, Adam was staring at me. I closed the book in my lap and crossed my legs.

"I know other doctors who are witches," he said. "Some are 'medicinal healers.' From what I understand of witchcraft specialties today, I think witches within your skill set mostly identify areas of concern with someone's health. But they don't heal them. They may soothe, but they use modern medicine once a diagnosis is confirmed."

Adam paused. "You are unique."

He took another long drink and finished his water bottle. He held it up. "Running and water consumption. That's my entire plan for health."

I must have appeared unconvinced because he went on. "Seriously. It works your cardiovascular system and if you do it long enough, it releases endorphins into the bloodstream that help reduce inflammation. They also make you experience a small sense of euphoria."

I raised my eyebrows, and he nodded. "Yeah, it's good stuff. We need to get you in on that. I'm going to get you some running shoes." He got up and went inside. I heard him opening drawers in the kitchen and then he was on his way back to the porch.

The screen door slammed shut behind him as he dropped to his knees before me and tugged on my slipper to take it off.

"Let's measure your feet," he said as he set my bare foot on the porch. He seemed to stall for a moment, and he ran his index finger along the line of my toes. I experienced the swift rush again of his skin on mine. He gave a short shake to his head and went to remove the other slipper. "Have to do both feet because one could be larger than the other."

While his head was down, I made use of the time to get my fill of Adam up close. His eyelashes were a thick fringe, and the shadow of his beard made me want to rub my hand over his jaw.

He placed a metal measuring stick against one foot and then against the other. "Perfect," he murmured. "Your feet are perfectly the same." He tapped my foot and with his warm hand on the back of my leg, he lifted it to fit the slipper back on and did the same for the other one.

Standing back up, he said, "What's your favorite color?"

I thought for a moment. "I suppose, red."

He said, "Do you mean wine colored, like my couch or brighter red like blood?"

"Couch," I said.

He sat down with his phone and began shopping online. I had learned this was the way he bought most things. Except for food, he bought that at a local market.

"I do not need red shoes, Adam."

He kept his eyes on the phone and raised his hand. "Nope! This is happening. Trust me, you absolutely do need running shoes."

"You may have noticed that I have not run anywhere while here in 2024."

"No doubt because of your appalling lack of footwear." He raised his hand again. "My bad. But I got you, Vivienne. The best women's size seven crimson running shoes are only a few taps away."

I smiled when, after a few minutes of scrolling on his phone and *many* taps later, he made a disgusted sound and changed tactics.

"Maria?" He held the phone to his ear. "Can you do something for me? Vivienne needs some running clothes and also the best size seven running shoes you can find." He listened for a bit. "I don't care. Yeah, just the best rated. Oh, and can you find them in crimson?" I heard her laugh and say something else. "Of course she wants them," he said. "Have them delivered the fastest way possible. Okay? Thanks. Bye."

He stood up and said, "See? No problem." He tapped my arm lightly to make sure he had my attention. "And when the FedEx guy shows up to deliver them, please don't kill him, okay? He's just doing his job."

I rolled my eyes, and he laughed on his way into the house.

Heaven help me. I imagined how I would look running from place to place in my village and I had a laugh of my own.

CHAPTER NINETEEN

Adam

July 17th, 2024

Vivienne could not wait another day to see the children's hospital. The only place she wanted to visit more was the Library of Congress and the manuscript. I had asked her to be patient about going there until I could make sure our protection detail was prepared for the visit. The security team was mostly large men in suits and not at all inconspicuous, but I felt better having them surround Vivienne. After our first outing, she asked that they give her a few meters of space and they argued until she gave them the steely eye and without question won that argument. The hospital was already on my daily schedule, so I let them know Vivienne was going too. And I tried to prepare her.

"Only children come here. Many of the patients have some form of serious disease. Many have fatal illnesses."

She nodded in sympathy. "It must be very difficult for those who work here."

"It is." I ushered her in front of me into the elevator, which I realized she had not encountered before. I asked the boys to take the next one. They frowned as the doors closed.

"This is an elevator," I said. "The elevator uses electricity to pull us up to other floors." Vivienne surveyed the interior from top to bottom and moved slightly closer to me when it began to lift.

"I'm going to introduce you as a colleague of mine from England. That way you can stay with me while I do rounds, but hopefully nobody will grill you about your work. I may say you study holistic healing. Maybe Reiki or something." She gave me an irritated look because we had already discussed the ineffectiveness of Reiki. "Well, I assume you'll want to help a patient, and that's the only thing I can think of to explain your weird jazz hands when you heal."

Her look promised to murder me soon, but the elevator dinged then and the doors opened.

When we stepped off the elevator onto the eighth floor and walked past the nurses' station, I was immediately bombarded with the usual requests. Also, I knew the sight of me on the unit with an unknown woman was raising some eyebrows and starting some text conversations. Right there in front of me. These people were always all up in my private life. Showing up with Vivienne just gave them enough to talk about for the next month. Or maybe year.

While I addressed what I could of the nurse's requests and dealt with some questionable claims about me having to provide lunch for the entire staff the next month, Vivienne was scanning the hallway. She took in the nurses' station and the patient rooms. There were sliding glass doors to some, and curtains acting as doorways of others.

Eleanor Rodgers was the head nurse of the unit and my friend of many years. Glancing at Vivienne she asked under her breath, "And who do we have here, Dr. Parrish? You have to give me something. Come on." Her brown eyes did not leave my face while she waited. Ellie was a forty something brunette and was beautiful in an amazon warrior sort of way. I loved her and loved that she took no shit from anyone ever, but I wished she had taken that day off. I decided to cut the chatter off at the pass.

"Eleanor, this is my friend Vivienne. She's here visiting from England. I also visited her there recently. She works at a hospital in London. We are not dating—we are just old friends. Much like you and I are. Please spread the word." She narrowed her eyes and cocked her head a little, silently calling bullshit on my peremptory strike at the gossip chain. Eleanor knew me too well and without a doubt could see that I was a little off when in the presence of Vivienne. I wished I could tell her how fucking hard it was to hold it together when standing next to Vivienne Lanier, and that she would be proud of me if only she knew, but instead I rolled my eyes at her and began to sign the stack of papers she held out.

The nurses were starting to take notice of our guards at the end of the hallway and I was forced to address that, too. "Vivienne comes with a security detail. Nothing to worry about. They'll just wait for her until rounds are done. If you need to explain it, say she's a visiting dignitary."

"Will do, Dr. Parrish." Eleanor's delight at my situation promised that there would be a thorough grilling the next time we saw each other. When the nurses were all finished with me, I took Vivienne's purse and stored it behind the desk. She gestured toward the sealed rooms and asked, "Are they at risk of infection?"

"Yes," I said. "Well, everyone in the hospital is. That's why we wash our hands so much. But we'll need to gown up for those."

We walked to the end of the hallway to the first of four curtained rooms. I said, "I'll explain the diagnosis of the patients for you later when we get home."

We entered quietly, and I approached a young woman dozing in a chair at the foot of the bed. She heard me log in to the medical chart from the computer next to her and stood up quickly, dropping the blanket she'd been wearing. I smiled at her as I pulled my reading glasses out of my pocket and put them on.

"Hi Dr. Parrish. How are you?" She gave me a tired smile. I really liked this mom. She was sweet and handled things with such grace.

"Hi Mary Lynn, I'm fine. How's my buddy here?" I read the notes on his chart then evaluated the eight-year-old boy covered by several colorful blankets on the bed. He wore a red knit hat with a Washington Nationals patch on it and held a TV remote in his hand.

"He's being good, so he's getting a surprise present today from his dad."

The boy's brown eyes lit up. "I know what it is."

I widened my eyes. "You do? What are you getting?"

"A Switch Lite!" he shouted.

"Vivienne, do you know what that is?" I turned to look at her.

Her eyes wide, Vivienne said, "No! Should I ask for one too? I've been very good this week."

"Jonah, this is my friend Vivienne. Can you please tell her about Switch Lites and see if you think she would like one?"

"You *would* like one." He began to tell Vivienne why Switch Lites were cool as she moved closer to hear him. I brought his mother nearer to the door to talk about the test results on his chart. I spoke to her softly. The update I had for her was not good. Jonah's results showed he was going to need more chemotherapy.

"This is not uncommon. Not at all. It's something we just deal with and keep at it." I gave her some specifics about medicines for the next few weeks and told her what to expect.

We turned back to the bed and saw Vivienne holding Jonah's hand while the boy drifted off to sleep, smiling. "Thank God," Mary Lynn said. "I need to make a call to his dad." She searched her purse for her phone while Vivienne and I left.

We faced each other in the hallway. Her eyes were serious. "Did you do that?" I asked. "Help him sleep?"

She nodded. "He was experiencing some pain. His body wanted to rest through it." We were silent for another moment. "You do this all the time?" she asked.

"Yep." I raised my eyebrows, acknowledging the enormity of the job. "But some days are better than others."

She said, "I heard you talking to his mother. You gave her hope."

"Well." I stared down the hallway. And then back at her. "There's always hope. That was only his first round of chemo." I realized I had not talked with her much about cancer and treatments for it. "I'll explain chemo to you at home."

We visited three more rooms and Vivienne managed to soothe three more children by touching a hand or humming a song. The parents each gave her a smile and a thank you. Then I got her ready for the remaining four rooms.

"These are the kids who are most ill."

In the hallway, she tugged on my sleeve and asked, "What's that?" She pointed to a wall of equipment. I pulled out my phone and took a 360 degree shot of the area. I leaned down to her. "I'll explain everything in this picture to you at home." She squeezed my arm in thanks.

We put paper gowns over our clothes and added gloves and masks. I pushed into the room using my back. Vivienne followed. Once in the room, her eyes swept over the toddler in the bed and I saw her concern.

"Hmm..." she murmured in sympathy.

I addressed the baby's father. "Hi Dr. Rawlings. How are you? This is my colleague, Dr. Lanier. She's visiting from England and observing rounds with me."

He turned to her. "Hello, nice to meet you." Jake Rawlings was a big man, dressed in a suit and tie, as if he came from the office. She returned his greeting. "Are you an oncologist too?" he asked.

"No," I said. "She trains nurses. Works mostly with relaxation therapies for adolescents in hospital."

I turned to her. "Vivienne, Dr. Rawlings works with infectious diseases." I moved to the side of my patient.

"How's my little angel?" I lightly lifted her hand and held onto her pinkie finger. The toddler did not move. She was breathing heavily, air tubes in her nostrils and patches with wires under them sealed to half a dozen places on her small body. Her shoulder-length blond hair and the well-worn teddy bear tucked under her arm were the only clues as to who this little girl was when she was happy and healthy. I read her charts carefully, knowing her father would have already done so and that he would be hoping for something new from me. Something that maybe only a pediatric oncologist would see. Anything.

Vivienne made her way to the bed and reached for the toddler's hand. "Don't wake her," her father said, sharply and too loud for the room. He shook his head slightly and tried to explain. "Sorry, her mother's at home getting rest, and I just want Emily to be asleep while she's gone. She gets upset."

"I understand," Vivienne said softly. She held the baby's arm with both her hands. Emily squirmed and made a small sound of distress. Her father frowned.

"It's okay," I told him. "She's a genius at soothing kids."

We watched while Vivienne began to hum softly to Emily. The toddler sighed. We both watched the monitor as her vital signs improved. Rawlings examined those numbers and his eyes darted back to Vivienne, sizing her up, wondering what this was.

"That's helping her," he said.

I drew him to the other side of the curtain to talk. I went over the numbers. Rawlings asked me questions. When did I expect her to get through this latest downturn in her health? Did I think it was being caused by the latest treatment? Have I seen this before? What was the outcome?

I paused. I looked directly at him. "I have seen children in all states of illness from pediatric cancer. And poor Emily is really in the thick of it right now. She is flooded with cancer fighting meds and her body is working really hard." Rawlings dropped his head. "But there's one huge thing to hold on to here, and that is that Emily is strong." Her father laughed a bit. I continued, "I'm not just saying that to make you feel better. She really is fighting the illness. So I expect to see that when I come back tomorrow." Her father nodded a thank you, still trying to compose himself, head down.

As we washed our hands and prepared to leave, Dr. Rawlings cleared his throat and spoke to Vivienne. "I'm sorry. Do you think you could come back? That was something to see. I'd like Sara to see that. Emily's mom."

Vivienne reached for his hand with both of her own. "I would be happy to come back. And I will pray for you and little Emily until then."

"Thank you," he said.

I was awed by what Vivienne had done on our rounds. I couldn't help wondering what my job would be like if I had that magic? As we left the room and took off our paper gowns, Vivienne pulled her gloves off slowly.

"You're tired," I said accusingly. "You said it didn't hurt you to use your soothing magic!"

She scoffed. "It does not hurt me. I'm happy to soothe a child."

"Alright," I said. *Time to lay down the law.* "Come on. You're going to stay in my office until I'm done down here." I took her arm to get her to come with me.

"I will not." She yanked away, refusing to move. "I need to see this. I need to learn how to heal in more ways. More modern ways." She was a full foot shorter than I was, but she still managed to stare me down. "I will not touch anything. Or anyone. For the rest of the day."

Holy fuck. In a battle of wills with Vivienne Lanier was not a place I wanted to be. The woman was not going to budge, this much I knew. I thought about it.

"After I've visited these last three rooms, I will need to work here and type in orders to the charts. You will stay in my office and rest while I do that."

"Yes." Vivienne beamed at me. "Thank you." She held up her hands. "No touching!" she said cooperatively. Right before she absolutely did manage to touch the remaining children we visited and, of course, leave them better.

CHAPTER TWENTY

Vivienne

July 31st, 2024

Adam had a day off at last. Finally, we would visit the manuscript. Then Grant at his office, and next we would visit Adam's mother, where he needed to retrieve a book. But first, he suggested we should walk and get lunch on the Mall. The Mall was a large grass field that was surrounded by museums full of art. Adam said we could visit those too, someday soon. Or maybe today I would find a way to get back to Alice. It felt wrong to make plans to enjoy myself. I needed to accept that it would be hard to leave, but that it could happen at any time.

I wore some new clothes Maria had dropped off for me after that second night of my stay in 2024 when I met her. Her note said, "I got a few more things for you to try. Some rich colors to go with your beautiful silver hair and some fabrics I think you will love. Please tell me if there is anything else you might need. I'm sure Adam would love to make you happy. —Maria."

I adored the fabrics; they were soft and shimmered and flowed over my hands. For our upcoming day of errands, I wore a short-sleeved pink shirt tucked into some black pants. Maria had brought me soft, black leather shoes that she said matched all my clothes, so I slipped them on and was once again grateful for all the modern luxuries of this time. Adam gave a nod of approval when I joined him in the hallway.

He said his friend Mel owned a 'mobile pub' on the Mall. He added that she was a witch and that we should not discuss anything of importance with her. Mel turned out to be a woman of our age with short gray hair and sparkling brown eyes. Those eyes scrutinized me while she prepared a sandwich for Adam.

"So this is what you've been up to. I was getting worried," she said. He introduced me as an old friend from Europe. "I wasn't aware you had any friends, Parrish," she said while handing him something in a silver wrapper.

"She's the only one," he said. "Give her a sausage all the way." He took a bite of his sandwich right there.

So that I would not watch him as he ate, I perused the clothing that hung all around her pub. The shirts featured paintings of the monuments we had seen and some writings that made no sense to me. One was black and said simply, "FBI." I rubbed the fabric of this one between my fingers and felt that it was heavy and soft.

"You want an FBI hoodie, Vivienne?" he asked me.

"Here you go, hon." Mel handed me a sandwich, too. It was warm meat that smelled delicious, surrounded by some bread. The toppings were plentiful, and I thanked her.

"Where are you from Vivienne?" She leaned over the counter to hear better.

"London," I said, taking a bite so she hopefully would not ask more. Oh my, it was delicious. I rolled my eyes and gave a small moan.

She gave a wicked smile and said, "Yeah, that's right. My brats are the best on the Mall. A little magic makes it mine." She winked.

So she knew I was a witch. Or made a good guess. Her gaze bounced between us. Adam was staring at me as I took another bite of my sandwich.

"I see this guy every morning after his run. He always stops to say hi. Eighteen years now, we've been a thing. You're not stealing my man, are you?"

I widened my eyes as I chewed. Adam scoffed. "She says that to everybody, don't worry."

"So you come here with many women?" I asked. Mel laughed.

He made a disgruntled face. "No! Not many. Mel's just a busybody."

She leaned over even farther to look me over. "Believe me, you are an improvement. I've seen some deplorable fashion choices with this guy's women. Some couldn't even make eye contact. And none of them were witches," she said with interest. "What do you practice, Vivienne?"

Still eating, I gestured for Adam to take over.

"None of your business. That's what she practices." He said, tossing his wrapper in the garbage bin on the sidewalk. "And keep your nosy thoughts to yourself."

She pursed her lips at him. But then some silent agreement passed between them, and she turned back to me. "He's grumpy. As you must know if you've been dealing with him for all this time. He also never deviates from his routine, so for you to have broken it, that means you've got him interested. So now, of course, I'm interested. Tell me more about yourself."

"I'm very boring," I answered. "I work as a midwife, helping birth babies in my small town near London." I hoped this sounded obscure enough for Adam's purposes. He did not prepare me well for this meeting. "And what about you, Mel? What type of magic do you practice?"

"It's kind of you to ask," she said. "I don't mind sharing, even if Adam is a big killjoy about it." She shot him an annoyed look. Motioning to herself with both hands, she said, "I'm an open book. My magic lets me see details others don't and helps me combine things. It's why I'm a great cook and a great salesperson."

"And a great spy," Adam added. "Mel here also works for the Council of Witches as an investigator. She sees a lot from this spot on the Mall, but her chief job is to keep tabs on me. Isn't that right?" He raised his eyebrows at her with amusement. She scowled back at him.

"Keep it down. You're such an idiot."

He laughed. To me he said, "It's a bit like having a friend who works for the Inquisition."

She shook her head and looked at me, ignoring him.

"Oh, I'm just kidding, buddy! Come on," he knocked his fist on the counter until she gave him her attention again. "I know you're on my side."

"Good luck with this one, Vivienne," she muttered as she motioned for a family behind us to come closer.

"We'll be back by later to get that hoodie!" Adam waved goodbye to her, and we walked on. When we had cleared her pub he said softly, "Mel's a friend. She gets paid by the Council to report on anything I do. I feed her some information sometimes about where I've been, and she shares it. But she doesn't share anything I don't want her to."

I threw away my wrapper in a trash bin. "How do you know?" I asked him.

He touched the small of my back to guide me across a busy street.

"Because I pay her more."

Inside the Library of Congress' main reading room, Adam insisted on giving me a tour.

"This is where I come and wait for Grant on Wednesday nights. And sometimes I come here on weekends to do some reading." He walked me around the outer circle of the room. The center was filled with people sitting at desks with books propped up in front of them and lamps lighting each seat. Adam took us into the outer ring of the room, which was lined with books on either side. As we made our way around, I saw there were small alcoves with comfortable chairs tucked into the ring. He watched as I touched the spines of some books on history. We came to a shelf with names and dates I recognized.

"Oh no," he grabbed my elbow and steered me on to the next section. "Grant says you're not allowed to know the history of your time. It could be dangerous to you and something about not violating the Prime Directive and not interfering with natural development, blah, blah, blah. He could be right; you never know with him."

He stopped at a winding metal staircase. "This is where I found you." He pointed down. I bent over the railing a bit to survey the area below. "Do you feel anything?" he asked.

I shook my head. "No. I barely remember it now."

"Let's go meet Grant in his office. We can see the manuscript on the way out."

Before we left the reading room, he stopped me and pointed to a woman seated within the round desk at the very center of the room. "That's Mary. She doesn't like me."

I found that hard to believe. Mary was a blond, attractive woman of about forty or fifty years of age. And he was... well, Adam. A more handsome man I had not seen here in 2024 or in my time of 1502. I was skeptical.

"No, seriously," he said. "She hates my guts. Insists that 'people should stick to their specialties,' and 'a master's degree is nothing to laugh at.' One time I tried to help a guy with his research, and you would have thought I had tried to fix a washing machine or cook a gourmet cake or, you know, something with real skill required." He shook his head at Mary.

"Just wanted you to see the best chair in here. She usually gets to sit in it during the day. I get it on Wednesday nights when I come here alone."

I watched him gazing over at the chair and realized he was totally serious. This was his place, and he was sharing it with me.

"Does this chair have special properties?"

"Absolutely. It twirls. And when you put it right under the dome and twirl, it helps you forget where you are." He looked up at the glass dome. "Who you are."

I nodded gravely. "That would be quite helpful. I'd like to try that sometime."

"I can arrange that," he said as he started toward a marble staircase.

While we waited for Grant in his office, I scanned the portraits on his wall. He stood with other men in the same uniform, next to a flag. A dog sat with the group directly in front of Grant.

Adam explained, "That's his army unit. He was a sergeant. This was in Afghanistan."

Grant seemed happy in the portrait. I realized that was not an expression I had seen on his face the evening we spent together. He seemed more at ease with his army unit, somehow more in his element.

"His dog was killed on a mission to sniff out explosives. Grant was injured, too. He had a really hard time. After his recovery, he was discharged." Still examining the portrait, Adam said, "I was glad. It's much easier to have a librarian son than a soldier son."

Grant came in then, holding a few books.

"Hi, Vivienne!" He greeted me enthusiastically, and a twinge of sadness hit me, thinking about my daughter Evelyn and her husband Robert. They died of a fever in the same week four years ago. I had been in another city helping a noble woman give birth and didn't hear of their sickness until they were gone. I waited for the pain of losing them to abate, but it had not. I wished for them to meet Grant and shook my head at the notion.

"How have you been?" he asked. "I hear you've become a legit doctor in the past month with your medical studies and that your modern English is so good you could write a dissertation."

I shot a look at Adam. "Not quite," I said. "But I do understand your words now. Much more than I did before."

His eyes widened, and he said, "Wow." He looked at Adam, who just nodded his head as if to say, 'I told you so.'

Grant said, "I've done some research on your manuscript." He placed the books on his desk and sat, offering us a seat in the chairs facing him.

Adam pointed at his portraits on the wall. "I was just showing Vivienne your unit picture and Lulu."

Grant smiled. "Lulu was my best friend. Smartest dog ever. Best bomb detector in the world."

Adam said, "Tell her how you were a Sergeant First Class and Lulu was a Master Sergeant."

Grant rolled his eyes. "Dad loves that she outranked me."

"All K9s are one rank higher than their handlers," Adam clarified.

Grant gave a quick glance at the dog and smiled again, a little sadly.

I thought again of Evelyn. Of having a picture of her, small like this, and perfect, and happy. In the world I was in, Evelyn had been dead for five hundred years. But the pain never died.

I asked Grant, "What have you found about the manuscript?"

He sat forward. "I found the artist. His name was Alexander Bryson. This whole thing is about him." He held up a large book. "I just found this so haven't been able to read it all yet, but apparently he's quite a mystery because he was working in a style of painting way ahead of his time. He used something called a two-point perspective, like hundreds of years before other northern European painters did. Also, there's something about how his colors were extra vibrant and they didn't fade."

I knew Adam was watching me as I stared at the book Grant held.

He asked, "What are you thinking?"

My eyes still on the book, I said, "Alexander Bryson is my father."

Chapter Twenty-One

Adam

I ordered the book about her father for Vivienne. It was not available on Amazon, so we would have to wait a week or so to get it from the small publishing house that carried it in England. She flipped through the whole thing while we were in Grant's office. When some tears began to fall, Grant pulled a chair up next to her and put his arm around her shoulders. Grabbing the box on his desk, I demonstrated again to her how to use a tissue and she laughed through the tears.

"Your father thinks he's funny," she said to Grant. She ripped the tissue from my hand.

"Made you laugh twice with that," I said. "That's proof."

She gathered herself together and placed both her hands on the closed book in her lap. "He would be so pleased that his art was appreciated and remembered like this."

Grant promised to research more about her exact manuscript and get back to us when he learned more. After a walk through the gallery where the manuscript was displayed, and a little time spent standing in front of it, I took Vivienne to the garage where my car was parked and we prepared to go see my mother. Tony and the rest of the security crew took their Rover that I was keeping parked for them in my garage.

Vivienne liked that my black Cadillac had sparkles in the paint job. I explained that it was called a diamond coat but was not made with diamonds. She ran her hands over the wood paneling inside. She was still not a fan of the speed at which cars traveled, but she appeared to like driving. She soaked in the scenery of Rock Creek Parkway and noted the details of every car we passed.

At eighty-five, Mom lived in the nicest assisted living facility on the east coast. She was sharp as ever and would still have lived with me if my hours were not so unpredictable. I didn't want her to ever need anything and be alone. Before we entered mom's apartment, I turned to Vivienne and asked if she would drop her guard and share her magic with my mother.

"Why?" she challenged. "You said I should hide it."

"I did. But this is my mother and I want her opinion. Can you do it just here at the beginning? Just for a minute?"

She pursed her lips, no doubt replaying my order at Bayham Old Abbey to never do that again. But she gave a short nod of agreement. My heart skipped a beat.

When we walked into the room, Vivienne smiled at my mother who was sitting in her recliner. I introduced them. "Vivienne, this is my mother, Isabelle Parrish. Mother, this is Vivienne Lanier. She is a nun who works as a midwife."

They regarded each other for some time, mom's brown eyes searching Vivienne's gray eyes. Mom has always looked very young for her age, keeping her shoulder length hair colored brown and wearing light makeup every day. One of her hobbies was to order clothes online to 'keep up with the Jones,' as she said. She wouldn't admit it to me, but I knew she had more than a couple of suitors at the residence and I was happy she kept busy and alive there.

Vivienne let her guard down but only slightly, sparing me from the embarrassment of not being able to speak in front of my mother. I was ready this time and tried to brace myself, but even with her shielding most of it, her magic and that scent had one hundred percent of my focus.

"You have magic," my mother said to her. "Such a refreshing life force, so different." She turned to me and registered my completely agitated state. "You must find it quite invigorating, son."

I barked out a laugh. "That's one way to describe it."

Vivienne surveyed my mother. "It's a gift I can share." She sat down on the stool facing mom and reached for her hands.

I said, "She has arthritis."

Vivienne said, "I can feel it."

Then she took mom's hands between her own and pressed them gently. Mom made a soft sound of surprise. Vivienne closed her eyes and hummed lightly as she massaged them. She had put her shield back up and was releasing only a small amount of her magic. Then, after a few moments, she squeezed both hands and with a light pat released them back to mom's lap. Mom lifted her hands, examined them and then sized up Vivienne again.

"The pain is gone." She looked at me. "Gone."

Vivienne said, "I'm a healer where I come from."

"And where exactly is that?"

"London," we both said at the same time.

"England," Vivienne added.

After some time spent marveling at her new hands and discussing all the new things she should try now (piano, cross stitch, video games in the entertainment room), mom asked Vivienne if she might bring us some sandwiches from the refrigerator and also iced tea. Vivienne said she'd be delighted to, and I watched her as she made her way there.

As soon as we were alone, mom pressed me for more information. "Her accent is not of London. Where is she really from?"

"London, a long time ago."

She waited for me to elaborate. When I didn't, she gave me an irritated look that said she could still whip my ass and I better know it. "How long ago?"

I leaned back in my chair and rested my fist against my cheek. "Shakespeare long ago."

She wrinkled her brow. After a few moments, she said, "Lord, Adam."

That is what I love about Isabelle Parrish. No hysterics, ever. Always the master of any situation she encountered. Kid about to be expelled from college for a frat party damage bill? No problem. She'd be right over to explain why not to the dean. Irate driver in the Target parking lot? She would bless their heart to their face and leave them wanting more.

"My magic says she's telling the truth. And when we went to London, I saw proof. It's for real. 1502."

Mother shook her head in wonder, her eyebrows raised at the concept. But there was some other look on her face that had me wondering if she had any experience with this sort of situation.

"Do you have something to share?"

She shook her head. "I just remember a story. From my college days, so I wouldn't expect too much from it."

She stared out her patio doors toward the courtyard. "There was a boy, first year of school, who I got to know a little. He was brilliant. From England. And once when we were walking, he said something about going back in time." She looked at me as if to say, *Right? Crackpot, obviously.*

"But something about it made me wonder if he was telling me the truth. He was smart enough to maybe make that science work. And he had powers that I recognized as significant. And different. But I was only a girl, just eighteen, and I thought maybe those were special European powers." She laughed at herself.

"We dated some, but then in the second year, I met your father in a literature class."

"And the rest is history," I said.

My mother and father had a fifty-year love affair. He studied literature and then practiced law, and she studied science and then practiced medicine. I got a little something from both of them and was grateful for it all.

"Yes. Your father got me through the classics, so I had to marry him."

"So this poor guy you dumped. What was his name?"

"Gerald McEntire. He moved back to England, or Scotland, or somewhere. Before he graduated, I think. I know it sounds crazy, but here you are with a friend from the literal past..."

"Thanks, mom, I'll check it out. Please keep this to yourself. It's safer for you if nobody comes asking questions."

She made a face at me. "But as you know, magic does not fade. If I can be of some help, please let me."

"I will, mom."

"And who was it that taught you every single spell you know?"

My mouth quirked up. "It was you."

"And now you are the most powerful witch in the world."

I dismissed that. "I think they separate that title among the continents now. Maybe I could claim North America."

She scoffed. "You could claim more than that."

We heard Vivienne tinkering in the kitchenette.

She raised her eyebrows at me. "Honey, you need to keep her hidden. You should know this. Do you not remember that group that tried to grab you in your teens?" Mom's expression grew serious. "I thought your father would kill them all."

I smiled, remembering the unholy amount of power my father had unleashed at that barn where I was being held in northern Virginia. I wasn't threatened again.

My mother shook her head. "That power of hers is too obvious. It's incredible."

I glanced out her patio doors at a couple strolling through the garden. They stopped to smell a shrub.

"She usually has her shield up and it's effective. I just wanted you to feel it." I turned back to her and asked, "And what you're getting from her is a life force? And it's refreshing? Really?" I couldn't fathom calling what she did to me refreshing. It was more like a total unraveling.

She softened her tone. "I can see you care for her. I don't know who she is or what that power is, but you know others will want what she has. You should know this better than anyone."

"I do," I said. We sat in silence thinking of the toll magic could take on a life. Thinking also of the glory of a spell that worked well.

I cleared my throat. "Actually, that's one reason we're here. We ran into a little trouble in England and I may need to make an official declaration of protection for Vivienne against a crazy priest we came across there who tried to kill her for her power."

My mother's expression went from tender to another one I knew well but had not seen since my college days. It said, "Are you fucking kidding me with this nonsense?"

I continued. "So I was wondering if you had dad's set of books on Magic Law so I can read up on what's required for a legal declaration? I don't trust the council to help with this. In fact, Cole told me I was on my own."

She gave me a death stare and after a moment said, "I would have thought by now you would have learned not to bury the lead, son." She stood and placed the blanket she had on her lap on the couch and walked into her extra bedroom.

Hey, that went about as well as expected.

Vivienne brought a tray in from the kitchen and I took it from her to set on the table. We heard mom rustling around in a closet and I said, "Do you need some help in there?"

In a clipped tone, she said, "No."

I shared a *yikes* face with Vivienne.

"What did you do?" Vivienne asked.

"I told her about Father Andrew Barry."

Vivienne said, "She will be worried for you now."

"Not so much him as you, honey." Mom came out of the room holding a thick, black leather book. "I think this is the one you'll want." She set it next to me on the table. "But there are four others in the closet to complete the set. You might want to take those, too. I also put the witch primer there. Vivienne might like that." Mom picked up her glass of tea and said, "Now tell me about this priest."

Fifteen minutes later, after eating a sandwich and hearing the whole story, along with my description of how he had tried to pull all Vivienne's magic from her, my mother gave me a knowing look and turned to Vivienne. "Adam is the best person to help you with this. Probably the best person in the world, and I'm not just saying that as a proud mother of his."

She turned her gaze to me. "Although I am that."

I tried not to show it, but there was really nothing better than your mom being proud of you. That lasted about five seconds. Then she asked me, "Have you explained to Vivienne what a declaration of protection means in this day and age?"

Vivienne turned to me with a frown on her face. "What is that? Who are you protecting?"

My mother looked to the heavens and said, "Adam Parrish. I know I taught you to communicate. Why do you not do that?"

"Hold on," I said, lifting my palms from the table. "I was going to tell her when I knew more."

Vivienne waited. Still frowning. It was more of a disappointed frown, as was my mother's. This was fantastic.

"Vivienne, Barry won't stop looking for you, and I think you know that. I need to take him out before he gets to you again, and in order to do that, I think I'll need to make a declaration of protection for you." She was shaking her head now. "Believe me, I *get* that you're a badass and can take care of yourself." She gave a loud sigh at that, propped her elbows on the table and dropped her head in her hands. My mother laughed.

"But I think I know his skill set and I have some experience dealing with criminals. I don't know where he might pop up again and if it's in public, I need to have an official declaration in place to do it. With a declaration of protection in place, I'm justified to use any means necessary to get rid of the problem."

Mother said, "Explain why witches don't do this every day."

I thought about it. "It's not great for business, I guess. Makes you look a little crazy."

Mother added, "Also, it can reveal your magic. Not something anyone with power wants others to know about."

Vivienne separated her hands and peeked out at me. "I don't like putting you in danger." She sat up. "But if I was the one to kill him, it would cause a stir for you. Explaining who I am." She looked at my mother.

Mother agreed. "Yes. Explaining that you're here from 1502 might be difficult."

After a moment, they both laughed, and I began to think that maybe I was going to make it out of that situation alive.

Thankfully, mom was with me on my plan. "I think Adam has the best solution here." Then she said to me, "Do your research with the books and if you still have questions, I can give you the number for one of your dad's friends to talk to about it."

Putting her glass down, she said, "Vivienne, would you mind if I have a moment alone with my son?"

"Not at all. I'll go for a quick walk outside if that's fine?" Mother nodded, and I opened the sliding glass door for her.

Mom waited until she was gone and then said, "I like her."

"She's very likable," I said.

Mom jerked her head toward the courtyard and said in a soft voice, "She's also beautiful." She raised her eyebrows.

"I know she's beautiful! I'm not blind," I hissed back at her. "I'm not going to chase after a nun!"

"She doesn't look at you like a nun would," mom observed.

"What does that mean?" I said.

"It means there's probably more to that story."

"There's no more to the story! Nun means nun in any era!" Vivienne was walking back in the door then and ended my rant to my mother.

"There's a couple out there having a private conversation," she said as she closed the screen door behind her.

Mom didn't want to let us go, and before we left, she gave us both a warm hug.

"It was very nice to meet you, Vivienne. I can't thank you enough for ridding me of the arthritis. I never thought I'd meet an equal to Adam, but today I think I have." Vivienne lowered her eyes and gave a nod at the compliment.

"It was lovely to meet you too, Isabelle. I hope we can do it again soon."

I leaned in to kiss mother goodbye and murmured to her, "I've increased the security."

She said, "The garden couple. I saw them."

She kissed me on the cheek. "And son," she said in a stern tone. "Please take this woman home and hide her from the rest of us."

Staring out her window on the ride home, Vivienne said, "What did your mother mean when she said you were the most powerful witch in the world?"

I raised my eyebrows. "You heard that?"

She turned slightly to look at me. *Not embarrassed by eavesdropping,* I noted.

I said, "Well, that was before you came to town, obviously."

"But how do you know? Are there games where you compete?"

"No," I answered. "There's a blood test as a baby. There are markers in the blood. And levels to determine strength. Families of witches have their babies checked." I thought of Vivienne's blood and how much other witches would like to have some of that. "And then there is teaching, from puberty through early adulthood." Her eyebrows raised at that. "There are many types of magic, and spells for the different areas of magic to practice."

"Do you have an area?" she asked.

"I do. I have two areas where I'm a master."

When I did not elaborate, she prodded me. "And they are…?"

Why not share with her? We had left discussing magic off the table while she was learning medicine and English, even though I was dying to learn about how it was practiced in her time. I guessed it wouldn't hurt to tell her now what I could do.

"I was born with the magic that allows me to disguise myself or other things, which is called cloaking. And the magic that allows me to make suggestions to people to make them comply with my wishes. That's called persuasion. It's a rare magical ability."

She frowned. "And…?"

I glanced over at her. "And what?"

She gave me a look like I must be kidding.

"You clearly have more magic than that. Much more. I can feel it. And," she continued, "I have seen you reconstruct a glass case."

"Kid stuff," I said, not happy with the direction of the conversation.

"I've shared my magic with you," she said, frustrated with me. "You've seen it more than once."

After a couple of minutes passed, she said, "Your mother knew someone who claimed to time travel."

"I hope she was right. I'll have my investigator look for him. Gerald McEntire of England or maybe Scotland. He'd also be a pretty advanced age, so we need to keep that in mind and hope he's still around."

More silence. She was not happy with me and I didn't like it.

"Mother gave me a Witch Primer today that you can look at. It details the areas of magic and the laws governing the use of witchcraft. It's what all witches get when they come into their power."

Fiddling with the glove compartment, she said, "That was kind of her. I like your mother."

The door dropped open, and she sat back quickly with a laugh.

"That's the glove compartment. Where you keep your gloves, if you have them, and insurance papers."

Without asking, she pulled things out and inspected them. A baggie of change, the car manual, the insurance papers. No gloves. When she was done spying, she returned them to the box and shut the door with a click.

"What about you, Vivienne? How do you practice your magic in the Middle Ages?"

She turned back to the window. "In secret," she said. "Everything is practiced in secret."

"You don't tell anybody?"

She shook her head. "You never tell a soul outside of your family. Witches recognize their own kind, but do not greet them. But, if you can help another witch, it's wise to do so. Then you can hope for help someday as well."

We sat at a stoplight. Vivienne waved to a toddler in the back seat of the car next to us. She smiled when he waved back with passion.

"And you never speak of magic to each other," she continued. "But when she was dying, my mother told my father about her witchcraft so that he would understand what to do with me when she was gone. Witches in my time are all women." She watched my face to see my reaction.

"*Really?*" I asked in amazement.

"Yes. Men do not hold magic. That is why you were quite a shock." She gave me a wry smile.

I wondered when that change came about. I also wondered about this lack of organization among witches. What would it be like to not have to answer to a group? No one governing your actions? How did they not have chaos? As strange as it was for me to imagine what a small circle of witches Vivienne had probably been exposed to in her life, she had to be struggling to grasp our current international network of witches, veined with rivalry and threats.

"But seeing that book today..." she murmured. "It reminded me of watching my father when he painted. The way the light filtered in from the windows... it seemed like colors were floating to him from the light. It seemed as though he gathered them with his brush and then stroked them gently onto his parchment."

She turned to me.

"I think my father had magic."

CHAPTER TWENTY-TWO

Vivienne

Adam pulled into a place to park. There were no other cars around and we were surrounded by greenery, almost like a forest. He undid his seatbelt and turned toward me.

"And I don't think my mother would have told him she was a witch unless she knew he had magic, too. She knew she was dying, and she told him what to do for me so I would be all right without her to guide me. Otherwise, I think she would have given me to another witch." I had been far from all right without her, but I realized my father had done all he knew to do when the time came for me to gain my powers.

"It's okay, you can take off your seatbelt." Adam gestured toward it, but I was too many years away. He opened his door, got out, and came around to my side of the car. Opening my door, he reached over and pushed the button down and let the seatbelt fall away to the side.

"Come on," he said, and he offered me his hand, but I got out on my own, aware that there should be no more touching between us. He led me to a wooden table set in a field of grass near the tree line. We sat next to each other on the bench.

"What was her name? Your mother?" It had been so long since I had spoken of her that suddenly I wanted to tell him everything.

"Her name was Marie. She was beautiful."

"Of course she was," he said with a smile. "How old were you when she died?"

My lips trembled, and the tears started again.

"Oh no, I'm sorry!" he said. He wrapped his arms around me. I cried in earnest then, letting the tears flow for my mother who died too soon, and for my father who had his own secret, and for all the people I had lost along the way. I had a tear for every one of them and a hundred more for the pain of our forced secrecy and the loneliness that did not need to be. Adam stroked my hair through it all and murmured to me that it was okay, that everything was going to be fine.

"I'm sorry," I said after too long in the comfort of his arms. "I don't usually cry." He made a skeptical face, and I laughed through my tears and hit him in the shoulder. "I mean it. I think it's you."

I tried to regain my composure by wiping my cheeks and breathing in deeply through my nose and out through my mouth. Adam gave a small laugh.

"What?" I said.

"It's nothing," he said. "That kind of breathing is just a technique I also use to try to calm down. It's good to see it's worked for millennia." He patted my leg and sat back, giving me space. "Do you want to tell me about her?"

I took another moment to compose myself, then I began.

"I was ten when she died. She was a healer like me, but I think more powerful. Everyone loved her. Especially my father." I was overwhelmed with memories of them that I had not thought of for years. My parents dancing in the yard of our house, holding hands on our walk to the village for church services. "They were very happy," I said. "*We* were happy. But it wasn't always perfect. They had some hard times. She lost a pregnancy, and I was an only child. But our life was good."

I noticed I was rubbing my hands together like my mother used to.

"She got sick when I was nine and she died when I was ten. It was the wasting disease, and it took her fast. It was your 'cancer.' She couldn't affect it at all. I had seen her attempt to heal others with it, and she had some success. She shouldn't have tried to heal that disease, because it made people suspect her of witchcraft, but she couldn't help herself. If a child was sick and she was able to help, she did so." Adam nodded his head in understanding.

"We had to move a few times to prevent families from finding us. They would want her to repeat the act. And if she wouldn't, they would say she was a witch." I pondered that. "My father had to know about her witchcraft. Probably even before she was sick."

Adam waited for me to continue, but I was done for the moment. I was exhausted. And I did not understand any more than I did before about who my father was or what type of magic he had. But I knew he had it.

Adam seemed to hesitate, but then he asked me, "Your mother was not able to cure herself of the cancer?"

I shook my head no. "And I have never healed anyone with the disease. My father was certain she took it upon herself when she helped others with it. I've been afraid all my life to touch it. I've wanted to," I hoped Adam would understand. "But I watched her die."

Adam shook his head firmly. "No one would fault you for that. You have no resources to work with in your time. For God's sake, it's all up to you and your magic! Even with everything we know and everything we can do for cancer now, we can't stop it when it's too advanced."

He stared back at the car. "I think you're onto something with your father. If he was a witch too, you maybe have some magic you don't know about. Maybe you haven't explored it all."

"There are many things I can do," I said. "I'm still discovering them."

But that's all you will get from me on this topic. If you won't share, then neither will I.

I stared at him.

"Like time traveling?" He raised his eyebrows. "That's a fun new thing you can do."

I stood up. "It's not fun."

He laughed and stood with me. "Okay, I'll try not to let that hurt my feelings."

Back in the car, he put his seat belt on again and waited while I did the same. With both his hands on the steering wheel, he faced the forest in front of us.

"I have an idea," he said. "You read about DNA." He gave me a side glance, and I nodded yes.

"I think we should take some of your blood, do a DNA test, and see if you have any living descendants. If you do, and we can find out what their talents are, maybe we learn something useful that might help you with this little adventure we're on to get you home."

I thought about it. "How would you find them?"

"All witches have their blood drawn at birth. I told you about that. The blood gets measured for markers of witchcraft. All results are kept. Your DNA would be compared to that of all other witches. If we got a significant statistical match, we could find out about that person or persons."

The idea of Alice having a son or daughter that might have born a chain of ancestors who extended to the present day... it delighted me. I suddenly needed to know this more than anything else. I was ready to agree to this suggestion of Adam's but there was something about it that worried me, I didn't know what. "Is there any reason not to do this?" I asked.

He smiled as if he was proud of me. "Excellent question. Yes. There's the possibility of your blood being noticed for its great and possibly mythical, magical properties."

I rolled my eyes at that.

"I'm dead serious, Vivienne. I don't know how magic worked in the 1500s, but in today's world, a person keeps their talents for a lifetime. That means as you age, if you are so lucky as to age, and if you have a significant power, you become somewhat of a sitting duck for unscrupulous witches who might covet whatever power you have."

He waited for me to absorb that.

"And how would they take it?" I asked.

"They wouldn't take it so much as force you to use it."

"It's the same in my time." I said. "We keep our power throughout our lives. But as no one ever knows our power..."

"Right. Not the same danger," he finished. "But today... you would not want to advertise that you have a huge amount. Or that your power is in any way special." He added, "Like the ability to heal anyone of anything."

"Fine," I said after a moment.

"Grant's mother, Connie, is a geneticist. I can ask her to test your blood. She'll do everything she can to keep it secret."

I took a look back out over the peaceful scene surrounding us. While we sat there in the quiet, I could almost believe we were outside London in a little glade I visited there. I liked to gather herbs deep in the center of it. But this was not London. And I needed all the help I could get.

I turned to him. "Yes. Let me give Connie my blood."

"Yes!" He hit the steering wheel. Starting the car, he said, "Let's call Connie and tell her we're coming to give her some blood!" I shook my head at his ridiculousness, and he laughed. Patting my leg, he said, "Don't worry, she has only the best leeches in her office."

Connie was not what I expected. She had short blond hair that was sleek and, I knew, very stylish for the present day. She wore a tailored blue skirt with a cream satin blouse and a white hospital coat over the top. I recognized this because satin was my new favorite textile weave. When Adam learned this from Maria, he ordered me seven new blouses of varying colors. The pink shirt I was wearing was satin. I was thankful to be appropriately dressed upon meeting Adam's mother and Grant's mother for the first time.

She was a beautiful woman, maybe in her early fifties, and clearly very intelligent. That much I would expect. But she was cool and measured in her greeting and handshake. Not at all playful like Adam.

We met her at her hospital. This was the hospital for adults, not the one where Adam worked with children. I was fascinated with the instruments and technology and Adam quietly explained it all while we waited for Connie to finish speaking with her co-worker. She did not ask me many questions beyond my name and age. She seemed surprised by my age and snuck a glance up at me when I spoke it.

"You look very young," she said.

"But my age indicates I am not?" I asked.

That made her laugh. "I stepped in it, didn't I?"

"What does that mean?"

"Stepped in some dog poo," she answered without any embarrassment. She added, "I'm fifty-seven."

I said, "You also look very young." We both laughed at that. I liked her.

After wrapping a plastic tie around the top of my arm and inserting a small needle into my vein, she unwrapped the plastic tie, and the blood flowed even stronger into the tube. She replaced the tube twice and when three of them were full, she gently pulled the needle out and covered the spot with a piece of cotton. Then she placed a bandage over it and patted my arm.

"All done," she said. "Adam has asked me to do some blood tests for a comprehensive health screening and to order a DNA test. Do I have your permission for all of that?"

"Yes," I said.

Adam took her to the side then and spoke to her. I couldn't hear what they said, but I knew he was asking her to do the work herself. And that he was asking her to do things she did not usually do. Maybe these tasks were beneath her station. I was so interested in their exchange that I did not notice the man who entered the room behind me.

"Well, that's a blast from the past." He jerked his head toward Adam and Connie. "Are you with them?" He wore a long white overcoat and his badge said, 'Doctor Samuel Marsh.' He held his hand out and I reached out mine to him.

Adam took notice of us at that moment and frowned.

"Sam Marsh," he said. "And you are?" When he smiled, he had wrinkles at the corner of his blue eyes, and I could tell he was used to a woman's attention. He was handsome, appeared to be in his fifties, and was very fit, like Adam. But Samuel's hair had turned mostly silver, like mine. There was something about him that I liked.

"Vivienne Lanier, I'm here with Adam."

His face was disappointed as he said, "Of course you are."

Adam was next to me then. "Get lost, Marsh, she's with me."

I gave him a dubious glance.

"She doesn't like to admit it," he said, still looking at his friend. "But you should definitely go away now."

Samuel rolled his eyes at Adam and said, "Whatever." To me he said, "I'm his best friend. In case he forgot to mention me."

Then back to Adam, "See you tomorrow morning at the tidal basin."

"Marsh," Adam caught his arm as he turned to go. "I got into some shit in England when Vivienne and I were visiting. I may have used your name and because of that, I might have added some security to your daily routine. Just FYI."

His friend eyed him with disgust. After a minute he turned to me and said, "Vivienne, trust me when I tell you that you can most certainly do better than this." Without looking at him, he pointed at Adam.

He turned to go. "Bye, Connie!" he called to her. She waved. "Bye, Vivienne." Samuel winked at me as he left.

Adam pursed his lips at his friend. "Come on, Vivienne. I just saved you from a lecherous lech, by the way. You're welcome. Let's go get some chili dogs."

I had no idea what a lecherous lech or chili dog was, but I was more than happy to follow that man to go and find some.

CHAPTER TWENTY-THREE

Adam

August 17th, 2024

Making a formal Declaration of Protection was both easier than I thought and far more complicated. Execution I had done before. Protection, not so much. Dad's witch law textbooks were clear on the exact wording I would need to use in the declaration and the procedure to file the document. The problems would come with the potential fallout after the fact.

Once it was filed with our North American Council of Witches, it would be available for every other council in the world to have. I had to believe Father Andrew Barry was associated with somebody of influence in our world. That would explain Cole's reaction to his description and the fact that Reeger had not found him yet. It would follow that he'd be apprised pretty quickly of my official plan to kill him. Since I'd be authorized to do whatever I had to, so would he. All I could think about was the possibility of Vivienne being collateral damage in a fight between Andrew Barry and myself. Or Grant, Maria or my mother. Would he try something at the hospital? What about the staff and my patients?

I needed to know more. Tom Reeger had been my private investigator for years, but before that he was special forces and he might have some experience with this. Maria set up a meeting for us at my office.

I'd known Reeger for over twenty years. He was tall, ripped, with dark eyes and a marine haircut. The asshole looked the same as the first day I met him.

"How's it going?" he greeted me and made himself at home in the chair across from my desk.

"It's kind of a fucking mess. Thanks for asking."

He laughed. "Yes. Sounds like you've outdone yourself this time. This is FUBAR, even for you."

"What the fuck am I looking at here? I just want to figure out what he might do if he gets the chance to come after me with no repercussions. I'm worried about everybody around me."

He got serious. "Honestly, it's not good that I haven't gotten anything on him yet. Takes some skill to be off the grid that completely. I'm going to need more than just a name and last known location at this point. A face to go with that would be good."

"I told you he looks like a fucking movie star. Even more so than you. With fucking curly hair. Brown hair. Blue eyes."

Reeger smiled at my lack of respect for Barry's appearance.

"Well, with that treasure trove of detail, I can't possibly miss."

Then I remembered how Vivienne drew Alice for me the first day she was here and hoped maybe she could do that again. "I can get you a picture," I said. "Vivienne is good at portraits."

"Excellent," he said. "I'd like to meet her. Vivienne."

I raised my eyebrows. Discontented.

"What was that look for?"

I gestured at his face. "I don't need your pretty boy face at my house. Thanks anyway."

"Are you fucking kidding me?"

"No. I really do not need your face."

He shook his head. "You know I'm married, right?"

I actually did not know that. "How long?" I asked.

"Two years," he said, reaching in his pocket for his phone. "My wife's a gifted witch in the field of earth magic." *Meaning she could make it quake. A nice skill to have.* He turned his phone around to show me a picture of him with his arm around a beautiful blond.

Glancing at it himself, he said, "That's why. I like to know what I'm getting into these days. It would be helpful to meet Vivienne. To see why you think Barry is after her. Then maybe we can come up with a plan for how to approach him when we find him."

That all sounded very sensible. It occurred to me that Reeger was a very powerful witch. In a relationship with another powerful witch. I wondered if his power came alive when his skin touched hers.

"I have a weird question for you..." I started, but just then Maria knocked on the door and stuck her head in.

"Sally Tolley just called. She asked me to remind you that today is the cookout at your house and not to forget the cake this time."

"Fuuuuck..." I dropped my head on my desk.

Reeger looked back at Maria. "This is just a guess, but I think he forgot."

"Oh, he definitely forgot. He only forgets when it's at his house, though. It's a quarterly cookout, the whole block comes. These people have known each other for decades." She shook her head. "That makes it so much worse because they never forget that stuff. Like, he will *never* hear the end of it."

Lifting my head from the desk, I said, "Maria, do you think it would be possible for you to pick up a cake at that horrible place over in that hotel owned by the accidental president? Right away? And then bring it over to my house?"

She said, "You told me not to ever give that establishment any of our money."

"This is clearly an emergency, Maria. I will donate a *million dollars* to the Democratic party tomorrow to make up for the hundred dollars we will spend there for the goddamn cake. *Okay?*"

She smiled. "Okay. I'll get the best cake ever. Anyway, he doesn't even own that anymore. You should pay attention to your surroundings. What else are you going to serve?"

I groaned. "Can you also call that barbeque place that does catering? We'll probably need enough for twenty-five people. Just... if you could have them be there before six?"

"You got it!" And she was off to the races. Thank God.

Reeger sat across from me, amused by my plight. I realized his idea had been good.

"How'd you like to eat some barbeque tonight?" I asked.

By the time I got home, the party in my backyard was in full swing. There was music playing and lanterns strung between trees. Grant was sitting at a table with Mom and Maria. All my other neighbors were there too, of course, and smirked at me as I arrived last to my own barbeque.

I was surprised to see the Justice and his wife sitting on a bench in the back digging into some plates piled high. Vivienne sat with them. Since nobody liked this particular Justice and had eschewed inviting him to any of their cookouts, I decided this was my mother's doing. Isabelle Parrish had connections to every branch of government in this town and loved to offer favors and pull strings with the best of them. I made my way over to their table.

"Mr. Justice, how are you? Glad you could come. How's the barbeque?"

"Excellent!" he stood and offered me his hand. "Thanks for the invite."

"Anytime," I said. "Make yourselves at home. There's a cake over there my assistant got at the president's bakery today. Enjoy!"

He smiled and gave a thumbs up.

"Vivienne, I need you for a minute, if you don't mind."

As we walked by Herb and Sally, he slapped me on the back and said, "Nice party, man. You always do it right." He was laughing at me for not remembering and it was fine. I'd be laughing at him later, no doubt. That was how we worked. He lowered his voice. "But what the hell? Why are you inviting the devil's minions?"

"To the barbeque I found out about a whole sixty minutes ago? I think your friend Isabelle might know more about that. Check with her."

He looked over to mother and nodded his head as if, yes, that tracked. Herb and I were only a couple of years apart, and his mother and mine had been best friends, helping to raise us as a unit. His mother, Janice, was gone, but Herb and Sally visited my mother at her home almost as much as Grant and I did. We were family. Family that gave each other shit every chance we got.

"Eat some cake, Herb. I got it just for you." I smiled at Sally and kissed her cheek. "Thanks for the call."

"No problem, Adam. You just need a little extra help sometimes." They laughed at me as I walked Vivienne up the stairs to the porch.

Once inside the kitchen, I said, "Why are you charming the Supreme Court Justice and his wife? Didn't mom tell you they're the bad guys?"

"She said they were delightful! And I should get information from them and tell her what they said. She said I could be the foreigner who does not understand your justice system and I could ask what they were working on."

"And you believed that horseshit?" Vivienne scowled at me. I really did not have time for the political intrigue my mother was starting.

I said, "They are not delightful. They are the enemy. But I'm sure mother thanks you for your service. Reeger's coming tonight. I was hoping you could draw a picture for him of the priest? Like you did of Alice?"

She was looking out the screen door at the get together in the backyard. Her eyes narrowed. "Your mother has surprised me." Then she laughed.

"Vivienne, focus. We need a picture to help Reeger find Barry."

"Fine," she said. "But I need to use my magic. I'll go to the turret and be down as soon as I'm done."

I stood watch at the entrance to the turret while Vivienne used her magic upstairs. Grant answered the door and steered Reeger toward me.

"Maybe you should see what I mean," I said. I pointed for him to head upstairs. I locked the door when I closed it behind me and followed him to the turret. Vivienne was concentrating and didn't hear us until we were on the top step and were getting the full force of her magic in use. It wasn't her healing magic, which had to be the most potent elixir on the planet, but when she used her creativity to draw, she still let loose a bit of that unbelievably sexy fragrance that could short circuit a man's brain instantly.

"Jesus," Reeger said.

Vivienne stood from the desk and held up her portrait of Father Andrew Barry. Like before, this one moved a bit, making it appear as if it was real. It added a dimension to the picture that gave you the illusion that you knew more about the person than you would if you were viewing a flat, still image. Barry was the kind of handsome that makes a person wonder how he used those looks and if he could be trusted with them.

"That's really good. Looks just like the son of a bitch. Vivienne Lanier, this is Tom Reeger. He's helping us find the priest."

"Pleased to meet you," she said and handed him the picture.

He was unable to speak.

"You should shield your magic," I said, also feeling the tug and wanting to pull her close. When her magic was covered again, the picture became static.

Tom sat down in one of the chairs facing the fireplace.

"Jesus," he said again.

After a minute, he stood and said, "Here's what I'd do. I'd write that declaration of protection up with no date on it. Leave it at the council and have Cole, or whoever you got there, post it when and if you need it."

He looked down at the picture of Barry and back up to Vivienne. "Okay. Well, that magic of yours is crazy strong." Then he said to me, "I think you're right. He's never going to give up. And I wouldn't put it past him to do anything to get what he wants, including hurting bystanders." He tapped the picture. "You just need to find him first. And hope nobody is around when you do."

CHAPTER TWENTY-FOUR

Vivienne

September 14th, 2024

Time was passing. And I felt guilty for enjoying the passage of time in the twenty-first century while my Alice was living without family in the sixteenth century. Adam knew this and made arrangements for the security guards to take me on a brief trip to the Library of Congress every day at different times.

It seemed like I might be reaching an understanding with the manuscript that was difficult to express. I explained it to Adam as a curtain swinging open gently and then falling back in place. In those brief moments, I felt a connection to the air of old and a slower pace that I recognized was my home. My anxiety as to the 'how' of time travel began to ease each time I experienced one of these bridges to the past. It felt as though when the time was right, I would be offered the way home again.

In the meantime, I was determined to suck all the knowledge out of this present day that I could. Adam and I had fallen into an easy companionship that we both valued. In the evenings, he had begun to share the wonders of the modern world with me. After describing an event or invention, he would sit on the couch next to me and show me pictures or videos on his laptop. He helped me with my modern English pronunciations of words, and I helped him with my 'Middle' English. Adam was not a good student, and he pretended to be hurt when I laughed at him.

My favorite topic he introduced to me was outer space. Adam showed me the latest ship flying through deep space and we sat in silent awe as the images unfolded. I liked that the James Webb Telescope was something new to him too. We could experience it for the first time together. The breathtaking pictures from space were proof to me of God's glory and the wonder of his universe.

Adam attempted to describe to me the concept of a 'Big Bang' theory and that all of space and matter are ruled by a science called physics. I told him I believed that physical truths may be governed by a set of scientific principles called physics. But then I reminded him that all of it was designed by our Holy Father in Heaven. He laughed and said he knew when to quit an argument, and that was usually when God got there. He conceded to my point.

He was really very kind. And a good teacher. I knew he was introducing the news of this world to me in small pieces so as not to overwhelm me, and I appreciated this approach. But I was overwhelmed by the twenty-first century, and I felt disconnected from God. I knew it was all of His making and that this world was the product of centuries of progress. But to me, it was all overnight. Here, I only prayed before meals and at bedtime. At home, I spoke to Him regularly throughout the day. I prayed with each patient, and silently on my own.

Adam, of course, noticed that I was experiencing anxiety. He noticed everything. It was both flattering and disconcerting to have this man so in tune with my moods. He arranged for Doctor Waltman to visit again. When she arrived at the front door, he asked if he might be allowed to stay for a moment before we talked.

She said, "If that's what Vivienne wants, of course."

They both looked at me and I nodded my agreement. We all took a seat in Adam's study, and Doctor Waltman started the conversation.

"How have you been? I understand you visited England and have also visited with Adam at his hospital. And you've met some of his family and friends. What was all that like?"

I thought for a moment about her question. "I'm very thankful for Adam," I said. "He's done everything he can to make me welcome in his home."

He countered, "But you're still anxious."

"Well, of course," I said. "I have a granddaughter who needs me, but I'm sitting here enjoying all the comforts of 2024 and not even praying with our Heavenly Father on a regular basis." My gaze moved between them. "I am off."

Sharon looked concerned, and I wondered then if Adam had spoken to her about our time in England. His next words answered my question.

"I wanted to stay and talk with you to update you on what happened in England. You and I spoke shortly after that, but I didn't fully fill you in." Adam paused and then spread his hands. "It was a very eventful trip. Turns out our friend Vivienne has been telling the truth. She *is* here from 1502. I knew you'd want to add that to your arsenal of facts when you work out how to help her through this experience."

We sat there in silence for a minute. Doctor Waltman looked at Adam closely and with a slight smile asked, "Any chance you're under her influence somehow?"

Adam laughed and shared a glance with her.

"Most definitely," he said. Then he shook his head. "But that's not it. I saw evidence, Sharon. There in England. I know how hard this is to imagine. And I'd appreciate it if what we discuss doesn't leave this room. The knowledge of this is dangerous."

"Well, it won't leave this room, I can assure you of that."

She looked at me then. "Give me a minute to try to get a handle on what you might be experiencing under these very improbable circumstances."

I agreed.

Dr. Waltman's brows drew together, and she concentrated on her notebook and began to write some things down. She drew lines on the paper to connect some of her thoughts.

Adam said, "I'll head out to the porch."

When we were alone again and after she had formulated her words, Doctor Waltman said, "Okay. Tell me, what is the main thing that's troubling you today?"

I took a deep breath in and let it out slowly. "What is troubling me today is that I do not feel connected to God like I should. He feels far away."

She nodded. "Normally, how do you connect to God?"

"I pray," I said. "At each important moment of the day. Before I heal someone, before meals, before bed."

"And what is keeping you from doing that here?"

I frowned. I didn't know.

Dr. Waltman did not press. We sat there for a bit while I tried to determine the cause. Then she said, "I suspect you would feel better if you could get your present-day routine to match your former routine at your home."

"My purpose here has been to learn all I can so that I can use that knowledge when I return to my time. It seemed like a noble purpose. But..." I raised my shoulders. "It also seems selfish. I'm enjoying the learning so much that I read to the exclusion of almost everything else."

She nodded. "So, you are experiencing some conflict? Do you feel guilty for doing this thing you enjoy that also takes your thought away from God?"

I did.

She saw my confirmation. "I think if you could introduce more prayer and regular worship time into your daily routine here, you may resolve your guilt about devoting time to studying medicine. It is a noble pursuit."

I realized that I admired her. Greatly. If I had been born in this time, I might have been like her. She may have been my friend.

I asked her, "How long have you been a doctor?"

She raised her head and looked up at the ceiling to think.

"Oh, god. So long." She laughed. "Thirty years." Then she asked, "What about in your time? Are women doctors?"

"I have never seen one."

She nodded. "How do you interact with doctors?"

I shook my head. "It's difficult. My magic tells me when things are wrong with a body, but the doctor doesn't know. And would not listen if I told him. They often treat for something else entirely and I have to reverse the damage from that treatment."

I could see that she understood. "It is both very different for women physicians today and sadly, sometimes kind of the same."

She looked down at her notes and tapped on the page with her pen. I saw that she had drawn a small church with a cross at the top.

"What if you visited church every day? There's a Catholic church just two blocks down on this street. Saint Joseph's Roman Catholic Church. I'm pretty sure they have mass every day. You could walk there. What do you think about fitting that into your daily routine?"

I nodded. My spirits were lifted just thinking about setting foot in a church again.

"This is good advice. Thank you. I also need to be able to work with patients again. I'll speak to Adam."

She said, "Without any licensure, you won't be able to do that."

I frowned.

"And, I admit, it's hard for me to believe that you might be here from the past. Honestly, I don't think I can get there. But I know Adam, and I have no doubt that he will still be working to help you and to find your family. So I'm inclined to leave it out of the equation for now."

"You don't have any other patients from 1502?"

She gave me a huge smile. "No, but I did have a patient once who said he was from another universe. That's a fairly common psychosis."

"Unlike the one where the patient thinks they're from 1502?"

We both laughed then at the insanity that was time travel and the fact that we needed to consider it at all.

Adam came back in through the front door and poked his head in the study.

"What did I miss?" he asked.

I turned to him. "We're going to church. That's what you missed."

⛬

When Adam heard about our solution to visit the church daily, he immediately arranged for the security detail to make that happen. I began to feel more like myself after sitting through a familiar Latin mass and worshiping alongside others. Adam came with me for the first few days, noting the surroundings, introducing himself to the priest. Once he decided it was a safe place for me to visit, he began to go to work when I went to mass.

I continued my studies in earnest then. I was saddened to learn that I should have read Gray's Anatomy before some of the other texts I had already read geared toward obstetrics and gynecology. Although Adam said those would be my areas of concern if I specialized as a midwife today, I needed a thorough understanding of the basics of the human body first.

It was so beautiful. God's plan laid out right in front of me to see. I was giddy with wonder all day long, reading those books. And when I learned the functions of the human brain and its connection to every part of the body, I began to understand the nature of some illnesses that had perplexed me as a healer.

Adam helped me comprehend things whenever I had a question. I didn't tell him, but he was correct when he asked if I retained things when I saw them. I had not had much to read besides the Bible, some Latin books and the Leechbook. But I found that every new medical term, condition or remedy that I learned was stored without effort in my own brain. I now knew I was quite up to the task of being a modern healer. Adam knew it, too. I could see he was impressed by how much I got through each day and by my questions for him.

I liked his approval. I had never had intellectual conversations with a man before. With anyone, really. Now that I could, I craved it. All this new knowledge was exhilarating. I wanted it all. And Adam was happy to share. I could see it in his attention to me when we spoke. I thanked God in my morning and evening prayers for bringing me to this age and to this man.

When he came home from work one afternoon, Adam asked if I wanted to watch the video he took during my hospital visit. He said he would explain all the healing tools for me. But first he went to the kitchen and made tea for me and coffee for himself.

"Americans love their coffee," he said as he placed a cup of tea in front of me. "More than almost anything. It's the caffeine. We get addicted to that jolt of energy first thing in the morning. Do you want to try it?" He held his coffee cup toward me.

I said, "I learned on YouTube that the English today drink tea all day long." I took a small sip of his coffee and did not know how he swallowed it; it was so sweet. He was amused by my distaste. He sipped from the same place I had and took a seat beside me on the living room couch. He set his cup down on the table in front of us and our thighs touched.

"And I only have one sweetener in there. Some people are so addicted to the caffeine in their coffee and the sugar that they'll buy a huge cup with half a dozen sweeteners in it or more." I winced at that and he said, "I know. They're taking in so many wasted calories, too."

I thought about it. "Well... surely there is something to indulging oneself. We're given this life. We should enjoy it. Who knows better than we do what makes us happy?"

His brown eyes were so close to mine, I saw him take in all of me. His eyes landed on my mouth. I was playing with fire. I wanted him, and here I was starting the conversation about it.

Adam continued to stare. "What do you like to indulge in, Vivienne?"

I would not toy with him. It would be wrong to become so close that it would hurt us when I left. I reined myself in and steered the conversation back to harmless topics.

I said, "I try to take the occasional nap. It's not easy."

He laughed at that and pulled the phone from his pocket. "Let's see if you can guess the purpose of any of these things from their name."

His head down, Adam hit play on the video and held the phone between us.

My eyes remained on his profile. I realized then that it was too late for me. It was already going to hurt when I left him.

Chapter Twenty-Five

Adam

September 27th, 2024

I was getting used to Vivienne welcoming me home when I got back from my morning rounds. As I set down my bag and hung the keys up in the hallway she said, "Adam, when you're comfortable, may I ask you about something I found on the Internet?"

"Of course," I said and walked in to see her staring at my laptop, a perplexed look on her face. I heard people then and recognized sex sounds.

Oh, shit.

Moaning, skin slapping together... *oh, fuck.* Right there in front of her was some pretty graphic porn playing out. With not just one couple, but two.

Shutting the laptop, I closed my eyes and rubbed a hand over them.

"Okay," I said. "Many things to talk about there."

She laughed at my distress. "Maybe not as much as you think, Adam. I'm a midwife. I was married. I'm not unfamiliar with the marriage bed. But these people..." she paused. "They didn't mind others seeing them?" She waited for me to gather my words.

I'm explaining porn. I was taken back to the sex talk I had with Grant when he was ten or eleven. I had told him for a couple of years that he could ask me about it whenever he was ready. Then he sprang it on me, and I was not ready at *all.*

Not good at surprise sex talks = Adam Parrish.

"It wasn't real," was what I finally came up with for Vivienne. "Let's see..." I was drawing a blank. Then, "Got it. It's called pornography. It's a performance. Meant to arouse the person watching."

She nodded thoughtfully. "Yes. It does do that."

I raised my eyebrows. Then I threw my head back and laughed.

She laughed with me, elbowed me out of the way so she could stand, and then shook her head.

"No. I mean to say it's lacking much."

After I recovered from the best laugh I'd had in a while, I sat on the couch. I knew what she meant about porn. "You're right, it lacks emotion. Connection."

Vivienne agreed. "Yes. Why is that?"

"Because those are actors. Real people in relationships don't film themselves having sex and put it on the Internet for the world to see." *Well, most people don't.* I gave a silent prayer to the universe that she'd never encounter 'Only Fans.'

"But is it acceptable to watch this? Is it common?"

"It's legal. I would guess most people have seen some type of it. I don't think that I'd say it's common."

I sat back and rested my arm along the back of the couch.

"I'd say it's mostly men who watch it. Mostly alone. Although couples watch it too. It can introduce new techniques and keep things interesting."

"Hmmm..." she processed that. "I was making tea," she said. I fiddled with my phone while she went to the kitchen and came back with a cup for both of us.

Reaching for the cup I said, "You don't have to do this." Seeing her worry I added, "But thank you. It smells great."

"Do you?" she asked, sitting down beside me. "Watch it?"

I coughed a little into my cup.

Vivienne watched me over the rim of her cup. She had a slight smile as she took a sip.

"We're still on this?" I asked.

She shrugged. "I'm a midwife. I want to know the mating ways of people today. What's successful. What's not."

"Ah." I set my cup down on the table and sat forward. "So you want to know about mating."

She frowned at me. "I know about mating! I know everything there is to know."

"Okay, well I'm going to need some proof of that. Go on."

Clearly irritated, she said, "I want to know about what methods work to obtain a pregnancy."

"Oh." I picked up my tea and sat back. "I can help you there. Assuming all systems are go with the male and female health, it's all about timing. There are kits you can buy to tell when ovulation is occurring, that's been the most significant development for improving conception rates. I'll get you a book about it. Or a less graphic website."

"Thank you." She set her cup down on the saucer.

"And, yes," I said. "I've watched it."

We held each other's gaze.

I added, "But a woman is always preferable."

Vivienne nodded sagely. "I would imagine so."

CHAPTER TWENTY-SIX

Vivienne

October 15th, 2024

When my new tennis shoes arrived and I did not kill the FedEx delivery person, Adam claimed to be very proud of me.

He was always teasing. We spent a good portion of our time poking at each other and fake fighting about which one of us was the most annoying. If he didn't think me a nun, I'd say we were acting like an old married couple. But my own marriage was very different from this, and I suspect Adam's relationship with Connie had been, too. We also discussed science and literature and he was introducing me to the poetry of my time, but we both looked forward to the times when we bickered.

It was my birthday and Adam took me to lunch at a local café to celebrate. There was a nip in the air but we sat outside and waited for our food to be delivered. My champagne glass had a strawberry perched on its rim. Sipping my drink I watched the passersby and wondered about their lives. What did they do to earn money? Were they married? A couple our age walked by and the man made the woman laugh. I wondered, were they still in love? He reached for her hand as they crossed the street and their hands remained clasped as they strolled away.

While my attention was on the couple, Adam threw a piece of paper from his straw at me and acted like he did not. Then we fought over whether or not it happened.

"Vivienne, I think it's possible, what with all your time travel, that you may be losing what's left of your sanity. Maybe it's time to get doctor Waltman to do another psych eval. We can call her after lunch."

I asked him, "Do you behave this way with all your house guests? And, if so, how do you ever get house guests?"

He sat back at that and folded his hands in his lap. He smiled at me. "I haven't really enjoyed having house guests in the past. You're my guinea pig. How am I doing?"

I returned his gaze and had difficulty hiding what I felt. Feelings I had never had before and knew I would never have again. This man was the closest thing I had ever had to an equal. He delighted me. I wanted to lean over that table and kiss him shamelessly.

But that could not be. I knew it. I still had to leave, and he needed to help me, not try to keep me here. I said, "My answer depends on one very important piece of information." He leaned in. "What is a guinea pig?"

Adam laughed loudly and then explained, "It's a rodent we use in medical experiments."

"Then I would say you are doing very well as a host because I feel exactly like a guinea pig in your house." He smiled at that and I wished again to be able to tell him everything I wanted.

What I wanted more than anything was more time with him.

He pulled a small package from his coat pocket.

"I got you a present." He laid the wrapped gift on the table in front of me.

It was wrapped in deep blue paper with a silver ribbon tied artfully on top. I smiled and pulled the ribbon apart and gently opened the paper where it was taped.

It was a small book. The cover said, "*The Poems of W. B. Yeats.*"

"Thank you," I said. The book opened to a page marked with a silver ribbon. I read the poem aloud.

He Wishes for the Cloths of Heaven
"Had I the heavens' embroidered cloths,
Enwrought with golden and silver light,
The blue and the dim and the dark cloths
Of night and light and the half-light,
I would spread the cloths under your feet:
But I, being poor, have only my dreams;
I have spread my dreams under your feet;
Tread softly because you tread on my dreams."

A message for me, from him. And just like that, my resolve was almost dissolved.

I looked up. "It's beautiful. I love it. Thank you, Adam."

"I marked a few more that are my favorites of his."

The waitress came with our food then and we returned to safer topics than poetry and feelings.

October 16th, 2024

Grant and Maria arranged with me to take a tour of the Smithsonian Museum for the afternoon. There were many museums to choose from, but they suggested the Natural History Museum as the best place to start. Maria said to wear tennis shoes, so I wore the new crimson colored running shoes that Adam had purchased for me.

I knew Adam had asked them to take me. He left to do some sort of business out of town and did not want me to be alone. Grant was staying overnight at the house, too. I said I didn't need a babysitter, but Adam would not budge.

The museum had a large dome on top and a staircase leading up to six columns. Inside, we were greeted by a massive beast from Africa called an elephant with a trunk that soaked up water or dust so it could spray all over itself. His name was Henry, and he was magnificent. I wanted to stay and look at him longer, but Grant ushered me into a hall of even more massive beasts, the dinosaur hall. My eyes were wide as they took in the skeletons of those creatures that roamed the earth before man. It was beyond incredible that they could be replicated here for current men and women to see. I read every bit of information in that room. Adam had explained to me about evolution and that one did not need to discount the scientific evidence in order to also believe in the Bible. I agreed.

Grant took pictures of me seeing the dinosaurs for the first time and sent them to Adam. When I was done, he steered me toward another hall full of even larger creatures. I stood under the blue whale and thought what an honor it was to see what Jonah must have seen and lived through. The replica of a great white shark was terrifying, and I pledged to myself never to enter the ocean, should I have the chance.

After hours of beast observation, Maria was done with that part of the tour and decided no woman should leave the Museum of Natural History without seeing the jewels. She was right. We did a tour of the gallery and decided to visit the gift shop next and then go home.

On the way there, Grant asked us, "Which gem was your favorite?"

Maria answered immediately, "The pink heart diamond."

Grant laughed. "Okay, got it. What if I can't find one that big? Would you take a smaller version?"

She made a mad face at him. "Don't skimp, Parrish. Women don't like men who skimp on the essentials."

"And eight carat heart-shaped pink diamonds are essential?"

She threw up her hands at me as if to say, "Look what I'm dealing with here."

I smiled. "Grant, when you decide to give a woman a diamond, she'll love it. Whatever size or color. Because it's from you." He smiled back at me and then gestured at Maria.

"Except this one," he laughed.

She glared back at him. "Have you ever *given* me a diamond, Grant?"

He looked incredulous. "Are you kidding me? You just, not ten seconds ago, told me to fuck off if the diamond isn't eight carats!"

"Oh my god," she said. "I was playing with you. You should know the difference by now."

Maria seemed more upset than the situation warranted, and I decided they needed a moment to discuss things. I stepped into the gift shop and began to look for something to get for Adam.

The museum gift shop was bright and loud and full of children tugging on their parent's hands. I understood their excitement because I wanted one of everything, too. There seemed to be a stuffed animal for every one that sailed on Noah's Ark. I fell in love with a mother elephant and her baby tucked up underneath her. There were rocks of every texture and color, cards and pens and, best of all, replicas of the gems we saw upstairs.

When we had stood in front of the Hope Diamond, Grant explained that diamonds could now be made by men in a lab. Machines could put as much pressure on basic coal to mimic what it took the earth a billion years to make. They were not inexpensive but compared to the gems mined in Africa, they were affordable and could not be distinguished from the originals by the human eye. I wondered out loud why a person would buy anything but the man made diamonds and Grant laughed at that. "You're a good woman, Vivienne."

As I viewed the replica jewelry, I felt a pressure. It was mental, not physical, and I did not look up or acknowledge it. I strengthened my shield around my power and knew that I was now completely undetectable by another witch. Nevertheless, I noticed a man staring at me from the doorway. My eyes skimmed over his, and I got the attention of the salesclerk. Handing her the credit card with Adam's information on it, I pointed to the pink heart replica diamond in the case. If it was not too much, I wanted to buy it for Maria. It wasn't eight carats, but I knew she would love it.

The witch was making his way to me, and I felt for his power. I sent a brief shot of pain toward his torso. It bypassed him and unfortunately, hit the elderly woman beside him. She gasped and clutched at his arm as she bent over with pain. Internally I winced, outwardly I continued to look at the jewelry. People sometimes got hit in the crossfire with magic. His shield had been stronger than I estimated, and my magic deflected to the poor woman.

Grant appeared in the gift shop entrance and immediately read the situation. In no time he was stepping between me and the other witch.

"You don't have to do that," I murmured.

"Pretty sure you're right about that, Vivienne. But I don't want to have to explain to dad why I didn't."

We inspected the gems in the case more closely. He pointed to another heart shaped pink diamond in the case. I indicated that, yes, I saw that. The man stood next to Grant now. I reached again for him and got a good estimate of his power level. His shield was strong, but he was putting out enough power to let me know he was not to be taken lightly. His level was high. Very high, maybe the same as Grant. Not close to Adam, though. And very far below mine.

I stood back from the counter and faced him. He was tall with dark hair and eyes. I noticed two more witches at the entrance, both with very high levels of magic. His men, I noticed, had a similar appearance. There was only one visible entrance. I had checked when I first came in. Grant's eyes also watched the door, worrying about where Maria was.

Before hurting anyone else, I thought I should address the issue with them.

"What do you want?" I asked the man.

To his credit, he didn't pretend to not understand. "We'd like to talk to you about your power," he said quietly. "We'd like to offer you a contract to work for us. My employer would like to meet you. He is extending an invitation for you to come with us and talk about it."

"Who's your employer?" Grant asked.

"None of your business," the man said.

"What about me? Is it my business?" I asked. There were now six or seven other witches in the gift shop ushering people out, using the gift of persuasion to do so. I had experienced Adam using this magic just once and did not want to risk it making its way past my shield.

All the witches in the room suddenly bent over in pain, their concentration shot. They looked to the man in front of me for orders. Unfortunately for him, he was also bent over, grasping his gut.

Grant's smile was wicked. "Fuck yeah," he said.

The salesclerk came back from the register and stopped short when she saw the room empty except for the ten or so people groaning and doubled over with pain. I reached out and grabbed Adam's card and the little silver bag she held in her other hand.

"Thank you," I said. "I think we'll leave now. It seems like there's some sort of virus going around." I took Grant's sleeve, and we turned from the case. Bending down to the witch in charge, I said in a low voice, "I am not interested. Do not approach me or these people again." I left him with one more sharp twinge in both his sides and, for good measure, in both his knees. He grunted and collapsed to the floor. The salesclerk squeaked and ran to help him. Grant and I gathered up Maria, who had been persuaded to sit outside the shop, and we swiftly walked out of the museum.

I didn't let go of their pain until we all sat in the back of a Lyft Grant called for us. Looking out the car window at the buildings that sped by, I realized that holding their pain for all those minutes had felt good. My magic had needed to stretch. I preferred that it be used for healing but sometimes the world presented other opportunities.

Chapter Twenty-Seven

Adam

October 16th, 2024

Chicago used to be one of my favorite cities. I had done all the tourist things like see the Cubs at Wrigley Field, go to the House of Blues, take the river boat Architecture Tour. But it was full of crime now and the only thing it had to offer me anymore was the primal fear I felt when I stepped out into the glass box on the side of the Sears Tower. It's called something else now, but in my mind it would always belong to Sears. Which I was pretty sure had filed for bankruptcy and was now out of business.

Staring down through the glass floor, I felt my heart rate pick up and my sense of fear kick in. Adrenaline coursed through my veins and I was reminded that this was a stupid thing to do. That glass should not hold an almost two-hundred-pound man and that at any moment I could plunge a hundred and eight stories down and die a horrible death. *Jesus fucking Christ.*

And then, time up. They rush you out to keep the line moving, but if they didn't, I would stay there for a good thirty minutes or so. Best remedy for God syndrome I have ever found. And being a doctor and a witch with my power, I was pretty well acquainted with that.

The witch I was there to see worked in one of the downtown buildings. He was a night security guard in a high rise that held business offices on the first floors and luxury apartments at the top. Jeremy Talbot, thirty-nine, a graduate of Southern Illinois University with a bachelor's degree in computer science. Talbot had not cashed in on that major, though, and I wondered what his problem was. A brief investigation was not going to get to the real problem. Was he just psychotic or did he have social problems as well and not fit in with regular society?

That seemed to be our uniquely American problem today. We raised young men, who, because of mental health problems or difficulty creating relationships, bought a gun in frustration and tried to shoot their way out of pain. I thought about trying to explain to Vivienne how Americans justified owning a gun in the face of all our gun tragedies. Would she see the folly of it all? She might have tended to wounds from swords or longbows. That was a whole hell of a lot more civilized than a child cut in half by semi-automatic gun fire. A common thread from both of our times was the inevitability of violence. And the pain that came with it.

The Council's report said Talbot was straight, had a revolving door of girlfriends, and no convictions on his record. My investigator Reeger had found a little more, as usual. He'd been asked to leave his fancy private high school because of a relationship with a teacher. She'd gone to jail for a while after being convicted of having sex with a minor.

Talbot also had been a person of interest in a molestation case involving a sixteen-year-old girl. Which, of course, he did. But somehow he was never charged, even though the evidence was sufficient to pick him up. This was the problem with deviant witches who also had the power of persuasion. They could get out of anything that came at them directly. The legal system did not know how to handle a situation with as many apparent fuck ups and as much red tape as a case like that.

At ten o'clock, I took a Lyft to the block where Talbot worked. It was on the edge of the downtown business district. The Lyft driver tried to tell me not to get out there. I got out anyway and headed for Talbot's building. Two kids across the street eyed me but stayed where they were. I pushed open the locked door using a field of power I took off a train conductor once when I was in college.

That night, I was half drunk, and I had walked all the way to the front car for some reason, probably thinking I'd rather sit in a car with a girl than in a car alone. The conductor was kicking the life out of a passenger on the floor, and the man was screaming at him to stop. I threw out a wall of my magic without thinking. When I laid it all on him, he collapsed immediately.

I wanted to walk to the passenger to get the conductor off of him, but I was pinned in place by another wall of power. As I felt it seeping into my blood, my knees buckled and a wave of nausea hit me. It didn't take long until I sensed the change. His power was mine now. Whether I wanted it or not. Since that time, I knew that sending out all my magic that fast, without reservation, all or nothing, would end the person I hit with it. And would give me what had been theirs.

That first magic I took had been some of the most useful and the most pointless. The conductor had the gift of opening locked things and of charming animals. I used the door opening frequently and the animal-charming almost never.

I knew Talbot had persuasion. I wondered what else he would have. Reeger had not found that for me and it was unusual for me to take a case without that knowledge, but I just wanted to get the job done and get back to Vivienne.

A schedule at the front desk had him maybe on the fifth floor at this hour. I took the stairs. Talbot wasn't there, so I went to the next place he was supposed to be, the sixth floor. Not there, either. I was getting tired of combing through office space when I heard a whistle. A taunting whistle. "Over here," it said. It came from the shadows, but I walked that way, anyway.

"Bold," he said from the dark. "Are you a witch? Must be." He stepped out and faced me. It was him. Tall, light brown hair, blue eyes. Not bad looking, I realized. I wondered again what had gone wrong with him and why.

"Yes." I never lied to people I was going to kill. It seemed the fair thing to do. "I came for you," I said.

He turned on his persuasion instantly. "You don't want me. You were wrong to come here. It was a mistake. The person who told you to do this was wrong. You should drop it."

His words washed over my head and landed softly behind me. That was the beauty of persuasion. It felt like a warm hug when administered. Or it felt like a waterfall flowing over and past you because you were immune. I just studied him. He narrowed his eyes.

"Shit," he said.

I thought of the girls he had taken advantage of and the lies he would have told them afterwards, and I unleashed my magic on him with a force I'd never used before. His face froze in surprise when it hit him, and then he crumpled to the ground. Bracing myself for the rebound of my magic and his, I found I was completely unprepared for the wave when it hit me. I dropped too and threw up while on my hands and knees.

Jesus. It was a lot. I struggled to get enough oxygen.

What was happening? His power of persuasion was added to mine, and I also noticed a new tingle in my brain. It was different from anything I'd gotten before. I couldn't identify it and knew this was not the time to try. I needed to clean up the vomit and get the hell out of there.

I made it downstairs and grabbed some garbage bags and bleach from the custodian's room. Sick to my stomach, I cleaned the mess and poured some bleach on it. With the garbage bag in my hand, I took one last look at Talbot. He was still dead. I headed for the security office. It would not do to leave a picture or video trail, so I spent a few minutes using my ability to fry the electronics with a touch, once again grateful for the acquisition of that skill.

I called the same Lyft guy. He gave me a curious look as I got in and asked him to take me back to my hotel. As I got out at the hotel, I persuaded him that he should not tell anyone ever that he had me in his car. And I gave him a great tip.

CHAPTER TWENTY-EIGHT

Vivienne

October 16th, 2024

Grant and I put Maria to bed at Adam's house when we got home. She was furious about what happened to her at the museum but thrilled when Grant described for her what I had done to the others. She took Grant's old room in the turret. I would sleep in Adam's room, and Grant would sleep in the guest room across from Adam's room.

When we finally sat together in Adam's study, I saw Grant using his phone to text. I knew he was talking to Adam.

"Tell him there was no challenge to it," I said.

Grant smiled down at his phone and typed the words. He said, "I have assured him no less than ten times now that you are fine and that we are all fine. He said he'll call you later on, when he can."

"Your father is a protector. That's what God made him."

Grant nodded yes. "To a fault, he protects. Everyone. He protects the world."

He scanned my face to see if I agreed. To see how much I knew about Adam's calling. I pulled my robe tighter around me and arranged it to cover my legs. I wouldn't talk of it with his son. Not until I spoke to Adam himself.

"Have you called your grandmother?" I asked.

"Dad already did. She has security assigned to her, his security, and he talked to them, too." Grant wiped a hand over his mouth and jaw. "This is so insane. I mean, you hear about witches abusing power, but I have never heard of anything like this." He shook his head.

I needed more information. "Who were those people? What's your best guess?"

He shrugged and said, "Maybe a wealthy witch who wants more wealth? Or any power hungry witch who wants more power... maybe the guy from Britain?" Grant stared at Adam's bookshelf while he considered it.

Then he changed the subject. "How is she?" Everything he felt for Maria was evident on his face. "She still seemed so out of it when we got here. Does she need a doctor?"

I gave him a look that said 'seriously?' and he laughed. "Right. Sorry. Forgot who I was talking to."

"I took care of her," I told him.

We sat in silence for a few moments, and then he said, "We dated. When I came back from Afghanistan. But I was fucked up and ended up fucking it all up." His hand plucked at the arm of the sofa. "She needed more talking, and I just couldn't talk. *At all.*" He made a face as if he couldn't believe how stupid he had been. "Don't tell dad, he didn't know."

I doubted that.

Grant gave a humorless laugh. "I still don't have any idea what she wanted. Or wants."

I reached down and picked up the silver bag from the museum gift shop. Tossing it in his lap, I said, "She wants a pink heart-shaped diamond. She was very clear."

He laughed as he pulled the ring box out of the bag. Opening it up, he said, "I thought about going back and getting this."

"Then you should give it to her. Sooner rather than later." I stood up and went over to the daybed to retrieve a book of poetry I had been reading. "You need to *gather ye rosebuds while ye may,* Grant. *Old time is still a flying. And that same flower that smiles today, tomorrow will be dying.*" He gave me a small smile. "Your father has been treating me to some noteworthy poems from my time. This one is called, *To the Virgins to Make Much of Time,* by Robert Herrick."

"Are you calling me a virgin, Vivienne?" he asked, a hand to his chest as if wounded.

"No more so than your father or I are virgins," I replied. "But we understand this poem written for virgins. Because we know the value of time. That's what this poem is about. Not wasting time. Read it." He laughed again as I shoved the book at him. I settled back in my chair, and Grant obliged me and read the poem out loud.

"Gather ye rose-buds while ye may,
Old Time is still a-flying;
And this same flower that smiles today
Tomorrow will be dying.
The glorious lamp of heaven, the sun,
The higher he's a-getting,
The sooner will his race be run,
And nearer he's to setting.
That age is best which is the first,
When youth and blood are warmer;
But being spent, the worse, and worst
Times still succeed the former.
Then be not coy, but use your time,
And while ye may, go marry;
For having lost but once your prime,
You may forever tarry."
Grant closed the book.

"You know...I've never seen him like this." He waited for me to look up at him. "Dad has never been this happy. Ever."

When I didn't say anything, he tried again. "Dad mentioned that your magic packs a punch. Said he's never experienced anything like that before. That it would be a hard thing to forget."

Adam had probably told Grant about my magic early on to warn him about me.

"That's just it, Grant. Once a man feels that he does not care to know the woman so much as the power she projects."

He shook his head sharply at that.

"Absolutely not. That's not what he cares about. Vivienne, he has not stopped talking about you since you got here. Every day, it's some new brag about how brilliant you are, how compassionate, how funny..."

I had to shut that down. "Well, I'm glad your father cares about me. I also care for him. But it's important to remember that I live in a nunnery. A nun cannot have a relationship outside of her vows." *Technically true.* "It will be very hard when I leave, but that's what will happen, and we will all have to live with that fact."

His look said he did not believe a word I had just said. But he was respectful and left it at that.

Grant opened the book and read the poem again. I watched the flames in the fireplace. He read another poem. I asked him, "Why were you in the Army?"

He tilted his head to the side, considering that.

I said, "You seem to me such a man of letters. A librarian seems to be your calling."

"I didn't want to be a doctor," he said with a small laugh. "I knew the hours involved and just really did not want to choose that. But, I did want to help people, so I joined the Army. Then worked the bomb squad. Got out from under the parental shadows."

"Those would be some very big shadows," I agreed.

After a moment he asked me, "What was your favorite gem today?"

I was happy to discuss that. "I liked the red diamond. Did you see it?" He shook his head no. "The information posted there said they are extremely rare. There was something so mysterious about it. It sparkled even in its depths."

After saying good night to Grant, I made my way into Adam's room and turned back the covers on his bed. I shook my head at the folly of this. I had just chastised his son for suggesting Adam and I could ever be anything more than friends, and here I was about to sleep naked in his bed and definitely touch myself as I imagined him lying there beside me.

I dropped my robe at the end of the bed and jumped as my cell phone rang on the dresser. Grabbing it quickly, I answered, "Hello?"

"Vivienne," his voice made me catch my breath. "How are you? I'm so sorry I wasn't there today."

I stood there naked, next to his bed, clutching the phone to my ear as if it were him.

"I'm fine. We're all fine. I told Grant to let you know it was no challenge."

He chuckled at that. "I realize that ten witches with persuasion would only be an imposition to you. But humor me and don't go anywhere until I get home and we figure this out, all right?"

"Yes," I said. I slipped between his sheets. "Mmmm..." The sheets smelled like Adam.

"What is mmmm?" he said.

"Your sheets are better than mine."

There was silence for a moment.

"Are you sleeping in my bed?" he asked.

"Yes. Your sheets feel like satin," I said.

More silence.

I heard a deep inhale and exhale. "Well, I will definitely upgrade the sheets in your room as soon as I get back. How's that?"

I laughed softly. "I would expect nothing less from you."

"Sweet dreams, Vivienne."

"And the same to you, Adam."

CHAPTER TWENTY-NINE

Adam

October 17th, 2024

I couldn't focus. I sat at my desk, flipping a paper clip end over end, staring out the window, imagining Vivienne in various states of undress. I kept an office near Union Station where Maria managed the schedule for my work with the Council of Witches. When I made a call to Richard Cole about what happened to everyone at the museum, he said he hadn't heard anything about it but would find out. He asked if I had decided not to file the Declaration of Protection. I told him it was coming.

I needed to study the information in front of me. Reeger had finally found something on the Internet about the priest and I wanted to follow up. He asked me to confirm that the picture he had was Father Andrew Barry. Barry couldn't have been more than eighteen, but that was clearly his face in the middle of a gaggle of Irish youth at a religious retreat.

So the priest part was for real? I would have bet a million dollars it was not.

Reeger said with that information he could get somewhere, hopefully soon. But I decided to go to Dublin myself to ask around at the church where the picture was taken. Something in me was howling to kill that man. I'd never felt like that before, but it was also not an unwelcome state. Knowing that he had fully intended to kill us in Britain and that he had most likely sent men after Vivienne at the museum while I was away made it even more obvious to me he needed to die. There was no conflict in me at all about my decision. It seemed like the pious little imp in my head had shrugged, dropped his pointer and shuffled off until this deal with the priest was all over.

I heard Maria making the plane reservations in the office outside of mine. She handled everything for me with no questions asked, ever. I did pay her well for that amount of discretion, but I still greatly appreciated her loyalty and abilities. Maria was a witch with impressive magic and intelligence and was extremely under-utilized as an executive assistant. She had worked for me for almost ten years and I knew she stayed out of gratitude for a long ago favor from me.

Her family life had been rough. Her stepfather had been taking out his rage on both witches and mortals alike for all of his adult life. He'd finally been reported by another witch, and the Council had confirmed he had not obeyed any of their warnings. That was how all Council of Witches sentences came about. A witch who was unwilling to stop abusing his power would finally meet up with me.

On the job to take out her stepfather, I discovered Maria and her mother cowering in a back room of his house. At the beginning of my tenure enforcing Council sentences, I had not been as organized. Back then, I did the investigating myself and sometimes failed to account for things like other members of a household being hidden in the house.

When Maria's mother found her husband dead, she sat down at the kitchen table and cried from relief. They had been punching bags for that pitiful excuse for a man and I was grateful to see the fear leave her mother's face. Maria looked shell-shocked, and for the first time I realized that I might leave others in the crossfire when I finished my work. What would the police say? Would Maria and her mother be charged with his death? I said I'd take care of the body. A week later I offered Maria a job and she'd been with me ever since. Over time our relationship had morphed into a father/daughter situation that made things both easier and harder for me. I worried about her as much as she worried about me.

I was there to work. But images of Vivienne filled my mind. I was at war with myself. She was a nun, and that meant hands off. But after just five minutes of exposure to the essence of her magic, now my very fabric of existence was unraveling. What was the point of anything if feeling that again was off the table? Ever since I asked her to shield her magic, I'd been trying to figure out an excuse to get her to share it again. Without it, she smelled tempting enough. The lotions or shampoos she used were heaven. A light touch of lilac followed by mint. It was both calming and invigorating at once.

My concentration was absolutely shot. What was *happening* to me? I was fucking *ensorcelled* by this woman.

And when she let her shield down... I leaned back, closed my eyes and imagined her in my room, lying on those sheets she loved so much.

"I've got you going out tomorrow morning, really early," Maria said from the doorway. She stopped there, taking in my obvious state of inaction. "You okay?"

"Yeah." I sat up and picked up the file in front of me. "Can you call Grant for me and see if he'll come over for dinner tonight?" I didn't usually staff out calls to my son, but it was getting late, and I needed to figure this trip out first. I wanted him to stay at the house with Vivienne again.

She smiled. "You like her. What you're doing... helping her? It's really nice. Vivienne's lucky she found you here. It was like fate."

I rolled my eyes at that.

"Seriously. What if somebody else had found her?"

That was true. But then again, she might have handled it.

"I've never met anyone as intelligent as Vivienne," I admitted. "She's clearly a genius. And, unfortunately for her, she was born a woman and a witch. Stuck in a time that didn't reward women for their minds. A time when people gleefully sentenced witches to be burned at the stake."

Maria's face was serious. Then she came out with, "You should ask her out. She's perfect for you."

I dropped the folder back on the desk. "Great idea. I'll get right on asking the nun out."

"Whatever. You're just chicken."

"I think you mean respectful of her wishes."

She turned to leave, and I raised my voice so she'd hear, "How about you, Maria? When was the last time you had a serious relationship?"

"Noneya," she called back.

I countered with, "What, *I* have to date but you don't?"

She yelled, "Father Time isn't after *me*, old man."

Damn. That was a good one. There was no comeback for that truth.

A few seconds later I heard her call to Grant. "Hello wanker," she said into the phone. "Your dad wants to see you for dinner."

I opened the file and began to read.

Grant came for dinner and peppered Vivienne with a million questions about the 1500s. She humored him. Before he left, he promised to stay over the next night.

After dinner, we sat down in the living room and I asked Vivienne if she'd like to hear some music. She asked for Mozart again. I mostly have albums from the seventies, but my father was a classical music lover, so I bent over and searched his collection, wishing I had ever once thought to alphabetize it. When I first introduced Vivienne to classical music, her pleasure was so great she let go of the shield on her magic for a while and I basked in its glow. I was, of course, ever hopeful I could pick another winner that would get me to that place again.

From behind me I heard her ask, "What does your travel have to do with your medicine?"

I stopped rifling through the albums and sat down on the floor in front of the stereo. We were both silent for a moment and then I surprised myself by telling her the truth.

"Nothing," I said. "It has nothing to do with medicine." I turned around toward her.

Vivienne nodded. She clearly knew this. "What do you do on your trips?"

I looked at her then, straight on. Taking my time to think about it, I decided to be completely honest with her.

"I take care of problems. For the Council. I take care of threats."

"Why do you do it?"

"Because someone has to," I said firmly.

She persisted, "But why do you do it? Surely no one can make you."

I laughed without humor. "No. They can't."

Swiping a hand over my head, I got up off the floor and sat down on the couch close to her chair. "But you know that," I said.

"Yes."

"No one else can," I tried to explain. "No one else has the power."

She said, "I don't doubt that. The other witches I have sensed here, on the street, and your friends... they don't have half your power. Not all of them combined."

I studied her. "But you do," I said. "You have more. Much more."

She gave me a sharp look. "But I grow my magic by giving life. Saving life."

I said, "I do too. I save lives."

"But you gain more from taking them, do you not?"

How the fuck did she know that?

I frowned. "I didn't choose this. I don't want to be the one who does the dirty work for them. But I'm the only one who can." I paused. "In the *world*, Vivienne."

I stood up and paced to the front door and back. "And some of these witches are beyond imagination. They're insane and power mad. Or just plain evil." I wanted her to understand why I did what I did. "They make the world dangerous for witches and mortals. Especially mortals."

"So you kill them," she said. "And you take their power."

My eyes searched hers. No one had ever suspected this. The Council of Witches thought I was just able to overpower, they didn't have any idea I gained powers as well.

I said, "How do you know?"

She stood up and laid her magazine down on the footstool.

"Your power increases after a trip. And it remains. You steal their power when they die."

I raised my voice. "I don't steal it! It just becomes mine. I don't do anything. I don't want it!" I needed her to know this, and more than anything, I wanted her to believe me.

Vivienne turned to go to her room.

"You may not ask for it, but you receive it." She stopped and added, "You could kill me and have my power, too."

"I would never hurt you. Never."

"You stole the secret of my binding spell."

"Because you used it on me first! I didn't steal it. You still have it."

We faced each other in the hallway. Her face remained impassive.

I said, "I can take the secret of magic that's used against me. I discovered that as a kid."

She said, "But there's more to it. When you kill them, you take it all."

I had already told her I didn't want it.

"Witches who abuse their power and don't change after they get warnings..." I wanted her to understand why I did what I did. "There is no witch jail, Vivienne."

She just stared at me.

"What about you?" I challenged her. "Is your magic always appropriate? Always used with discretion and decorum?"

She frowned at me.

I raised my eyebrows. "Come on. You've told me of other times you used magic when you didn't want to. How does your magic manifest itself?"

"When I'm healing people. When I want it to."

"And never when you don't want it to or how you don't want it to?"

She hesitated. Then raised her chin. "With strong emotion. Joy, anger, fear... passion. Sometimes a spark will show before I can grasp it."

"Just a spark?"

She stared at me stonily, unwilling to participate in this line of questioning anymore.

"We're not that different, Vivienne. I just acknowledge the truth of my magic use. It's not always pretty, but it's always necessary."

She turned and walked to the stairway. Before she entered, she said, "We are very different."

I heard the door to the turret close firmly and felt the seal rise around it.

CHAPTER THIRTY

Vivienne

October 18th, 2024

Adam's overnight bag was in the hallway, and I heard him getting a cup of coffee to go. No doubt he had already called a driver to take him to the airport. I hated that we had argued the night before. Who was I to judge how he used his power? I knew he only did what he thought was right. His reasons were noble and the consequences of his actions obviously weighed upon him heavily. When he walked into the hallway, I started to tell him so.

"Adam, I'm sorry about what I said last night. Almost everything I said was wrong." But he did not acknowledge me. He raised a hand to his head and leaned against the entry to his study. When he slid down the wall behind him, I ran over and tried to cushion his fall. But he fell hard and held his forehead with both hands.

I reached out a hand to place on his face but he grabbed my wrist and said, "Don't touch." I tried with my other hand and he grabbed that wrist, too. His face was ashen, and he held his eyes squeezed shut tight.

"Look at me, Adam. What is it?" I asked him. "Should I call Grant for you?"

He pushed my arms away, and I went flying across the hallway. I ended up on the floor too, winded from hitting the wall.

"No! Don't touch me! It's hell. It's in my brain." One hand clutched his hair, and the other shielded his eyes from the light. "From Chicago. I want to hurt you. I want to hurt everyone." He moaned. "Please leave before I hurt you." He writhed on the floor, rolling from side to side in agony like I had only seen from women in childbirth.

I had observed the previous night that he was not quite himself. Now I knew it must be some dark magic in him, something new from his visit to Chicago. It had appeared right after that. I would take it out, like I did with illness. This was like an illness; I could do it. There was no time to second guess. I stood and went to him again.

"Get away," he roared and went to throw me again. I stepped back to be out of his reach, and I dropped the shield around my magic. Then the hallway was filled with my healing magic and Adam calmed instantly. He opened his eyes to me and I saw the pain in them. I took up his hand in mine and said, "I'm here."

"No," he said. "Don't want you to feel this."

I touched his forehead to determine what to do. There was a malignancy in his brain. *Something wrong, something wrong.* It felt inflamed. He whimpered, and I wished it were over for him already. I vowed it would be soon. Gathering my resolve, I sent in my magic, directing it through my finger, pointing directly to where I sensed it. Adam's body jerked, and he closed his eyes again. He was unconscious, and I thought that was probably for the best.

The darkness was coming out. I felt it rising. The only thing I didn't know for sure was if I could dispose of it like I did with other sicknesses I brought forth from patients. Would this dark magic dissipate in the air like an infection would?

As it reached for me, I knew the answer was no, it wanted a host. I felt it begin to seep into me and I allowed it until I perceived that Adam was relaxing and knew it had left him and was trying to work on me. I stood and opened the front door. The sun had not yet risen. I walked out into the middle of the street and threw my arms wide, pushing the madness out into the world. It was a small thing, but it left me with a powerful boom as I willed it toward the sky, hoping our Heavenly Father would strike it down before it could live again in another.

Just then, I noticed the Lyft car parked by the curb just a few feet from the front of Adam's house. The motor was running. I walked to the driver's window and leaned down.

"I'm sorry. Your passenger was sick this morning and will not be able to use your car. I'm sure he will pay you for your trouble."

The young man inside nodded quickly and said, "That's cool. No problem." He faced the front and drove away.

Back in the house, Adam was sitting up again, still leaning against the wall. When he saw me, he closed his eyes and gave a weak laugh. "Thank God," he said.

"I sent your car away," I said. "I told him I would make sure he got paid."

Adam let out a real laugh at that. "Yep," he said. "Will do."

He looked at me and his face sobered. "Are you all right?"

"Yes," I said. "I made it leave you, then I made it leave me."

"I told you not to do that," he said.

I shook my head at him sadly. "As if you get to tell me what I can or cannot do."

He closed his eyes again and smiled.

"It was a risk," I admitted to him. "I wasn't sure I could do it or what would happen. But Adam, if it had been me and I was suffering like that... what would you have done?"

"Right," he grunted. "Can you help me up? I may need to throw up. Don't want to do it here."

I reached over for his hand and steadied him as he stood. He sucked in his breath when he saw the redness on my wrists from where he held me before.

"Was this *me*?" he asked.

"I'm fine," I said. "It doesn't hurt. You weren't yourself."

He shook his head and rubbed his thumbs over my wrists where the bruises were starting to blossom. His touch there was so gentle and light, but the tingle came as I knew it would. Then he skimmed his hands over my shoulders and down my arms, checking for injuries. "Where else? Where else does it hurt? God, I'm so sorry Vivienne. You saved my life and I threw you across the room."

I scanned him to make sure it was truly gone. His heart was beating fast, but he was clear of the dark magic.

He pulled me to him in a hug. "Thank you, by the way. For saving my life."

I hugged him back. "Of course. I know you would do the same."

He rested his chin on the top of my head and said, "I would do anything for you."

"I know," I said. I steered him toward the bathroom. "Now freshen up and then lie down for a while. You're not going anywhere today."

CHAPTER THIRTY-ONE

I didn't get on the plane. In fact, I didn't move much from the daybed in the living room all day long. I protested that Vivienne should take the daybed, but she insisted. It was so alien to me to have someone pamper me that I just said okay and let it happen. She said she wanted to keep an eye on me after my fall and after the exorcism.

That's what I was calling it. I had a demon in my head from that asshole Talbot in Chicago until Vivienne brought out the holy water of her healing magic and banished that demon back to hell. At least I hoped that was where it was. I kept watch on her too, all day long, waiting for any signs that fucking devil magic still lived in her.

That was a first for me. I'd never gotten anything evil from a witch I had dealt with. The magics I accumulated were often more of the same thing I already had, and I would just end up with a larger dose to use. I didn't sense anything different with Vivienne, but I realized I had lived with that shit for a couple of nights before it made itself known. If Vivienne did, in fact, still have that dark magic in her, I didn't know what I could do about it.

We met Marshall in the sculpture garden on the Mall. He was sitting on a bench typing a text when he caught sight of us and stood.

"Vivienne, it's so good to see you again." He held out his hand, and she shook it. He examined me then and said, "Want to tell me what the emergency is now?" I gestured toward the bench, and both he and Vivienne sat. I stood in front of him.

"I need your help."

His eyebrows raised at that.

"You're the best in the world at what you do, and I need the best right now. I want you to determine if Vivienne has been subjected to a type of magic that could harm her or her ability to heal."

He was concerned. "How was she exposed to this magic? Is she able to absorb other magics?"

Both Vivienne and I shook our heads no.

"Adam is being overly cautious. But I am willing for you to perform your divining magic."

I said, "You don't need to know the rest. Just look to see if her magic is tainted with anything dark."

He checked with Vivienne for her approval again. "This will just take a minute. Adam, pull me out of it if I go longer."

She lowered the shield over her magic and he leaned in toward her. He was concentrating. Then he dropped his eyes and held a hand to his heart. I understood what he was feeling because I was feeling it, too. There was a couple entering the garden at the other end and from their immediate stop, I knew it had also reached them.

At exactly one minute, I grabbed his shoulder and pulled him away from her. He was looking at her with wonder and no small amount of desire. She raised her shield again. To his credit, he stood and walked a few paces away and stayed there with his back to us.

"I didn't feel anything dark. And I did get through the depths of her magic." He turned. "It's incredible. Yours is such an array of healing arts. And other things I couldn't determine."

Then he focused on me. "You need to take better care of her. Why was she exposed to dark magic?"

I thought that was to his credit, too. He was right. Vivienne would not have been exposed to the demon magic if not for me.

"Congratulations on being right about something, Marshall." I held out my hand for Vivienne, and she took it automatically. Our magic was happy with this state of affairs. I knew it. I wondered if she did.

"She could do anything she wants, Adam. She should know that."

I turned my head back toward him.

"Did you send those witches after her?" I asked in a low voice.

"No, but I know who did. It's a witch from the Middle East. His wife has cancer. He heard of Vivienne and would pay anything for her to try to cure his wife."

I dropped Vivienne's hand and took a quick stride toward Smith.

"And how did he learn about Vivienne? I'll give you a try with me right now, Marshall. Divine me and see what I can do to you if you ever do that again."

His mouth tightened. "I know what you can do. But it wasn't me." My magic told me he was telling the truth. "I just found out for you who was after her. You should look a little closer to home for who spread the word about Vivienne."

"What the fuck does that mean?" I stepped closer to him. I felt Vivienne pull on my arm.

"Adam."

I took a breath. Then I closed my eyes and turned away from him.

Vivienne turned to him as we were leaving and said, "Thank you, Marshall. I won't forget that you did this for us."

Chapter Thirty-Two

Vivienne

November 1st, 2024

Adam woke me at the crack of dawn to go running with him, and I cursed him. Literally, I sent a pain to his side, and he groaned and said, "Was that you?"

From under the covers I said, "Was what me?"

"Oh no," he laughed. "No, you don't." He ripped the comforter off and a burst of cold hit me.

I sat up and covered my eyes in protest at the overhead light. "Adam, it's still dark outside."

He didn't say anything, so I uncovered my eyes.

He was staring at me, his face full of desire. He seemed unprepared. I had more skin exposed than he had probably seen as yet, and I pulled my bare legs up to my chest to keep from shivering.

After a moment he said, "Get it together, woman. We leave in five minutes."

When I had dressed in my new black lightweight running pants and white short-sleeved shirt, I joined him on the porch. I tied a light, purple jacket around my waist and nodded to Tony and Caleb, our guards who were waiting on the sidewalk for us, and apparently tasked with running as well.

"Nice shoes," Adam said. Despite the chill in the air, he was dressed in only his black shorts and a gray t-shirt that said, 'Georgetown.'

"Thank you. My best friend bought them for me."

His lip quirked up at that. "Don't try to suck up. You've put this off long enough. This is going to be brutal. A challenge like you have never experienced before. Are you up to it?"

"Please, Adam. I'm in perfectly good health. How hard can it be to run from one place to another?"

He smiled again. "Alright Lanier, let's go."

He jogged down the porch steps, and I followed.

"Our goal for you today is to run to the Reflecting Pool, and then you can walk back. When you need to, just walk a minute and then get back to a nice and easy jog."

It was quiet outside and very few cars were on the streets. I could see why he liked the mornings. The cool air caressed my cheeks, and I breathed in and out with pleasure. The sound of our feet hitting the roadway was soothing somehow, and I felt myself falling into rhythm with him. After a block, he gave me a side glance and said, "You're a natural."

My pleasure at this praise was immense. I wanted to hear more of his praise, in all places. In bed especially.

I looked ahead again and tried to get back the settled feeling of running next to Adam on a quiet Washington D.C. avenue. But my concentration had been shattered when he praised me and on top of that, my lungs were beginning to burn. My steps faltered a bit as I tried to think this problem through. Adam adjusted his pace for me. I sent a small wave of healing to my lungs and as they re-oxygenated, I picked up my pace again. Adam raised his eyebrows at that and held his arm out to prevent me from running across the street until the light changed.

We ran a while longer and then he steered me toward the Reflecting Pool that sat between the Washington Monument and the Lincoln Memorial. He slowed when we came to the first set of benches, and he jogged in place while I sat and tried to regulate my breathing again.

"Alright, be honest. Did you do something to your breathing to be able to run this distance?" he demanded.

I gave a small laugh as I leaned back on the bench and closed my eyes for a moment.

"I may have asked my body for a bit more oxygen at some point," I said.

He sat next to me. "Oh my god, no cheating Lanier! I'm not sure you'll get the benefits if you add extra oxygen along the way." He seemed to me to be thinking that through while I still struggled to get my breathing normal.

"Why would I not? I'm still pushing my cardiovascular system to work harder than normal and for longer than normal."

"Yeah, maybe," he said. Just then, we both noticed his friend Samuel running along the sidewalk toward us.

"Vivienne! Did this asshole make you get out of bed this early on a Saturday morning? Why did you let him?" He stopped by us and stretched his arms, and then walked in a circle for a couple of minutes to cool down.

"Sam and I meet here some mornings to run over by the Cherry Blossom trees and then back here." Adam pointed to a line of trees in the distance. "We can't help trying to outrun each other and it makes for a good workout."

Samuel said, "It's true. We are nothing if not predictable."

"Marsh," Adam began, "hypothetically," *I knew where this was going,* "if a person could run with a steady stream of oxygen to their lungs, would they reap the benefits of running?"

Adam said to me, "Marsh is a heart surgeon."

Samuel considered some unknown point in the sky. "Well, it's been proven to be effective for athletic recovery. The NFL keeps it on the sidelines of every game. But do you mean the benefits like improved cardiovascular health?"

"Yes. And endorphin release. Would a runner get the same results if he had a constant supply of oxygen flowing?"

It was not like I had a constant supply of oxygen flowing. It was more like a light wash of it when my lungs became uncomfortable. I willed Adam to know this, and his mouth twitched as if he felt my righteous indignation.

Samuel pondered some more, jogging in place, and then said, "I don't see why not."

I swiveled toward Adam in triumph, but he was looking at Samuel and shaking his head in disgust.

"What?" Samuel said, "You asked. Don't ask if you don't want to know."

Adam stood.

Samuel asked, "You want to come, Vivienne?"

"Oh, no," I said. "I think I'll stay here and watch you two challenge each other."

Adam looked back at me as they headed for the trees, checked on the security team to let them know to stay with me, then glanced back again as he got further away. I knew he was worried. I wished he would accept that I was the last person on earth he needed to be worried about. But I was also warmed by his concern. It was nice to have someone who wanted to take care of me again.

My husband, John had been protective, too. He was a good man, a hard worker who loved bringing me flowers and sometimes baked goods so that I would not spend a whole weekend baking for the week ahead. Thinking of him made me smile. The years when our Evelyn was young were the best years of my life. He was a skilled sculptor of stone and worked mostly on cathedrals. In the early years, we had to move a few times for him to keep steady work. But I didn't mind because I always had sick people to heal and expectant mothers to help. Later, he worked for the King in the Tower Complex, and we stayed in one place.

John was worshipful of me in the bedroom. It had been very good with us. After he died in an accident at his work site, I missed him and his warmth fiercely. I refused any suitors after that for many years and made sure his memory was kept with reverence.

Other runners passed me by as did a couple walking a large shaggy dog on a leash. They waved at me and responded to my "good morning" with greetings of their own. I leaned back on the bench, closed my eyes and raised my face to the sun.

Thanking God again for Adam and the lovely place called Washington, D.C., I had a nice communion with my Holy Father in Heaven and made some peace with the fact that I would need to leave here soon. Thinking of Alice still made me flush with guilt. I vowed to myself that tomorrow I would halt my selfish exploration of modern medical knowledge in order to spend the whole day in pursuit of an answer regarding how to travel home. To my time.

After a while, Adam and Samuel made their way back to the bench. Samuel sat next to me and took a long drink of his water. He said, "Adam said you asked him to take you running. I know this can't possibly be true. Please give me the honest story of how you came to be brainwashed by this buffoon."

"It did not quite happen that way," I said.

Adam finished his water bottle and said, "Marsh, she might have lain in bed all day if I didn't get her up! She was just lying there." His eyes swept over me on the bench. "In those ridiculous pajama shorts and shirt. With Snoopy on them."

Marsh glanced up at Adam looking at me and said, "Well, now you've made it uncomfortable."

He got up and said, "Go home and sleep all day if you want, Vivienne. You've earned it." He patted my shoulder, said, "See you later," and jogged off in the opposite direction from where we came. With Adam back with me again, Tony and Caleb veered off to the grass to give us privacy.

Adam sat next to me and leaned back to let the sun hit his face.

"Is that what you want?" He asked with his eyes closed. "To lie in bed all day?"

I watched him while I could. His beautiful lips and firm jaw. I wanted to taste them.

"No," I said after a moment. "I need to explore options on how to get back to my time. To Alice."

His mouth tightened. He opened his eyes. "I was thinking…"

I raised my eyebrows, inviting him to go on.

He took my hand and laced our fingers together. We both felt the rush of our magic racing to meet. Hungry to meet. Adam focused on our hands, linked together and resting on his leg.

"I don't want you to go. I was thinking you could stay here and help me heal sick children. And stay at my house forever and let me teach you world history from the beginning until now." He smiled at that. "Or you can do whatever you want to do, here. I'll help you. You could go to medical school and be the best doctor on the planet."

My heart was breaking for us both. Because of course I wanted exactly that. But now was the time to make it clear why I needed to return to my time. We couldn't pretend any longer that my staying in 2024 was an option for us.

"Adam," I said gently. He closed his eyes again, knowing the answer was going to be no. "I want to tell you why I need to go to Alice."

He stood up then, placing my hand back in my lap.

"All right," he said. "Tell me." He did a slow walk back and forth in front of me as I told him my story.

"My father raised me. He was a good man. He did his best. But as I turned fourteen and had my first cycle, I gained my powers earlier than most girls. I knew they were coming." I paused. "But my powers came on so much stronger than I imagined. Suddenly my blood ran fast with the possibilities of my magic. I wanted to explore it. I needed to explore it."

Adam stopped pacing. "That wasn't your fault. It was natural."

In a soft voice, I said, "I didn't say it was my fault."

Then I said firmly, "No, what happened was not my fault. It was their fault. Two boys. They found me in a field where I was letting my magic flow free." Adam turned away from me. "They raped me. I didn't know how to stop them yet. It was so new, my power." His hands curled into fists. He started pacing again.

"So I ran home to my father. Crying, such a mess." I shook my head. "He cleaned me up and cared for me. He said it was not my fault and that God would judge the boys. That we would move, and I would never have to see them again."

I caught his hand as he paced by me. "But Adam," I pulled him down to the bench. "It wasn't enough for me. Moving away in defeat was not an option for me." I searched his face, knowing he would understand this part. "My fury grew over the next night and day until I had to act. I don't know how I knew it would be so, but I understood that I held the power to hurt them, and that's what I did. I found them, and I killed them. Both of them."

Adam said, "They deserved it."

I took a breath in and then exhaled. "God help me, I agreed with you. This is how we're the same, you and I."

"But," I continued, "As time passed, I saw what happened in a different light. I put myself in their place. Young boys, exposed to my magic."

Adam shook his head firmly. "No. Rapists don't get an excuse, Vivienne. That was not because of you."

"I know it wasn't my fault. They could have chosen differently. They should have left me. But I also regretted the life I had taken from them and the vengeance I had taken. I asked forgiveness from God and I promised to help his children from then on instead of hurting them."

We sat there for many minutes until he said, "Is that how we're different then? I exact vengeance and you don't?"

"It's not as simple as that. You help so many. All your choices are made to help people."

"But people do get hurt along the way," he finished for me.

I needed to add more. "It harms you, Adam. Taking lives."

He sat back on the bench. "I know. I took a class called 'Killology' at the Naval War College. On the way into the building, I had to persuade everyone that I was some commander. Every time."

"What is killology?" I asked.

"The study of killing. As it happens in wartime." He stared at something in the distance. "I wanted to know how others experienced it. If justifying killing in war was different somehow."

"And what did you learn?"

"I learned that sometimes justification works and sometimes it doesn't."

I leaned toward him.

"Adam, I don't want Alice to be alone and have to face learning how her magic works without me there. No one else will be able to explain how to harness this kind of power. There is not another witch alive, then or now, who can help her with it. I can't let that happen."

His eyes searched my face.

"I have been trying, you know. To help you get back." Adam ran a hand through his hair.

"Tom says Gerald McEntire keeps moving on him. He gets close and then Gerald is gone." Adam looked at me. "But Reeger's good. He'll find something."

He reached for my hand and threaded our fingers together again. He held them up.

"But what about this, Vivienne? Why is this happening? Don't you want to know? I do."

Where our hands touched, the electric feeling thrummed again. It was both new and old. Our magic wanted this. Wanted us to get closer. I closed my eyes and tried to imprint the feel of him on my soul. I wanted to keep it and take it with me forever.

"I don't know why it's happening. Our magic is strong. Like calls to like."

He shook his head. "I've been with powerful witches before. I've never felt this. Nothing like this."

He squeezed my hand tighter and our magic roared to the surface again, this time demanding that I get closer, that I let our powers join. I pulled away and stood up.

"This can't happen, Adam. We cannot be."

His brown eyes challenged mine. After a moment, when I did not add more, he said, "Fine."

Standing up, he said, "All right then, enough sitting around. Let's see if Grant can have lunch. I have questions about that manuscript."

CHAPTER THIRTY-THREE

Adam

At the house Vivienne and I went our separate ways to recover from the morning's revelations. I wanted nothing more than to figure out what was happening between us, but she was steadfast in her need to return to 1502, and I had to respect that. When Grant came over for lunch, I asked him about access to the manuscript. Vivienne and Grant sat at the kitchen table while I stood in front of the opened refrigerator.

"Can't we come see it sometime without people around?" I dropped a plate of turkey and cheese slices on the table a little too hard. Grant looked at me. I added mustard and a loaf of bread. Vivienne had her head down in a medical text, as usual. I went to wash some green grapes in the sink.

Grant said, "You'd have to come after hours. Why don't you just do it on a Wednesday when the security guards are used to seeing you there?"

"Fine," I said. Vivienne's rejection of me, my lack of progress in finding the priest and at helping her with her need to return home... it was all hitting me. Reeger was making the trip to Dublin instead of me to ask around there and I was just waiting around, it seemed, for information to be delivered.

Vivienne said, "I'm studying sexually transmitted diseases. I see that syphilis is a death sentence for both men and women. If not treated." She checked in with me.

I confirmed that it is serious. "And cases are on the rise in the last few years. A man's cock could become gangrenous if not treated."

We shared a look of mutual consternation. Then she said, "Is cock the term most used for a man's penis?"

I debated what the most common term would be. "I don't know. Dick is pretty common. I think that's probably more common than cock. It's also the short version of the man's name, Richard."

"What is, dick?" she said, her head still down, highlighting something in the text.

"Yes," I said.

Grant was looking back and forth between us.

"That is unfortunate," she glanced up. "For the Richards."

I nodded and turned off the faucet.

"Or is it?" she said. "In my time, men are very proud of their cocks."

Grant slumped back in his chair and covered his face.

"Oh, we're proud in 2024 as well," I smiled at her. "That's as inevitable as death and taxes."

"I have read that testicles are called balls. What about the vagina? What is the common term for that?"

I set the bowl of grapes down on the table between us.

"Pussy," I said. I sat down across from her. "It's said with great affection."

Grant dropped his head down face first on the table.

Vivienne and I shared a smile over his prudishness.

I decided to go all the way.

"Also snatch, cooch, honey hole..." I counted them off on my fingers.

"Vajayjay..." Grant's muffled voice came from his covered face.

I hit his arm. "What are you, twelve?"

"Beaver," he said. Still behind his hands.

I ate a grape.

"And twat. And cunt," I said. "But those are derogatory. Meant to insult. Pussy is the nicest."

"I know the word cunt," she said. "I have been called that word." She pulled a grape off the stem.

Grant sat up. We both scowled as she ate her grape.

After a moment I said, "Did the person who called you that die a horrible death?"

She laughed. "Oh, it wasn't serious. Rude words are used by rude people."

Vivienne saw that we remained unsatisfied. She made a concession to us.

"He may have gone home with some extreme nausea."

We both smiled our approval of her handling of that situation.

"Like a boss," Grant said with admiration.

She raised her eyebrows at him, asking for further definition.

"The person in charge. Or Dad, anywhere he goes." Grant rolled his eyes.

I shook my head no and contemplated Vivienne's profile as she went back to her reading.

"Not when I'm in the same room as her." She peered up at us and gave a small, satisfied smile.

She knows it. I am putty in her hands, and she knows it.

"I kind of love that, Vivienne. His ego could use a check," Grant said.

I kind of loved it, too.

Grant and I ate our sandwiches in silence for a bit.

"What's the penis called in your time?" I asked her.

"A pen or a pudding prick. And a vagina is sometimes called a pudding, a purse...," she thought for a moment. "Or a quiver."

"I like quiver," I said. "The penis should be called an arrow, to go with quiver."

I poured more lemonade in Vivienne's glass.

She continued her highlighting.

"Oh, and prick!" I was pleased to remember. "For penis. But that's derogatory, too. But you can say 'my dick' and it's not derogatory, but calling someone a dick would be. I think mostly just dick and cock are the acceptable colloquial terms for penis." I turned to Grant to see if he agreed.

He looked dubious. "What about cocksucker?"

"Right..." I agreed. "That's definitely derogatory."

No one said anything for a few moments.

"But cock on its own..." I began.

Grant scraped his chair back and stood up with the rest of his sandwich.

"I'll be in the study." He walked out.

Vivienne looked at me.

I said, "I think we broke him."

We shared a laugh at his expense. After a pause, she said, "And what is the act itself called?"

"For vaginal or anal penetration, it's called fucking."

She raised her eyebrows. "It is called that in my time, too."

I raised my eyebrows. "Huh," I said. "Interesting."

Very interesting. Also, this talk was going so much better than the porn talk.

"And the rest?" she asked.

Might have spoken too soon.

To stall for time, I said, "I have to say, I love your interest in this subject."

She didn't touch that one. Just sat waiting for an answer.

"For oral sex, when a man does it for a woman, it's called 'going down' on her, or 'eating' her. And mostly it's called a 'blow job' when a woman does it for a man."

And then there she was in my mind —between my legs at that very table —my hand in her silky hair, guiding her mouth over my dick.

"And the climax of the intercourse? What is that called?"

Jesus, Mary and Joseph. She is cool as a fucking cucumber. She is definitely winning this.

"I promise, this is the last intercourse question." She gave me an encouraging nod.

I tried to regain my doctor chill. "Vivienne, you can ask me anything."

Leaning back with my elbows on the chair, I clasped my hands together, my thumbs touching. Then I gave her the stirring speech I gave Grant back in the day when he had asked me about the birds and the bees.

"Intercourse is the formal term. Sex is the informal term. During sex, when a man or woman has his or her orgasm, the climax, we say he or she has 'come.' So one person might tell the other person, 'I'm coming.' The medical term when a man comes is 'ejaculate.' The bodily fluid from the man is his semen, also known as 'cum.' Spelled c, u, m."

"Dad!" Grant bellowed in protest from the study.

"Shut up!" I bellowed back. "She asked me!"

Vivienne shook her head at our lack of cool.

"It's the same in my time," she said.

"What is?" I asked.

"Coming," she replied. Those gray eyes with those dark eyelashes staring directly into mine. "Another common word for climax is to spend."

She went back to her book. "It's remarkable how the joining of a man and woman hasn't changed in centuries. The acts are the same. Only a few words are different." She turned the page.

How the fuck was she just sitting there, talking about coming to me? I was hard enough to come right then and there.

I twiddled my thumbs and watched her read her medical book. Ready to answer more questions. Really hoping they were about the flu or the common cold or skin rashes.

Chapter Thirty-Four

Vivienne

November 28th, 2024

I was restless. The need to get back to Alice was ruining my sleep, and the need to use my magic was ruining my waking hours. I had been to see Emily at the hospital a few times when Adam was away. Using my magic for her had kept me sane. Allowing her to waste away there was just not something I could do. I knew Adam wouldn't approve of me exhausting myself at her bedside, so I didn't tell him. At each visit, I flooded her with my life force and was rewarded with her improvement afterwards. It wouldn't last, of course. But it was helping her to stay alive.

I'd never been so long without helping to heal on a regular basis and my magic wanted to be released. When Dr. Waltman told me that I could not heal in this era without a medical license, I forgave her, since I knew she had not experienced my magic. Adam agreed to see if there was any place I could be of use.

I mentioned that I would like to work with homeless people. They were called "unsheltered," and I thought it somehow a more kind way to describe their plight. The small bits of magic I had used in 2024 were with unsheltered people who we saw on city streets. Adam said in cold weather they slept on grates on the sidewalk that were warmed by gusts of air from below. He wasn't sure where the heat came from. They covered up with whatever they could. Sometimes they used papers with the news on them.

I used my cell phone to alert the guards Adam had hired that I was going to go out and take a short run while Adam was at work. I could help any unsheltered person I saw and also get an errand done along the way. And I wanted to check in with my father's manuscript. When I stood in front of it with a clear mind now, I sometimes felt pieces of my time reaching out to me. I wasn't ready to leave Adam yet, but I needed the daily commune with the manuscript to remind me that there would be a journey to come.

And while I was out, there was some other business I needed to take care of.

Mel smiled at me when I jogged up to her hot dog stand. She was helping a family with two children to buy hotdogs, chips and shirts for the children. When they left, she greeted me, "Vivienne! Where's your shadow? Is he letting you out on your own now?"

She leaned over the ledge of her stand, taking in the details of my clothing and shoes. "I see he's made you into a runner. God help you. I'm glad to see you. It's Thanksgiving and nobody's in the mood for sausages today."

I stepped closer to her and said in a low voice, "I know it was you."

Her face lost its pleasant smile at that, along with all its color. She stepped back a foot and braced her arms on the ledge, as if she'd need to hold on in a moment.

Smart.

We both spent a bit of time digesting that information. She had sold out her friend of many years, Adam, and me, for what was bound to have been a huge amount of money.

"If it had just been me in peril at that museum, I wouldn't be here now. But you endangered Grant and Maria, and that I cannot abide. Adam will not be able to accept it either."

She started to speak, but I stopped her with a raised hand.

"What you say now doesn't matter. What's done is done. I came to tell you I think you should retire now. You should take the money you were paid and live somewhere far away from here. Because if I know it was you... it's only a matter of time before Adam realizes it was you. He may already know."

A couple came up beside me and I turned away from her and began jogging again. This time toward the Library of Congress. First, to see my manuscript then to go home and be with Adam's family for the celebration called Thanksgiving.

The house smelled delicious when I came through the front door. Isabelle greeted me from the study where she was watching television. In the kitchen, Grant was bent over a pan he had pulled halfway out of the oven. Behind him Maria was swiping her finger along the inside of a bowl and bringing it to her mouth for a taste when he whirled around and brandished a spoon at her.

"No!" He shouted. "I saw that! There is no tasting until the dish is on the table..." Setting my keys down in the hallway, I saw him grab her around the waist as she broke into hysterical laughter at his reaction. Walking into the study I shared an amused glance with Isabelle as we heard a scuffle and then the sound of bodies hitting the wall and then silence. We raised our eyebrows at that.

Adam walked in the front door and said, "Why is the oven door open?"

Grant responded with laughter in his voice, "Maria was stealing dinner. Had to address it."

Adam looked at us and shook his head. "Please just finish cooking. I'm starving." He came in and sat next to his mother on the couch. Kissing her on the cheek, he said, "Did you make the mac and cheese?"

Isabelle looked at me. "He only loves me for my mac and cheese." She addressed him. "Yes, I made the mac and cheese."

Adam nodded his approval. "And did Grant make the stuffing?"

She rolled her eyes. "Yes. Grant made the turkey and the stuffing."

He said, "And the potatoes? Should I do that? He doesn't always do them right."

Maria came in then and said, "Relax. I did the potatoes. There's nothing left to do."

He frowned. "But... the rolls...and the gravy..."

Isabelle patted his leg. "Adam likes his traditions, Vivienne. He needs to get all his favorite foods at Thanksgiving and watch all his favorite movies at Christmas or there's hell to pay for the rest of us. He's been that way since he was a boy."

"I wouldn't say it's hell, exactly..." his voice trailed off.

Maria said, "No. Just a hell of a lot of pouting."

Isabelle laughed.

Grant called from the kitchen, "Dinner in ten minutes! The table setting needs to be finished."

Adam put his hand on my shoulder and pushed me back down in my chair when I rose to help. He and Maria went to complete the setting of the dining room table and Isabelle explained for me the Macy's Thanksgiving Day parade. Bands of teenagers played instruments and marched, people walked gigantic balloons down the thoroughfare and actors and singers performed. It was spectacular.

Isabelle saw my rapture and said, "I'll record it and you can watch it later with Adam."

My eyes still on the show, I said, "We don't watch television much."

"I know," she said. "Adam told me that you said it was bad for him."

I looked at her.

She said, "Thank you for that. He needs someone to care for him, too."

She held my gaze.

"I would do anything for Adam," I said.

Isabelle stood and took my arm, leading me to the dining room.

She said again, "I know."

As he was pouring wine into glasses on the table, Adam said, "Vivienne, Americans use this day every year to gather with family and celebrate the feast the first Europeans held with the

Native Americans in 1621. Most businesses are closed and people travel from far away to get home to their families for Thanksgiving. There's also very real potential for fighting at the table." Maria laughed.

She was lighting candles in the center of the table when Grant came in carrying the last dish, a large bird on a platter that he set in front of Adam's seat at the head of the table.

"You want to fight?" He asked. "I'll fight you."

Adam said, "Please. You wouldn't last thirty seconds in a fight with me."

Maria took a seat and said, "Can we just eat now and you guys can fight later? I'll referee. Just, food now."

Adam pulled a chair out for me next to him. Grant did the same for Isabelle on the other side of Adam. When Grant was seated at the other end of the table, next to Maria, Adam said, "Vivienne, would you like to say grace?"

I bowed my head. I thanked God for those people, for the bounty provided on our table and for our health. I also wished for the health of Alice and my sister friends at the convent. When I said 'Amen,' Adam took my plate and added some of the sliced meat to it.

Grant said, "Vivienne, that's turkey. You've never seen it, right? I mean, outside of a sandwich? It's an American bird. Used mostly for this holiday."

After he set my plate down Adam showed me a picture of a turkey on his phone and said, "It tastes way better than it looks."

"It would have to," I said. The turkey was not handsome.

He laughed. "Okay, now. Don't disparage our poor, almost national bird."

Grant plopped some mashed potatoes on his plate. "Yes. Benjamin Franklin wanted turkeys to be our bird but thankfully saner minds prevailed and we got the eagle."

Adam held my plate again and was walking around the table filling it to his specifications. I was apparently going to have a little of everything and enough for two grown men to eat. He laid it down before me and sat in his chair to my left.

"Thank you," I said, amused at his offering.

"I want to see you taste the sweet potatoes. Do you like those?" He looked at me expectantly.

Maria pointed at the sweet potatoes on her plate.

I took a small bite of the orange potato dish and closed my eyes with pleasure at the sweet taste.

Adam smiled. Then he began to fill his own dish.

"Okay," he said. "Let's get all the gratitude out of the way so I can stuff myself."

Grant said, "I'll go first. Vivienne, we each say something we're grateful for. It's usually a lot of the same stuff. But this year I can start with something new. I'm grateful for Vivienne." He gave me a smile. "For her good advice and for her friendship with Dad. And I'm grateful for Dad, Grandma and Maria." He reached out and took her hand, lacing their fingers together.

Maria said, "I'm also grateful for Vivienne. And for the people at this table. And for the fact that Grant learned to cook in Home Economics class."

Everyone laughed and agreed with that. Isabelle said, "I'm grateful for Vivienne, too." She nodded her head at me. "And my family." She looked around the room. "And for magic. For all the gifts I've been given through the use of my magic. And I'm grateful for so many good years on this Earth."

Adam's arm rested on his chair and his hand covered his mouth as he listened to his family speak of their gratitude. With all our eyes on him he took his hand away from his face and said, "I'm grateful for my job. And for all of you." He paused and then his eyes met mine. "I'm especially grateful that Vivienne came into our lives." He looked at Grant. "I'm more grateful for her than you are."

"No, not possible..." Grant said loudly. "We've bonded."

Maria said over Grant, "I'm the most grateful for her. She's kept him busy, and he's so much less grumpy now..."

Isabelle shook her head and began to eat.

Adam said, "What about you, Vivienne? What are you grateful for?"

Looking at the faces around the table I wished his family was mine. I wished he was mine.

"I'm most grateful for you, Adam." He smiled at me. "And I'm so very thankful God allowed me to come to this time to meet you all."

When wert thou born, Desire?
Edward De Veer, Earl of Oxford, (1576)

"Will ever age or death
Bring thee unto decay?
No, no, Desire both lives and dies
Ten thousand times a day."

CHAPTER THIRTY-FIVE

Adam

December 1st, 2024

Vivienne was going away. Sooner rather than later. These were the phrases that floated around in my head as I made my rounds. My charting was lackluster. I moped and stared into space for so long that the nurses asked me what was wrong.

I did have valid reasons for being depressed at work. Emily was losing her battle with cancer. I didn't have much good news for her parents today except that their toddler was still fighting. But it was heartbreaking to see her suffer in that hospital bed and know I had no real solution for her other than more of the same toxic medicines to try to kill the cancer that was killing her.

All I wanted was to go home and sit with Vivienne in the study. Just her presence alone calmed me. There was no question about it, I'd been better with her there. Even when she confronted me, she did so with the sole purpose of helping me. I tried to remember the last time I looked forward to doing something even half as much as I looked forward to seeing Vivienne's expression when she learned something new. Or when she tasted something she liked. The bottom line was, she made living worthwhile. I tried to push away the thought of what things would be like when she was gone. That was not a world I wanted to live in.

On the porch steps I heard *Primavera,* one of my favorite classical pieces. Vivienne had been enjoying the radio lately and was thrilled that all she had to do was turn a knob to get sound floating on the radio waves surrounding her.

Opening the door, I was drawn in by that intoxicating scent that belonged to her alone and I watched with wonder the beauty of her magic playing with the music. She made it visible somehow—notes from violins and the piano intertwined and danced in the air in pink and lavender flashes. Her magic made real each stroke of the bow and each strike of the piano key. She stood with her back to me, head down in concentration as if she were a conductor bewitching the orchestra to follow her every command. Gentle waves of pink and gold flowed from her hands when the piano entered and soothed. Her body swayed in time with the music and when the violins surged, more bursts of purple light filled the room.

I was overcome.

In two steps, I took her by the elbow and turned her to me. Vivienne's mouth opened in surprise and I took it—my lips on hers, as it should be. To my everlasting relief, she didn't push me away but parted her lips for me and returned the kiss. I reached around her waist and pulled her to me.

Finally.

My pulse rocketed at the first taste of Vivienne. Her tongue was sweet and fresh, and where our lips met our magic mingled. I tangled my hand in her silky hair and tugged her head where I wanted, deepening the kiss. Golden magic surrounded us and I was lost to the sensation of Vivienne.

She was soft, silky skin and she smelled fucking unbelievable.

We explored each other like we had finally found it, the thing we needed. She was warm and real against me, better than anything I had imagined and the only thought I could form was...*mine*. I wanted more of that, and I wanted to keep it forever.

My magic wanted more of her too. It wanted to bathe in the perfume of her power, and it was not taking no for an answer. Although I had never done it before, I had no choice then but to lower my shield and let my power loose to play with hers. Vivienne's knees buckled at the force of our magic meeting, but I held her tighter to me.

Her mouth was heaven, pure and simple. There was no way I could live without it now that I knew it.

Then the music ended and the announcer spoke.

What did I do? I wasn't supposed to do that.

Somewhere in the deep recesses of my brain, I realized that I had pushed up against her, and she was trapped between me and the wall. I tried to pull my lips from hers, but she made a satisfied hum and her hands around my neck reached up to clutch my hair, keeping us connected. Her sounds drove me wild and, forgetting completely that I was supposed to be stepping away, I kissed along her jawline, then kissed the other side and took her lips again.

A pounding on the door made us both jump.

Vivienne pulled away, her eyes wide and darker than normal.

I didn't know what was going on in that head of hers, but I knew desire when I saw it.

What I didn't know was whether she would forgive me for it.

She walked over to turn off the radio and raised her shield. Then she covered her mouth with her hand.

My brain started to function again, and I tried to will my power to obey. *Fuck.*

"Shit. I'm sorry. I didn't mean to do that..." I turned away from her and wiped a hand over my face. A delivery truck pulled away from the curb out front. We stood there for a moment more. It was too quiet in the house.

She said, "It's not your fault."

I scoffed at that. "Yeah, it was my fault. I felt your magic and just lost it." I took a deep breath in and then let it out. "I'm so sorry."

"Adam," she tried again, "it's okay."

I shook my head no and went back out the front door. I walked off across the street toward the Supreme Court Building.

Vivienne had been straight with me, all along. She had made it clear. This was not in her plan.

Jesus. What the hell is wrong with me? I kissed the nun. The nun who is leaving me as soon as she can.

I laughed a bit at that. I hated myself for what had just happened but also thought it inevitable that I had fucked things up so royally. I needed to tell someone about it, so I called Marsh. He said he'd meet me at the Red Lion just a few blocks away.

Thirty minutes later, he slid into the booth across from me and said, "All right now, what is this about, young man?"

"You're six months older than me." I pushed a whiskey his way.

"Yes, but years ahead in wisdom." He raised his glass to me and took a sip. "What have you done?"

I looked at him and then closed my eyes as if I couldn't bear it. "I kissed a nun."

When I opened my eyes again, he was squinting at me.

"You kissed a nun?"

I nodded yes.

"Where did you find a nun?"

"It was Vivienne."

"*Vivienne* is a *nun*?"

I raised my glass to the bartender and signaled for another. "Yes."

I drank the rest of my whiskey. I couldn't remember the last time I had more than one drink, but it seemed like this was the right day to break that streak.

Marsh was struck dumb by this news. All he had for me was, "But...she's so sexy!"

I groaned. "Are those years of extra wisdom going to kick in anytime soon? Because now would be great. I'm fucked, and I do not want to go home to face it."

He shook his head, and a smile broke out on his face. "Goddamn. You really do bring me the best stories, though." Then he lost it and laughed at my expense for a solid minute. I rubbed my hands over my face.

When Marsh finally stopped laughing, wiping his eyes, he said, "Okay, I'm sorry." He drank his whiskey down and called for another for both of us. "Come on, let's think about this," he said. "It's probably not that bad. What did she say?"

I tried to remember her words exactly. "That it was okay, she was fine, no big deal..."

He was unconvinced. "Was it no big deal, or was she into it?"

She definitely kissed me back. And she waited to shield her magic again. And to stop me. It almost hurt more that she had responded to me. Now I knew what I was missing. What I could never have.

Marsh read my face correctly.

"Uh huh, I thought so," he said. "She was into you when I saw you guys on the Mall. No question about it. I thought that was already a locked-down situation."

Now it was my turn to look skeptical. He argued his point.

"What is *wrong* with you? This insecure loser in front of me is not the Adam Parrish I know. What's really happening here? How did you come to be in possession of a nun, and why is she a nun?"

Marsh was my best friend, but he was not a witch, so I had to be pretty vague with some of my story. But when I was done, he said, "Well buddy, it sounds like maybe Miss Vivienne is re-thinking those Jesus vows. Maybe she wants some Parrish to wed now. You know, instead of Jesus? Isn't that what nuns do?"

"Oh my god," I said. "You didn't hear anything I just told you! Nothing. She does not want to marry me! She has made it very clear she has to get home to her family. They need her. And she has all this charity work she does for her convent. She's leaving."

We both lifted our glasses to take a drink.

"Well," he said. "That sucks."

"There's that wisdom," I said.

We laughed. And drank a couple more. Maybe a few more. Marsh caught a Lyft, and I tried not to sway all the way home.

Although it was only early evening, I was ready for bed. If I could make it there. Inside the house, I dropped my keys in the dish on the hallway table and turned to lock the door.

"I have dinner made if you would like some," Vivienne said from the daybed in the living room. She was there, surrounded by her books. That's how I thought of them now. Her books. Would they keep any of her scent when she was gone, I wondered? I imagined cracking them open and burying my face in them, desperate to catch any bit of her essence.

"Thank you." I headed for the kitchen. Might have underestimated the nearness of the doorjamb and might have hit my shoulder into it. But I did make it to the plate on the oven and uncovered it to find some potatoes and beans and a piece of chicken. I ate it standing up and drank a whole bottle of water before making my way back to her.

I sat down on the couch and wished it were the beginning for us again and I had all the wonders of the twenty-first century to share with her once more. At some point I noticed that she had covered me with a blanket. I was lying down on the couch now and she kneeled beside me, her hand gently moving through my hair.

I grasped her hand and held on. "Vivienne."

She laughed softly. "Yes?"

"What if I came with you?" I said.

Vivienne covered my hand with her other hand. Our magic relaxed and settled in together at her touch. All was right with the world.

"Let's talk about that tomorrow morning, all right?"

I fell asleep like that. My hand surrounded by hers. As it should be.

Translation of Ovid's Elegies, Book One, 5
Christopher Marlowe (1599)

"In summer's heat and mid-time of the day
To rest my limbs upon a bed I lay,
One window shut, the other open stood,
Which gave such light as twinkles in a wood,
Like twilight glimpse at setting of the sun
Or night being past, and yet not day begun.
Such light to shamefaced maidens must be shown,
Where they may sport, and seem to be unknown.
Then came Corinna in a long loose gown,
Her white neck hid with tresses hanging down:
Resembling fair Semiramis going to bed
Or Laïs of a thousand wooers sped.
I snatched her gown, being thin, the harm was small,
Yet strived she to be covered therewithal.
And striving thus as one that would be cast,
Betrayed herself, and yielded at the last.
Stark naked as she stood before mine eye,
Not one wen in her body could I spy.
What arms and shoulders did I touch and see,
How apt her breasts were to be pressed by me?
How smooth a belly under her waist saw I?
How large a leg, and what a lusty thigh?
To leave the rest, all liked me passing well,
I clinged her naked body, down she fell,
Judge you the rest: being tired she bad me kiss,
Jove send me more such afternoons as this."

CHAPTER THIRTY-SIX

Vivienne

December 15th, 2024

It had been two weeks since the kiss. For the first week, after he had apologized to me again, Adam refrained from being in my presence or even talking to me much when he finally got home from work. He retired to his room and put his light out soon after.

But for the last week I had been waking every morning to find a poem on the pillow next to mine. Beautiful poems of love from my century. When I thanked him for the first one, he stopped his preparations to leave for the day to give me a small smile. "I'm glad you liked it," was all he said.

The poem I found in my room that morning had stuck with me all day. It was carnal, about a man and woman having a tryst in the afternoon. I wondered at Adam's boldness. I wondered again how he got the poems there without me knowing. He had insisted I seal the stairway and the turret room every night, as if someone could bypass the security detail outside, get through his own shield around the house and then get past him. But I set my seal each night and, apparently, Adam stepped through it each night.

I wondered if he knew I was rehashing the words and images of the poem all day?

Grant was joining us for lunch and I welcomed his presence. I knew Adam was holding back from saying what he wanted from me, but I felt all too keenly the desire to tell him the truth. I wanted him to know they were not wrong, his feelings. And they were not unreciprocated. He deserved to know. Despite my efforts to remain uninvolved, things had progressed too far between us to be ignored. But how to begin that conversation?

I was given an opportunity as we were setting the kitchen table for the meal.

Grant asked, "Dad says your convent is one that works with sex workers. What is that like? I've read that some sex workers were even canonized."

"I do live in the nunnery and help with their work, but I do so as a healer. The nuns are the ones who help fallen women. I'm not a nun."

Adam's head snapped up at that. He stared at me from across the table. Observing his father's reaction, Grant let a smile spread across his face that led to a burst of laughter.

"Oh my god, Dad…" he clutched his chest and dissolved into laughter. "Your face!"

Adam's eyes did not leave mine.

"People outside of the nunnery don't distinguish between us, healers and midwifes and nuns." I attempted to smooth it over. "One is either a fallen woman or a nun. So, the village people and nobles I serve all consider me a nun. But I have taken no vows."

Grant was now covering his face, trying to hold the laughter to a minimum, but clearly losing the battle.

Adam's chair scraped back as he stood and clapped his hand down on Grant's shoulder. "Time for you to go, son." He raised his laughing son by the collar and piloted him out of the room.

"Aww, no!" Grant protested as Adam hustled him down the hall. "I'm sorry! I'll stop! I want to hear this!"

"Goodbye, Grant!" Adam pushed his son out onto the porch. He flipped the lock and turned to face me. He slipped his hands in his pockets and leaned back against the door, studying me. We were rooms apart, and we stayed that way for a minute. He was obviously working through what it meant that I had let him believe I was a nun. I found myself trying to remember to breathe.

"Do you not want me?" he finally asked.

I shook my head slightly. "That's not the reason I didn't explain myself."

At that, he pushed off the door and began the long walk back to me.

"Vivienne." Adam sat at the table and turned my chair toward his. He took my hand in between his own. The tingle of his touch promised pleasure. "I know that you know how much I want you."

His eyes searched mine. He turned my palm upright and brought it to his mouth for a kiss. His touch was reverent and so full of need I thought I would die of it. He turned my hand over and kissed each of the knuckles there, his tongue tasting me. Worshiping me.

As always when our skin met, our magic began to stir.

"Adam…" I struggled to find the words. "I have to go back. Alice needs me. I don't know how, but I will be leaving. And I hope it will be soon." I needed him to know this could end in nothing but heartbreak for both of us. If we did this, what would it do to us to live apart for the rest of our lives?

He stared at me for a moment more, considering what I said.

Finally he said, "I don't care." He made a fist in my hair at the nape of my neck and brought my lips to his.

It was as electric as before. This time more so because I knew we would not stop there. Adam stood and pulled me up close to him.

"I could have been kissing you all this time," he said against my neck. He kissed me again, deeper, his hands moving into my hair, and kiss after kiss Adam convinced me that this was what had been missing, this was what we were made for. Then his lips moved over my jaw, down my neck, and he began unbuttoning my blouse, tasting the skin above my bra. I lifted his shirt and stroked my hands over his broad back and felt him shudder under my touch.

But I was the one coming undone. With every trace of Adam's mouth along my skin, I felt my magic rise as if he was calling it to him.

He ran his hand over the sheer material of my bra, his thumb stroking my nipple and the sensation made us both take a quick breath in. He brought both his hands to my breasts then, and we watched as he touched me there. I leaned in to kiss his temple and his cheekbone, and then he claimed my mouth again, hard and needy.

There was only the press of his lips, the taste of his tongue, and my need for more of him. I had been in his arms for mere minutes and already I knew I would crave that feeling for the rest of my life.

Adam had made a disciple of me.

With any other man that feeling would chafe. But shivering at the touch of his lips against the shell of my ear, I knew I would follow that man anywhere.

He took a slow breath then, trying to find some control. His hands, I noticed, were not steady. I was shaking, too.

"Are you all right?" His breath was warm against my neck.

I gave a small nod. "It's just... you."

His face buried in my hair, he inhaled and said softly, "And *you*." Reaching up to hold my head in his hands, he pulled back to look at me. "I wanted to do this slowly. I've imagined this..." he gave me a small kiss. "I wanted to take my time with you."

He almost managed it. Adam brushed his lips over mine once more, softly, and then again. Gentle, careful kisses that tugged at my bottom lip as if he couldn't quite bring himself to stop. Then he was back, his mouth demanding and insistent, until he broke away to say, "Jesus. Vivienne, please." His voice rough, he dropped his head to kiss the hollow of my throat. "Please let me feel you."

I let it all go.

The warm golden glow that was my magic filled the room and charged our every breath, every kiss, every touch. It was desire unbound. Then his hands were everywhere, his mouth back on mine, and I was lost in Adam again—the heat of his chest against me, the urgency of his hands at my hips pulling me closer. I grabbed his hand and pulled him with me out of the kitchen toward the bedroom, but in the hallway, he stopped me again for another kiss that left me breathless. He lifted me, and as I wrapped my legs around him, I thought he would have me there against the wall. I was more than willing.

Then I heard a noise from outside. "Adam. Wait," I said. He ignored me, but there was knocking at his door.

"Adam!" I said louder. "Someone is here."

Pushing into me against the wall, he said, "They can wait." He kissed me again, and I reached up to cup his face, feeling the stubble there, breathing in the scent of him. But through the fog of our desire, I became uneasy. The person at the door was Marshall Smith, and what he wanted was urgent.

"Stop." I managed to say. "Adam, stop."

He stilled but held onto me as if I might get away.

His breath was hot against my neck, and when he sucked there, it occurred to me that this was the most aroused I had ever been in my life.

"Dear God, Adam." I gave a shaky laugh. "You make me unable to think."

I felt his smile on my neck. "What is it? Why do you want to stop?"

"I don't." I ran my fingers through his hair. "I don't ever want to stop this."

I pulled my magic to me and shielded myself again. "But... Marshall Smith is here."

The knocking at the door started again. After a moment, Adam exhaled in frustration and slowly lowered me to stand on my own. He placed his hands on my shoulders and then, without looking at me, he turned to head toward the door. He stopped with his back to me and I saw him wipe a hand over his face. Taking a deep breath, he ran a hand through his hair and adjusted his pants.

His back still to me, Adam said, "And why is it so important I see him now?"

"I don't know," I answered. "I only know he is very intent on getting something done."

He turned to glance at me then, his eyebrows raised.

"You can read intentions?"

I raised my hands, palms up, and shrugged a little. I said, "Be nice."

He shook his head and went to open the door abruptly.

"What?" he said loudly. "Why the fuck are you pounding on my door?" I peeked around the corner and saw Smith on the porch. His eyes were busy scanning the room behind Adam, and I moved back quickly.

"It smells good in here, Parrish. I take it Vivienne is here?"

"Yes." Adam replied. "I'm busy. What do you want?"

"Cole said not to bother you, but this case is bad. I really need someone to take it like right fucking now. This guy has somebody he works with who we think is next in line."

I heard Adam open a folder and flip a paper over.

Smith entered the hallway and closed the door.

After a minute, Adam said, "Why are you going around Cole's orders?"

"This just needs attention right now. I'm actually trying to get the bad guys, just like you." He paused. "We're on the same side."

Adam was quiet. Then he said, "Do me a favor."

"What?"

"Stop trying to divine me every time you see me. It's fucking exhausting trying to block you every fucking minute of the day."

Smith had a smile in his voice. "Sorry. Comes with the territory. But fine, I'll stop. You'll do this?"

"Yes. Go away now."

Smith laughed and said goodnight.

As the door closed, I stepped into the hallway.

"Did you two make up?" I asked.

Adam narrowed his eyes at me. "You've been very bad, Vivienne. Making me answer the door because I thought Marshall was here to fight. Waiting all this time to tell me you are not actually a nun." He shook his head. "This will need to be addressed."

Yes. Please address it. I laughed softly.

Closing the space between us, he said quietly, "So you've been able to read my intentions all along?" He crowded into me and put a hand on the wall beside my head. I laughed at him again. With his other hand, he tucked a piece of hair behind my ear and cupped his hand around my neck. His thumb lightly stroked my throat, and I felt my pulse quicken.

I shook my head. "I'm only certain of feelings when they're intense. When the body ramps up, I can tell. Marshall's not a threat. I think he wants to do good." Adam shook his head slightly, as if dismissing forever the very insignificant thought of Marshall Smith.

"So, after the kiss? You've known my intentions since then?" Adam's eyes searched mine, waiting for me to confirm. "The first kiss," he clarified.

"Adam. I've known your intentions toward me since my first week here. And the daily poetry left on my pillow this past week was also a clue."

He gave me a slow smile. "Good."

He leaned down to kiss my neck. Breathing in deeply, he feathered kisses up over my jaw and to my mouth. He gently kissed one cheek and then the other. I shivered as he trailed a finger along my collarbone. His eyes on my lips, Adam said, "There's so much I want to do to you." I stopped breathing for a moment. The finger traced slowly down the middle of my chest, between my breasts. His eyes moved up to mine. "Will you let me?" He saw the answer on my face and gave a short nod of approval like he knew just what I wanted.

Then he took a deep breath in and sighed, as if he couldn't believe what was coming next. He said, "I have to pack now and catch a flight to Lisbon. I'm sorry."

I could not help my response. Reaching up with both hands, I pulled his head down and kissed him.

I broke away to tell him, "No."

He raised his eyebrows at that and said, "No what?"

"No, you're not packing for Lisbon." He huffed a short laugh that I caught with my mouth, and then he was mine again. Our passion reignited, and he pushed me back against the wall. I felt him straining against his pants. My hands went to his zipper, and he drew a sharp breath as I unzipped it and reached for him.

"Fuck, yes," he said into my mouth. My magic was loose, painting the hallway with gold and silver. I turned him so that his back was against the wall. Then I dropped to my knees and pulled his pants down. Looking up at him, I smiled as I took him in my mouth. I made a sound low in my throat at the rightness of it. The rightness of us. He was silky and salty and so hard for me. Adam stared down at me with dark eyes as I licked the tip and reached up to cup him. Then I took him in all at once, and he threw his head back, hitting the wall.

"Fuck," he said, the word torn from him. My mouth smiled around him, relishing my power in that moment. I loved seeing him unbound. I sucked him back up to the tip and took him in again. He was big, but I took all of him and I felt the thrill of it, knowing what was to come. He recovered after a moment and placed his hands on my head, guiding my mouth over him as he pushed into me over and over. I felt his magic rise to the surface of his skin and I reveled in its depth and darkness. We were alike in power, alike in our need. He held my head in place and used my mouth as he took control from me. With three final deep thrusts he said in a low voice, "I'm coming," and he spurted into me, down my throat. I swallowed and smiled, licking the final drops from him.

When I sat back, he dropped to his knees and pulled me to him, his heart beating fast.

"You took me by surprise there, Lanier." His hands gathered my hair into a ponytail and he gently tugged me down to the floor until we lay there face to face. "I think you might have given me a concussion just now. I might have to take you to court."

I laughed. He cupped my cheek and ran his thumb gently over my lips.

Then he said, "I think that may be the highlight of my life."

"What about the birth of your son?"

He shook his head no. "He's nice and all but that…" he gave a weak laugh. "There are no words."

His eyes scanned my face as if he wanted to savor the moment forever.

"I have never wanted anything as much as you right now." He sat up and reached back to pull his shirt off over his head. Then he lifted the hem of my shirt and I sat up, raising my arms to let it flow over me. I pulled my already undone bra off and then we were bare to each other. Adam braced me from behind with one arm and gently laid me down with the other. He held himself over me with one arm and palmed my breasts with his other hand. Kissing me deeply and leisurely, he stopped only to kick off the rest of his clothes. When he reached for my skirt, I stopped his hand.

"Wait. We're in the hall."

He ignored me and pulled the skirt off easily.

"Yes. We are. And you are out of your mind if you think we're done here. You started this in the hall." He gave a soft laugh. "I'm finishing it in the hall."

I raised up on my elbows and watched him pull my panties down my legs slowly. His hand caressed my legs all the way down, waking every inch of my skin that he touched. Adam gently lifted my shoes and then socks from my feet and tossed them behind him. He kissed my ankle and I felt a tingle there as he slid the panties off and then pushed my bent leg to the side. I spread the other for him and he hummed his approval.

"So fucking beautiful..." his hand grazed my mound and I arched into him. It had been so long for me. So long since anyone but myself had touched me there. He parted me gently and the cool air against my center made me catch my breath. Then his mouth was on me and I gasped at the heat surrounding me there and the sensation of a million nerve endings sparking to life. I bucked at the first swirl of his tongue, but he laid his palm over my waist, holding me firmly in place. Gripping his hair in my hands, I fell back, helpless. Adam tasted me like that for minutes—causing me to slowly lose my mind and make noises I didn't know I could make.

Then he kissed me softly between my legs and lifted himself up so he bracketed my body. I made a sound of protest.

"Not yet," he said. "I want this to last." He kissed me deeply, and I felt him hard against my stomach.

"Please," I whispered.

"In the immortal words of Vivienne Lanier... No." He stretched my arms over my head, and I felt an invisible bond holding them there. He also bound my legs, already spread for him. Never had a man taken control from me, and I wondered briefly if I could let him.

Adam's eyes met mine. "Is this okay?"

He watched me as I realized that it was more than okay, and I thought again that I had never been so aroused in my life.

"Yes," I said.

But two can play at this game. I let more of my magic loose. I knew he loved my fragrance, so I let it wash over him, along with a refreshing light song of pink that tingled when it touched us both.

Adam stilled and then rained hot kisses down my neck. The hollow of my throat. Each breast in turn, as if he had needed me for so long. He kneaded them and bit and sucked, one hand working slowly down over my stomach, then running a finger through my folds and finding my center.

"Adam," he kept up his pressure between my legs, "I want to touch you too." I tested the hold of his bond on my wrists, but it held firm. I needed him inside me, and I desperately wanted to taste him again.

"When I'm done with you, you can touch."

His gaze swept over my breasts, and my arms held over my head.

"You are so fucking sexy. You're a dream, Vivienne."

Giving both of my breasts a final nip and drawing a gasp from me each time, he was back between my legs. His fingers found me, sliding inside, his thumb finding exactly the right place.

Adam did not rush. True to his word, he took his time with me, more time than I was used to. More time than I even gave myself. I felt the pressure build in me slowly, the way it should. Then the whole universe condensed down to the single point where his thumb continued to stroke me.

I had tended bodies my entire life. I thought I understood them. I did not know my own.

"Can you read minds?" I breathed.

He gave a soft laugh.

"I know what you need," he said and continued his complete takeover of my senses—his fingers hard and fast and just where I needed them. Then an explosion of lights flashed against my closed eyes, and I cried out, lost. My entire body quivered while the rush roared over me, down to my toes and back again. Adam stilled, then pushed his thumb down at my core and kept his fingers pressed firmly against my inner wall in the perfect spot. My body jerked again and again at the pressure he kept there, and it was suddenly clear to me why people abandoned good sense for the touch of a lover.

When I finally settled and he released my bonds, I threw an arm over my face and laughed for a moment. "Adam."

He crawled up to lie down beside me. He held my hand, and we both stared at the ceiling.

"My back," I said.

"My knees," he said.

And we laughed.

"Vivienne." He turned and clasped my face and kissed my lips gently, over and over. "I have never in my life had so much fun. The hallway is my new favorite room." He got up slowly and offered me his hand.

"The hallway is freezing," I said.

He pulled me up.

"Maybe next time you should start things in the bedroom."

He put his arm around my waist and pulled me against him. "That plane isn't going anywhere without me. Let's make round two a bedroom thing." He was hard again, and I wanted nothing more than to feel him inside me.

But I said, "Are you really leaving soon?" He hummed his agreement against my neck.

"Then I would like to wait," I said. "Until you can stay."

He raised his head to see if I meant that. Because who in their right mind would postpone what we would be together? I wavered. But then he nodded and smoothed my hair down from the roots to the tips. He gave a slight tug at the end. "All right then. I'll be back in two days, Vivienne. Be ready."

My heart flipped. *Dear God. What he does to me.*

In his room, Adam tucked me gently into his bed with the sheets from heaven, and I watched as he packed a small bag. When he was done, he leaned down to kiss me goodbye.

"I'd like you to stay naked while I'm gone. Right here. Send me pictures."

I smiled.

He pulled away with a frustrated sound. When he reached the door, I said, "Adam!"

He turned to look at me.

"Maybe it doesn't have to be all or nothing. I took the evil magic from you, and you didn't die."

Adam paused, gave a small nod, then walked out the door.

Chapter Thirty-Seven

Adam

December 17th, 2024

I had never been to Lisbon. I hoped to never go to Lisbon again. It was vibrant and beautiful, and it was so far away from my house across from the Supreme Court Building. Where Vivienne was breathing the air and walking around and eating and bathing. I was like a sixteen-year-old with a crush on the prettiest girl in school. Only, miracle of miracles, she liked me too. God help me. It was exhausting having my brain and my hormones working against me every waking moment.

Love was clearly a disorder that should appear on page one of the DSM.

And that was what it was. I was in love with Vivienne, and I could not imagine living without her. If I could, I would go back to 1502 and live with her there. We hadn't talked about it, although I suspected it had come up on my drunken night. I had obviously been working through the Vivienne dilemma for some time in my subconscious. Vivienne was the only path to happiness for me. I wondered what she was doing at home.

I stood up quickly, disgusted with my juvenile obsessive behavior, and tried to get my head in the game. The night would not be easy. Tom had emailed me a quick summary of what he learned from a friend in town about the target I was there to see. He was a doctor. Someone entrusted to care for the health of patients who, instead, took their lives for his own pleasure. I recognized the irony of a physician coming to kill another physician because he was a killer. But I was going to try to switch things up this time, and not kill the evil witch. Because of Vivienne. I just hoped I didn't die while trying.

Dr. Jorge Dalez was an OBGYN. Thirty-five years old, he was married with three kids and had a thriving practice with his partner Emily Montegro. Dr. Montegro had recently died of an embolism. Caused by her partner, Dr. Dalez, who wanted to prevent her from outing him as a serial philanderer. As a side perk, he was hoping to buy out her side of the practice for practically nothing.

The cheating on his wife part was just sleazy behavior. The real problem was that he was murdering the women he dated and dumped. That was him having fun. He was inventive too, using a different method for every victim. I wondered why he wasn't on the police radar for any of this until I saw he had the magic of cloaking, and I understood how he kept things secret. But apparently, not from his business partner.

He was handsome. Tall and blond, with an easy smile. I watched him eating dinner with a co-worker. An attractive female co-worker. I hoped things had not progressed to the bedroom for them yet, so he might not be enacting a murder right before me. I thought of the dozen lives he had taken and of the countless more he might take using his witchcraft to accomplish the deaths. It was a perversion of magic. I disapproved of it with all of my being, using magic for evil. Of course, I understood that I used my magic to end life and almost any way you look at it, that was also a corruption of the beauty that was magic.

But if I could do what Vivienne suggested, take his magic without ending his life... that would be worth the trip. The whole nightmare of taking lives to save lives. Vivienne was right, of course, that it harmed me. The truth was that I didn't have many more trips in me.

Maybe one doctor can't save the world. It was time to accept it.

Dalez laid bills on the table and left with the co-worker, placing his hand on the small of her back as they walked out to the sidewalk. Once there, he walked her to her car and took her hand in his to kiss her fingers as they parted.

Just at the beginning then. She's lucky.

I pulled out just before he did but waited until he left to drive down the road behind his yellow Porsche. It made all the right roars, and I acknowledged to myself that I was envious of the killer's car. He drove away from the part of the city where he lived and I realized this may be my opportunity. I didn't want to do this at his home. If things went south, I did not want kids to be present.

He stopped his car in front of a small house on a hilly street. I heard him put the parking brake on and the electronic beep when he locked the doors. Once he was in the house, I did a quick Google search to confirm where I would find the fuel line on his Porsche. When I figured out what to look for, I pierced a small hole in the line and hoped my timing was going to work out. Then I used my magic to unlock his car and leave a present inside.

About fifty minutes later, he jogged down the steps of the house and got into his car. He took off with another roar and I followed far behind, just catching his tail lights. I was pleased to see the steady stream of gas flowing from under his car. Five minutes later, he came to a stop on a dark hillside road. No houses in sight. If he weren't in possession of such a noticeable car, I'd worry less about the location and my options. But as it was, I thought I'd better try this thing and get the hell out of Dodge.

I pulled up behind him slowly and parked. Getting out, I realized he had probably already called for help, so I needed to be even quicker about things. Dalez made me as a witch right away. He pretended he didn't though and said something casual in Portuguese.

"Hey," I said. "What's going on? You need some help?"

I approached him and he held up his hands as if to say, "No thanks." But that motherfucker was working a spell with them, and it took all of my willpower not to throw one back at him. Instead, I grabbed the spell he was sending at me and kept pulling. I pulled and pulled until there was nothing left to receive and he fell to the ground. I felt his magic flood into me. He had persuasion, cloaking, pain and a surprising understanding of numbers—*Jesus, that would have helped in med school*—and I realized I didn't get the hit of nausea that usually floored me. When I made it to him, I also noticed that Dalez was stunned and not able to move but was very much alive laying there on the ground. His eyes said he would kill me when he was mobile again.

I laughed down at him and said, "You got lucky tonight, Dalez. You don't know how lucky."

Walking back to my car, I said to him over my shoulder, "Don't go too far. The police should be here soon to check out the scene. There's a nice explanation of all your crimes waiting for them in your back seat. I'll make sure they know it's there."

Driving away, I thought of all the unnecessary deaths I had caused. I wished I'd known sooner how to use this magic of mine that could take other powers. Wished I'd understood any part of it. But I said a short prayer to ask for forgiveness and also to thank God. For Vivienne.

CHAPTER THIRTY-EIGHT

While Adam was away, I pined. There was no better word for it. I sat and stared out the window and waited for him to return. In a moment of clarity, I saw myself as I sat there on the daybed surrounded by books that I could not will my mind to read.

Get up, you lazy witch.

I decided to return to my work with the unsheltered in earnest. Adam hadn't found me an official job with this group yet. But I had become acquainted with some individuals who lived on the street. They stayed in one area by working their way around one or two city blocks each week in an effort not to draw the ire of merchants or police.

I pulled out my crimson running shoes from under Grant's bed and then opened his top dresser drawer. I felt slightly guilty when I saw the selection there for me to choose from. Thanks to Adam and Maria, I was in possession of two weeks' worth of undergarments and at least one week of sleeping clothes. The colors and different fabrics pleased me. I frowned at my selfishness and thought it was too much for one person. I had the idea to give some away to my new unsheltered friends, so I went to get a paper sack with handles from the kitchen and began to fill it with a few things I thought would be useful.

The season had turned cold and since I did not know how long I would be gone; I dressed for it. I wore loose black slacks and a black turtleneck cashmere sweater. And under that I had on a white silk set of what Maria called "under-alls," and under that I wore a teal set of lacy underwear and a matching bra. I pictured Adam as I dressed, knowing he would hate the layers but love the undoing of them. I finished with thick socks and my crimson tennis shoes.

In the hallway I put on a long cream colored woolen coat Adam had purchased for me and slipped my hands into soft leather gloves he had left in the pockets. I was hit by a wave of love then for this man who cared for me so and provided me with all I needed. I gazed around his house, at the elegant furnishings in his study and the books lining the walls. I would miss it all. I wondered, when I returned to my time and thought of this place and Adam, would my mind be comforted that I had been here and felt this? Or would I despair?

The Library of Congress was on my way and Caleb and I made a stop there as usual to look at the manuscript. Once or twice when I stood before it, I thought I caught an echo from my village. A fleeting moment of awareness that there was somewhere else for me, a place I belonged, buried in the pages of that book. I felt it a little more, a little deeper in my soul each time I visited.

But on that day, the guards at the front door would not allow me inside with my bag. The guard explained that sometimes they had security concerns and changed the rules on entry. So I decided to ask for Grant and see if he could store my bag. Moments after the guards called him, he came jogging easily down the steps. I was surprised to see Maria behind him.

He swept me up in a hug when he reached the bottom, and I laughed and hugged him back.

"What are you up to?" He wore a brighter expression than I had seen from him, and I noticed as Maria's hand reached for my bag that she was wearing the heart-shaped pink diamond ring. I smiled but did not mention it.

"Thank you, Maria. Could you both hold on to this for me for just a moment? I'd like to visit the manuscript but can't take this inside the hall."

"Of course," Grant said. "Come see us when you're done. Do you remember where to go?"

I said I did. Caleb gave me my space when I entered the hall. The manuscript was being viewed by a school group, so I busied myself with looking at the other offerings in the hall. There were beautiful statues and other historical books on display. None as old as mine. I stood before a marble statue and closed my eyes. Yes, I could feel the manuscript, even from across the room. I was definitely developing a connection to it, but I didn't know how or why or what to do about it.

When I got to stand in front of it, I saw that it was turned to a particularly lovely illustration my father had made of a stained glass window with a nun and priest standing before it. Library staff turned the pages regularly, and I had not seen my illustration with the *V* since I got here. I studied the nun a little closer and saw a hint of my mother. And the priest, he was a bit of my father. I smiled.

In Grant's office, I sat next to Maria in the chairs before his desk. He typed away on his computer and she said, "He's trying to get away for lunch. Do you want to come with us? We're walking."

I explained my plan and where I was going. She said, "That's kind of on the way. Grant, can you take enough time to have lunch and then go with Vivienne on her errand?"

"Yes," he said, still typing away. "As soon as this email is done, I can be done for the day."

When he finished, he read through it and pursed his lips.

"Would you proof this for me?" He looked at Maria. She stood and went around his desk and leaned in to see his screen. "Here, sit." He stood behind her as she read. They were clearly comfortable sharing a close space.

When Maria had made one little change to his email, Grant hit the send button. He was getting ready to go when I pulled Caleb aside in the hallway to speak to him.

"I want to spend this afternoon with some of my friends who live on the streets. You know they're intimidated by you, Caleb, I'm sure you understand. Grant and Maria will be with me and we won't be long."

Caleb didn't understand. In fact, he disapproved. He said Adam had hired him to stay by my side at all times when Adam was not there. I was becoming frustrated with his inflexibility when Grant stepped into the hallway and showed him a text from Adam that approved of our outing without his presence. "Fine. I'll see you at the house," he said.

Leaving the library, Grant held the bag, and both he and Maria followed my lead. After lunch, for our first stop, I took them to see Derrick Johnson. We found him sitting in his tent in an alley between two buildings. It wasn't a street, so he liked this position because he didn't worry about getting run over by a vehicle if he slept.

Derrick was older than I, with a scruffy gray beard and even scruffier mane of gray hair. His blue eyes were always alert. I realized when I spoke to him that Derrick was always prepared for strange possibilities. Adam told me many unsheltered people have mental health issues and Derrick might have schizophrenia or any number of other psychoses. Adam asked me not to see him alone. *Adam would be happy Grant is here.*

But I could see that Derrick did not like that I was there with new people. At least Caleb was not there, Derrick *really* did not like him. I crouched down to speak to him. "Hello Derrick, these are my friends Grant and Maria. We just had lunch. I had some leftovers; would you like some soup?"

He took the bag from my hands and opened the container. He began to slurp the soup, and I reached in Grant's bag for some hand warmers. "Here, take some hand warmers for tonight. They might be good for keeping feet warm, too."

Derrick took the hand warmers from me and put them in his tent. He went back to his soup, ignoring us completely.

"God be with you, Derrick," I said. "I hope we can meet again soon."

Our second stop was to see Martina Welton. She was a veteran from the United States Navy and had been unfortunate enough to lose her custody fight for her children when she returned from her overseas duty. She admitted to a bit of a drug problem that had gotten worse after the judge decided against her. Now she was as clean as a whistle, she said, but mostly because she had no money whatsoever. Martina laughed as she said that it was a blessing and a curse.

I learned all this over coffee at a Starbucks one morning while Adam was at work. Martina was a woman in her thirties with dark skin and unruly hair that she shoved into a cap. She carried all her worldly goods in a giant over the shoulder bag. When we came upon her, she was sitting on a couple of layers of blankets on the cement, leaning against her grimy green bag full of goods.

"Vivienne!" She threw up her hands and stood up to greet me with a hug.

I introduced her to Grant and Maria and they shook her hand. I told Martina that Grant was a librarian at the Library of Congress and that maybe he could help her find some resources for veterans who lived on the streets of Washington, D.C. She was interested. Grant seemed surprised, and Maria looked amused.

Martina said, "You just got voluntold."

"I did," he said with good humor. "And I know nothing about it, but I should. And I'd do anything for Vivienne, so I'll find out what I can."

I took the bag from Maria and dug down to the bottom. "I made some sweet bread. Do you like that?"

Martina grabbed the loaf I held out to her and said, "Give me that now."

We all laughed at that. I reached in and found her more of the hand warmers I had gotten from under the kitchen sink and an extra set of the silk under-alls I was wearing.

"And I want you to put these on when the night gets too cold. It's an extra layer that will keep you insulated." She accepted those more quietly but thanked me and said she would do that.

"Last thing," I said. "I worked on your hands and your knees last time because you said they hurt. Did that work?"

"They haven't hurt once since!" She pointed at me and said to Grant and Maria. "This woman is a miracle worker!"

I said, "I want to do another little massage to keep them that way."

She sat down and motioned for me to sit in front of her.

I handed Grant the bag and as I was taking off my gloves, I said to him in a low voice, "I'm about to attempt something new. I may need to put her to sleep to do so. Please keep an eye out for people passing by. I can't be interrupted."

His brow furrowed. "Do you need me to cloak you?"

"I don't think so. But that's up to you." Now that I had decided that, I was anxious to get started.

I sat down in front of Martina. On our last visit, I'd detected a hint of cancer in her right breast. I felt it then too when I held her hands before me. I didn't usually get to have patients who were asleep or alone in a room, therefore my methods were hidden. I generally sent a wave of my magic from my hands to theirs or from my hand to their lungs or their temple. Depending on the ailment. But ridding Adam of the evil magic had called for a concentrated stream of magic directly to where it was in his brain. I don't know how I knew, but that was what I needed to do for Martina. I sent a warm wave of sleep over her and she slumped to the side.

Maria gasped and stepped closer.

"Grant. Now would be the time to cloak us," I said. I closed my eyes and said a quick prayer to our Heavenly Father to use me to help Martina. I began to hum. The cancer was small in her right breast. I raised my hand and lightly touched the place on her breast where I felt it. I sent a strong stream of healing magic directly to the spot.

In the past when I had healed people of a fever or infection, I would always draw it out and disperse it into the air. I could see it, but no one else had ever said they did. I didn't know what would happen with cancer. Would it disperse as the lesser ailments did? I prayed that would be so.

The cancer was dislodging from its cavity. I felt it loosen, felt the weight of it, so much heavier than the small pea it had seemed, and I realized it was coming toward me. My magic stream was indeed evicting the cancer from Martina's breast, but it would need another host and that was me. I had a moment of panic when I realized I was facing the thing I had studiously avoided all my life.

But that was human, was it not? Fear for one's own life?

I decided in that moment not to be small, as I had always been when facing the challenge of cancer, but to be large, like Adam, and fight for the world.

I didn't have to do it alone, though. I prayed to God that it would work the same. That when the cancer reached me and tried to stay, I would be able to expel it as quickly and efficiently as I did the dark magic that had cursed Adam.

The hardest thing I have ever done was to hold still while that cancer tried to claim me. I did it though. I held on until I felt it all gone from her body. Then I broke the stream and stood quickly. I walked away, out of the safety of Grant's invisible shield around us, and I stood facing the building next to us and away from the street. I raised both my arms and pushed the cancer from my body with a force I had never before summoned. My eyes were closed, but I sensed a flare of heat leaving me. When it was over, I dropped my tired arms and turned toward Grant and Maria. They were dumbstruck.

I felt immense satisfaction because I knew the cancer was gone from Martina and from me. I had done it. I couldn't wait to tell Adam.

We needed to get to his hospital. Soon.

CHAPTER THIRTY-NINE

Adam

December 18th, 2024

In the last thirty hours I had gotten about three hours of sleep. I didn't care. Dropping my bag in the hallway, I stood and listened for Vivienne. Water was running in the kitchen and dishes were being rinsed underneath it. Walking that way, I called out, "Vivienne!"

The water stopped, and I came upon her, drying her hands with a dishtowel. Her eyes lit up and the smile she had for me, just for me, was everything I ever wanted. She tossed the towel on the table and ran to me. I grabbed her and lifted her off her feet, twirled her around in the hallway, and kissed her.

God, yes. She tasted so good. She ran her hands through my hair and kissed me back frantically, like we had been apart for years. We were so hungry for each other, both of us filled with a need to be close and never let go again. When we broke for breath, she laughed. "I have news for you, Adam."

"I have news for you, too. Can we share the news naked?"

She cupped my face with her hands and kissed me again. "I wish."

My hands made their way to her ass and her hands made their way to mine. I pulled her closer.

"*Please.*" I put everything I had into that word and, truth be told, thought about using persuasion. "It's almost midnight and I've been awake forever."

"Not yet," she said. I groaned, and she laughed at me. "We need to talk. Come sit." She grabbed my hand from her ass and began to drag me to the living room.

She pushed me down on the couch and I pulled her down onto my lap.

"Whatever. Let's do this fast," I said. She wrapped her arms around my neck and leaned into me. "Here's my news: you were right. I neutralized a witch, captured all his powers from him, and did not leave him dead." Her eyes widened. "That asshole was definitely still breathing when the cops rolled up."

Vivienne's eyes began to tear.

"No, no, no! This is happy news." I wiped my thumbs over her cheeks and pulled her into another deep kiss. "It's because of you that I even knew to try."

She feathered kisses all over my face and I wondered how I had ever lived without this.

"Vivienne, I love you. I am head over heels in love with you."

The crying started in earnest then. "I know," she said through tears. I reached back and got a tissue from the table and handed it to her.

"You *know?*"

She closed her eyes and laughed. When she could, she answered me. "I love you too," she said. "Of course."

Vivienne sat back from me then to prepare me for her news.

Placing a hand in the center of my chest, she said, "I cured a person of her cancer."

I felt the world stop. My brain needed to hear that again.

"What?"

"Grant and Maria were there. I felt it in the woman, Martina. It was breast cancer, small, not much, and I pulled it out with my magic."

I sat up and set her down next to me on the couch. The realization of the danger she had faced hit me all at once. All I could say was, "Why did you do this without me?"

Her look to me said, *Really? What were you going to do?*

"Adam, it was time for me to try. Like it was time for you to try."

"Where were you? When did this happen?" I needed details.

"I was visiting one of my unsheltered friends, Martina. And

I just needed to do it. I can't explain it other than that," she said with some irritation.

"And how do you know..." I didn't even want to voice the words.

"I treated it the same as I treated your dark magic infection. As it came from her, it wanted to claim me. As soon as it was out of her, I stood and pushed it out of me. Grant and Maria saw a red light shoot into the sky." My eyes widened at that.

"Is it...?"

She knew what I needed to hear. "It's gone. It never got a hold of me."

"But what if it did?" I didn't want her to do this again.

She shook her head, knowing the path my mind was taking. "It was exactly the same as with the dark magic. I willed it out of me and it answered immediately. I have no fear of doing it again."

I was not convinced.

"Adam," she said gently. "We need to go to the hospital now. For Emily."

Of course I had been thinking the same thing, but I hadn't processed yet that Vivienne felt it was safe for her to perform this incredible magic again. I ran my hands down the side of her head and threaded my fingers through her silky hair. She watched me come to terms with the reality of things. This was her magic. She understood it. I could only listen to her and believe what she said.

"Okay," I said. I stood and pulled her up with me. "Let's go before I change my mind. Now, while we can maybe sneak in and not be seen by as many people." I texted for a Lyft and we both bundled up and headed out the door. We held hands in the backseat, and I prayed to God the entire drive there to please let this work. To please keep Vivienne safe.

CHAPTER FORTY

Vivienne

Adam persuaded the Lyft driver that we were never there. Then he persuaded the guards at the front desk that they never saw us. Before he spoke to them, he said to me, "Shield yourself." I barely had time to do so before he was using words with such effect that my mind almost shut down. Even with my shield, I felt the pull of his voice.

There were cameras that Adam needed to disable, so we went to a room full of computers and screens first. He rewound some video and then touched a keyboard. The picture on the screens went fuzzy and then blank. Taking my hand, he led me from that room to the elevator. He pointed to the number eight button. I pushed it and when it lit up, I could not hide my delight. He shook his head.

"So easily pleased," he said, patting me on the head.

There was no one in the hall when the elevator doors opened, but the nurses' station had three women sitting behind it. I was ready this time when he persuaded them to continue monitoring all the rooms, but to forget we had ever been there. That was a key component to his gift of persuasion, I realized. The command to forget it was used. We gowned up for Emily's room and Adam peeked through the window in the door.

"Shit," he said. "Sara's here."

"You persuade her we were not here and I'll help her to sleep," I said.

He pushed into the room. Sara smiled when she saw Adam, and it was not long before he had her sitting in a chair and I had her dozing off comfortably.

We both brought our masks down at the same time and took our places on either side of Emily's bed.

"You don't have to do this," he said. "It'll be different from an early breast cancer. This will be more. A much bigger tumor. And I worry about your technique of removal and the effect it could have on Emily's brain."

He was just advocating for his patient. I would do the same with an untried cure.

I regarded Emily, so still in her bed. She was fragile, and I was moved by the dark sweep of her lashes on her pale cheeks. I was itching to touch her and relieve her pain. But I waited for Adam's approval of this endeavor.

I raised my eyes to his. "She'll die without any intervention, correct?"

Adam's eyes moved to Emily. He was studying her, too. "There are some impressive results with pre-surgery immunotherapy..." he seemed to be speaking to himself. Picking up her wrist out of habit, he felt for her pulse. He laid her hand back down gently and said, "But it's too late for that. Yes. She will die without any intervention."

"My magic has never hurt a patient. Never. It has only soothed and relieved them of their pain. But I'll treat this as delicately as I can."

He nodded then, trusting me completely.

"And what will you do when you draw it all out? Where will it go?"

That was an excellent question. I surveyed the room. "No window," I said.

We both looked around then. Adam reached under the cabinet and drew out a metal waste can.

"Well, this seems like a terrible idea," he said with a short laugh.

Adam's eyes looked to me, dropped down to Emily, struggling to breathe on the bed, and back then to me. I could see he was fighting to keep his panic at bay and that he was terrified for both Emily and me. His trust in my ability won out.

"Go for it, Lanier. Leave it here when you get it." He set the can on the floor at the end of the bed. The metal top flipped open.

"Step back," I told him.

He reluctantly took a few steps back to stand beside Sara, still asleep in her chair.

Adam had discussed Emily's cancer with me at length. He detailed the type, 'glioblastoma,' which in Emily was a level four type of brain tumor. It was growing at an alarming rate and would shut down her brain function soon. I said a silent prayer to God to let her still have brain functions and to let me do no harm to her young body and brain with my healing magic. I closed my eyes and placed my hands over her head.

I felt the tumor immediately in the back of her skull. It was so much larger than I imagined a tiny child could withstand. Lifting Emily's head with one of my hands, I brought the index finger of my other hand to the spot where it was. My magic took over then. It raced to the site of the tumor and I felt the tumor rattle when it was touched. The monitors began to ding, and I heard Adam at the door telling someone to turn off the alarms at the desk and forget they rang at all.

The tumor was resistant. I couldn't yank. I had to surround it with my magic and let it flow to me. Sweat rolled down my back. I felt like I was lifting a great boulder and walking backward as I pulled it along to me. It began to dissolve into my stream of magic. And just like with Martina's cancer, this disease needed a host. I allowed it to come through my finger and into me. Again, I had to battle the desire to let it go and flee the room, but I pictured Emily, her mother, and her father and I stayed put.

Martina's cancer had moved almost instantly. Emily's cancer was so dense it took minutes to abandon her brain. I felt it searching for its favored place within me and as it reached my brain and tried to roost there, I began to panic. What if I couldn't make decisions by the time it left Emily, and I needed to oust it from me? I prayed again to God to let me keep my reasoning.

When my magic had cleared Emily's brain of the cancer, I pulled my hands from her head and willed all the cancer in me into my arms. I lurched to the end of the bed where the trash can stood open and I thrust my hands downward and let the cancer flow out. Grant and Maria were right, it was a red field of energy. It was ugly, and it pulsed and raged, making a soft hissing sound as it hit the bottom and sides of the trashcan. As soon as the stream of energy stopped falling from me, Adam slammed the lid down. He reached for me and gathered me in his arms.

"How are you?" he murmured against my hair. "Check yourself. Do you feel it?"

I was exhausted. I could barely stand. When I felt my legs buckle, he tucked me up closer to him and held me upright.

"Let me see," I whispered. I tried to regulate my breathing again, tried to slow my heartbeat so I could evaluate myself from my normal state. It felt good to be in his arms. I breathed in his scent, that heavenly pine forest, and I gave a contented sigh as I breathed out. Much calmer after a minute, I did a scan of myself. This was a regular practice of mine, to make sure no infection lingered with me. It had become almost an unconscious practice, but this time, I concentrated on each part of my body as I assessed myself. I felt tired, but there was nothing different in my body than had been there before the treatment.

When I was done checking myself, I let Adam continue to hold me while I scanned him, too. He made it difficult to concentrate by repeatedly kissing my head and my temple. But I was relieved to confirm that he was clear of cancer as well.

Finally, I pulled my head away from his chest. "You and I are both free of cancer." He kissed my lips and turned me around to look at the monitors. Emily's vital signs were stable. She was breathing easily and color had returned to her face.

"We need to get out of here now, but... look what you did," he said. "You're a miracle worker."

I was thrilled to know this was a part of my magic. That I could help children and families with this devilish illness. But I knew where it came from and told Adam so.

"God gave me this magic. All the glory is to Him."

Adam turned me back around. "He certainly gave it to the right person."

His eyes turned to the can behind us and he frowned.

"Should we look at it?" I asked.

"God, no! Who knows what state it's in? I need to contain this thing." He dug around under the sink again and got out a garbage bag. Carefully lifting the can, he pulled the bag around it so it closed tightly at the top.

"Let's get out of these gowns. We can put them in here." We took off the paper gowns and threw them away in the bag. I gave one last look to Emily, and then to her mother. I wished I could see the joy of her mother and father when they saw her healthy again.

Adam carried the bag with extreme care. He persuaded all we saw that we had never been there.

At home, he placed the bag on the table in his study and sat down on his crimson couch in front of it. The last thing I saw before I fell asleep on the daybed was Adam staring at the can.

CHAPTER FORTY-ONE

Adam

December 19th, 2024

That damn garbage can of cancer was still on my living room table when I woke up three hours later. I had crashed on the couch, Vivienne on the daybed. We might have slept all day if my phone had not scared the shit out of us both. It was the hospital telling me Emily had a change in her status, and I needed to get there as soon as possible. Usually, this was a terrible call to get, but I knew this was going to be different. I did a quick check on Vivienne to see how she was and she laughed at my hand across her brow and lips on her temple.

"I'm fine," she said. "Still no cancer."

"Go back to sleep," I told her. It was just after 5:00 am and there was no need for both of us to feel like hell all day. I took the can with me to my bedroom. I started the shower in my bathroom and opened the closet door. Mostly I kept linens on shelves in this closet, but I also had a boxed vacuum cleaner and a couple of boxes from my childhood and Grant's childhood. I pulled it all out and stored the can in the very back. I replaced the personal boxes and put the boxed vacuum on top of them. Once the can was hidden, I felt my stress reduce by about fifty percent. The hot shower took care of the rest. There were going to be a million questions about Emily's recovery, but I felt confident I could answer them with, "I don't know how this is possible."

Because, really, how could I explain this miracle? I had no idea how Vivienne worked that magic of hers. I truly did not understand how she did it. The one thing we could both agree on was that God had blessed her.

Yes, I thought it. There was a God, and he gave Vivienne a gift like no other. It followed that my own magic had been heaven sent as well. My hand on the wall of the shower and my head down in the hot spray, I smiled.

Well, this was quite an interesting turn of events. Vivienne had turned me into a believer.

When I got to the hospital, I was cornered as soon as I got off the elevator by Eleanor. She did not pause for breath.

"Jesus Christ, you are not going to believe this shit when you see it, Parrish. It is a fuckin' miracle." She hurried me to Emily's room. She pushed through the door into a room full of people. Both Sara and her husband stood on opposite sides of Emily's bed, their hands all over her. Emily sat up in bed with a juice box in her hand and a smile on her face. I caught my breath at the sight of her.

I surveyed the group and asked anyone who was not family to please leave the room. Eleanor stayed as everyone else shuffled out. Rawlings called Sara over to his side of the bed so I could access the computer with Emily's chart. He knew I'd want to evaluate the whole situation. The last vitals were at 11:30 or so. They were terrible. I looked at her blood work from earlier on the day before. Also terrible.

Then I looked at the vitals displayed on the monitor above her bed. Perfect.

I said, "Emily! You look so much better today! Can I listen to your heart?" I showed her my stethoscope with Sesame Street characters on the lanyard. She nodded yes, shyly. Her heartbeat was beautiful. Her lungs clear. Her eyes and mouth, perfectly clear.

"Are you hungry?" I asked. Her eyes widened at the thought. "Would you like some Jello?" An enthusiastic yes. Once Emily and I determined that red Jello was best, I asked Eleanor to get me blood work and a scan of Emily's brain as soon as possible and some red Jello, stat.

Then I turned my eyes to the Rawlings. Sara was crying. Trying hard not to because she didn't want to scare her daughter, but the tears kept coming.

"Is this remission?" Jake asked.

I took a breath and said, "I don't know what this is." Their eyes were laser focused on me. "It's unbelievable. I've never seen anything like it. I want to get these tests done and see the results before deciding anything or calling it anything." Rawlings searched my face like he didn't quite believe something. "But I am very encouraged by how healthy Miss Emily is looking this morning. If she wants to eat, you can feed her all her favorites." Emily's eyes lit up.

"In moderation," I added. "I'm going to put a rush on the tests. I'll let you know when they come back." I grabbed Emily's foot and shook it, and she laughed.

Rawlings stopped me as I started out. He pulled me to the side of the room behind the curtain.

"What is this?" He asked. His eyes were fevered. He wanted so badly to believe this was real, but as a physician, he knew that this was not supposed to happen.

I put my hand on his arm. "Well, it looks like this is a miracle," I said. His eyes filled with tears. "Let me get the tests back so we can call it that, all right? In the meantime, it's perfectly fine to have hope. Okay?"

Rawlings gave me a fierce hug before I left.

The MRI could not be done for a couple of hours and the blood work would take that long, anyway. Before I laid down on the couch in my office, I ran through the likely scenarios I might face in the next few hours. Explaining a miracle was not hard in the world outside the hospital. Inside the hospital was another matter. My colleagues who faced this day in and day out would want every single detail. I wondered if Rawlings would put together the miraculous events of the day with how Vivienne had soothed Emily to sleep so effortlessly that her vitals had improved after being touched by Vivienne. I was sleep deprived and couldn't focus on the next steps. It was time to call in reinforcements.

The receptionist at Grant's office said he was in a meeting, so I called Maria and asked her to get a message to him.

"A lot has happened in the last twenty-four hours. Can you please ask Grant for me to read his mother in on the nun situation so I can talk to her later about some hospital stuff and she'll be up to speed?"

There was silence on the line for a moment while Maria processed that request. Then, "How much of the nun situation do you want him to discuss with her?"

"All of it," I said.

She whistled. "Wow." Then, "God, I hope he lets me sit in on that."

"Thanks, Maria."

I wondered if Grant would finish the nun situation story with the fact that I was definitely in love with the nun who turned out to not be an actual nun. Connie would love that.

I dropped down on the couch in my office and immediately began to sink into sleep. My last conscious thought was that I hadn't done anything more about the people who had threatened Vivienne at the museum.

CHAPTER FORTY-TWO

Vivienne

After Adam left for the hospital, I couldn't get back to sleep. It was always this way with me when I've done a particularly difficult healing. I'm weak immediately after, but with the smallest amount of rest, I'm rejuvenated and full of energy. My magic is made stronger with every use of it. I didn't know if this was normal for witches, in my time or this time. But it was five in the morning, and I didn't know what to do with my excess energy.

I decided to run. Putting on two layers of pants and three layers on top, I added white cotton gloves and a black knit hat with a furry knot on top. I tucked my cell phone in the pocket of my running pants. My crimson running shoes were the last item, and I tied them with satisfaction.

So many things I've learned in this new world. I'll miss it. I felt a physical pain in my stomach. *I'll miss him.*

Jogging down Adam's front steps, I saw my breath in the air when I exhaled and felt the cold nip at my cheeks. I took the same path we usually did and made my way to the National Mall. With satisfaction I saw that Mel's mobile pub was gone from its location of many years. Adam and I still had not spoken about it, and I hoped we could do so soon. I didn't like keeping something from him.

As I turned at the Washington Monument to make my way back down the Mall, I saw the man who had spoken to me at the museum walking toward me with his hands in his coat pockets. He was alone. He nodded to acknowledge me and I fortified my shield and sent a wave of pain to his side. He fell onto a bench and withdrew his hands from his pockets. He held them out to me as if saying; I mean no harm. I lessened the pain but did not release it completely.

Tony jogged ahead of me and stopped in front of the man. "Who is this?" he asked.

Caleb stopped directly behind him.

I took stock of the man and realized he was not there to abduct me. Having already bested him once, I had no qualms about doing it again. I was actually a little glad to see him. The waiting around for someone to possibly attack had become tiresome. Maybe now we would get some answers. I gestured to Caleb and Tony and shrugged at the man. "I don't think they're going to leave." Sitting down next to him, I said, "What's your name?"

"Martin Becker," he said. He grunted. I eased the pain a bit but kept it present.

"Mr. Becker was the man who approached us at the museum," I told Tony. He frowned, pulled out his cell phone, and rapidly typed a text.

"What do you want?" I asked him.

He held his side and got straight to it. "I'm here to apologize. My employer is a desperate man who used desperate measures to try to gain your assistance. I advised him not to go that route." I released the pain in his side. He took a deep breath and then slowly sat up straight.

"Thank you," he said.

"Your employer's name?"

He hesitated. "Sheik Farhad Al-Masri. Of Oman. He heard there was a great healer. His wife has cancer. He is... anguished."

"I understand. And I'm sympathetic." We sat in silence for a moment. It was wise of him not to push. I looked to the sky. Two jets appeared to be headed directly for each other. Adam had told me the planes were probably a hundred miles apart or more, but I still watched until they passed each other and their white trails crossed in the deep blue sky.

"My healing has been limited to common illnesses. If I was to heal someone of a complicated illness... something deadly..."

I saw that he understood. He said, "Word could spread. I can assure you that any help you provide would be kept secret."

Looking back up at the sky I replied, "No offense to you or your employer but no, it would not."

Despite successfully removing Martina's tumor, I didn't know what an attempt to cure a metastasized cancer might do to me. I sent a quick prayer to ask for guidance. Standing, I said to him, "Stay here."

Walking toward the middle of the lawn I thought about what it had felt like to remove Martina's cancer. Difficult, yes. Terrifying, yes.

Exhilarating, yes.

I realized there might never be a better time to flex my healing magic. With Adam by my side, using his own formidable power, ready to help however he could. I wouldn't have to try this in secret, by myself. And I did want to try it. God had given me this gift. I needed to use it to the best of my ability. It was time to test that ability. I walked back to the man on the bench.

"I make no promises..." I said, "but I will see her here in Washington."

He brightened, and I added again, "No promises. Make sure he knows that. But I will visit with her. In return, I may need to ask for assistance from your employer. I assume he's very wealthy?"

"Incredibly so," he said.

"Hmmm..." I said. There was something telling me I would need his help. I just couldn't crystallize the idea to know exactly how.

"For a future favor from him, I'll see her."

He stood and bowed to me. "I thank you and my employer thanks you. We are so very grateful. I'll call him now to make the arrangements."

As he turned to go, I thought how nice it would be to have just one day with Adam with no responsibilities between us.

Tony said, "Adam would want us to detain him."

I stared at them both. "Did you not hear me just invite them to a meeting? Mr. Becker and his employer will be back. Also, do you think I could not handle that one man?" I stood and placed my hands on my hips.

They hurried to agree that of course I could take that one man, I could make him run home screaming for his mother. They were just doing their job and wanted Adam to know they offered.

I nodded and began my jog back to Adam's home, Caleb and Tony close behind.

Chapter Forty-Three

Adam

Emily's MRI came back clear. Her blood work, also clear. She was eating and laughing and her parents needed my assurance over and over that she was cancer free. I gave it to them, along with permission to take her home. I took a picture of the three of them, gave Emily a hug, and asked Eleanor to get an appointment set up with them for one month later.

When my rounds were finished, I trucked back home and saw that Vivienne was on the daybed reading her medical books. She glanced up when I stepped into the room and gave me a small smile. I stood there and just looked. The sun sparkled in her silver hair. Her hands were so elegant resting on the pages. Those long slender fingers... her mouth parted as she saw me taking her in. And then I was next to her on the bed, scattering the books so they hit the floor. She laughed into my mouth as I leaned back on the pillows and pulled her with me. Her body was over top of mine, finally, and her hair fell all around us in a fragrant cloud of bliss. I ran my hands up under her sweater and undid her bra.

"Adam," she said.

"Nope, not stopping again," I said against her mouth.

She pushed off of me. "Grant is here," she said.

"Son of a bitch," I groaned loudly.

"Well, that's not very nice." Connie's voice from the doorway was the last thing I expected to hear.

Vivienne laughed. "I'll leave you two so Adam can apologize for that." She picked up the books on the floor before she left.

Connie called down the hall to her as Vivienne went upstairs to her room, "Okay, but come back quick. I want the whole story!" She sat down on the couch, crossed her legs, and gave me an amused glance.

So Grant had filled her in. Good. I held my hands up like, *"Can you believe this shit?"*

She shook her head a little like, *"No, I cannot believe this shit."*

Then she surprised me with, "It's so good to see you happy." I ducked my head. "Thank you."

Then I frowned and added, "She has to go back, though."

"So Grant said. But you don't really have that piece worked out yet, do you?"

"No."

"So maybe you still have a while."

Connie was trying to make me feel better about it, and I was touched. I sat in a chair in front of her on the couch.

She said, "I understand now why it was so critical to get her DNA results and possible matches. We should have them soon. It took this long because you didn't want to call attention to her sample." She paused. "You could have told me, you know." She wasn't being accusatory. Maybe just a little hurt.

I said, "I know! That was the plan. We were just at the hospital. And then Marsh was there..."

She held up her hand. "I get it." Her look was concerned. "But what about this group of persuaders who cornered them at the museum? What are you doing about that?"

Vivienne walked in then and said, "I have some updates on that." She sat down in the chair next to me.

"Were you planning on discussing the happenings at the hospital today?" Vivienne raised her eyebrows to me, asking if this meeting with Connie was about that.

"Yes," I said.

"Then your update should go before mine." She sat back.

What is this now? There was really no telling with Vivienne. I realized the sort of constant surprise and challenge she brought to me every day was exactly what I had needed in my life. I called out to the kitchen for Grant to join us.

When I finished the tale of how Emily was cured of cancer by Vivienne and how I had stored the proof in a garbage can in my bathroom closet, both Connie and Grant sat across from us on the couch with their mouths ajar. I turned to Vivienne. "We keep doing this to people," I said.

"Poor Grant has been through it twice," she said.

Connie could not stop staring at Vivienne. "It's miraculous. What you did. You are miraculous."

"Thank you," Vivienne said. "But it is a gift given to me by our Father. I cannot claim the miracle."

Connie considered that. "Yes, it's a gift from God." Her voice was thick with emotion. "My mother died of lung cancer. I have always feared it, feared for myself and for Grant." He put his arm around her.

I remembered the picture then of Emily I had on my phone and I showed it to them all. Vivienne took the phone in her hand and continued to stare at it.

"That's my update. Top that, Vivienne."

She raised her eyes from the phone. "My update. I agreed to meet with the wife of the man who sent the other men to get us at the museum." Grant's eyes widened at that, and I frowned. "She's very sick with cancer," she continued. "He's very rich and will grant me a favor just for seeing her. I made no promises because life is never certain."

"When did this happen? How did they get to you?" Grant was upset that she had somehow been put in danger and I was mad at myself for the same reason.

"I was jogging."

I turned to her and gave her an incredulous look.

"The man approached me on the Mall. The same one from the museum," she said to Grant.

"You were *jogging?*"

She said to me, "Yes. The man didn't threaten me. Caleb and Tony were there, but I didn't need them. It was fine. I took care of it."

I looked at her with disappointment and shook my head slightly. "And you said you didn't want those running shoes."

She rolled her eyes. "Fine. I love them and I use them. Every day, okay?"

Connie seemed to be riveted by our griping. Then she laughed out loud. "God, I *love* this," she said.

I wondered why Caleb and Tony didn't grab that man or call me with this information. I rubbed a hand over my eyes.

"You look like hell, Parrish," Connie observed.

"There's one more thing, Adam," Vivienne said gently.

I opened my eyes and looked at her. She took my hand and squeezed it. "It was Mel who let my secret be known."

I was confused at first and then I felt a rage wash over me that I know darkened my expression and made Vivienne take her other hand and cover mine.

"She's gone now," she said. "We had a short conversation where I informed her that I knew, and that when you did, you would not be happy."

Not happy. What I felt was so much deeper than "not happy."

I tried to calm down. I breathed in deeply and out a couple of times. I realized I was jiggling my leg, so I stopped. The room was watching me, so I said, "I'm fine." Vivienne squeezed my hand again and let it go.

"Well, this has been a lot," Grant said.

I gave a short laugh. "Yep."

Then everyone laughed, and we sat for a moment to take it all in.

Grant summed it up. "So Vivienne is in danger now because the whole world will want what she has if word gets out." He surveyed everyone to see if we agreed. I nodded. "And she has to work this magic again because a rich man is bringing his wife here from... where?" He looked at Vivienne.

"Oman?" she said, asking if that sounded like a real place.

"Good. Oman," he said. "And she'll need a place to do this."

"The backyard?" I looked at Vivienne. She considered that. "We can do it at night. I can cloak it."

"And there's still a can of cancer in the bathroom," he finished.

Connie said slowly, "Cancer outside of a host should not be something to worry about. But I understand you wondering what state this cancer is in after being removed with magic."

I said, "I was thinking about Jake Rawlings." It didn't look like she knew him. "He's Emily's father. He's got some authority at N.I.H." She saw where I was going with it then. "If I can figure out how to do it, I might give it to him to have it worked up. With all precautions in place, of course."

She agreed. "Could it be anonymous? And then later you can pick his brain for the findings?"

"Yes. I don't like to do it, but that's what I was thinking."

We sat there again in silence.

"Okay then," Grant said. "We got everything figured out."

Vivienne said, "Not quite everything. I still need to travel back to 1502. Let's work on that next."

CHAPTER FORTY-FOUR

Vivienne

Connie made Adam take a nap. I liked her even more when I saw the sway she held over both Adam and Grant. Their relationship had not worked out, but Connie obviously still cared for Adam and wielded some influence. I was glad he would still have them when I was gone. I fixed my gaze on his sleeping face and thought about shedding my clothes and getting in bed with him, but then he would not sleep. I decided instead to cook him some soup for when he woke up.

Cooking in the twenty-first century was not a chore. The ease and quickness of it allowed me to get creative. While I chopped the vegetables and started the beef stock, I hummed and let my brain work. I also did this when I cooked at home. Cooking was a time when I was alone and no one talked to me or needed anything from me. Except for sometimes Alice. I remembered the time I tried to teach her to make a basic pie crust. Her face and hair were covered in flour before we were done. When I saw her again, it would be time to teach her how to cook a bird. How to cook all the meals. Her mother had loved to cook.

Suddenly I wished Alice could come of age here in the twenty-first century. She could attend college and learn all there is to know about the heavens or the human body. Standing at the kitchen sink, I thought how much richer my life would be when I returned to my time. When I cooked dinner there, my mind could be listing all the bones in the body or reciting a poem that had yet to be written. But Alice would never know any of those things. The water rushed over my hands as I cleaned the vegetables.

I glanced out the window as a robin zoomed by. Adam had a bird feeder in his backyard that took frequent pictures of the birds who came to visit. He had been texting me bird pictures with his own captions for a few weeks. In spite of my blue mood, I had to smile remembering some of them. Then I pictured Alice in Adam's backyard. Pouring seeds in the bird feeder.

Still staring ahead, I turned off the water and dried my hands with a towel. In my mind I loosened just the tiniest bit my grip on 'what had to be.' My resolve remained intact to go back to my time and help Alice. I just allowed a thought to float to the surface. That thought was, *Alice has my blood. Alice has my DNA.*

CHAPTER FORTY-FIVE

I awoke to the smell of vegetable soup. Or beef broth, or both. "Mmmmm…" it smelled delicious and pulled me out of bed from a dream I did not want to leave. I stepped into my kitchen to find another dream standing at the sink. Vivienne tasted a spoonful of soup. She pinched a dash of salt from a dish and tossed it in the pot. Humming lightly to herself, she reached up to open a cabinet, and I took that opportunity to put my arms around her from behind. She started, and I felt that power rise to the surface of her skin, ready to give her whatever she asked of it.

"Gah! Adam! You should know better."

She tried to turn around, but I held her there, one hand under her shirt on her stomach. I swept that long silky hair over her shoulder and softly kissed her neck. I asked her, "Is this your go button? Right here?" I tasted the spot on her neck right behind her ear and she gave a small gasp. I smiled, "Thought so. Other side too?" I swept that hair over her other shoulder and tested my theory. She gave another gasp and a shiver when I tasted her skin there. My hands wandered as I lightly kissed every inch of her neck. One hand opened the button of her pants and slid lower and the other found her breast and lightly pulled at her nipple. "I can't wait another minute. Please, can I take you to bed?" Her nod was quick, but I was already scooping her up in my arms and carrying her to my bedroom.

Once there, I tossed her on my bed, and she laughed.

"Take everything off," I said, while I pulled off my shirt and dropped my boxers. I watched her lift her shirt and toss it at me. I smiled when she took off her bra and threw that at me, too. She scrambled out of her pants, and I ripped them the rest of the way off and dropped them on the floor.

Vivienne stroked my midnight blue sheets, which she said felt like satin, and then stretched like a cat, raising her arms above her head. We looked each other up and down and smiled. Her silver hair spread out over my pillow. Her legs were slightly parted. I crawled up the bed and over her. She spread her legs more for me and I settled between them. Propping myself up on both arms beside her, I said, "This is what life is about."

She smiled. "It is."

I smoothed the hair at her temple and stared into those incredible eyes.

This love.

What I would do for her.

I kissed her jaw and then the left corner of her mouth, the right corner, and then she opened her lips and kissed me back. She brought her hands to my head and played with my hair.

Then she lowered her shield and her magic filled the room. Gold and silver light shimmered over the walls and ceiling. Everywhere our skin touched, I felt my nerve endings react. The room smelled of her—that wild, sweet fragrance that was her magic unshielded. I wanted it to stay there forever in my sheets and curtains and pillows.

I lowered my shield then and our magic finally met as it had been wanting to. I heard her breath catch as she felt the rush of our power sweeping the room. My deep blue swirling through her silver and gold. We both hummed at the sensation as it flowed over us, a rich, satisfied sound that seemed to come from the room itself as much as from us. The possibilities of our magic combined were heady. I wondered if she knew it too, that together we could do anything.

Reaching for her breast, I lowered my head to kiss the tip of it and then sucked her nipple into my mouth. She gave a small gasp.

"When you were here in my bed without me...did you touch yourself?"

"Yes," she murmured.

I kissed the other breast and got another quick intake of breath from her when I sucked and nipped there too.

"Did you come?"

"Yes," she said without hesitation.

That image in my mind confirmed, I had to close my eyes for a moment to keep myself in the game.

Starting with her throat, I kissed down her slender body, sucking one nipple and pulling the other until she whimpered and I had to stop and breathe. I wanted to know every inch of her skin. I kept going—her rib cage, her belly button, the bone of her hip—but I kept returning to her breasts.

Then my mouth was on her. When I kissed her mound reverently, she said, "Please, Adam. I want you." She tried to pull me up, but I pushed her back and held her in place with my hand over her stomach. She watched on raised arms as I swiped up over her clit with my tongue, then back up again. "God!" Her head fell back.

She had been living front and center in my mind since I'd first tasted her. I wanted to learn her, to know exactly what she needed and to make her come again and again this way. When I thrust my tongue inside her, Vivienne arched for me and I hardened more than I thought possible. She tasted like her magic and her warmth. I stroked her clit with my thumb as she pushed against my face and whined her frustration as her need grew. I felt her still, and knew she was close to coming. Keeping up my rapid pace between her legs, I heard her breath stall and the small desperate sound she made when she was almost there.

"Yes..." she whispered. Then she was pleading, "Adam... don't stop. Don't stop," and I wanted her right there on that edge forever. When she cried out and bucked her release, I watched every second of it. At last her trembling stopped, and she stretched again and made adorable, contented sounds like a kitten purring.

Vivienne reached out her arms to me. "Come here," she said.

"No," I said and climbed up her body. She laughed underneath me as I reached across her for the bedside drawer.

"You seem to be in quite a hurry," she said.

When I fumbled the lubricant, nearly losing it off the edge of the table, she said, "Do you need some help?" I gave her a look.

"Not a word."

That made her laugh even harder. Then I had some lubricant in my palm, and I covered myself and then her, my finger slipping inside her and making her breath catch and her laughter fall away.

I drew her legs apart and settled between them. I held myself over her on both arms and looked down at her face. Her eyes on mine, wide open and ready.

I entered her slowly, waiting for her to stretch for me. We both held our breath as I did, and when I was finally there, I stilled.

She exhaled on my name, "Adam."

Whatever I had been about to think or do or say was gone.

Then I began to move and she pulled up to whisper in my ear, "You fill me."

I had never felt anything like that in my life. Not just the physical sensation of being inside her, but her voice telling me she felt it too, her eyes finding mine again as I began to move inside her.

If there was ever a place made for me in this world, it was this place in this woman.

I couldn't be gentle after that. I pushed deeper and she met me, her hips rising to mine, her hands cupping my face and pulling me in for a deep kiss that let me know the moment was the same for her as it was for me. Then those hands began to move —slowly, deliberately, her fingertips tracing the muscles of my stomach, down and down until she reached the place where our bodies were joined. Vivienne touched us there, lightly, with the same careful attention she gave to everything.

It nearly stopped my heart.

We found a rhythm that was urgent and then slow and then urgent again. I buried my face in her hair and breathed her in. The scent of her magic was everywhere, and knowing no other man would ever have it, I thrust harder into her. I said her name against her neck and felt her shiver under me. Her breath came faster and I pulled back to watch her face, unwilling to miss a single second of what I was doing to her. She brought my head back to her for another kiss and then we stayed like that, breathing the same air, moving together, and I thought, *I can't live without this.*

"I'm close," I managed.

"Just a little more," she said, her voice strained. "Give me a little more, Adam, please…" The sound of her asking undid the last of my control and I couldn't watch anymore. I gave her everything I had.

When I felt her inner walls clench around me, I lost it, and she cried out at the same moment I did. Then it felt like the world slowed, shuddered, and stopped.

I was dimly aware of a blue cloud with what looked like electrical sparks popping off all around us.

She let go of me and we collapsed together. I pulled her close against my side, my heart hammering, and drew the sheet over us both.

When we woke in the dark a while later, Vivienne sat up abruptly. "The soup!" she said.

"I got it," I said. I rolled out of bed naked, turned back to her and pointed. "Stay!"

She did not stay, of course, and I heard her padding along behind me in the hallway. Most disappointingly, she had put on clothes and was wearing my t-shirt.

"Huh," I said as I noticed it was dark outside and my neighbor's backyard light was not on. The stove was off, but the pot was still warm. I took her hand and walked us to the front room where I saw that there were no lights on anywhere in front of us either. No streetlights, no house lights.

"Huh," I said again. "I wonder what happened to the electricity."

This time it was Vivienne putting her hands around my waist from behind. "I know what happened to the electricity. We happened."

I turned to her and pulled that shirt up in the back to grab her ass with both hands.

"What the fuck? Seriously?"

She laughed and covered her face with her hands. "Didn't you hear it? When we both came? Together?" She was almost shy when she said that and I was charmed even more by this facet of her.

"I'm afraid I was out of my mind at that particular moment and did not hear anything."

"There was a loud groan," she started.

I nodded and said, "That was you."

She pushed at my chest and I pulled her back toward me.

"No! It was the world. It felt like the world groaned around us and then stopped."

We stared at each other in the dim light of the living room and I remembered the first time kissing her here. And I did it again. I would have taken her again right there on the daybed, but Vivienne stopped me with, "We need to figure this out, first."

She tugged my hand back toward the bedroom. "Let's get dressed and eat and think about it."

I protested that it was dark outside and we probably should be having sex in the dark and then sleeping, but she ignored me and after she washed up in the bathroom, she was dressed in her pajamas and a robe. I did the same.

I found some candles in the hallway drawer and we lit them to use in the kitchen. Vivienne served us some soup that was still warm with some of her homemade bread with butter, and I thought my life could not get any better than that. I stared at her in the candlelight.

"I did see a sort of cloud around us with some sparkles," I said. "Right after."

Her eyes widened.

"Yeah," I said. "I thought it was weird, but I was still on top of you and that was more interesting."

"More interesting than a cloud with sparkles? In your bedroom?"

"So much more interesting," I said.

We ate our soup for a minute.

I remembered something then. "There's this urban legend among witches…"

She waited, knowing an explanation was coming.

"An urban legend is a tall tale that people tell that may have some basis in reality, but then again, could be entirely made up. I was just thinking about this one story that claims that two witches of immense power could knock out electrical grids if they climaxed at the same time."

Her eyebrows lowered as she contemplated that possibly true or entirely false fact.

I took a sip of water. "We may have blacked out the entire metro area. That's something to consider for next time."

Vivienne said with a straight face, "What makes you think there's going to be a next time?"

I frowned at her. "Oh, there'll be a next time. I'm thinking within the next five or ten minutes."

We ate some more. Then I set my spoon down decisively and said, "It's next time."

She squealed when I threw her over my shoulder and took off down the hall.

"Try not to knock out the lights at the White House this time, kitten."

CHAPTER FORTY-SIX

Vivienne

December 20th, 2024

Adam's investigator had located Gerald McEntire. Apparently, Isabelle's friend from college had not wanted to be found. He had disappeared after a first attempt at communication and only agreed to meet with us when Isabelle's name was mentioned.

Adam and I held hands as we walked into the senior living home. Grant was clearly pleased with our new relationship, as I assumed Isabelle would be as well.

We were happy, too. There's nothing like new love. At any age, it's intoxicating. Appetite decreases. Stamina increases. Thoughts race and spiral and regularly return to the loved one and when you will see him again. How it will be when you do. Adam and I were as smitten with each other as any teenagers ever were.

Isabelle took in our clasped hands, and a smile blossomed over her face. "Vivienne! It's so good to see you! It looks like you conquered this son of mine. Thank God. He's never looked so content."

Adam leaned down to kiss her cheek. "What makes you think she conquered me? I could have conquered her."

She was skeptical. "Did you?"

Grant piped in from behind us, "No. He did not. Vivienne is definitely the conqueror in that relationship."

Adam smiled and shrugged his shoulders in agreement.

I hugged Isabelle and whispered in her ear, "I'm the lucky one."

We sat together on stools behind Isabelle's recliner. Gerald had said yes to a Facetime call with us and at the agreed upon time his face came into view on Isabelle's computer we had positioned in front of her. Someone was helping Gerald to fix his computer so he could see us all and we waited while he dismissed the person and turned back to his screen. He appeared to be in a study with bookshelves behind him and a fireplace to his left. Gerald was a handsome man with a head full of gray hair and sparkling blue eyes.

He smiled. "Hello, Isabelle. It's lovely to see you."

She said, "You as well, Gerald. Thank you so much for taking the time. My son needs some of your knowledge and I knew you would be willing to talk to him if you knew that."

"Anything for you," he said.

They took a moment to see each other. "You look so young, Gerald," she said. "Time has barely touched you."

Indeed, he did look younger than her. Maybe twenty or thirty years younger.

"It's a side effect," he said.

"Of your time travel?" Grant spoke up from his place in our back row.

Isabelle said, "That's my grandson, Grant. His father, my son, Adam," she pointed to him. "And this is Vivienne. She is here from the past."

Gerald's eyebrows raised at that.

I spoke up then. "I came here from London in the year 1502."

We were all quiet for a moment to allow that to sink in. The enormity of the years separating us from that time.

"It was an accident. I need to know how to get back. I have a granddaughter that needs me."

He wrinkled his brow. Gerald seemed worried.

"I..." he paused. Starting again, he said, "I have never spoken of this to anyone else. Not of my own traveling. I've done a thorough study of the theory of time travel in my life and have conversed with many scholars on the topic. But never have I met anyone else who claims to have done it. Not witches or mortals. This has been a solitary pursuit for me."

He leaned forward. "Tell me how you did it."

I cast a side glance at Adam and he gave a nod. "I was touching a manuscript from my time that my father had illustrated. He was a gifted artist. I believe he was also a witch." I watched for his response to that.

"That was unusual for your time." He confirmed my belief.

"Yes," I said. "I think he used magic in his art. I think that when I ran my hand over one of his illustrations, it brought me to the manuscript in this time. Is that possible?"

"Yes."

We all sat for a moment with that.

"Why, then, did it not work when I did the same thing here in 2024?"

He said, "When did you try? You would not have been able to do it again right away. Did you not feel a weakening when you landed here? There is a complete re-ordering of cells. It takes many weeks to recover to your previous state of power."

I remembered back to that time and realized he was correct. That first night at Adam's, I was so tired I fell asleep immediately upon lying down.

He asked, "How long have you been gone?"

Adam responded, "Six months."

Gerald sat back, deep in thought. "I have not been gone that long," he said.

Adam got straight to the point for me. "Is it possible for her to go back and what can she expect?"

Gerald sat back up straight. "I think it is very possible she could do it in reverse. What you can expect, Vivienne, is that you will look a little younger. Maybe a few years for that amount of time gone. You can try to explain it by saying you had a great rest. But I would be very careful about standing out in any way in your time. The fear of witches and witchcraft was so strong." He was right about that. "And this is just what I know from my own travels. Your magic may work differently."

I said, "Is it as simple as just touching the manuscript again in the same place?"

He shook his head. "Nothing about time travel is simple. Every aspect is complicated. Intention is key to any trip. Your mind needs to ask clearly to go to a very specific time and place. For me, I also need an anchor to that particular time to get myself there. My anchor to the present day is always a current coin. At the very worst, I will travel back to the date on the coin, which would be within the year I left."

I must have appeared as worried as I felt because he tried to reassure me. "The manuscript is your anchor to *then*. But you'll need to be extremely precise in your request of your magic. Specify the exact date. The exact place. And for you, the time of day would be key. You would not want to show up in front of anyone."

We all grimaced at that, agreeing that timing was indeed key.

Grant piped up again. "Gerald... where have you been?"

Gerald said, "Perhaps you'd like to read my historical novels someday, young man? I have several series. Under a pen name, of course. Look for Alternate Histories with Jerry Spangenberg."

Isabelle chuckled. "You made his day, Gerald."

"And what about you, Isabelle? How have you been? Are you married? Any other children?"

"My husband died over ten years ago. We had just one son, Adam. And then we were blessed with Grant for a grandson. It's been a wonderful life."

Gerald said, "I'm glad." And then, "I missed out on that."

I asked him, "Was that your choice?"

"Yes," he said. "I only recently perfected my traveling. There were times I accidentally left this time for the past and had difficulty returning. Now I always have a coin. But when I came back, I looked younger. I had to explain the sudden absences... it was too hard to keep friends without a good excuse for all that change. And my family is gone."

He turned serious. "You should be careful too, Vivienne. This is a magic many would pay for, or even worse. Some might kill for this."

Adam said, "We're not advertising it."

Gerald said, "Good. Vivienne, you should also try hard not to effect any real change in the past. Don't bring any sort of modernity into the past. Other than a coin, of course, should you choose to use one."

Grant leaned over and looked pointedly at Adam, who rolled his eyes.

Adam had one more question. "What can she take back with her? Could she bring a person?"

I think we all held our breath, waiting for his answer.

Gerald shook his head. He spoke to Adam with some sympathy. "I don't think so. I don't know for certain. But when I travel, even though I don't understand it, I feel like I am using my magic." In other words, if you do not have that magic, you will not be traveling. More silence from our group.

Grant stepped in with, "Gerald, thank you so much for helping us to get Vivienne home. We may have more questions. Would you be willing to talk again?"

"Of course," he said. "It was a joy to see you again, Isabelle. Please visit sometime if you are ever in London."

She laughed. "I think I should extend that invitation to you, Gerald. You seem more likely to be traveling the world these days than I am."

He said, "And best of luck to you, Vivienne."

"Thank you," I said.

Adam squeezed my hand as Grant shut down Isabelle's computer.

He would have left his modern life for me. We all knew it.

I squeezed his hand back. This had been hard. Realizing that my own blood, my own magic was likely the key to my time travel, not the manuscript. I knew we had both held some hope that with his great store of power, Adam would somehow be able to withstand a trip through time and go back with me. But it was not to be.

I'd be making the trip on my own.

CHAPTER FORTY-SEVEN

Adam

December 21st, 2024

The sheik's man contacted Maria to let me know that they were here and ready to meet. Maria called me at the hospital to tell me.

"Does Vivienne want to do this?" she asked. "She was weak afterwards when she did it on the street."

I heard the concern in her voice and felt the same concern building in me. I was rebelling against the idea of her putting herself in danger again. If the woman was sick enough to need this kind of last ditch effort, then what would it do to Vivienne to heal her of it?

"She insists," I said. "Tell them tonight at 8:00. My place."

Maria hesitated. "Should I come?" Then, "Should Grant?" Grant had filled her in on everything and I was glad. I knew they were dating again, but neither one had spoken to me about it, so I wasn't about to bring it up. I just hoped it lasted this time. "Yes, both of you come over. We could probably use all the help we can get."

When I was done charting, I sat in my office and called Connie.

"Hey! What's up?" she asked.

"The sheik is in town. Vivienne's going to help his wife. Tonight at my house. Do you want to come?"

I heard her intake of breath.

"Yes. Of course I want to be there. What time?"

"8:00. Come early if you can."

She said, "I can. I will. Do you need anything?" I told her no.

Then I shut off my computer and gathered my things to go home to Vivienne. To see if she would have me once more in bed before the world needed her again.

She was asleep when I got there. On the daybed. Reading a history of the world textbook. "Tsk, tsk, tsk..." I muttered. "Grant will get you for this." I pulled the book off her lap and gathered her in my arms to take her to our bed. She woke up and gave me a sleepy smile. I laid her on the bed and undressed her so she could feel the soft sheets. Pulling the heavy white comforter over top of her, I said, "Enjoy your nap, kitten. The sheik is coming tonight with his wife."

"No," she reached out a hand and put it on my pillow, but she sounded tired, so I tickled her palm and closed the door softly behind me.

Vivienne was still in bed when Connie arrived. I let her in and she made herself at home in the kitchen. I closed the bedroom door behind me and went to wake Vivienne but she was already awake. She smiled like she had a secret when I entered.

"What do we have here?" I said. She flipped the covers back and revealed her legs spread with her hand between them.

I took a sharp breath in. "What the fuck..." I locked the door.

"Take your pants off and sit down," she said. Her eyes went to the large leather chair in the corner of the room.

I said, "Connie's here. People will be here any time," while I one hundred percent obeyed her and dropped my pants and kicked off my shoes. She dug around in the drawer and squirted some lube in her hand. Rubbing them together, she walked to me and motioned for me to sit down in the chair. The leather was cold on my ass, and the lube was cold on my dick and I'd take that or anything in the world, really, to have that woman ready for me.

She sat herself down slowly, taking me in inch by inch, and when she had taken all of me her eyes closed and she was still for a moment. I held my breath. My hands on her hips were the only thing keeping me from losing my mind altogether.

"I've wanted this all day," she breathed.

I usually liked to control things in the bedroom, but she was fucking perfect.

"Take what you need, kitten." I ran my hands up her rib cage then, over her perfect breasts, and I rolled her nipples roughly. She gasped at that sensation and sat back to let me pinch them harder, her head thrown back and her hair cascading down over my legs. I pushed up into her, and she began to rock back and forth on my lap. "Oh my god..." I managed. "Fuck. You feel so good."

As she moved, the sounds she made spun me out of control. My eyes swept from her elegant throat, over her breasts, her beautiful stomach, to where we were joined.

I touched her there and she raised her head to look at me. Her hair was wild, her eyes dark and determined.

"You're a fucking goddess," I said. She smiled and began to push up and down off her knees nesting around my lap.

When she came down, I thrust up. We were rough on each other. She put her hands on the back of the chair and rode me harder. I felt her clench around me and knew it would be soon.

"Vivienne," I ground out. "We *cannot* come together again." I felt her give a silent laugh at that. I said, "You come first." I stroked her clit hard and fast the way she liked and just a minute later she gave a strangled cry when she came.

"That's it," I said, approving of every single second of that interlude. She collapsed around me, trembling.

I couldn't wait and thrust up into her then with my own release. She captured the sound I made with her mouth, and we kissed like that until I stopped spurting inside of her. We rested then, my hands moving up and down her back, our hearts pounding.

"Sex is also good cardio," I managed to get out.

She lowered her head to my chest and dissolved in laughter.

"Oh, Adam. I think the word for that is...lame? Is it lame?"

"What?" I said as she pulled away and stood up.

"It's not lame if it's a fact. I'm just saying this is an activity we should engage in more often for our health."

She shook her head at me over her shoulder on the way to the bathroom. I watched her ass sway as she walked away and thought, not for the first time, that I was in serious trouble.

I held my hands up. "I'm just thinking of you!"

She closed the door as I sat there with my dick out and boxers around my feet. Totally unraveled. Completely undone. Hopelessly in love with a woman who would be leaving me soon, probably forever.

I washed up after Vivienne did and found her in the kitchen with Connie swapping stories about obstinate children. Connie was saying, "Grant hated that class so much we had to bring in Isabelle to get him straight."

"Home Economics?" I said.

They both laughed. "God, yes," Connie said. "He was willing to throw away his whole GPA to ditch that class."

I said, "I know. Mom told him girls would like a man who knew how to cook and he turned it around."

The doorbell rang. Vivienne's power surged and then receded. I patted her on the head and said. "Good girl." She swatted at my hand, but I was already on my way to get the door.

The sheik was not what I expected. He was young, maybe 35 or 40, in an expensive suit. He held the arm of his wife, a beautiful woman with a green scarf over her head. She was too thin and had dark circles under her eyes. I recognized by the pallor of her skin that she was someone who had been through too much chemotherapy.

"Come in," I said and made way for them. "I'm Dr. Adam Parrish," I pointed to Connie and Vivienne in the hallway. "This is Dr. Connie Jewell, and this is Vivienne Lanier. She is who you came to see."

The man said, "I am Sheik Farhad Al-Masri. This is my wife, Nora."

Vivienne stepped forward and took Nora's hand. "Hello, please have a seat." She pointed to the living room.

When we were all seated and Vivienne had offered refreshments that were politely declined, Farhad said to Vivienne, "I want to thank you for seeing us. I understand your terms that we should not expect a miracle. But, of course, we are always hopeful."

Nora said to Vivienne, "And we obviously want to compensate you for this help. Anything you ask."

Vivienne said, "I only ask that you offer your help to my friend Adam, whenever he may need it."

Farhad nodded. He said to me, "You will have it."

"Why did you send men to abduct Vivienne?" I wanted to say this to him in private. I wanted to slap him around and ask him what the fuck he thought he was doing, sending persuaders to work on Vivienne and Maria and my son. But he was here with his sick wife and I knew my being an asshole was not going to go over well with this crowd.

He had the decency to look ashamed. "Please accept my apology. I was out of my mind that day. I was wrong to do so." I gave him a dissatisfied look and moved on to his wife.

"Nora, can you give us more information about your cancer? Where and when did it begin? What treatments have you had?"

Nora seemed beat. I was sorry I had addressed her and glad when it was her husband who replied. "She was diagnosed with stage four ovarian cancer six months ago. She's been through four rounds of chemotherapy and it has metastasized to her stomach and possibly her lungs. We don't know where else." Farhad took his wife's hand in his.

Grant and Maria were entering the hallway then, and I made introductions again. I explained that we would work in the backyard. We made our way through the kitchen to the back porch and down those steps to the back yard. Once there, I asked Grant to stand by in case I needed him to help with the cloaking of us all. If Vivienne needed me, I wanted to be ready.

It was a cold but beautiful night. The air was crisp and the smell of fires from my neighbors' fireplaces distracted me. I wished I was taking Vivienne for a walk after dinner, holding her hand all the way. I worried that this session would drain her and make her effort to return to her granddaughter even more dangerous. More than anything, I wished that it was all over.

Vivienne guided Nora to one of two lawn chairs. She had carried a soft, beige blanket from the living room and she spread it over one of the chairs. She had Nora recline on it. Vivienne sat on her own chair and her look told me she was ready to begin. I said to the group, "I'm going to cloak us now." I raised the illusion over and around us. While I knew this magic was rare, Farhad didn't even react. He might have someone on his payroll who could do the same. But that was no time to collect information about magic.

Vivienne spoke to Farhad. He bent down and kissed his wife and said something to her in Arabic. She took his hand and kissed it. He reluctantly took a few steps backward. Farhad stood in a line with Grant, Maria and Connie. I stood on the other side with a clear view of Vivienne.

Vivienne laid her hands on Nora's chest. She had done this with Emily too, helping her to sleep before beginning. We had discussed the possibility of this cancer having metastasized and how she could handle it. I hoped Vivienne would stop if she felt it was too much, but knowing her, I doubted that would happen. My mind was racing. I'd seen her do this before, but it was still so nerve-wracking I found myself clenching my fists.

One minute passed. Vivienne's brows drew together. Two minutes passed. Her breathing became labored. Her face had a slight glimmer of sweat. I wanted to intervene. Why hadn't we talked about a signal that I should look for in case she was in trouble? Nora continued to breathe normally and appeared to be at ease. Another minute passed. Vivienne suddenly slumped over and slid off the chair.

"Grant!" I yelled for him to take over the cloaking. I lifted Vivienne and held her in my arms. She was hot. Burning up.

"Grant," I said in a lower voice. "Just cloak us now. Just Vivienne and me."

He did, and we were immediately in our own private space.

"Vivienne," I squeezed her a little. "Tell me what to do." I wanted to run her in the house and sit her in a cool bath. But there was no time for that. There was no time for anything.

Vivienne, what should I do?

I kissed her forehead and laid her down on the grass. Her pulse was weak. Her beautiful face had lost its color. I'd seen this so many times. In the last moments of a human life, time seems like it slows down. But I knew for a fact that those last seconds were flying by.

I prayed to God. *Please show me how to help her. Please let her live through this. Please.*

Then I did the only thing I could think to do. I began to take her power. Slowly, because she was already dying, so slowly and carefully. When I felt it coursing through my veins, I stopped. I hoped just a jolt of this might be enough to wake her. Enough for her to take over and rid herself of the cancer inside. I laid my hands on her chest and prayed again that God would show me how to heal her with her own magic. I imagined her magic flowing from my hands into her body. I imagined a waterfall of healing magic. Incredibly, I felt it leave me and pour into her.

Her eyes opened. She took a deep breath in.

"Get rid of that cancer, Vivienne."

She sat up then and I helped her to stand. I held her up with her back to me. She raised her arms and screamed as two rays of red shot into the sky. An enormous jolt of energy pushed me back a step. When it stopped, she collapsed and I gathered her up in my arms. I stepped out of Grant's cloaking then to the amazement of the rest of the people in my backyard. Farhad had his arms around a healthy Nora and everyone stared at us with wide eyes.

"Good to see you feeling better, Nora," I said. "Vivienne is done for the night. I'm taking her to sleep. Everybody come back tomorrow."

Carrying Vivienne into the house, I made my way to my room and laid her in the bed. I took off her clothes and pulled the comforter over her creamy white shoulder. I undressed myself down to my tee shirt and briefs and crawled in behind her. I scooped her close to me and breathed in her hair.

"Vivienne."

She didn't stir.

"Vivienne," I shook her slightly. "Are you healing yourself?"

"Yes," she said, barely audible.

"I love you," I whispered in her ear.

"I love you, too," she whispered back.

Listening to her breathe, I placed my hand on her heart, feeling it beat.

Willing it to beat.

Chapter Forty-Eight

Vivienne

December 22nd, 2024

I awoke in the dark with Adam behind me, his arm flung over my waist. I tried to review the events from the night before but found that some parts of the evening were just blank. I must have passed out while freeing Nora of her cancer.

It occurred to me that was a significant flaw in the process. I would have to always have backup, but even then, what could they do? I was too committed to the cure to leave the job unfinished. If I attempted to rid someone again of a cancer that far advanced...it would be the end of me.

Unless my backup person was Adam. Adam's will to save me... I knew how great that would be because I would do the same for him. I did a quick scan of myself and Adam and was relieved to find no cancer. Nora should be free of it too, but I desperately wanted to see her, to be sure. I did remember sending the cancer to the sky. It was so much. So heavy. I gave a small groan, remembering the taking in of that disease and the excruciating process of releasing it. Adam pulled me to him and whispered, "Are you awake?"

"Yes," I whispered back and pulled his arm closer to me. He squeezed me and hopped out of bed to come around to my side. Handing me a cup of water he said, "Drink." He put on slippers while he watched me drink it. Kissing my forehead, he said, "I'll be right back."

When he returned, he turned on the lamp and I saw that he had brought a tray with cups of steaming hot tea and two chocolate croissants on a festive Christmas plate.

"My favorite!" Sitting up, I pulled the covers up over my chest and he set the tray in front of me. He came around and sat on the bed next to me and watched as I ate both croissants in record time. He didn't speak.

"Was one of those for you?" I asked, taking the last bite. He smiled and shook his head no, wiping a crumb from my mouth.

"What are you looking at?" I asked him.

"How are you feeling?" he asked.

I took a sip of tea. "Do you mean how does it feel that some of my magic is gone?"

He remained still.

"It feels fine."

"Really?" he asked.

"What you did for me worked. Nothing else would have worked. And my magic is not diminished. I always have more after I heal someone." I touched his hand. "Thank you."

"You were dying. I didn't know what else to do. I would never steal your magic, Vivienne. Please know that."

"Of course I know that," I said. "You saved my life." I squeezed his hand to reassure him. "How do *you* feel?"

"I feel incredible." He shook his head. "Shit, Vivienne. If we could bottle your magic, we'd be the richest people on Earth." He brought my hand to his lips and kissed it. "Do you think it'll stay with me?" he asked.

"I have no idea," I said. "Think of when you've gained magic from others. Does that stay?"

"It does," he said. "Do you think it will replenish like yours does?"

I raised an eyebrow. "I think we should check that out, don't you?"

The doorbell rang and Adam scrambled to put on pants and a shirt to go answer it. I got dressed as well and joined him in the living room, where Farhad and Nora sat on the couch. Farhad said to me, "I'm sorry for coming so early."

I shushed him. "It's fine. We were awake."

Adam was taking Nora's pulse. "Your pulse is good." He said. "You look wonderful. How do you feel?"

"I feel reborn," she said with tears in her eyes. Farhad was crying too, and he stood to hug me.

"How can I ever tell you what you have done for us? For me? Thank you."

I squeezed him tight. "I'm so happy for you both. I want to check Nora, is that all right?"

He stood back and allowed me to sit on the other side of her. I placed my hand on hers and did a quick check. She was cancer free, and I told her so. Her tears fell in earnest then and Adam brought out his trusty tissue box for both Nora and Farhad to use.

Then Farhad asked the big question. "Are you the only person who can heal like this?"

Adam answered. "Vivienne is the only one, and it's a secret that cannot be shared." He looked Farhad in the eye. "No one can ever know what she is able to do. It's too dangerous for her to attempt removing this much cancer again. She's going away, so the world will not ask her to."

There was no negotiation in Adam's tone. Farhad got the message and replied, "Nora and I are grateful you granted us this miracle. I can't work miracles, but I will happily do whatever it is you need, Vivienne. If it is within my power, it is yours. Forever."

After they left, Adam took me back to bed. We disrobed and Adam laid down first.

"My turn," I said. "Put your hands away."

"I think you also had the last turn but okay." He placed both of his hands under his head on the pillow and kept his eyes on me as I touched him.

Starting sweet and slow, I ran my hands over his muscled chest, down over his stomach and then over each of his legs. I was not ready to name what I was doing, but I knew it. I was learning him by heart. Every ridge of muscle, every scar. Taking inventory of a man I would not have much longer. I rubbed both of his feet for a minute and he made a low sound of appreciation. On my way back up his body I cupped him and kissed the tip of his erection.

"Get up here," he said and pulled me up to lay on his body. I kissed his mouth gently and, as ever, our tender kisses became fast and fevered. When he couldn't wait any longer, Adam rolled me over so that his body was on top. He breathed, "I need..." then he entered me. I felt the pressure in the room shift at the rightness of it. He made a surprised noise, and I knew he felt it too.

Running my hands from his forearms to his shoulders and then back down over them again, I said, "Should we stop the world again?"

He gave a short laugh. Then we both let our magic loose and the feeling of it —his power reaching for mine, mine answering. Our magic was inseparable. As were we.

Holding my arms above my head and clasping his fingers through mine, he stilled for a moment and looked down at me. His beautiful brown eyes roamed over my features and my hair. He said, "How are you mine?"

I squeezed his hands and said, "You were quite the surprise, too." I raised my hips in invitation. He smiled, sudden and unguarded, and released my hands. Then he gathered me in his arms and began to move. He was not gentle.

I loved that Adam knew I wanted it and that I could take it. That he knew me like that...it was what we both had needed. To be known so thoroughly by another was a gift.

I did not let myself think about what came after. I gave myself instead to the feeling of Adam —the fullness of him moving inside me, the warmth and the weight of him above me. The sounds he made without knowing he made them. *God...* breathed against my neck. *So good...* said to himself. *Yes...* when I moved beneath him in a way that pleased us both. This man who commanded every room he entered, utterly lost. And I had done that. The knowledge of it sent a rush of desire through me so acute it was almost pain.

I gripped his waist as he thrust into me over and over, his eyes on mine. I was close and told him, "Now, Adam. I'm coming now." I closed my eyes, but he took my chin in his hand and said, "Look at me."

We watched each other then as we both came apart. I heard the power shut down again at that moment. I knew Adam did too because when we stopped trembling and he lay on top of me, gently stroking my arm, he said, "They'll be fine. It's daytime."

I laughed, and he joined me. Rolling off me, Adam rubbed a hand over his eyes. "Urban legend confirmed. I guess we need a better plan." I glanced around the room and saw remnants of sparkles like the ones he told me about the first time we were together.

"We made sparkles again."

He turned to his side and looked at me. "And I bet there are rainbows above us."

We smiled at each other.

"Let's take a shower and get dressed," he said. "I'm taking you out for lunch. And shopping."

Adam drove us to an area called Georgetown, which was full of beautiful shops decorated for Christmas. When I protested that I couldn't buy his present with him standing next to me, he gave me a credit card and told me I had one hour and that the card would let me spend fifty thousand dollars.

I said, "Adam. That's ridiculous."

"Fine," he said. "But I'm going to be very disappointed if you don't spend at least ten thousand."

"I think I could buy shelter for many people for that much."

That stopped him in his tracks. He pulled me into an embrace on that city sidewalk and smoothed the hair away from my face.

"Is that what you want for Christmas? To help unsheltered people? We can buy a building. Downtown. You can run it. I'll do it today."

I pulled his face down to me for a kiss.

"Not yet," I whispered to him. "But I do want that. Thank you."

He knew I couldn't commit to anything because I had to leave him soon and the small smile he gave me did not reach his eyes.

Tony walked with me and Caleb went with Adam. In my hour of shopping, I found a beautiful black cardigan sweater for

Maria, made of the softest yarn. For Grant, I found a book about nuns in the middle ages and one about illuminated manuscripts like my father's.

And for Adam, I spent the most. In the same clothing shop where I bought Maria's sweater, I saw one for men that tempted me. It was dark blue with buttons and so soft to the touch. I envisioned Adam hanging it in the hallway and putting it on in the evenings when he sat in his living room or on his porch. I could wear it and leave some of my scent for him. I bought the sweater.

In the jewelry store next door, I saw a beautiful gold band for a man with diamonds gracing the top. Tony was impressed with my choice and gave me a thumbs up. I had the salesclerk wrap it in gold paper and ribbons. I wanted Adam to remember me when he wore it. It wasn't kind of me to do so. He would have been better off if he could forget. But I knew I would never forget him and, selfishly, I didn't want him to ever forget me.

CHAPTER FORTY-NINE

Adam

December 23rd, 2024

There was finally a rainy day where I was off and could have Vivienne all to myself. My plan was breakfast and then back to bed. We were just finishing up on the daybed in the study, so Vivienne could watch the rain. She leaned against my chest. I recited to her Shakespeare's sonnet eighteen, stopping every other line to kiss her.

"Shall I compare thee to a summer's day?" – a kiss to her cheekbone. *"Thou art more lovely and more temperate."* – a kiss to her lips.

Vivienne sighed. "Do you think he's called the Bard in my time, too?"

I looked at her askance. "No!" I squeezed her tighter. "You do not go looking for Shakespeare! He's a cad. Definitely to be avoided at all costs." She laughed at me.

Grant came in the front door and set his umbrella down in the hall.

"Grant, can you believe this cruel woman is going to her time to find Shakespeare to bed? Next thing you know, there'll be a whole new group of Shakespeare sonnets 'For Vivienne'!"

He gave a soft laugh. "She deserves them. But aren't they like, a hundred years apart or something?" He came in and sat in one of the chairs, pulling it around to face us.

"I have the results," he said. "I got them today." He looked at me to see if I was ready to explain this to Vivienne.

I sat us both up and turned her to me. "After we talked to Gerald, I had a hunch that I asked Grant to look into for me. Connie has been checking for a match to your DNA. She was held up because she needed somebody in her office to be gone when she did it. Since they hadn't done it yet, I asked Grant to get Connie to check into Gerald's DNA, too. Did she?"

"They're related." He looked at Vivienne. "Gerald is a distant relative of yours."

Her jaw dropped. "Gerald. Is my relative?"

He nodded. "Yes, the match is very good. There is almost one hundred percent certainty that he is descended from you in some way."

I was silent.

She cupped my face. "This means that the time traveling is definitely tied to me. To my DNA. My magic."

"Yes," I said. *This also means you will be leaving.*

Vivienne gave me a quick kiss. "You brilliant man."

Then, all business, she said, "Grant, I need to speak to him again. Can you get him on the computer? What time is it there?"

This is happening too fast. She's going to leave me, and soon.

Grant took one look at my face and figured out I was having an internal meltdown.

"Yes, I can get Gerald. But I think you may need to deal with him first," he pointed at me. "I'll go make coffee and get the laptop set up in the kitchen."

When we were alone, Vivienne pushed me back on the pillows and laid on my chest. She propped herself up on both arms and gave me a small smile. I couldn't help cataloging each of her features. Her finely arched brows, her thick eyelashes, those light gray eyes with their dark ring. I rubbed my thumb over her soft cheek and her luscious lips. She reached up and lightly drew a finger over my temple and down my cheek. When she ran it over my mouth, I felt her begin to soothe me and I caught her hand with my own, raising it back to my lips for a kiss.

"Don't heal me," I said. "Don't."

She kept her hand in mine but did not soothe me with her magic.

"Losing you should hurt," I said. "I want it to hurt."

She laid her head on my chest, and I stroked her long silky hair.

"I need you to stay through Christmas Eve," I said.

She nodded yes, and I felt her tears as they fell.

The Passionate Shepherd to His Love
Christopher Marlowe (1599)

Come live with me and be my love,
And we will all the pleasures prove,
That Valleys, groves, hills, and fields,
Woods, or steepy mountain yields.
And we will sit upon the Rocks,
Seeing the Shepherds feed their flocks,
By shallow Rivers to whose falls
Melodious birds sing Madrigals.
And I will make thee beds of Roses
And a thousand fragrant posies,
A cap of flowers, and a kirtle
Embroidered all with leaves of Myrtle;
A gown made of the finest wool
Which from our pretty Lambs we pull;
Fair lined slippers for the cold,
With buckles of the purest gold;
A belt of straw and Ivy buds,
With Coral clasps and Amber studs:
And if these pleasures may thee move,
Come live with me, and be my love.
The Shepherds' Swains shall dance and sing
For thy delight each May-morning:
If these delights thy mind may move,
Then live with me, and be my love.

Chapter Fifty

Vivienne

December 24th, 2024

It was the day of Christmas Eve. Adam said he wanted to take me to a church service. I dressed carefully, in the white lace dress Maria had provided and low-heeled leather shoes the color of bare skin. I arranged sparkly combs in my hair and looked at myself in the mirror.

Being in love had changed me. There was a peace in my eyes. Whether he was with me or not, I would always have the knowledge that a man like Adam had loved me with his whole heart.

He wore a dark suit tailored perfectly to his broad shoulders with a crisp white shirt beneath. He never gave a thought to how he looked and never needed to. Adam was the most handsome man in any room he entered, and he had eyes only for me. When I came out of the bedroom, he grabbed the nape of my neck with one hand, anchored his other arm around my waist and bent me backward in a kiss. I fisted my hand in his hair and kissed him back wholeheartedly.

Grant cleared his throat from the hallway. "We're here. In case anybody wondered." We continued the kissing, and I heard Maria's laugh.

"Adam," I tapped his arm.

He lifted me to a standing position. "To be continued," he said.

Grabbing keys from the hallway dish, Adam said to Grant, "Is your mother coming?"

"No, she had to work," Grant said, "but she sends her best."

As Adam locked the door and we all walked down the front steps, Grant asked, "What about Marsh?"

"Yes, he'll be there," Adam said and gave Grant the car keys. "You drive."

I thought it was nice that they all worshipped together at Christmas.

In the car, Adam kept his hand on my leg and said he had a surprise for me.

"What is it?" I asked.

"Something from your time to make you feel at home at Christmas," he said.

Fifteen minutes later, I saw what he meant when we pulled up the driveway to a massive cathedral. It had elegant white spires and towers and intricate carvings on every surface. It rivaled any church in London in sheer size and beauty. He pointed out the gargoyles as we walked up the pathway and I thought of John, who would have known every one of them by name. I wished he could see them.

When we entered the main hall, the organ was already playing—that familiar, enormous sound filling every inch of the vaulted space above us. Winter light poured through the stained-glass windows in rivers of color I had seen before, in another century, in other churches. And then the choir joined it, voices rising with words I knew and melodies I had sung in another life.

Adam watched my face as I took it in. "Do you like it?" he asked, as if he'd had it built just for me.

"Yes." My head spun from side to side, trying to take it in. "It's magnificent."

"The service starts in twenty minutes," he said. "Come with me, I want to show you something else." He pulled me gently toward a small chapel to the right that was empty of any congregants. We walked to the front altar, and Adam offered me a seat in a pew. He dropped to one knee then in front of me and I stared at him in surprise. He took my hands in his.

"I wish your father were here for me to ask him for your hand in marriage. I would," he said. "I would tell him that God made you and I for each other. That you and I were so inevitable that we found each other through time. I would promise him that I would love you forever, no matter how near or far apart we are. For all my days, Vivienne, I will be yours. Will you be mine? Will you marry me?"

He reached into his pocket and pulled out a small box, which he opened and held out to me. It was a delicate silver band. I held one hand to my face and picked the ring out with the other.

"Look inside," he prompted. In a beautiful script it read, 'A loves V, 12.24.'

"No year," he smiled. "That could be problematic."

He was keeping me safe. Even five hundred years away.

"Yes," I said. "Of course I will marry you."

We both stood, and he pulled me up off my feet to kiss me and spin me around. I heard clapping and cheering from the hallway and saw that Marsh had arrived with Isabelle and they all stood watching Adam's proposal. He slid the ring on my finger. I widened my eyes at him. "What if I had turned you down?"

"Not possible," he said. "Let's go to this service and then get ourselves married."

And we did. During the church service, I was full to the brim. The entire time I held Adam's hand, leaned on his arm, and thanked God for this gift. During our vows, when the priest asked us to exchange rings, I went back to the pew, fumbled in my purse and got out a box for Adam to open. His smile when he opened it would be forever how I remembered him.

"Do you like it?" I whispered.

"I love it," he said. I placed it on his finger.

And then he kissed me, and we were husband and wife. *At least we had this day. At least we will have this night.*

Adam took us all to a celebratory early dinner. We laughed and toasted our union and everyone, even strangers, wished us well. When they did, I saw a flicker of sadness in Adam's eyes, which he quickly dispelled by kissing me and squeezing me tight. I could not keep my hands off him. Knowing I would soon not have him near, I held onto his arm and couldn't let it go.

When we finally made it home, Adam picked me up in his arms and carried me over the threshold. I laughed as he did and he said, "Be quiet, kitten. It's your honeymoon night. I'm going to do this right."

He closed and locked the front door and pushed me up against it. Then he cradled my head and kissed me until my knees were weak.

We shed our clothes on the way to the bedroom. Our touch at first was soft, slow, erotic. He laid me down on my stomach and ran his fingers over my body, feather-light caresses down my arms and my legs that made me shiver. Then he kneeled over me, his legs on either side of my body, as he massaged my shoulders, my back, my buttocks and my legs. When he came to the base of my spine, he lowered his head and gave me a gentle kiss there. "I love this place," he murmured, almost to himself. He gave me a light caress there.

His hands felt safe.

All the while he praised me and claimed each part of my body as his own.

Adam turned me over and saw a single tear roll down the side of my face. He wiped away the trail of it with his thumb.

"Happy or sad?"

I said, "You have to ask?"

He covered me with his body then and gave me a tight squeeze. He kissed the shell of my ear, then my cheekbones and the tip of my nose.

"Both," he whispered.

For a while there was no more conversation between us. Just murmurs as we loved each other slowly, deliberately, making it last. When my climax came, he watched my face and I didn't hide from him how he moved me. And then I watched him above me, full of need, desperate to keep me but knowing he could not.

We held each other then, and Adam whispered things in my ear, sweet things that I could take with me. He said that I was his wife. That our love would last forever. He said that I was strong and I could do anything. That I had saved him and that no one had ever loved anything as much as he loved me.

Drowsing in his arms afterward, when I felt his breathing even out, I knew it was time. I sent a wave of deep sleep over him. Then I got up and retrieved from my purse a poem I had copied for him. I placed it on the pillow where my head had rested. I dressed in the clothes I wore when I arrived in Washington, D.C., and I leaned over to kiss his lips one last time.

Before going, I stopped and let my eyes wander over Adam's study. The Christmas tree with its sparkling lights and presents underneath, the books, the daybed.

I made sure the door was locked and closed it softly behind me.

How Do I Love Thee?
Elizabeth Barrett Browning (1845)

How do I love thee? Let me count the ways.
I love thee to the depth and breadth and height
My soul can reach, when feeling out of sight
For the ends of being and ideal grace.
I love thee to the level of every day's
Most quiet need, by sun and candle-light.
I love thee freely, as men strive for right.
I love thee purely, as they turn from praise.
I love thee with the passion put to use
In my old griefs, and with my childhood's faith.
I love thee with a love I seemed to lose
With my lost saints. I love thee with the breath,
Smiles, tears, of all my life; and, if God choose,
I shall but love thee better after death.

Chapter Fifty-One

Adam

December 25th, 2024

She was gone. Even before I opened my eyes on Christmas morning, I knew.

The automatic coffee maker smelled like it had brewed me a cup of heaven. I debated whether or not I should lie in bed all day and wallow in pain or whether I should get up and face it. Since there were still sick kids who were going to need me later on, I rolled out of bed and stepped into slippers.

That's when I saw the poem on her pillow. I picked it up and read it. *How do I love thee?* By Elizabeth Barrett Browning. Written in Vivienne's beautiful cursive handwriting. I traced a finger down the page as I read. In the kitchen I kissed it, then placed it under a magnet of Monticello, next to the dinosaur I colored for her.

Pouring myself a cup of coffee, I played with the wedding band on my left hand. How would I explain that at the hospital, I wondered? I shrugged and took a sip. I'd say we had gotten married but were in a transcontinental marriage. I'd visit her in the winter, she'd visit me in the summer. That would get me at least six months.

In the living room, the Christmas presents lay under the tree, wrapped and ready to open. There was one I knew I had not wrapped. I picked it up and read the tag. 'To: Adam, From: Vivienne.' I tapped her name lightly for a moment, wondering if I had the fortitude to open this thing she had touched so recently.

I sat down on the couch and unwrapped it carefully. It was the size of a box for a shirt. I pulled the tissue apart and saw it was a sweater. A blue button up sweater. Unbelievably soft. There was a note.

"Dearest Adam, I hope you will put this on and be comforted. I hope you feel my arms around you when you wear it. Yours always, Vivienne." I pulled it up out of the box and held it to my face. She had worn it. Her scent filled my head. I took off the robe and put on the sweater.

I reached for my phone. "Grant? Merry Christmas."

"Same to you!" he said. "Maria and I were going to come over pretty soon."

"Can you do me a favor? Can you get me in to see the Manuscript?"

He hesitated. "Now?"

"Yes. Now."

I heard him turn to Maria. "We need to meet him at the Library first, then we can go over there."

"Okay," he returned to the phone. "We'll meet you. The back entrance."

Once we all reached the Library of Congress, I asked Grant to get me to the manuscript. There was a guard asleep in the front hall. When he didn't rouse at our entrance, I assumed that was Vivienne's work. We hurried to the manuscript display and saw that the glass had been smashed. It lay on the podium, open to the same illustration she had used to travel to me in the first place. The broken glass crunched under my feet as I walked closer to it.

I saw it then. To the left of the V, in the smallest writing ever... a note for me. I took my phone out and took a picture. It read, *"Though it were ten thousand mile."*

Tears filled my eyes. "She made it." I said. I turned to Grant and Maria and said louder, "She made it, and she's coming back."

After I repaired the case and the manuscript looked like it was supposed to, we went home and opened presents. Vivienne's stack stayed undisturbed under the tree. Grant and Maria did not want to leave me when afternoon turned into evening, but I said I was going to be fine. I knew Vivienne would move heaven and earth to come back and I could live with that.

Also, she had left me with a purpose. I now had the ability to heal cancer. And I was going to do everything in my power to find a way to give it to everyone. I'd need help, but I knew just the guy to do it.

January 8th, 2025

Two weeks later, Jake Rawlings and I stood before a door at the National Institute for Health. I had convinced him that I was able to draw cancer out of someone if it was small enough and early enough. I had demonstrated it twice for Jake at the Children's Hospital and he obviously knew all the details of Emily's miracle. Now we were here to pitch it to the one person who might be able to make a plan to get this ability out of me and into a vaccine or cure. I read the nameplate on the door again, Dr. Abe Goree.

When he opened his door, I confess I was both a little starstruck and intimidated. This man had guided our country through a worldwide pandemic with knowledge and grace despite all the idiocy of those in power at the beginning of it. He was also known to not suffer fools lightly, and I often wondered how he had functioned during that time.

Goree was short and wiry with a firm handshake for both of us. As we sat, Jake said, "Abe, we are here with incredible news."

Thirty minutes later and after several head shakes from Goree, we all three were on our way to demonstrate it again. Goree said, "If you are wasting my time, I will kill you both."

Jake and I agreed that would be reasonable.

Then, "Do these people even know you're experimenting on them?"

Jake said, "Of course. We have signed permission."

And lastly, "And I hope you know nobody is going to fund this kind of amateur hour adventure."

I said, "I have funding." *Thank you, Farhad. And Vivienne, for somehow knowing we'd need him.*

Goree needed to observe the procedure five times and examine the results himself and read all the medical charts front to back at least a couple of times. Even though the participants had signed an NDA, word was starting to get out about a miracle cure. When we came back a week later, he said, "I had you both checked out. You're respected physicians in your field. I can't believe I'm saying this, but it appears to be real."

He walked around his office a bit and fiddled with a blind to check out the parking lot. He examined me again. "You're going to need to be a whole lot more transparent with your methods. If this is all coming from you, from something special about you, we need to know why and how. Also," he shook his head slightly, "you need to know that half the world is going to be suspicious and accuse you of trying to insert a chip in them or trying to poison them." He sat at his desk and faced us. "I have some experience with this."

"I know you do," I said. "That's why we're here. And I have a plan to make it known how and why this is possible." I wasn't happy with it yet, but a plan had been slowly formulating in my brain.

He nodded. "Here's what you need. A trial. It has to be secret. It has to show a significant impact at the six-month post recovery mark. You should work on a cure and a vaccine."

We nodded in agreement to all of it.

Then he said, "It needs to be free."

I said, "Of course."

"The only reason I would consider this kind of insane crapshoot of an idea is that I was planning to retire, anyway. If this goes sideways, and it probably will, I'll be drawing retirement and it won't matter."

He held his hand out to me. As we shook, he said, "Let me know when your plan for transparency is in place. Then we can get to work."

Chapter Fifty-Two

Adam

January 31st, 2025

My plan for transparency involved asking the witches of the world to out themselves in order to provide a cure for cancer to the rest of the world.

It had many flaws.

Chiefly, that witches would willingly consent to spilling a secret they had kept for thousands of years. I understood how difficult it would be to give it up. It became ingrained in the very cells of your body. Every conscious thought was filtered through the question, "Is this going to reveal my secret?" Not to mention the countless death sentences imposed every year on witches who gave up the secret willingly. They were mostly new witches who couldn't get a handle on their power. Usually, they came from powerful families. Families who had used their powers to benefit themselves and create a legacy.

Witches were big on legacy. Marrying someone with equal or greater power was encouraged. That was why witches had developed the ability to let off some of their power like steam from a teapot. That way, a witch would know not to fuck with you or that it was okay to fuck with you. I remember being attracted to Connie because I could tell she was formidable. I needed that. Someone to keep the twenty-something me in check.

I thought about Grant and how he didn't let any of his power shine through, ever. When he was fourteen and came into that power, I had prepared him for what it could be like, of course. I told him he might receive several rare powers because Connie and I were both chock full of witchcraft. I told him we would be with him every step of the way and he could always ask either one of us anything.

He handled it with grace. I knew each and every one of the things he could do, and they were many. He got my persuasion and cloaking abilities. He got Connie's ability to hear the truth and her gift of telekinesis.

I loved that he did not abuse his magic. In fact, he rarely used it. Persuasion in particular was anathema to him. He could never abide the abuse of power, and persuasion was nothing but that. Grant was all the goodness in the world, a gentle, old soul from the very beginning. As I walked into the office of the International Council of Witches, I was thinking about my boy and how the decisions made on that day would affect him.

Louise Carmichael was not at the desk. That was my first clue that this day was going to be different. The new receptionist pointed me toward the boardroom where everyone was apparently waiting for me.

There was one empty seat at the huge conference table, in between Cole and Louise. She looked great, as usual, her blond hair shining in a ray of sunlight from the floor to ceiling windows overlooking the river below. She was trying to signal something to me with her eyes. Cole looked haggard, as usual. Those who couldn't get a seat at the table lined the walls of the room. Some sitting, some standing. I rolled back the empty chair and greeted the fifty or so witches in the room. "Hello, everyone. Sorry to be late. Thank you for coming today."

I sat down and looked up to meet the blue eyes of Father Andrew Barry. Sitting directly across from me. The bastard I had been trying to find for the better part of a year. He smiled.

I felt my power surge and saw everyone in the room brace in alarm.

"Hello, Adam," he said. "Or is it Samuel Marsh?"

I needed to get a hold of myself. Everything in me wanted to end that man right then and there. But I couldn't do that in a room full of witches I needed to get on my side. Killing him there would ruin everything.

Louise laid a hand on my arm and I gave a brief nod that I was okay.

"It's Adam Parrish. I think you know that."

I looked around the room. The heads of every witch council in the world were there to listen to what I had to say. Cole had done his job of wrangling them to Crystal City.

"I know you've traveled from every corner of the earth to be here, so I won't waste your time. I'm here today to let you know we've discovered a cure for cancer." I heard a gasp. Chatter all around. Andrew Barry watched my every move but remained silent.

"It's magical. In my blood." Barry's eyes narrowed at that. "I'm a physician and have personally been able to remove the cancer of over half a dozen patients."

Ironically, that statement was just the lead up to my real motive for this meeting. I held on to my words for just one more second before I sprung it on them.

"I'm working with researchers to develop a vaccine and a cure. When we've achieved this, we want to make it available to the world." I paused. "Mortals included."

This pronouncement led to silence. Everyone was running through the problems associated with offering a magical solution for illness to the entire world.

Then I dropped the bomb.

"This would necessitate giving up our cover. To offer this magical cure to the rest of the world, we would need to reveal the secret of witchcraft."

The room erupted. Everyone spoke at once, some in conversation with those next to them, some heatedly towards me. One man at the far right end of the table stood and said to me, "Give me one good reason why I should not kill you right here and now. For that statement."

I expected this. He seemed like he could make a good effort to kill me. My shield was already at full power, but I knew he would be a threat. "Please announce your name. If you're going to threaten to kill me, we should at least know each other."

He was unfazed. "Enzo Conti. Europe."

So he was the new head of Europe. I'd heard good things. He was known to be a bit abrasive but effective in running his area of the world.

"Mr. Conti. Here's my one good reason for not killing me. I'm suggesting that we reveal ourselves to the world because mortals make up the majority of the world's population. We are a small minority. We need them to continue to live as we want to." I paused, hoping they would acknowledge that to themselves. I could see Conti was not on board with me yet.

Then I went for the throat with the real reason these witches should get on board with my plan. "To deny mortals this cure would be morally wrong. Not to mention that if they ever found out we had it and kept it for ourselves, we would be forever hunted and despised. If we reveal magic to them through the vessel of this gift, we stand a chance at living in harmony." I let that sink in. "No more secrets. No more needless deaths."

A woman sitting by Father Andrew Barry stood and looked at me as though she was ready to kill me right then and there. She wore a dark maroon tailored suit. Her long brown hair was styled into a ponytail that hung to the side. A large diamond graced her hand. Her brown eyes pierced mine. "My son Robert was killed because he couldn't handle it. His power ruled him at first. He made one mistake," she pointed a finger at me. "One!" She shrieked the last word.

The room fell silent again. Everyone knew someone who had not made it through puberty because of the terrible nature of gaining one's power. It was our tragic shared experience.

The woman was not done yet. She picked up her glass of water and threw it at me. I stopped it midair using telekinesis, not spilling a drop. I used my power to set it down gently in front of me.

I looked down at my pad of paper. "I am sorry for your loss." I glanced around the table. "We all are, I'm sure. Almost every witch has experienced the death of a loved one because of our need for secrecy. What I am proposing would mean an end to the deaths of our children. I hope you will take that into consideration."

Enzo Conti sat down. The woman pushed away from the table and left the room, sobbing quietly as she went. Andrew Barry stood then.

"Parrish is right. This is a chance to offer something to the world to appease them when we tell them about witchcraft. It's a chance for us to finally be free. We will never get another chance like this to share our secret in a way that doesn't harm us."

I hated that he agreed with me. I needed everyone in there to get with me, but I just did not want to agree with him on anything. He saw my discomfort and enjoyed it.

He said, "We should take a vote. All those in favor of revealing our secret, raise your hand."

He and I raised our hands. Louise did as well. The rest of the room did not. Barry made an impatient noise. "For Christ's sake," he said. Loading his voice with persuasion, he said, "Everyone, raise your hand in affirmation of my motion."

Every hand in the room went up. People sat glassy eyed and still, for the most part. His persuasion was good, as good as mine. I could not believe there wasn't another witch in there with persuasion. If I didn't say something, everyone would think they made this decision on their own.

"It won't stand if they don't agree. We need them to emotionally agree with this, you dumb son of a bitch."

He made a face at me. "Why do you care if they agree or not? You and I both know this needs to happen. It's the right thing to do. Witches deserve to come out of the shadows. Now is the time."

Something about his fervor made me uneasy, but then was not the time to dig into Andrew Barry's psychosis. I just needed that group back to normal and for him not to fuck with them again.

"Everyone, please lower your hands. We need to take another vote. Let me explain more about what I hope will happen."

Two hours later, I had convinced over half the room to vote yes to the proposition and the historic measure was passed. No persuasion was used. It was determined that I would be the ambassador for the witches of the world and would make the announcement on television. But not until the cure was synthesized, and the vaccine was complete.

Andrew Barry was the first to leave.

CHAPTER FIFTY-THREE

Adam

December 25th, 2025

The National Mall was a feast for the eyes at Christmas time. Lights and decorations adorned every building, bush and tree. I slowed my jog down out of habit when I came upon the place where Mel used to have her stand. The new occupant raised his arm in greeting, and I waved back. Lonnie was okay. His food was crap, though. I missed Mel's brats. And after some time had passed, I was surprised to find that I missed her, too.

Vivienne had been gone then for a whole year. I told myself she had her hands full with Alice gaining her powers and maybe she was having trouble getting access to the manuscript. Even though we had speculated that it wasn't necessary for her time travel, she had used it twice that way. Maybe it had been moved from the monastery while she was there or what if it had been destroyed? And at night I entertained worse thoughts that I then tried to banish in the light of day.

When I got home, I said goodbye to Caleb and Tony, my loyal protection detail, who had been assigned to Vivienne when she was here but now always ran with me. They missed her too.

I gave the street a look up and down before heading inside. Turned out a significant portion of the witches of the world were not happy with the idea of being outed to mortals. As a result, my guard detail had been upgraded by Farhad to Secret Service level coverage. I also accepted his offer to provide security for mother, Grant, and Maria. It was one less thing on my plate and I trusted him to have only the best. I agreed to security for myself because I needed to stick around for Vivienne.

The witches in opposition were going to have to come to terms with the way things were going to be. The council had voted in favor of my proposal, and it was going to be necessary to discuss witchcraft when we explained the process used to create the cancer vaccine. Scientists weren't going to find any of the stuff that made up this vaccine in the periodic table of elements. It was made of magic. And it was looking like the vaccine was going to be effective in targeting not only most cancers but also most major maladies of the twenty-first century.

So I didn't give a damn anymore if witches wanted to remain a secret society. The world needed that vaccine. Witches and mortals.

Grant and Maria were coming over to have dinner and open gifts. When I was done with my shower, I checked on the roast in the oven and was pleased with the progress. He liked the potatoes and carrots, so I made sure those were covered with broth and getting soft.

The doorbell rang, and I came out of the kitchen and saw one of the security detail in the window beside the door. When I opened it he said, "Dr. Parrish, you have some guests." He stepped aside and at the foot of the stairs, I saw Vivienne with her arm around Alice. Gerald McEntire stood behind them.

I dropped the towel I was holding and bounded down the steps to pick her up. I buried my face in her neck.

She smelled the same. "Thank God. Thank God." My heart was beating so hard. "You're here." I set her back on her feet, and we shared kisses on the lips and cheeks and then hugged each other even tighter.

"I'm here," she smiled up at me and ran a hand through my hair. It was longer now and streaked with gray.

"I haven't had time for haircuts," I said.

She shook her head. "Don't cut it. I love it."

Then she reached down and gathered Alice close to her. "*We* are here." Alice was a mini version of Vivienne with beautiful wavy red hair and big blue eyes that were looking a little shell shocked at the moment.

I wiped a hand over my face and said, "I'm sorry, it's cold out here." I pulled Alice into our embrace. "I've been waiting to meet you for almost two whole years, young lady. Let's get you inside."

When I had Gerald seated in a chair and Alice on the sofa, I took Vivienne's hand and pulled her along behind me to the kitchen. Once there I yanked her to me and kissed her deeply. "Never again, Vivienne. I can't be without you again."

She rested her cheek against my chest, her arms around my waist.

"I know." She turned her face to kiss my chest. "I love you."

I pulled back to see if she was real. Her beauty stunned me then, as it sometimes did, and I thought ahead to having her in my bed with me later. Then I couldn't help asking, "What took you so long?" Her face registered that familiar irritation with me and I smiled.

"Don't start with me, Adam! I had a lot to do—Alice didn't take to using her shield until very recently."

My smiling at her made her even madder. She added, "And she didn't want to come."

"To the *future*?" That was surprising to me.

She shrugged. "She is a medieval girl. I had to convince her." Vivienne paused. "Did you not get my message?"

"I got it." I pulled her closer again, breathing her in. That wild sweet fragrance, still there. Still hers. "Thank you," I said. "It helped me."

She softened against me.

I said, "I've been busy too."

She looked up at me with those eyes that saw everything. "Tell me."

"Farhad and I developed a vaccine. For cancer." I watched her face. "Several cancers, actually."

Vivienne went still. "Adam."

"No big deal," I said.

She covered her mouth with her hand, and I saw her eyes fill. She shook her head at me.

I kissed her forehead. "It was because of you. Your healing magic was our base."

"Also," I said, "the witches have agreed. We're going to tell the world about witchcraft so everyone can get the vaccine."

Vivienne stared at me for a long moment. Taking in all that meant. Then she said, "*Everything* is going to change."

I knew she was thinking of Alice. Of things she had promised her.

"Hey." I tilted her chin up. "We can handle it. Whatever comes."

She searched my face the way she did when she was trying to believe something she wasn't sure of yet.

I said, "Together, there is nothing we can't do."

She nodded slowly. "Together."

"Stay here." I pointed at her and then quickly retrieved a black box from a kitchen drawer. She looked down at it and then up at me. "I bet you can't guess what this is," I said.

She pursed her lips and said, "Well the last small box was a ring."

"Damn, you're good."

She tried not to smile, but a corner of her mouth gave her away.

"It's tradition to have an engagement ring before the wedding band. So, I'm a little behind with this."

She drew in her breath at the sparkling red diamond inside. Taking it out of the box, I slid the ring onto her finger, above the silver wedding band. Vivienne held her hand up and watched it catch the light.

Then she looked up at me with those eyes, and I thought with satisfaction, *this is what I do now. I make my wife happy.*

"I love it," she said. "You'll spoil me."

"Forever," I agreed.

I pulled her back to me. In the other room, Alice and Gerald were waiting. Outside, the world was waiting.

But for just another moment, they could all wait.

EPILOGUE

Adam

Barry had surfaced again. He was like a new virus. Just popping up when least convenient. Threatening to kill you and everyone around you for no good reason at all.

The message he left with Maria said he would meet me in Times Square at ten a.m. the next day. I sat in an outdoor cafe right in the heart of it all, knowing he'd find me.

At ten on the dot, he walked up and took a seat at my table. He smiled at the waitress as she approached. He asked her what was good. As she talked, he watched her intently and ignored me completely.

In his best Irish brogue, he said, "Great. I'll have the eggs benedict and a hot latte, thanks, love."

She gave his stupid, handsome face a big smile, and he watched her walk away. Then he turned his attention to me.

"Thanks for coming," he said. "I thought this might be the best place in the whole world for us to meet."

"It's definitely harder to kill somebody here."

He smiled. Then he said, "You smell like her."

I willed my face to remain impassive at his mention of my wife. The woman he had tried to kill for her power.

"She's back, I see. Where'd you have her all this time?"

"What do you want, Barry?"

He sat back, irritated that I wasn't going to discuss Vivienne.

"Well, I wanted to let you know that people are going to try to kill you." He clarified, "Other people. Besides me."

"This isn't news. I'm about to announce witchcraft to the world. I know there are factions who are opposed."

"It's a bit more than 'factions.' That piddly little security detail you have on Vivienne isn't going to cut it. That's what I'm telling you."

"And here I thought you were concerned about me."

The waitress came with his latte and he thanked her.

He took a sip, then shook his head.

"No, you're not in the equation. I tried to talk to you about it. There was room for us both. But you didn't want to work together in the new world order to come. So this is just about me telling you to better prepare, so Vivienne stays alive."

"What makes you think you're going to have any part in a new world order? Your days are numbered."

"On the contrary. I feel like my best days are ahead. In fact, I feel like time is on my side."

Just then, everything came to a halt. The cars in the street, the people on the sidewalk, the videos on the buildings. They all stopped in place. Times Square was deadly quiet.

My eyes met his as he took another leisurely sip of his drink.

"What did you do?" The very air seemed wrong, and I felt sick.

The world very slowly began to move again, and the noise returned. Our waitress brought Barry's plate, and he raved about how good it looked and thanked her.

I kept my eyes on him.

As he cut up his food, he said, "That's something I picked up from your wife. Don't know quite how to use it yet and I'm not sure where it will be most useful, but I'm hoping Vivienne can enlighten me when I see her next." He took a sip of his latte.

"So keep her safe for me, would you?"

SNEAK PEEK!

Thank you for reading A Witch to Change the World!

Keep reading for a look at the next book in the series, *A War of Witches:*

"So you're a fucking witch."

Samuel Marsh, my best friend of over forty years, stood on my doorstep and looked as though he was about to deck me. There was fury there, just below the surface, and I steeled myself just in case he was about to let it out. I wanted to let him, I just didn't know if I had it in me to stand still with a fist coming at my face.

"Yep. I'm a witch."

His eye twitched.

Oh, fuck. Here it comes.

After a few seconds he said, "And you didn't think to mention that even once in the past forty years?"

"Couldn't."

"But now you can."

"Yep."

His mouth tightened. We faced each other, our breath visible in the cold December air, and for some reason, I thought about our first day of med school, and how he had asked out every pretty girl we ran into until he had a week's worth of dates lined up. I'd opened my front door thousands of times to find Marsh standing there.

Suddenly, I found myself scared to death that I might lose my best friend.

Then he said, "Why the fuck aren't you a warlock?"

That made me smile. Maybe this was going to be alright. I said, "Why don't you come in and I'll explain the world of witches, and we can drink some whiskey?"

He muttered, "Witch motherfucker," and shoved past me into the hallway.

I followed him a few steps into my study.

"Vivienne!" He smiled when he saw my wife sitting on the couch. She had been gone for a year, back in time to 1502 to bring her granddaughter Alice with her to the present day. Of course, Marsh didn't know any of that, and I realized the day was going to be even rougher than I had anticipated.

I clapped him on the shoulder. "Marsh, this is Alice." I motioned to the pretty fourteen-year-old sitting beside her grandmother on the couch. But he was looking at Vivienne and putting things together.

"I suppose you're a fucking witch too, Vivienne."

She frowned.

When he went on to say, "And you too, young lady. Everybody here is a goddamn witch..." Alice frowned, and Vivienne stood. I felt her power rise and tried to calm everyone down.

"It's just Marsh. He's being an ass. Let's give him this day to adjust. Marsh, say you're sorry to Alice."

"Yes, Samuel and to me as well." Vivienne leveled a glare at Marsh that made me glad I wasn't him. "This is a nice way to greet me after I've been gone for a year. I thought we were friends."

"I thought we were, too!" He threw his hands in the air in frustration.

Vivienne took pity on him and said gently, "Samuel, this is my granddaughter, Alice. Alice, this is my good friend Samuel. He's having a bad day."

Alice said, "I'm pleased to meet you, Samuel. Grandmother says I have bad days, too." I watched Marsh take in her not quite right British accent, similar to Vivienne's but just a touch stilted.

Marsh sighed and rubbed a hand over his eyes. He gathered his words together and said, "I'm sorry. It's not you I'm mad at, it's him. I'm sorry, Alice." Then he looked at my wife. "Sorry, Vivienne." Without even turning my way, he said, "Let's do this out back." He made his way through the kitchen and down the steps to the backyard.

Grabbing a bottle of whiskey, I put some ice in two glasses, and I followed him to the rocking chairs in front of the fire pit. I set the glasses down and poured us both a tall drink. When he took the drink I offered him, I picked my own up and toasted, "To forty years."

He lifted his glass and glared at me as he said, "Forty fucking years."

I set my drink down. "I take it you saw the news this morning?"

He yelled at me. "Yes, asshole, I saw the fucking news this morning because you called to tell me to watch the fucking news this morning! You want to tell me why I had to hear this shit on the fucking news instead of face to face?"

I held my hand up. "I'm sorry. It should have happened that way. But I just found out last night that there are some groups in our world who are not happy with my revealing the secret. It had to be done now, before they could get to me and stop it. Overnight, I had to prepare a way to introduce the fact of witchcraft to the world and explain about the vaccine. It was a lot."

His brows drew together. "Well, that sounds great."

Then after a moment, "Are you in danger? Are they in danger?" He jerked his head toward the house.

"Most likely, yes, for me. I don't know for sure about them." Our eyes met. "Or you, or mother, or Connie, or Grant, or Maria. I'll have security for everyone. You won't have to talk to them. They'll just be around."

We both took a big drink and rocked in our chairs for a minute. He held a hand up to the side of his head. I stood and went up the back porch steps to get him some Tylenol. Vivienne was at the kitchen sink, watching him with sympathy.

"Does he have a headache? Should I help him?"

"Definitely not. But thank you." I kissed her temple and headed back down with the medicine and water for him. He swallowed the pills. We both rocked in our chairs again in silence, Marsh with his eyes closed.

"I'm sorry," I said at last. "You're my best friend in the world, and I have wanted to tell you for forty years. But it's something we could never say to a mortal." His eyebrows raised slightly at my description of him as a mortal. "It takes a toll on a witch. To never be completely honest with those you love. I'm actually grateful for this chance to tell the world about us." I could see he was not yet swayed, so I said, "Nothing will be different for you and me."

He scoffed at that. "How can nothing be different? You're a lying motherfucker, that's a change. And you didn't trust me enough to tell me this very important thing about you."

I stopped my chair.

"It meant death to tell the secret. If anyone found out I told you, I'd be killed, and my mother and father would have had to go into hiding. I could not tell you."

"But why?" he said and set down his drink. "Why all the secrecy? And for so long? It's just some extra abilities, right? Like superheroes. For Christ's sake, everybody loves those guys."

I shook my head.

"In movies, they love those guys. But not that long ago in real life, they were burning those guys. Also, there was this little thing called the Inquisition. You may have heard of it. Witches are not universally loved."

He made a face like that was bullshit.

"You just need a good branding campaign. Get some celebrities or TikTokers to say you're cool, and that's that."

I laughed. "Marsh, I appreciate that you're not judging. I really do. But I think you may be underestimating the fear people will have when they find out their neighbor can tell if they're lying. Or that their neighbor can move cars with their mind. Or can hide from them by cloaking themselves."

He perked up at that.

I added, "Like they become invisible."

He whipped his head my way. "Are you serious?"

I nodded.

"Can you do that?"

I shrugged my agreement.

"Fucking show me right now!" he demanded.

I laughed again.

That's more like it.

Buy *A War of Witches* now!

https://www.suzannesnowden.com/a-war-of-witches

The Witch Wars Series
Book 1 —*A Witch to Change the World*
Book 1.5 —*A Time Apart* —Summer, 2026
Book 2 —*A War of Witches* —Available now!
Book 3 —*A Witch to Save the World* —2026

ACKNOWLEDGEMENTS

From start to finish this first book took me years to write and I have many people to thank for their support. First, special thanks to my good friend Lydia Netzer who was the first to read this book when we traded novels on New Year's Eve. Hers was an amazing work of sparkling prose and unforgettable characters while mine was a pretty much unformatted mass of telling not showing. But, kind person and writing guru that she is, she read it all and ended up giving me the most useful advice ever… get a bad guy. That idea turned this one book into a three-book series. Then, after I took her advice, she read it *again* and her suggestions made it a million times better. Lydia, I can't thank you enough.

More thanks to Lydia and also Joshilyn for writing like fiends with me for thirty days straight during NaNoWriMo, 2023. And thanks to my Chesapeake Romance Writing buddies for their support during an intense revising week at our retreat in Duck, N.C.

I also want to thank Taylor, my work bestie. Taylor, thank you for listening to every outrageous plot point along the way and telling me each time that it was incredible. Also, thanks for joining me in celebratory hot chocolate when I finally typed "The End" and then celebratory animal crackers when I finished the final edits. I can't wait to force an entirely new plot upon you.

My sincere thanks to the people who read this book and gave me really useful feedback, Mary, Chris and Margaret. I'm thankful for my good friend, author M. Jayne LaDow who has been so generous with her knowledge as she navigates this self-publishing world along with me. Thank you for going first! And I was lucky to have two seasoned writers take the time to message with me along the way, thanks to Donna McDonald and Lydia M. Hawke for your encouragement and advice. Thanks also to Megan Gallt at Novel Grounds bookstore for her industry advice, and to my *amazing* book cover artist, Danielle Fine. Opening an email from her with book cover art has become a bigger thrill than my birthday and Christmas morning put together.

Finally, all my love and all the thanks in the world to my family. At this point my sweet husband and kids have heard from me every possible story idea ever proposed. Despite that, their trust in my abilities and pride in my accomplishments remains steadfast. You guys bring me joy, I love you so much. Thank you for believing I could do this and supporting me like you have.

(And Katie, thank you for "Don't forget about the dungeons." You're a genius.)

ABOUT THE AUTHOR

I almost died while editing and formatting this book.

Not really, but it seemed like a distinct possibility. It was *hard*. I work full time at a public library, and this book writing was *supposed* to be my fun, new (and expensive) hobby.

But this year I learned that while writing is joy, editing and formatting is hell.

Before I worked at the library, I was a teacher of high school kids and before that, a radio DJ who hosted a Lovesongs Show. (Earning my street cred to write romance books.) I have three grown-up kids, and my favorite thing to do is sit on the couch and read a good book with my dog Luna on my lap.

My husband Gary would probably like a mention in this section about my life. That is only fitting since he is my best friend, and the main reason I know anything at all about romance.

I look forward to finishing *The Witch Wars* Series in 2026. After that, I'm going to write a series about wolves, then there's going to be some magic at the library and then some mystery at the radio station. (There's a whole plan.)

Check out my website at suzannesnowden.com
I also have a Substack:
https://suzannesnowden.substack.com/subscribe
And a newsletter called *Romance for Grownups*:
https://suzannesnowden.kit.com/09427b0950

You can also find me on all the social media that mankind has to offer: @suzannesnowdenbooks

Books by Suzanne Snowden

The Witch Wars Series

Book 1 —*A Witch to Change the World*

Book 1.5 —*A Time Apart* —Summer, 2026

Book 2 —*A War of Witches* —Available now!

Book 3 —*A Witch to Save the World* – 2026